Map of Albion

Place Names

Place names in Dark Ages Britain vary according to time, language, dialect and the scribe who was writing. I have not followed a strict convention when choosing what spelling to use for a given place. In most cases, I have chosen the name I believe to be the closest to that used in the early seventh century, but like the scribes of all those centuries ago, I have taken artistic licence at times, and merely selected the one I liked most.

Ægypte	Egypt
Æscendene	Ashington, Northumberland
Afen	River Avon
Albion	Great Britain
Bebbanburg	Bamburgh
Beodericsworth	Bury St Edmunds
Berewic	Berwick-upon-Tweed
Bernicia	Northern kingdom of Northumbria, running approximately from the Tyne to the Firth of Forth
Cantware	Kent
Cantwareburh	Canterbury
Dál Riata	Gaelic overkingdom, roughly encompassing modern-day Argyll and Bute and Lochaber in Scotland and also County Antrim in Northern Ireland
Deira	Southern kingdom of Northumbria, running approximately from the Humber to the Tyne
Din Eidyn	Edinburgh
Dommoc	Dunwich, Suffolk
Dor	Dore, Yorkshire

Dorcic	Dorchester on Thames
Dun	River Don
Elmet	Native Briton kingdom, approximately equal to the West Riding of Yorkshire
Engelmynster	Fictional location in Deira
Eoferwic	York
Frankia	France
Gefrin	Yeavering
Gipeswic	Ipswich
Gwynedd	Gwynedd, North Wales
Hefenfelth	Heavenfield
Hibernia	Ireland
Hii	Iona
Hithe	Hythe, Kent
Liminge	Lyminge, Kent
Lindisfarena	Lindisfarne
Mercia	Kingdom centred on the valley of the River Trent and its tributaries, in the modern-day English Midlands
Muile	Mull
Northumbria	Modern-day Yorkshire, Northumberland and south-east Scotland
Pocel's Hall	Pocklington
Rendlæsham	Rendlesham, Suffolk
Sandwic	Sandwich, Kent
Scheth	River Sheaf (border of Mercia and Deira)
Temes	River Thames
Tuidi	River Tweed
Ubbanford	Norham, Northumberland

PROLOGUE

FRANKIA, AD 635

"Be careful there, you two!"

The cry came from old Halig. He worried like a maid.

Wuscfrea ignored him, leaping up to the next branch of the gnarled oak. The bark was damp and cold, but the sun was warm on his face as he looked for the next handhold. They had been enclosed in the hall for endless days of storms. Great gusts of wind had made the hall creak and moan as if it would collapse and when they had peered through the windows, the world had been hidden beneath the sheeting rain.

After so long inside it felt wonderful to be able to run free in the open air.

A crow cawed angrily at Wuscfrea from a perch high in the canopy of the trees. The boy laughed, echoing the bird's call.

"Away with you," Wuscfrea shouted at the creature. "You have wings, so use them. The sun is shining and the world is warm." The crow gazed at him with its beady eyes, but did not leave its branch. Wuscfrea looked down. Fair-haired Yffi was some way below, but was grinning up at him.

"Wait for me," Yffi shouted, his voice high and excited.

"Wait for me, *uncle*," Wuscfrea corrected him, smiling. He knew how it angered Yffi to be reminded that Wuscfrea was the son of Edwin, the king, while he was only the son of the atheling, Osfrid. The son of the king's son.

"I'll get you," yelled Yffi and renewed his exertions, reaching for a thick branch and pulling himself up.

Wuscfrea saw a perfect path between the next few branches that would take him to the uppermost limbs of the oak. Beyond that he was not sure the branches would hold his weight. He scrambled up, his seven-year-old muscles strong and his body lithe.

The crow croaked again and lazily flapped into the sky. It seemed to observe him with a cold fury at being disturbed, but Wuscfrea merely spat at the bird. Today was a day to enjoy the fresh air and the warmth of the sun, not to worry about silly birds. For a moment, he frowned. He hoped Yffi had not seen the crow. Crows were the birds of war. Whenever he saw them Yffi recalled the tales of the battle of Elmet, and how the corpse-strewn bog had been covered by great clouds of the birds. The boys had frightened themselves by imagining how the birds had eaten so much man-flesh that they could barely fly. It was a black thought. As black as the wings of the crows. To think of the death of their fathers brought them nothing but grief. Wuscfrea shook the thoughts away. He would not allow himself to be made sad on such a bright day.

Glancing down, he saw that Yffi was struggling to reach a branch. He was a year younger than Wuscfrea, and shorter.

"Come on, nephew," Wuscfrea goaded him. "Are you too small to join me up here? The views are fit for a king." Wuscfrea laughed at the frustrated roar that came from Yffi. Yet there was no malice in his words. Despite being uncle and nephew, the two boys were more like brothers, and the best of friends. Still, it was good to be the superior climber. Yffi, even though younger, was better at most things. The long storm-riven days had seen the younger boy beat Wuscfrea ceaselessly at tafl and Yffi had joked that someone with turnips for brains would only be good to rule over pigs. The words had stung and Wuscfrea had sulked for a while until Yffi had brought him some of Berit's cheese as an offering of truce. Wuscfrea loved the salty tang of the cheese and the insult was quickly put aside.

Now, as he pulled his head and shoulders above the thick leaves of the oak, Wuscfrea wondered whether he would ever be king of anything. Certainly not of this land, rich and lush as it was. This was Uncle Dagobert's kingdom. Far to the south of Bernicia and Deira, the kingdoms his father had forged into the single realm of Northumbria. Far away and over the sea. A safe distance from the new king.

Wuscfrea breathed in deeply of the cool, crisp air. The treetops on the rolling hills all around swayed in the gentle breeze. The leaves sparkled and glistened in the sunlight. High in the sky to the north, wisps of white clouds floated like half-remembered dreams.

One day, he would travel north with a great warband, with Yffi at his side. They would have ships built from the wood of this great forest and they would ride the Whale Road to Northumbria. They would avenge their fathers' slaying and take back the kingdom that should have been theirs. Wuscfrea's chest swelled at the thought.

"Vengeance is a potent brew," Halig had said to him when they had spoken of the battle of Elmet one night over a year before. "Drink of it and let it ferment in your belly. And one day you will wreak your revenge on the usurper, Oswald," the old warrior had touched the iron cross at his neck. Wuscfrea had thought of how Jesu told his followers to turn the other cheek when struck and wondered what the Christ would think of the lust for revenge that burnt and bubbled inside him. But then Wuscfrea was the son of a great king, descended from the old gods themselves so they said, so why should he care what one god thought?

Glancing to the south, a smear of smoke told of the cooking fires of the great hall. They had walked far and would need to return soon. Suddenly hungry, Wuscfrea's stomach grumbled.

Several woodpigeons flew into the bright sunshine. Where was Yffi?

Wuscfrea peered down into the dappled darkness beneath him, but there was no sign of his younger nephew now. Had he gone too far with the jibes? He sighed. He would ask for Yffi's pardon and let him beat him at a running race. He did not want the day spoilt by Yffi's pouting.

"Yffi!" he called. "Come on. I'll help you up so that you too can see the kingly view." He couldn't help himself from continuing the jest. "Yffi!"

No answer came. The crow flew close and cawed. The pigeons circled in the air above the wood, but did not settle.

"Yffi!" he shouted again. Silence.

Letting out a long sigh, Wuscfrea began to climb down. It seemed Yffi was not in a forgiving mood. Perhaps they should return to the hall and find something to eat. When hungry, Yffi was impossible.

Carefully picking his way back down from branch to branch, Wuscfrea shivered at the shift in temperature. It was much cooler in the shade of the trees and he would have liked to have spent a while longer basking in the warm sun-glow.

Dropping down to the leaf mould of the forest floor, Wuscfrea scanned around for signs of Yffi. Surely he had not run back to the hall without him. Halig would not have allowed him even if he had wanted to. The grizzled warrior was as protective of them as a she-wolf of her cubs. But where was Halig? All Wuscfrea could see were the boles of oak and elm.

"Come on, Yffi," he said in a loud voice that he hoped veiled the beginning whispers of unease he felt. "I'm sorry. Let's go back and get some of Berit's honey-cakes."

No answer came and Wuscfrea strained to hear any indication of movement. But there was no sound save for the wind-rustle of the trees.

Cold fingers of dread clawed at his back.

"Yffi! Halig!" He didn't care now if they heard the fear in his voice.

What was that noise? Relief rushed through him. He had heard a stifled sound, choked off as one of them tried to remain silent. Perhaps Yffi suppressed his giggles from where he hid with Halig to teach Wuscfrea a lesson in humility.

He had them now.

Wuscfrea ran in the direction of the sound. Did they seek to make a fool of him? He would show them. His soft leather shoes slipped in the loamy soil as he skidded around the gnarly oak trunk. His face was flushed with excitement.

He passed the massive tree, laughter ready to burst forth from his lips. But the laughter never came. Instead, a whimpering moan issued from him. He skidded to a halt, his feet throwing up leaves and twigs. He lost his footing and landed on his behind. Hard.

Yffi and Halig were both there, but there were others behind the tree too. Strangers. Wuscfrea's gaze first fell on a giant of a man, with a great, flame-red beard and hard eyes. In the man's meaty grip was a huge axe, the head dripping with fresh blood. The corpse of old Halig lay propped against the tree, sword un-blooded in his hand, a great gash in his chest. The old warrior's lifeless eyes stared up at the light shining down from the warm sun above the trees.

Some movement pulled his attention to another man. He was broad-shouldered, dark and scowling, his black hair in stark contrast to his fine blue warrior-jacket with its rich woven hem of yellow and red. In his left hand, this second stranger held the small figure of Yffi by the hair. Wuscfrea's eyes met those of his nephew. He saw his own terror reflected there a hundredfold. The stranger's right hand was moving. There was a knife in his hand. With a hideous sucking sound the knife sawed across Yffi's throat and bit deeply. Yffi's eyes widened and a gurgled scream keened from him. Hot blood spouted in the forest gloom. The knife cut through flesh and arteries and with each beat of the boy's heart, his lifeblood gushed out and over Wuscfrea in a crimson arc.

Wuscfrea felt the hot wetness of the slaughter-dew soak him. His nephew's blood covered his face, his chest, his outstretched legs. Wuscfrea could not move. He wanted to scream. He knew he should bellow his defiance of this dark-haired warrior and the red-bearded giant who had given him more deaths to avenge. A king would leap up from the cold leaf-strewn ground and launch himself at these strangers. He would scoop up the sword from his fallen gesith and slay the man's murderers.

But Wuscfrea just stared. His breath came in short panting gasps as he watched the dark-haired man casually throw Yffi's twitching body onto Halig's corpse. Halig slid to one side, his dead hand finally losing its grip on the sword.

Wuscfrea knew he should do something. Anything. To die lying here was not the death of a great man. Not the death of a king for scops to sing of in mead halls.

Hot tears streamed down his face, smearing and mingling with Yffi's blood. But he was yet a boy. He was no man. No king.

And, as the death-bringing stranger stepped towards him, an almost apologetic smile on his face and the gore-slick knife held tight in his grip, Wuscfrea knew he would never rule Northumbria.

From the fungus-encrusted trunk of a fallen elm the crow looked on with its cold black eyes as the bloody knife blade fell again and again.

Anno Domini Nostri Iesu Christi
In the Year of Our Lord Jesus Christ
636

Part One

Fire and Feud

Chapter 1

Beobrand smelt the smoke before he heard the screams.

The scent of burning wood was not uncommon. They had passed many small steadings as they travelled south. Each hut or hall had its own hearth. Sometimes, the aroma of baking bread or roasting meat would waft on the wind from some unseen farmer's hovel, or from a shepherd's camp nestled in the shelter of a valley. At such times, it always surprised him how far smells could travel.

Sounds of anguish, shouts of terror and shrieks of pain, could not be heard from so far away. And were less common.

There was a light breeze blowing into their faces and at the first scent of smoke Beobrand had wondered whether there was a hall nearby. They had been travelling for days and had not slept with a roof above them in all that time. The days were warm, but the nights were yet chill. A place by a fire and some warm food would be welcome. Perhaps even some ale or mead.

Then he had seen the broad smudge of grey, like a blurred heron's feather, hanging in the flax-flower blue sky and he had known they would not be sleeping in a hall that night. Judging from the amount of smoke, something big was burning.

A piercing scream came to them on the wind. No, there would be no rest any time soon. Someone was in agony just the other side of the next rise. Beobrand's black stallion, Sceadugenga, lowered its ears and snorted.

Beobrand pulled the beast's head back with a tug of the reins. He could feel the great muscles bunching beneath him, ready to gallop forward; towards the screams. Towards danger. Sceadugenga was a true warrior's steed.

"Are we yet in Mercia, Attor?" he asked, twisting in the saddle to turn to the slim rider beside him.

"I cannot say for certain, lord. We are in the land of the Gyrwas, I believe, but we may already be in the territory of the Herstingas. It is all fen and forest in this part of Albion." He shrugged. "I cannot be sure." Another scream drifted to them. Attor's mount tossed its mane and rolled its eyes.

Beobrand had hoped to make this journey without incident, but the island of Albion was seldom safe. He rode at the head of a small band of mounted warriors. Not large enough to be called a warband, but hopefully enough of a show of force to avoid most confrontations. They numbered thirteen men in all. Beside Beobrand rode Wynhelm, fellow thegn of Bernicia. He was several years Beobrand's senior. Black-haired, with a close-cropped beard, he was aloof and sometimes haughty, but had fought bravely at Hefenfelth and Din Eidyn, and King Oswald trusted him. Wynhelm brought four warriors from his retinue, all battle-hard, grim-faced men. Killers, if Beobrand was any judge.

In the centre of the group rode the monks, Gothfraidh and Coenred, whom they were charged with protecting. Gothfraidh was an elderly man, his grey hair thinning. Kindly, and uncomplaining, he was always quick to offer his help when they were setting up camp. Coenred was much younger, barely a man, though Beobrand knew that despite his youthful aspect, he was brave and had proven himself to be a true friend.

Beobrand quickly cast his gaze on those of his own retinue, his gesithas, who accompanied him. Dour Dreogan was closest to Attor, the black lines of his soot-scarred cheeks making his face savage. Behind him followed Gram, tall and powerful. He was a mighty warrior, who never seemed to show fear or excitement; a steadfast shield-brother whom they would be glad to have at their shoulder, if it came to a fight.

Broad-shouldered Elmer rode towards the rear of the group. He was brave and bold, and despite the horrific sounds of pain that came to them on the breeze, he had a wide grin on his face. He was still so pleased to have been asked to ride with his lord. He felt that in the past he had too often been left behind with the women, children and old men, and no matter the number of times Beobrand had told him this was due to the trust he had in the muscular warrior, Elmer had taken it as a slight. The last two riders were the inseparable Ceawlin and Aethelwulf. They were woven from the same cloth, each taciturn and stocky, savage in combat but quick to jest and laugh when the mead flowed.

They were all good men. Strong warriors. Loyal gesithas. Beobrand was proud that they called him lord. And yet he wished Acennan was with them. He missed his friend. He had not seen him since before Solmonath, the month of rain and mud. Summer had long since begun to warm the land and Beobrand had expected Acennan's return weeks before.

Another scream.

Acennan would have to wait.

The trail rose up a shallow bluff. To the west huddled a stand of alder.

"Whether Mercia or no," said Beobrand, reaching his damaged left hand down to touch the hilt of his sword, Hrunting, "I will not ride by while someone faces torment. Come, let us see what is burning."

He dug his heels into Sceadugenga's flanks and gave the horse its head. He did not wait to see whether his men followed him, he knew they would. The stallion, ever happy to gallop, surged forward. As always, Beobrand revelled in the sheer power of the steed as they thundered up the shallow incline. Beobrand's fair hair flew back from his face, the wind bringing tears to his icy-blue eyes. He had hoped to reach their destination without trouble, but after the long cold winter cooped up in the smoky hall of Ubbanford, Beobrand's blood rose at the prospect of combat.

"Wait," cried Coenred, "we should not tarry here." Beobrand ignored him. He should probably have commanded the men to ride wide of this place, to ensure the monks and the gifts they carried reached the lands of the East Angelfolc as quickly as possible. He recalled King Oswald's words to him: "You are to see these men of God safely to the land of my brother in Christ, King Sigeberht. Let nothing detain you. The gifts they carry are of great value and importance." He had given his word to his king.

But he could not simply ride past.

Cresting the hill, Sceadugenga hurtled down the other side. Beobrand took in the scene in a heartbeat. He adjusted the stallion's direction slightly, without pausing to think.

Some distance away, further than he had expected, a hall was burning. Great gouts of smoke billowed into the air as the thatch of the roof collapsed with a groaning crash. Flames leapt upward, sparks spiralling to be lost in the pale sky. Even as Sceadugenga carried him down the hill, Beobrand could feel the heat on his face like a furnace.

Smaller buildings were dotted around the hall. Some of these were also aflame. Figures ran amongst the buildings. A group of mounted men sat astride stocky steeds, watching the destruction impassively. Iron glinted in the sunlight. Byrnies, shield bosses, spear-tips, swords.

On the packed earth before the burning hall stood a pitiful band. Unarmed women and men in dark robes cowered from the blades and savagery of the men who corralled them. A few paces closer to Beobrand, two women were prostrate on the earth, held down while warriors pleasured themselves. The women were screaming, which only seemed to more inflame the passions of their attackers, who laughed and shouted encouragements to each other. They spoke in a sing-song tongue, with slippery words. Beobrand did not understand what they said, but he recognised the language.

Waelisc.

Dark memories flooded his mind at the vision before him. Another burning hall, the dead heaped on the ground before it. A freezing forest. Cathryn's pleading eyes. But that was in the past. Winter was gone and the day was not cold. And he was mounted, armed, with trusted gesithas at his back; no longer a frightened boy.

He was almost upon them now, a couple of the men had looked up, eyes wide at the sight of the fair-haired warrior on the great black steed charging down on them. They reached for weapons. One snatched up a spear, another a large, jagged-bladed knife.

Beobrand felt the battle lust sweep through him. Part of his mind screamed at him. There were too many men here. He could not face them all and survive. One of the women screamed pitiably. A beam fell into the conflagration of the hall with a choked crash. Beobrand could not turn away, any more than he could stop the sun from rising in the morning. He pushed aside thoughts of defeat and welcomed the battle-fury like a long-lost brother

Tugging savagely at Sceadugenga's reins, Beobrand swung his leg over the stallion's back and leapt to the earth. A dull twinge in his right leg reminded him of past injuries, but the winter's rest had done him good. His wounds were healed and he was once again hale and strong. Dragging Hrunting from its scabbard, he bellowed his defiance at the men before him. One black-bearded man jabbed a spear at Beobrand's chest. As fast as thought, Beobrand deflected the spear-point to his right with a push of his blade. Without pause he closed with the Waelisc warrior in two steps, the spear haft sliding harmlessly along his midriff. Beobrand brought Hrunting back in a vicious, glittering arc, slicing through flesh, sinew and bone. Blood fountained from the man's neck and he fell back to lie twitching on the earth. His head, eyes fear-stricken and wide, toppled from his shoulders and rolled to a halt beside his corpse.

The moment of shock and surprise had passed now. The other men were leaping up, scrabbling for weapons, fumbling with breeches.

Beobrand shifted his attention to the knife wielder. The man's face was pale, his features pinched. For an instant Beobrand believed the man would flee, but then, the eyes narrowed. The shoulder muscles bunched. And Beobrand knew he would attack. He almost laughed aloud. His blood coursed through his veins. Hrunting sang in the air. The sword-song was his tune and he was happy to let its music wash over him.

Flashing his teeth at the Waelisc, he leapt towards him. The man was fast, flicking the wicked knife at Beobrand's throat. But few could match Beobrand's speed. He watched as the Waelisc warrior's hand moved, his mud-clogged boots shuffled forward on hard, packed earth. Following the man's motion, Beobrand lashed out his left hand, catching his opponent's right wrist. Beobrand's hand was not whole, his grip weakened as a result of losing the best part of two fingers a couple of years before, but he had sufficient strength to grasp the wrist for long enough. He yanked his opponent forward, off balance. At the same moment, he swung Hrunting upward in a deadly swing. The fine, patterned blade sliced deeply into the man's groin. Hot blood gushed and the knife-man let out a piteous scream.

Blood and piss splattered Beobrand's leggings and shoes. He pushed the man away.

Around them, his mounted gesithas reined in, drawing blades. Beobrand cast a glance up the hill. He was pleased to see that Wynhelm and his warriors had also followed him. With a shout, Wynhelm led his men off to one side, away from the burning buildings. Where was he going? Then Beobrand saw what he was about. Wynhelm had blocked the approach of the mounted warriors who had been surveying the scene.

For a moment, nobody moved. The women sobbed from where they lay on the ground. They shuffled close and wept, each burying their faces in the robes and hair of the other, clinging together as if that could save them from the terror that surrounded them.

More armed Waelisc came from between the huts. Beobrand reckoned that there must be more than twenty in all.

As if of one mind his gesithas suddenly dismounted. Dreogan came quickly to his left, Attor to his right.

"You looked lonely down here all on your own," said Dreogan, a wicked grin twisting the soot-scars on his cheeks.

The endless days of training back in Ubbanford were evident as the others rapidly and silently formed a small shieldwall.

The Waelisc bunched together, interlocking shields and facing Beobrand's small band. Smoke wafted around them as the wind picked up. The heat from the flames brought beads of sweat to Beobrand's brow. He gazed at the furious faces of the Waelisc. They stood strong and firm. These were no brigands, they were warriors. Raven-feeders. It was ever his wyrd to rush into battles, but this had been foolish. There were too many of them. Those flames would likely be his bone-fire. The pyre of his recklessness on which his men would burn.

Between the two lines of warriors, lay the corpses of the Waelisc that Beobrand had slain. Friends and shield-brothers of the men yet lived and longed for nothing more than to rip the life from Beobrand and his gesithas. Death and violence hung in the air, as palpable and acrid as the smoke.

One of the Waelisc, a tall man, with close-cropped hair and beard, and a nose so twisted it didn't seem to fit his face, called out something in their burbling tongue. Evidently the others listened to him, for they all took a step forward.

"Hold firm, men," Beobrand said. "There may be more of them, but we are men of Northumbria. We do not crumble before a few sheep-swiving Waelisc scum."

The men closed more tightly about him. He could smell Dreogan's sour breath. The Waelisc took another step toward them. Spear-points lowered. In a few heartbeats, the shieldwalls would meet, and then the killing would start in earnest.

Beobrand clenched his jaw. So much for arriving without incident. Another piece of the roof structure fell into the swirling furnace of the hall, sending fresh sparks into the sky. Did the gods look down upon them? The gods loved mischief. Beobrand tightened his grip on Hrunting. Well, let's give those bastards something worth watching.

He drew in a deep breath, ready to shout with his battle-voice. He would scream his defiance and his men would join him. They would deal more death this day before the end.

But before any sound passed his lips, another voice cut over the din of the fires and the approaching shieldwalls.

"Halt!" came the cry.

Beobrand turned to see that one of the mounted warriors, evidently the leader, had ridden forward. Wynhelm had stepped aside, allowing the man to approach. What in Woden's name was he thinking? The Waelisc had black hair and a spotless white cloak. At his neck shone a golden torc. He reined in his mount and spoke in a clear, ringing voice.

"I know you," he said, "but you are far from home, Beobrand Half-hand." The man spoke the tongue of the Angelfolc well. Beobrand had no idea who he was.

"If you know who I am," said Beobrand, reaching up to wipe a splash of crimson from his cheek, "then you know how I deal with treacherous Waelisc curs."

The man did not react to the taunt.

"Well, you will not be killing any more of my men this day," he said.

"Believe what you will, but the wolves and foxes will feast on Waelisc flesh this night."

"The animals will not go hungry, but no more of my men will feed them." The man ran his left hand through his black hair. "You will turn and ride from this place now. There will be no more bloodshed."

Beobrand looked at the pallid, fearful faces of the unarmed men and women. The younger of the two ravaged women stared up at him, her eyes glistening, tears streaking her face. She was a plain girl, but he had seen eyes like hers before. She was lost without his aid.

"What of these people?" he asked. "No more harm will befall them?"

"Oh no, they must be punished. My lord Penda has willed it, and these are his lands. You have no right to intervene."

"He's right, Beobrand," said Wynhelm. "Mercian problems are not ours."

Curse the man. Why did he speak?

The Waelisc leader grinned at Wynhelm's words.

"This has all been rather unfortunate. But you will ride on your way now. Later, I will send someone to collect the weregild for my men."

Beobrand's ire rose in him like the flames of the hall.

"Pay weregild? You are mad."

"Oh, but you will. As your wise friend here so rightly says, Mercia is not your land. Would King Oswald be happy to know you had broken the peace he agreed with Penda?"

Beobrand recalled the anger of his king when violence had threatened the truce with Mercia. He did not reply to the smug Waelisc horseman.

"If you do not leave now," continued the Waelisc leader, "I will give my men the order to attack. You will surely kill some of them, but you will be overrun. You will all die."

"Listen to the man," said Wynhelm. "We should never have got involved here."

"Hold your tongue, Wynhelm," snapped Beobrand. He trembled with rage. He longed to rush at Wynhelm and pull him from his saddle. But he did nothing save for gripping Hrunting so tightly his knuckles cracked. The words of both men were true. Oswald would never forgive him if he broke the fragile peace between Northumbria and Mercia. And their mission was to take the monks safely to the king of the East Angelfolc. Beobrand knew that he had been foolish to enter this fray, but he could not bear the thought of leaving these people to their fate at the hands of these Waelisc savages.

He glowered at Wynhelm for a moment. The fool would pay for speaking out against him. The eyes of the women who yet huddled on the earth, pleaded with him. The younger one shook her head slightly as she saw that he had made his decision. The Waelisc leader had spoken true. Beobrand could not hope to save these poor folk. All he would be doing is throwing away the lives of his men.

He swallowed the hard lump in his throat.

"Mount up, men," he said, his voice cracking. He hawked and spat into the dust. "We are riding out."

Beobrand beckoned to Sceadugenga. The black stallion approached and lowered its head. Did it look disappointed in its rider? Beobrand swung himself into the saddle. Around him, his men climbed back onto their horses, slinging shields over their shoulders. All the while they watched the gathered Waelisc furtively for any sign of attack.

Beobrand spat again, but the bitter taste lingered.

"You cannot leave us."

Beobrand looked down. The girl clung to his foot. Fresh tears washed down her face. She shook like a tree in a strong wind.

"Please," she went on, "they will kill us all."

Beobrand surveyed the scene. Most of the huts were burning now, adding their smoke to the roiling grey column that issued from the hall. The faces of the Waelisc men in the shieldwall were grim, hard and unyielding. She was right. As soon as Beobrand and the Northumbrians rode away, the unarmed men and women would pay the price of the warriors' humiliation. He looked to the two corpses. The head of the first lay at an impossible angle next to the body. Its sightless eyes stared up into the smoke-smeared sky.

Yes. They would pay, and it would be a high price.

He could not save them all, but perhaps he could rid himself of the bitter gall-taste of utter defeat. He reached out a hand to the girl.

"Come, I will take you from here. You will be safe."

She stared up at him, eyes wide. She shook her head.

"I cannot. What about the others? My sisters and brothers?"

The older woman raised herself up then and spoke in a clear voice.

"Go with them, Edmonda. The Lord has seen fit to send these men here for a purpose."

"But you will all perish," Edmonda said, her voice almost lost to the crackle and roar of the fires and the wind rustling in the alders.

"Perhaps that is God's will," said the older woman. "But we must not question Him. Salvation is offered to you. Take it, Edmonda, and carry the word of the Lord with you, so that all may know of His love."

One of the huts collapsed with a muffled crunch. Sceadugenga shook his head nervously.

"Come, girl," said Beobrand. "I know naught of the gods, but better to live than die, I would say."

One last look at the other woman and then Edmonda grasped his hand. Beobrand pulled her up behind him with ease.

"God bless you all," she said, sobbing.

"Hold on to me, girl," said Beobrand. "Tight, mind, or you'll fall when we start to ride."

She did not reply, but her slim arms encircled his waist.

Swinging Sceadugenga's head around, he turned to the mounted Waelisc warrior in the white cloak.

"You say you know me," said Beobrand. "And yet, I know you not. What is your name, Waelisc?"

The man offered him a broad smile.

"I am Gwalchmei ap Gwyar. And you have now stolen two things of mine."

The name meant nothing to Beobrand.

"What two things? What riddle is this?" How he would love to ride the man off his horse and smash that smile from his face.

"Well, now there is that girl. But she is nothing. That however," he said, indicating Sceadugenga, "is another matter."

What was the man speaking of? He made no sense.

"What do you mean?" Beobrand asked, his words as sharp and cold as shards of iron.

"That fine stallion you are riding," said Gwalchmei, "is my horse."

Chapter 2

"Your horse?" Beobrand said, immediately regretting having spoken. The Waelisc leader was toying with him surely. Trying to unnerve him.

Gwalchmei still smiled, but his eyes showed no mirth. They were dark and cold, like the deep Northern Sea. Around them Wynhelm's warriors were moving out. Beobrand's gesithas had all mounted, but held back, waiting for their leader. The flames of the buildings breathed and sighed like living things, the wind fanning them to greater heat. It was hot on his face from this distance. Closer, where the gathered men and women moaned and cried it must have been unbearable. Beobrand scanned the set, impassive faces of the Waelisc warriors. The prisoners would not have to bear the pain of the heat for long. What horrors yet awaited them on this earth, Beobrand did not care to dwell on. He pushed the thoughts away.

Edmonda's hands were clasped at his waist. Her body trembled like a bird against his back.

"Yes," replied Gwalchmei, no sign of a smile in his voice, "my horse. You stole it from me at Hefenfelth."

Beobrand recalled the moment when the Waelisc corral had been broken and the horses routed. It had been the turning point of the battle. One animal, half-crazed with fear from the crashes of thunder, the clash of weapons and the screams of the dying, had galloped towards King Oswald. Beobrand had stopped it and the great black beast had carried him in pursuit of Cadwallon, King of Gwynedd. After the battle, Oswald had gifted the horse to Beobrand and the stallion had been a trusted companion ever since, always leading him safely through shadows and danger.

"Taranau is his name," Gwalchmei said, something like longing in his tone.

Sceadugenga's ears pricked up, and it pawed the earth with a hoof.

"See, he remembers me," said Gwalchmei.

"Enough of this," replied Beobrand. "If it was your horse once, it is so no longer. And his name," he patted the coarse mane, "is Sceadugenga."

Gwalchmei spurred his mount forward a couple of paces. Beobrand could almost reach out and pull him from the saddle. He gripped his reins tightly, willing his hands not to shake.

"Mark my words, Half-hand," all sign of the smile had gone now and Gwalchmei's words were clipped and sharp. "I do not have time to deal with you now. Too many of my men would have been injured or slain in a fight and I have matters of more import to attend. But heed me well. Next time we meet, I will take back what is mine, and you will pay weregild for what you have stolen from me."

"I shall pay you nothing."

"Then the next time we meet, I shall slay you."

"You can try, Gwalchmei. Many have tried before you, and yet I still breathe."

Beobrand did not await an answer from the white-cloaked Waelisc lord. He swung Sceadugenga's head away and dug his heels into the stallion's flanks, praying that the girl was holding on tightly. The horse, seemingly wanting to be far from its former master, jumped forward. He appeared not to notice the extra weight of Edmonda. Beobrand clung to the reins and gripped the broad back of the steed with his thighs. Attor, Dreogan, Elmer, Ceawlin and Aethelwulf spurred their own horses on. Galloping up the slope, they approached Wynhelm and his retinue.

Behind them the fires raged.

As they cleared the ridge, leaving the settlement behind them, Beobrand heard the first screams. He closed his ears to the sounds and rode on.

They slowed to a canter and Coenred and Gothfraidh fell into pace with them. The monks must have waited for the warriors to return, and had not approached the burning buildings or the Waelisc.

"What has happened, Beobrand?" asked Coenred, his voice eager and curious. "Who is this girl?" Beobrand did not answer him. He could not bring himself to talk of it so soon. Perhaps never.

"What has happened?" Coenred repeated in breathless tones.

Beobrand again ignored the monk and kicked Sceadugenga onwards. More wails of anguish drifted to them over the thrum of their horses' hooves. Beobrand dug his heels in savagely, Sceadugenga was beginning to blow and would need to slow soon, but Beobrand wished to be far from this place. His hands shook now as they always did after battle. He could feel the blood of the men he had slain drying and cooling on his skin. He had killed two of them in as many heartbeats and had lost none of his own men. His charges, the monks, were safe, and he had saved one of the defenceless people from violation and likely a grisly death. Surely this was good.

A victory.

But as they rode away, the screams receding into a whispered memory on the rustling-leaf sound of the wind, with only the smudge of smoke in the sky to remind them of what they had seen, he could not stop feeling he had suffered a terrible defeat.

Chapter 3

"By Woden and all the gods, you dare defy me?" Beobrand had held back his anger at Wynhelm all that long day as they rode into the land of the East Angelfolc. But now, with the men setting up camp around him in the well-practised rhythms that came from a long journey, Beobrand allowed his ire to bubble over, like a pot of milk left too long on a hearth.

"Lord Beobrand," said Wynhelm, his voice calm and soothing in the face of Beobrand's anger, "let us go to the stream and fetch water together. We can speak there."

Beobrand wanted nothing more than to scream his fury at Wynhelm, but he bit back his words. The older man's soft tone made his own brash rage seem petulant and childish, which only angered Beobrand further. Snatching up two of the leather flasks they used for collecting water, he stalked off towards the stream without waiting to see whether Wynhelm followed.

The men did not comment on Beobrand's outburst. His gesithas knew of his temper, and had seen all too frequently what happened to those who crossed him. Wynhelm's men did not need prompting to keep out of the way of the huge Cantware thegn as he stamped his way past them and down through the trees to the small brook. Beobrand's anger was legendary, and they had all witnessed how he had ridden amongst the burning buildings and slain the two Waelisc who stood against him.

Beobrand had pushed the men hard all that day, not wishing to pause in case Gwalchmei was able to call upon reinforcements and follow them. It was unlikely. He had let them leave without a fight, but there was a chance that his enmity would lead him to strike out after them, especially if more Waelisc or Mercian warriors could be gathered in pursuit. Would he risk riding across the frontier marches to the east, away from Mercia? Beobrand doubted it, but he might. The further from Mercia they rode, the safer they would be and so they rode on without pausing to eat or rest until the sun was low in the sky at their backs and there was nothing for it but to halt.

The land they had ridden into was low, flat, and dotted with lakes, meres and waterways. As they had pressed south, with the fens to their left, they had seen no way eastward. They had thought to continue south until such a time as they could follow a road into the east. But they had not been riding long when Edmonda spoke to him.

"If you turn from the path here, there is an old causeway, a raised path built by men long ago, that we can follow."

Beobrand could only see boggy land, a few stands of alder and the glint of large expanses of water. There was no sign of a path.

"Are you sure?" he had asked.

"Yes. It used to be a major road, such as Wæcelinga Stræt and Earninga Stræt, but it is not used now. Parts of it have fallen into the water, but it is passable and only those who live in these parts know of it."

Beobrand had thought for only a moment before ordering the men to ride in the direction the girl had pointed. It took them a while to find the beginnings of the built-up track. It was overgrown with brambles and nettles, but the girl had spoken true. For long stretches they rode along the dry, crumbling road, with the quivering reeds and rippled waters of the fens rolling away to north and south.

The road would be of no use to carts or waggons. There were many sections where the stones and rubble had been washed away in long-forgotten floods and storms. At these places, they sometimes needed to dismount and lead the horses, but still they made good time, putting distance between them and the Waelisc warband.

Eventually, they had found a small thicket of rowan on a small rise, with a stream running to the south of the slope. Beobrand had ordered them to make camp, ensuring the fire was lit on the eastern side of the hillock, so that it would not be seen by any pursuers in the west.

All the men had been subdued on the ride eastward. Beobrand wondered what they thought. He could not stop thinking of the terrified faces and pleading eyes of the people they had left behind. He had saved one girl, but would all the others be slain? Or perhaps Gwalchmei would make slaves of them. That would surely bring him more profit than their deaths.

The memory of their screams echoed in his mind as he knelt beside the stream to fill the skins. The cool water washed over his hands. His anger lessened.

"I am sorry," said a quiet voice from behind him, "for speaking against you before the men, and that Waelisc bastard." Beobrand had not heard Wynhelm approach. He covered his surprise by reaching for the second skin. He did not look up at the older thegn.

"I am sorry," Wynhelm repeated, "but you would have got us all killed."

As if a bellows had been pumped hard into a forge fire, the flames of Beobrand's fury were rekindled. He threw down the skin with a splash, and surged to his feet.

"That bastard was going to slay all of those people. They were defenceless… What would you have had me do? Ride by without a second glance?" Again, he heard the echo of the screams in his mind.

"You did what you could, Beobrand. We were outnumbered. Surrounded. We could not have fought them all. What good would it have done to throw our lives away too?"

Beobrand let out a long, shuddering breath. As quickly as his ire has burst into life, so it was now doused by the sense in Wynhelm's words.

Beobrand knelt once more, snatching up the discarded water skin and resumed filling it. Once it was full, he stoppered the skin. He splashed fresh water onto his face, washing some of the grime of travel away. Standing, he turned to Wynhelm, who stood by patiently.

"It is I who should ask your pardon," said Beobrand, feeling foolish now, a child before his elder. "I should not have charged in without a thought for those I lead."

Wynhelm's mouth curled in a rare smile.

"It is what you do. Your men love you for it."

Beobrand snorted.

"They will not love me if I get them all killed."

"I doubt they will much care then," said Wynhelm, now stooping to the water with his own skins. "The men and the king love you because you have luck. Or the gods smile on you. Most men would long ago have perished if they had performed the deeds you have."

Men often commented on Beobrand's luck. He seldom felt it himself. To him it seemed that death stalked the land in his shadow, taking the life from those he loved. His was not the life of a lucky man.

Uncomfortable with the praise, Beobrand turned the conversation to the question that had been gouging at his thoughts ever since they had ridden away from the Waelisc warriors.

"Why was Gwalchmei torching Mercian homes, if he is an ally of Penda's?"

Wynhelm stoppered the skin and pushed himself up.

"Now that," he said, drying his wet hands in his hair, "is a very good question. I've been pondering that all day. In fact, I wonder whether we have not been tricked."

"Tricked? You think perhaps he is not Penda's man?"

"Perhaps, or mayhap he is. But you are right to question the events we witnessed. All is not as it seems. Come," Wynhelm said, leading the way back up the slope in the gathering twilight, "let us ask one who may be able to give us answers."

*

The shadows were deep and heavy by the time they got back to the camp. The fire was burning well, cracking and popping, sending sparks into the darkening sky. The trees would shelter much of the light from the road. The mood in the camp seemed to have lifted, perhaps because Beobrand had taken his brooding anger away from them for a short while. Whatever the reason, the men seemed lighter of spirit as they prepared a meagre meal and got the camp ready for the night ahead.

"Elmer, Attor," Beobrand said, "take the first watch. We'll bring you some food soon."

The two men nodded and made their way out of the camp without comment.

"Be wary," Beobrand called after them, "if those Waelisc are following us, they should not see our fire, but it does not do to expect the best when considering an enemy."

Attor grunted something, and then they were gone, out of the circle of light from the campfire and into the thickening dusk.

The girl, Edmonda, sat close to the fire. She stared into the dancing flames, perhaps reliving the moment when all she knew was destroyed. Her arms were wrapped tightly about her legs, her chin resting on her knees. The firelight lit her face in a ruddy glow, softening her features, making them more pleasing. She was no beauty, but something of her fragility reminded Beobrand of Reaghan, the young Waelisc woman he had left back in Ubbanford. He shook his head. Reaghan may look fragile, small of form, slim of limb, her angular face surrounded by cascades of dark brown hair, but in many ways, she was as strong as any man. He missed her.

"Edmonda," he said in the soft voice he saved for frightened animals. She started, then turned her face toward him. Her eyes were dark, sunken in shadow, full of despair. "Edmonda," he said again. She did not reply, but raised her eyebrows in question.

"Why was Gwalchmei burning your steading?"

"Not steading," she said, her voice hollow.

"What then?"

"Monastery."

Of course. Again, Beobrand felt foolish. It should have been clear. All those rounded up by Gwalchmei's men had been wearing plain robes, much like those worn by Coenred and Gothfraidh.

"But why attack the monastery?" A thought came to him. "Is it because Penda forbids the worship of the Christ in his lands?"

"It's true, Penda is no lover of the Christ," she answered, "but he does not forbid His worship in the lands of Mercia."

"Then why send Gwalchmei to attack, if they are indeed allies."

"Oh, I am sure they are allies. Though I do not know if Penda sent the Waelisc to torment us. Rather I believe he has been told to scout ahead for a larger warhost."

The night suddenly grew colder. A wind shook the branches of the rowan, making them creak and moan. Beobrand looked at Wynhelm. The older man's features were drawn and harsh in the fire-shadows.

"But why burn buildings in his own kingdom? And why kill his people or…" he could not bring himself to talk of what the warriors had been doing to Edmonda.

"He was not causing harm to his own people, lord," Edmonda said, her tone making it clear she had thought this much was obvious to all. "The monastery is in land that is oft-disputed between Mercia and the East Angelfolc."

"And to which people does the monastery belong."

"The monastery lies in the kingdom of King Ecgric."

"Ecgric?"

"He is king of the East Angelfolc."

"Not Sigeberht?" Beobrand asked, thinking of the strange, sombre, pious king he had met the previous summer. He had seemed more monk than king then. His hall had been a mean place where the warriors grumbled into their bowls of thin pottage. Perhaps they had turned on their lord. "I had not heard of Sigeberht's death."

"Oh no," she said, a look of surprise on her face, "Sigeberht is not dead. He has given himself to God. He prays for the souls of all the folk in the land." Her eyes were wide in awe at the devotion of this holy king.

Beobrand had never heard of such a thing.

"So, the king has become a priest?"

"Not a priest, but he is very holy. His prayers will be listened to by the Almighty."

"He will need more than prayers if Penda is coming and is freshly allied with the Waelisc."

Edmonda suddenly lunged forward. She picked up a fresh log and threw it into the fire. Sparks showered. Gone was the softness of face of moments before, the dancing light now made her face a hard mask, grim with shadows.

"I will pray that God brings his righteous punishment upon the Waelisc."

Not so unlike Reaghan after all. There was iron beneath that soft female flesh.

"So, who is this Ecgric?" he asked. "And where can I find him?"

"He is the king, lord. Kinsman of Sigeberht. He rules now, but I know not where he is."

Wynhelm, had remained silent, but now stepped forward into the light. Beyond the small light of the fire all was dark now.

"I have travelled the lands of East Angeln before," Wynhelm said. "There is a great hall to the south and east. Rendlæsham is its name. If the king is not there, we can learn of his whereabouts. It is not far from where we were headed anyway. News of the Mercian host may well precede us, but we should make haste. The king will wish to prepare the defence of the land."

"What of Gothfraidh and me?" said Coenred, his youthful face glowing in the red light of the flames. His head was shaved from forehead to crown, but his hair fell thick and long to his shoulders. "We have gifts for King Sigeberht from Holy Abbot Aidan and our lord king, Oswald." He ran his long fingers nervously though his hair and Beobrand noticed how the monk's hand fell to the finely-carved casket. The chest never left his sight and Beobrand wondered what could be so valuable that it required so many warriors to protect it. He knew it was not heavy, so it could not be gold, or silver. Gems perhaps.

"The land is not safe, Coenred," Beobrand said, noting the tension in the young monk's jaw. "You ride with us. The old king can wait for his gifts."

Beobrand sensed that Coenred meant to argue with him. But Beobrand was done with discussions. Tiredness washed over him as he turned, without waiting for a response, and walked into the darkness.

*

The low murmur of the voices of the men drifted to Beobrand on the cool night air, but he could not make out their words. They spoke quietly as they prepared food and readied the campsite, aware that sound travelled far at night. A gust of wind rustled the leaves of the rowan above him, further masking the sounds of the men. He pulled his woollen cloak about him. He needed these moments of peace and would often step away from their camps to stand and listen to the night.

And to think.

Someway off to his right he could see the shape of Elmer, silhouetted against the darkening sky. The large gesith had heard his approach, turned and raised a hand to Beobrand, but he knew his lord well enough and did not come near or attempt to speak. Beobrand was glad of it.

For a moment, he thought of Acennan. Where was his friend? Beobrand had heard from Eadgyth in Eoferwic that he had headed south at the end of the winter. At the first sign of a thaw, he had mounted up and told the dark-haired maid that he would speak with her brother or father to seek their approval of their marriage. In the darkness Beobrand smiled. Acennan had been smitten, and he could see why. Eadgyth was a beauty no doubt, and with a quick mind and strong will too. She was a woman worth fighting for.

Beobrand's brow furrowed. He hoped his friend had not ridden into trouble in Mercia. He had been gone for weeks. Well, there was nothing that he could do. For all he knew Acennan had returned to Eoferwic already and was laughing at having missed his lord.

An owl hooted somewhere off to the north-west. A fox shrieked.

As if in answer, a blaze appeared just below the horizon to the west. It was hard to judge how far away it was, but it must have been at least half a day's walk. The last light from the sun had faded from the sky and the fire stood out bright and flickering against the gloom. Its light glinted off the surface of one of the meres they had passed. For such a fire to be so clear, it must have been huge. Were the Waelisc burning another hall? Even now, were men, women and children being murdered, enslaved, violated? He found himself holding his breath and straining to hear, but no sound came to him beyond the rustle of the trees and the murmur of voices. The scent of cooking meat wafted to him. His stomach clenched at the smell as it mingled with dark memories.

He shuddered. There had been so many fires in his life. His wyrd seemed interwoven with flames. He recalled his home in Hithe, engulfed in smoke and flame. Sunniva's father, Strang, charred flesh pulling back from grinning teeth as his body smouldered on a charcoal mound. He remembered seeing the flames of Gefrin leaping into the sky to light the clouds as Scand led them to Bebbanburg and safety. The searing heat and chaos of Nathair's hall as it burnt and illuminated a night of terrible slaughter.

And then, closing his eyes, he could see the shape of Sunniva as she was consumed by the great bone-fire he had built for her.

A light step on the leaf mould alerted him to someone's approach. He felt the cooling of the tears on his face and cuffed them away angrily.

"The Waelisc?" said Coenred.

Beobrand relaxed. Coenred was a true friend. He'd nursed Beobrand to health after the battle of Elmet and risked his life for him more than once.

"Probably," answered Beobrand. "Or another warband of Penda's. They mean to savage the land until this new king, this Ecgric, has no option but to face them in battle."

They were silent for a time, each gazing into the night at the distant flames.

"It was a good thing you did, Beo," Coenred said as last.

"What?"

"Rescuing the nun, Edmonda."

Beobrand thought of all those he had not saved. All the ghosts that would come to him in his dreams demanding vengeance.

"Too many remained," he said. He hawked and spat into the darkness. The taste of failure was sour in his mouth.

"You could do no more."

Beobrand was not convinced. What good had he done saving Edmonda? But deep within him there was a flicker of pride in his action. Surely saving one was better than allowing all to die?

"You saved Edmonda from terrible torture, and God alone knows what her life will bring. Perhaps she is destined for greatness." On the horizon, the fire flared up. Perhaps the roof of the building had fallen in, feeding the flames. "Many more will suffer torment or death in the coming days it seems," said Coenred. He did not speak of Tata. He had no need. Beobrand remembered all too well Coenred's sister, her pale bruised and blood-streaked form on the altar, after she had been used and murdered by Waelisc warriors. Tata was another ghost that haunted his dreams.

For a long moment, neither of them spoke. The flames in the distance continued to burn with intensity.

"Will war never cease?" Coenred asked.

"I doubt it," said Beobrand. "It pleases the gods too much."

"It does not please the one true God," Coenred said, his voice taking on an edge of anger.

"If your god does not like it and is so powerful," Beobrand snapped, bitterness making his tone jagged and harsh, "then why does he not stop it?"

Coenred was silent. He had no answer.

Beobrand spat again and strode back to the camp.

Beobrand lay wrapped in his cloak, listening to the night sounds. A log shifted on the small campfire with a creak and a sigh. All about him, the men slept, snoring and grunting. He could not find sleep so easily. He had taken the second watch, thinking to tire his body past the point where it could resist the embrace of slumber, and yet here he lay, eyes glittering in the firelight, while memories flapped in his mind like a murder of crows caught inside a mead hall.

He had used to be able to sleep in an instant, and had seldom dreamt. But those days had gone, fled along with lost loved ones. He tried not to dwell on the past, as Bassus always counselled. He knew he could never change what had happened, but he could no more prevent thinking of those who had died, than he could ignore the loss of his fingers on his left hand when lacing his shoes.

He had pushed himself hard through each short gloomy day of the long winter, training with sword, spear and shield, rebuilding the strength in his battered body, honing his battle-skill. When it was raining, he would have the hall cleared of boards and benches and practise weapon-play with the men there. They griped and complained, but Beobrand could not bear the alternative: to sit drinking, eating, talking and thinking. He did everything he could to keep them all occupied and tired. A good day for him was when he fell into the bed he shared with Reaghan, coupled ferociously and then collapsed into a dreamless sleep. But such days came all too rarely.

His nights had been plagued with vivid dreams. Faces of those he had loved would come to him. And also, the terrifying, blood-streaked features of those he had killed. He would awaken then, sweat-drenched and panting, as if he had run a long distance. Sometimes, Reaghan would stir, and mumble something to him. He would stroke her smooth slender back and she would quieten, her breathing slowing, leaving him alone with the darkness and his thoughts.

He had been short-tempered for much of the long, frigid winter. He knew he should have been content with his lot. He had loyal gesithas, friends, a fine woman in Reaghan, and a son. And yet every part of Ubbanford, especially his great hall, reminded him of Sunniva, of the fact that her defiler, Wybert, yet roamed free and that he had failed to slay him when he had been given the chance.

One of the wardens coughed in the still night, rousing Beobrand from his thoughts. The ghost of sleep had been tugging at his senses, but now it fled once more and he was alert again.

He had made a decision in those long, silent winter nights, where the only sounds were the snores of his warriors, and the wind moaning under the eaves of the hall. He would not rest until he had found Wybert and taken from him the blood-price he was owed. He vowed this to Woden, Tiw and Thunor. He even swore it to Frige, the goddess that Sunniva had often prayed to. He hoped they would all witness his oath and help him to exact revenge. Perhaps then, he would know peace. Maybe, with Wybert dead, he would be able to sleep without the shades of the past disturbing his rest.

One bitter day, when the Tuidi had frozen over completely and the ice cracked and groaned, Coenred had come to Ubbanford. The young monk came with a group of the Christ brethren from Lindisfarena. They came once every few weeks to preach to the people of Ubbanford and Beobrand welcomed them. Attor was always overjoyed to see the Christ followers, and earlier in the year he had been baptised in the river. Abbot Aidan had cured him from a terrible wound that had been festering and ever since, he had been a devout follower of the new god.

Coenred had come down to the river where Beobrand stood alone swinging his sword and hefting his shield. His breath had clouded around him like fog.

"I remember seeing you practising like this back in Engelmynster. Remember?" Coenred had said.

Beobrand had paused, lowering his sword.

"Aye," he'd said, wiping his fast-cooling sweat from his brow with his sleeve, "I remember." He had been injured and left for dead after the battle of Elmet. Coenred had helped to nurse him back to health.

Coenred had given him a long, appraising look.

"You have that same intensity now." He'd frowned. "The same anger."

Beobrand had sighed.

"I wanted vengeance then. And I want vengeance now."

"Has nothing changed, then?" Coenred had asked.

For a moment Beobrand had said nothing, just staring down the river. The land was cloaked in ice and snow, making it strange, quiet, still and forbidding.

"All that has changed is that I have more enemies. And more need for revenge."

Coenred had cast his gaze down, sadness washing over his face.

"Our Lord the Christ says that whosoever shall smite you on your right cheek, turn to him the other also."

Beobrand had scoffed at the idea.

"I have heard the priests say as much. But I have also heard them say that the punishment should match the injury: 'An eye for an eye, and a tooth for a tooth.' That is a god I could follow, for he speaks as Woden."

"You should turn away from this path, Beobrand. It will bring you nothing but pain."

"I cannot. I have sworn the bloodfeud. It is the only way I can hope to find peace."

As soon as the snows had melted and the frosts of winter had receded into the north for another year, Beobrand had been summoned to Bebbanburg.

There, in the great hall atop the rocky crag that overlooked the slate-grey Whale Road, Oswald had told Beobrand he wished him to lead an escort for holy men who would carry gifts of great value to Sigeberht, king of the East Angelfolc.

Beobrand had stepped forward, close to the great gift-stool of the king.

"Cannot another perform this task?" he had pleaded. "I would seek your leave to go in pursuit of my enemy, Wybert. You know I have sworn the bloodfeud with the man, and I cannot find peace while he yet walks upon this middle earth."

Oswald had not wavered.

"No, Beobrand," he had said in his soft, even tones, "I need you to accompany these men of Christ southward. I know you burn for revenge, but your vengeance will have to wait." At least he had not attempted to preach to him of turning his cheek. Oswald knew him too well for that.

And so, Beobrand had ridden south, putting aside his bloodfeud for a few weeks more.

Somewhere, out in the darkness of the fens, a bird shrieked. One of the guards placed a fresh log on the fire where it crackled and popped for a moment, sparks drifting into the blackness.

Beobrand closed his eyes and willed sleep to come. The last thing he remembered seeing in his mind's eyes before drifting into slumber was the sneering face of Wybert, goading him from across a sun-licked meadow while a host of Northumbrian and Mercian thegns watched on.

Chapter 4

Reaghan looked down at the little round face of the babe. Octa's eyes were closed and his mouth slightly open. He had flung off his blankets and now lay in a tangled mess of limbs and bed clothes. He was on his back with arms and leg flopped out with abandon in the crib. He was a good child. He hated being swaddled and always fought his way free of his blankets, but he seldom woke her in the night and was quick to smile during the day.

She loved Octa as if he were her own child. The thought scared her. Reaghan had never said the words to anyone, but she had long since admitted as much to herself. Of course, he was not hers and despite Beobrand's vigorous attentions throughout the long winter nights, his seed had failed to find fertile ground within her. How had she been so foolish? She had carried his child before and had longed to be rid of it, and now she wept silent tears of regret whenever her monthly blood came. For the briefest of moments, she remembered the cramping pains as her body had voided the unborn babe. No, she would not think of it. It was an evil thought and she could not change the past.

Stupid, stupid, girl.

She sniffed. Octa had soiled himself, the sickly pungent stench of baby-shit oozed from where he was sprawled. He smirked in his sleep and she could not help but smile back. How he seemed to love lying in his own filth! She could scarcely believe it, such was the stink, but it never seemed to wake him.

She would clean and change him soon, but while he yet slept, why wake him? She knew he would bawl and scream once she began to wipe him with a wet cloth. After that, there would be a long while of grizzling before he would find sleep again. So, she would wait.

But not so close, the smell was terrible.

She carried the rush light back to her bed, sheltering the small flame with her hand as she walked. The stink of the sizzling mutton fat that she usually hated, seemed almost pleasant following the smell of Octa's soiled cloth wraps. She lay down on the straw-filled mattress. It was a large bed, big enough for two. Her tiny form was lost in it without the bulk of Beobrand beside her.

She looked at the dancing shadows of the roof beams as the rush light guttered on the stool where she had placed it. Sleep was a long way off. She found it hard these days to find slumber. Her days used to be marked with arduous chores. Lady Rowena would chase her about Ubbanford, never happy to see her idle. And after a long day of cleaning, mending, cooking and carrying water up from the river, Reaghan would collapse into her small cot, sleep washing through her almost before she was still. The only times she had found it hard to sleep then was if Rowena or her daughter, Edlyn, had seen fit to take a hazel switch to her. Then she would lie on her front uncomfortably, every movement causing the welts to sting.

Now she was not pushed to complete her chores, nor did Rowena or Edlyn dare to strike her. And the only other thing that would send her to sleep was not possible without Beobrand. The pleasing memory came to her of his weight. His callused hands caressing her, the feel of his heavily-muscled arms around her, his hips thrusting…

She shivered in the gloom of the hall. How she missed him.

A year before she would have scoffed at the thought. She had hated the Angelfolc. They had killed her family and enslaved her. She had been ill-used by Ubba, his sons and some of his gesithas. She had been largely accepted by the women, until she had begun to turn the heads of their men. Jealousy had made the womenfolk spiteful and Reaghan had merely sought to get through each day without a beating. As each drudge-filled day had passed, her hatred of those who had made her a thrall deepened. She had dreamt of her family, the freedom to do as she pleased, the warmth of her father's embrace after a long day working the land.

And then, one autumn day, Beobrand, son of Grimgundi, had ridden into Ubbanford on his huge black steed and just like that, she no longer hated all of the Angelfolc.

Beyond the partition she heard a cough, then a loud snoring.

She smiled. No, she no longer hated them all. Bassus, Beobrand's friend, was gruff, but he was a good man. He doted on Octa as if he were the babe's grandfather, and he treated Reaghan with respect. And sometimes, when he forgot himself, even with tenderness.

But it was Beobrand who had changed everything. Lost in his grief for his wife, he had turned to her for solace, as Ubba and his sons had before him. And yet, there was something different about the young thegn from Cantware. Something had stirred within her at his touch. Then, in that terrible night of flame and horror, he had risked all to rescue her. From that point on, she had known she was his, and not merely as thrall and lord.

Evidently, he had felt it too, for after the Blotmonath feast he had given Rowena a small sack full of hack silver and trinkets in payment for Reaghan. Then, he had led Reaghan and a large group of witnesses out on the path towards Berewic. When they had come to the first joining of paths, Beobrand had stopped and, blushing, had haltingly declared that Reaghan was no longer a thrall. Just as she now stood at a crossing of tracks, so she was now free to choose her own path from this day hence. He had turned then and limped his way back towards Ubbanford, for his leg had still troubled him after his fight at Din Eidyn. For a moment, everyone had stared at her, as if they expected her to run off into the wilds. She had looked upon the faces of those gathered there. Some, like Bassus and Maida, had been pleased for her, smiling encouragement. Rowena had frowned and turned her face from her. Reaghan had looked down the paths that led away from Ubbanford, and then turned to watch Beobrand's back. He did not turn to see which path she would choose.

A strong wind had rustled through the woodland that surrounded the track. She had shivered. Then, taking a deep breath, she'd set off after him.

She could still scarcely believe this thing had happened. Her sudden freedom had frightened her. Still did. She would always be thankful to him for what he had done, but she wondered whether he had ever given a thought for what she would do while he was away. She longed for his return. When he was at the hall, laughter and song rang out in the night as his men revelled and riddled by the firelight. When he was away, the hall was quiet and she never felt at ease; never fully safe.

Her eyes had closed now, and she was at last slipping into the embrace of sleep.

A wailing pierced the night-silence. Instantly awake, she sat up, her heart hammering.

And then the smell of shit wafted to her. It was Octa. He had finally decided that he had had enough of the stink. She climbed out of her cot and padded softly across the rush-strewn floor to attend to the baby. Despite the stench as she approached and the loud screams that split the quiet of a moment before, she smiled.

Chapter 5

"I have never been in a land so flat," said Elmer, shielding his eyes from the setting sun.

Beobrand did not reply, but he could not argue with the bulky warrior. They had ridden all that day through woods and past great ponds and meres. At times, they had ridden through large areas of open land, where little grew save for bracken and stunted grasses, but at no point had they encountered anything higher than the low rise they had camped on the night before. There were wrinkles in this land, but nothing that could be called a hill and certainly no mountains.

They now stood atop one such rise in the earth. They were surrounded by trees on all sides, but for some reason none grew atop the rise.

"Like Birinus' hair," Coenred had said, smiling at his own jest.

Beobrand offered the monk a thin smile. It was true, the bald crown of land surrounded by trees was reminiscent of the strange shaved pate of the bishop of Wessex, but he did not reply. He was too tired. And he was nervous. The land was strange to him, and he feared they were riding into a war.

Beobrand nudged Sceadugenga closer to Elmer's mount and peered into the west, following Elmer's gaze. The sun's orb was hazed by a pall of smoke. It seemed the Waelisc, or perhaps other warbands, had been busy.

"How far to Rendlæsham?" asked Beobrand.

Wynhelm reined in beside them. He too looked tired, his face drawn and pale.

"If we ride hard," he said, "we should reach there tomorrow."

A cry came from the head of their small band. Turning to face the south, Beobrand saw Attor approaching at a canter. He had been scouting some distance from the group, vigilant for danger and seeking out likely spots for them to pitch camp.

Clattering past the other riders, Attor made straight for Beobrand. The hands around Beobrand's waist tightened, reminding him of Edmonda's presence. She had been silent for most of the day. At midday he had asked her to ride with one of the other men for a time, to spare Sceadugenga from carrying two riders, but she had shaken her head, eyes wide with fear, so he had not persisted. He had felt the warmth of her against his back now for so long he had almost forgotten she rode there. Sceadugenga appeared not to notice the extra burden.

"Riders approaching," Attor said.

All around them, the warriors began checking their weapons. Shields were unslung from backs, seaxes and swords loosened in scabbards.

"How many and how far?" asked Beobrand.

"I only saw two, lord," Attor paused to spit into the dust of the path they followed. "They could be out-riders for a larger warband. But I don't think so."

"Why not?"

"They are riding hard. I'd say they are messengers, or they are fleeing from someone."

"How far?" Beobrand asked again, absently caressing the hilt of Hrunting with his half-hand.

"Not far, lord," said Attor.

A shout went up from some of Wynhelm's men. Edmonda's grip tightened.

Beobrand nudged Sceadugenga forward. Two riders had burst from the elm woods to the south and were galloping towards them. Quickly, Beobrand assessed them. The lowering sun did not glint from byrnies or helms. They bore no spears.

"Not far?" he said, turning to Attor with a raised eyebrow. "They are practically in our laps."

Attor grinned and spat again.

"Sorry, lord, they were coming on fast and hidden by trees."

Beobrand glanced back at the approaching riders. They were bearing down on them. There was no more time for talk.

"Elmer, Dreogan, Attor. With me. The rest of you stay here."

"Careful," said Wynhelm.

"Do not worry, Wynhelm," Beobrand said, sliding Edmonda to the ground. "Watch the girl, and if they try anything, ride them down and slay them."

Edmonda clutched at his hand for a moment. Her eyes were wide, tears brimming. He could feel the trembling of her. She was terrified; the events of the monastery still raw and fresh in her mind. But there was no time to put her at her ease.

"Wynhelm will keep you safe," Beobrand said, pulling his fingers from her grasp.

He tugged Sceadugenga's head to the side and kicked his heels into the horse's flanks. With a great burst of speed, the black stallion sprang forward. The power of the beast always amazed him. Even after a day of carrying two riders, Sceadugenga was willing to gallop. With Dreogan and Attor beside him, Beobrand rushed down the shallow slope towards the riders. Elmer followed a couple of horse-lengths behind.

The approaching riders slowed their mounts and awaited the four warriors. In a few heartbeats Beobrand was pulling Sceadugenga to a halt before the two men. Beobrand noticed they were both young, slight of build, with only seaxes at their belts. Each was dusty and sweat-streaked, as were their mounts. It seemed Attor was right. These men were riding somewhere with haste and did not plan to fight.

For a moment, none of the men spoke. As Beobrand had taken their measure, so now, they sized up him and his men. The younger of the two riders, a sandy-haired youth with wispy beard and freckle-splashed cheeks, seemed to come to a decision.

"Are you Lord Ordway?" he asked, nudging his horse forward a few steps.

"I am not," answered Beobrand, who had never heard of the man.

The freckled rider thought for a moment, clearly at a loss for words.

"Are you Lord Ordway's men?"

"We are not."

"Then who are you?" An edge of concern entered the young man's voice, and he glanced back at his companion, who started to edge his horse back, away from Beobrand and his gesithas.

"Why don't you tell me first who you are?" Beobrand said. He held the boy's eyes in his blue gaze.

"I… I mean… We…" Another glance at his companion, who had now moved his mount several paces back in the direction they had come. His eyes flicked from side to side, taking in the men on the rise and the warriors before them. All were heavily armed with swords, shields, spears and iron-knit shirts. His face was pale, but he offered his friend no aid.

"Don't look to him," snapped Beobrand. "Who are you?"

The boy swallowed and must have decided there was nothing for it, or there was no harm in giving his name.

"I am Brun, son of Iuwine," he said, jutting his chin in a show of defiance.

Beobrand smiled.

"Well, Brun son of Iuwine, where are you riding in such haste?"

Again, Brun sought out his companion for support, but found none. Having now decided to speak, he seemed almost eager to impart his news.

"We are sent to call upon Lord Ordway and any other man of worth to do his duty to his lord and king, Ecgric, son of Rædwald," he spoke in a breathless rush. "The land is under attack. Penda of Mercia has a warhost and Ecgric rides to meet him. He has called the fyrd to protect the land."

So, it was as Edmonda had suspected. Penda sought to take East Angeln, the kingdom of the East Angelfolc. By the gods, what had they ridden into?

When Beobrand did not respond immediately, Brun squared his shoulders, brave now that he had spoken his mission aloud.

"Whatever your name, you must ride to do your duty."

"And what is my duty?" asked Beobrand.

"You must serve your king and lord," answered Brun.

"But Ecgric is not my lord or my king."

At hearing these words, the man who had pulled some way from them wheeled his mount around and kicked it into a canter southward.

"I told you they were Mercians!" he cried over his shoulder.

"Halt!" shouted Beobrand in a voice that could cut through the tumult of clashing shieldwalls. "We are no Mercians."

The man reined in, but looked ready to gallop away at the slightest provocation. He was about a spear's throw distant now, so Beobrand raised his voice for all to hear.

"We are no Mercians," he repeated. "Nor are we King Ecgric's men. I am Beobrand, lord of Ubbanford, thegn of King Oswald, who is king of Northumbria. We are your allies, not your enemies. Now, tell us where the fyrd gathers so that we may ride to your king. I would speak with him."

*

The two messengers had been hard to convince that Beobrand and the other warriors from Northumbria were not in fact a warband from Mercia sent to strike deep within the heart of the land of East Angeln. Though what they thought they could do about it, outnumbered as they were by armed and mounted men, Beobrand did not know. In the end, it had been Edmonda who had convinced them.

She had walked down the slope towards them. Beobrand noticed she had ensured her plain wooden cross pendant was clearly on display, resting atop the rise of her breasts. Plain as she was of face, her slim form was feminine beneath the rough linen of her habit. None of the men could look anywhere but that bouncing rood as she approached.

"What the lord Beobrand tells you is the truth," she said, her voice firmer than Beobrand had heard it before. "These men rescued me from Waelisc allies of Penda. They now mean to seek out King Ecgric with news of the attack on his kingdom."

"But Ecgric knows Penda plans to attack," said Brun.

"That may be so, but we did not know that. Besides, there are two other holy men who travel from the sacred isle of Lindisfarena with gifts for the most Christian Sigeberht."

Eventually, they either believed them, or had come to the conclusion they could do nothing to stop them if they tried.

"Follow this path and soon you will see the campfires of Ecgric's host," Brun had pointed south. "Godspeed to you, lady," he had nodded to Edmonda. "Mayhap we will see you, lord Beobrand, on our return."

With that, Brun and his nervous companion had galloped northward into the gloom of the trees.

Chapter 6

They rode into the encampment the next day, shortly after the sun pushed itself over the horizon. Clouds had gathered at dusk bringing with them an all-drenching drizzle. Before the land was cloaked in darkness, they had seen the smear of smoke from many fires against the gloaming. Ecgric's host was not camped far away, but they had decided to wait until morning to approach.

"Riding into a host of warriors who are expecting battle is not wise," Wynhelm had said. Beobrand had not argued. The two messengers had been tense, full of the tension of impending war. To surprise a host of such nervous men would not end well.

And so they had spent a miserable night, huddled around a guttering and spitting fire that only Aethelwulf's fire-skill had been able to kindle. The light rain had fallen incessantly and by the first watery glow of morning, they were all cold, wet and irritable.

Despite their concerns the night before, none of the men assembled at the encampment seemed interested in their arrival. Their mounts churned up earth that was already a quagmire, while around them men crouched beneath any shelter they could find or craft. There seemed no order to the camp. They continued slowly through the camped warhost, scanning the small collection of tents that some of the wealthier warriors possessed for sign of a royal standard or sigil.

"Look at that," said Ceawlin.

They reined in and spread out, so as to all be able to see what the warrior was staring at in open amazement.

"It looks as though a giant carved out the land," Aethelwulf said, awe in his voice.

"Do you think this was made by the same men who built the Wall?" asked Beobrand. It was the only thing he could think of that matched the scale of what lay before them.

The land fell away into a deep, steep-sided ditch. As deep as the height of many men, it was a formidable defence. It disappeared into the rain-misted distance to the left and right, cutting straight into the earth until lost to sight.

"Who can say?" said Wynhelm. "But it is a good place to make a stand against an enemy. It would seem this Ecgric is no fool. A small force," he looked about him, "however slovenly, could hold off a larger host here, atop this ditch. Even Penda, the great warlord, will be unable to take this position from a stout defence. As long as the men hold this ridge, none shall pass."

Beobrand gazed into the south-west. The path they had been following stretched to the horizon. Who knew how far it went? Perhaps it too was a reminder of the men from the south who had long ago ruled the land of Albion, but he did not think so. This was something more natural, less tamed. Perhaps it was even older than the men of Roma. He pictured Penda's host as he had seen it at Elmet. He imagined the great wall of men beneath their lord's wolf-pelt standard. They would darken the land with their numbers. Looking back at the fyrd-men gathered around them, he shivered. Could these men stand against the might of Penda?

He hoped that Wynhelm was right about being able to defend here, but doubt tugged at his mind.

"You," Beobrand said suddenly to a scraggly-haired man who stood gawping at them. "Where is the king?"

The man sucked at his moustaches and shook his head.

"No king here," he said.

"Then who leads?"

"I don't rightly know," answered the man, scratching his head. He wore such an expression of vacant stupidity that Beobrand wanted to leap from Sceadugenga's back and beat the man. Did he not see that they would all perish here, if they did not organise a strong defence? He gripped his reins until his knuckles hurt. It was not the man's fault. Someone must lead here.

Wiping the rain from his eyes, Beobrand selected the largest tent he could see, a taut leather structure, surrounded by three smaller shelters, and spurred Sceadugenga towards it.

Men cursed as they passed, splashing rain and mud. A man bearing a spear leapt to his feet and hurled abuse at the riders. Gram's mount shied from the man, trampling over the campsite of a small group of men. The horse whinnied in fear as it crashed through the smoky fire, sending sparks and sputtering logs flying. The men threw themselves aside, screaming their anger. Gram wrestled with his mount, for a moment looking like he would be unseated. But he soon had it under control once more and joined the rest of them as they reined in before the collection of tents.

"Well done, Gram," Aethelwulf said, no hint of a smile on his face. "That will have woken the bastards up."

"This bastard is already up," said a brawny man who strode forth from the shelter of the large tent. He was not a young man, but broad of shoulder and strong of arm. His beard was dark, but streaked with grey at his chin. He wore a sword at his side, the finely-wrought hilt protruding from a red leather scabbard, adorned with embossed metal. He took in the scene at a glance with the practised eye of a warrior and leader of men.

"Who are you?" he asked, voice sharp, but not raised. "I recognise none of you, but you are clearly men of worth. Whence do you come?"

"We have ridden from Northumbria," said Beobrand. "From the land of our lord king, Oswald, son of Æthelfrith. Who are you? Do you lead here?"

The man squared his shoulders. The arm rings he wore strained against the muscles there as he folded his arms across his wide chest.

"You have ridden into my camp, Northumbrian," he said, voice as cold now as the rain that trickled down Beobrand's neck. "I would know your name before I speak mine, and I would have you do me the courtesy of dismounting before we speak further."

Beobrand clenched his jaw. Wynhelm shot him a look of caution. He took a deep breath of the damp morning air. It was redolent of churned mud, cooking fires and midden pits. Slowly, he swung himself down from Sceadugenga's back. Then, reaching up, he helped Edmonda dismount too.

Wynhelm and the rest of the men followed his lead and a moment later they were all standing at the heads of their steeds, holding their reins.

Beobrand handed Sceadugenga's reins to Edmonda and took a step towards the man.

"I am Beobrand, lord of Ubbanford, thegn of Bernicia," he said, keeping his tone flat.

"Truly?" the bearded warrior surprised him by smiling broadly. His eyes flicked down, and Beobrand realised with a start that the man was staring at his left hand. "Beobrand Half-hand is here," he said, turning to the men who had congregated outside the tents. "Tales of your exploits precede you, lord Beobrand. We have oft heard the scop's sing the lay of how you slew Hengist."

Beobrand frowned.

"The scops tell many lies," he said.

The man, rubbed his beard thoughtfully, but his smile remained.

"Mayhap that is so. But you are here now, and you can tell us your tale yourself."

"I am no story-teller." Beobrand thought of his friend, Leofwine. There was a man who had possessed a true gift for songs and tales. Alas, he was not gifted in the sword-play and had fallen at Gefrin. Beobrand wondered whether he would ever enjoy again the telling of a good story. Perhaps, but not one that told of his own life.

Nobody spoke for a moment, then the man raised himself up to his full height and lifted his head. He was still at least a head shorter than Beobrand, who towered over most men.

"Well, you have told me your name, now I will tell you mine. I am Offa, son of Alfric, and yes, I lead here."

"Where is the king?" asked Beobrand. "I would speak with him."

Offa's face clouded.

"My lord Ecgric is not here."

"Where is he?"

Offa hesitated

"Come, let my men tend to your horses. Break your fast with me in my tent and I will tell you of the king."

*

"King Ecgric is where?" Beobrand struggled to keep his voice even.

"Your ears do not deceive you," said Offa. "The king has retired to Beodericsworth."

Beobrand could scarcely believe what he had heard.

"But Penda is approaching," he said. "He is allied once more with men of Gwynedd, perhaps other Waelisc kingdoms too. We have seen his men torching your buildings, murdering your people." Beobrand looked to where Edmonda knelt. She had refused to be separated from him and had followed them silently into the tent. She had not spoken, but Beobrand saw the glimmer of her eyes as she watched everything. "Does your king not believe his place is here with his fyrd?"

Wynhelm reached out and placed a hand on Beobrand's arm. Beobrand glanced at him. Their eyes met. He understood the man, despite the older thegn not speaking. They did not know these people. Offa seemed a good man, but no warrior took kindly to men insulting his lord.

Beobrand took a sip of the ale Offa had offered them when they had first entered the tent. It was sour. The three men were seated on stools. A great helm and shield rested against a wooden chest. In contrast to the encampment, the tent was ordered and tidy. It reeked of sweat and wet leather.

They were all silent for a moment. Offa looked forlornly into his cup before taking a gulp of the ale.

"Ecgric is not a bad man," he said at last, quietly. "He is a good lord, generous and honourable."

"Then why is he not here?" snapped Beobrand. From the corner of his eye he saw Edmonda flinch.

Offa looked up sharply, his brows furrowed.

"I cannot speak for my lord king's decisions. But, lord Beobrand," said Offa, an edge of iron creeping into his tone, "I know you are a warrior of renown, but do not forget yourself. I have carried shield and sword for longer than you have breathed. I will not hear an ill word spoken against any king of East Angeln." He drained his cup, grimacing at the taste of the ale. "I will fight the man who insults my king."

Wynhelm raised his hands in a placating manner.

"It seems to me we are allies here," he said. "Beobrand means no harm. He is but young. Headstrong. And you will be needing to save all your fight for the Mercians and the Waelisc."

Beobrand said nothing. Wynhelm's words angered him, not least because he knew them to be true. He took another sip of his ale.

"How far is this Beodericsworth," asked Wynhelm.

"Not far. Half a day's ride. Less in good weather." The wind picked up outside, shaking the walls of the tent. The leather slapped and cracked and the tent was filled with the sudden sound of heavy rain thrumming.

Offa smiled ruefully.

"Half a day's ride," he said. "The king has told me to send word the moment the enemy is seen, and he will ride here with all speed."

Beobrand could contain himself no longer.

"But what does he do at Beodericsworth that he cannot do here?" he asked. "Is there a woman there whose company he seeks?"

Offa sniffed. "Perhaps." The previous tension had dissipated like the rain running off the skin of the tent. "There are many fine women in Beodericsworth. But I believe Ecgric seeks the company of a man, not a woman."

Wynhelm, his cup to his lips, spluttered.

Offa grinned now, pleased at the reaction to his words.

"He seeks the counsel of his kinsman."

"His kinsman?" said Beobrand.

"Aye. His kinsman. Sigeberht." At the mention of Sigeberht, Offa's face lit up.

"The old king is at Beodericsworth?"

"Of course, he is. It is where he built his monastery school. A fine place to teach boys the ways of the Christ god."

"And Ecgric seeks Sigeberht out so that he can help the fyrd with the Christ's magic?" Beobrand finally thought he understood the king's decision to leave the host and travel to a monastery. The Christ's power was strong. Perhaps it could help them defeat Penda.

"He may want Sigeberht to pray for him, but I believe he wants his advice."

"About what?" asked Wynhelm.

"This battle of course. Sigeberht was not always a man of God." Offa's tone grew wistful. "He was a great warlord. A man to lift the spirits of his gesithas. Men would fight to the death at his command."

There was something about the way Offa spoke of Sigeberht.

"You were one of his comitatus?" Beobrand asked. "Sigeberht was your lord?"

Offa looked at him as if he were slow-witted.

"Of course. And he was the best of lords."

"But now you serve Ecgric."

Offa nodded.

"Now I serve Ecgric." Offa set his cup down on the chest. He took a long slow breath. Outside the rain had subsided. A horse whinnied and a dog barked. "I serve Ecgric for my lord Sigeberht ordered me to," he said. "My lord commanded and I obeyed. He chose Ecgric, and I trust his judgement." Beobrand thought he sounded as if he were trying to convince himself.

Beobrand stood up quickly, handing his empty cup to Offa.

"Can you spare us a man to lead us to Beodericsworth?" he asked. "This camp is no place for a holy woman," he offered his hand to Edmonda, who, after a moment's hesitation, grasped it and allowed him to pull her to her feet.

"And I would speak with both of your kings."

Chapter 7

Rowena pulled the antler comb through Edlyn's long, dark hair. A thrall could easily have done the task, but Rowena liked to spend this time with her daughter each day. The teeth of the comb snagged on a knot and Rowena teased the tangle free and continued with the long smooth strokes. Edlyn's hair tangled so easily. It always had. Across from where they sat on the porch of the hall, several children shrieked as they were chased by a dog. The shouts were shrill, the dog's yelps piercing, but Rowena did not mind. To have a life full of sound and laughter of children was not a bad thing.

For a moment, she ceased combing, allowing her gaze to wander further, beyond the huts and barns of Ubbanford to the hills and trees that surrounded the village. Soon, all too soon, Edlyn would be gone somewhere beyond the valley. She was of age already. Rowena frowned. She should probably have found her a husband before now, but she could not bear the thought of seeing her leave. Ubba's hall was too quiet already, the nights long and cold. When Edlyn left, Rowena would be totally alone.

"Mother?" Edlyn broke into her reverie.

Rowena realised she had paused, her hand resting on her daughter's head. She recommenced brushing.

"Sorry, child, I was just thinking."

She thought too much, that is what Ubba had always told her. Perhaps he was right. But he was not there now to tell her. He had left her alone, and taken her two fine sons with him to a cold grave at Hefenfelth. And for what? So that a new king could rule over them? She cared no more for one king than another. No king had kept them safe in this valley by the Tuidi. They had always fought their own battles. It was their sweat and blood that had fed this land. Not some atheling who had come from exile far to the north-west.

Absently, she began to braid Edlyn's hair, her fingers nimble at the task they had performed countless times before. The girl had such silken hair. She was truly beautiful. Rowena smiled. Of course she would think that, she was the girl's mother. And yet she knew it to be true. She had seen the way the men looked upon her daughter. The way their eyes lingered on her hips, her slim waist, the curve of her breasts. Men were all the same.

Her thoughts returned to Ubba and she frowned. She missed the old goat. He had often been cantankerous, grumbling at everything, but still she missed him. Missed his solidity in the hall. His presence had seemed to ground everything, to keep her world steady. And she missed the warmth of his bulk beside her in their cot at night. Perhaps not all men were the same, but they were all governed by one thing. They could be mighty warriors, able to feed the wolves and ravens with their prowess in battle, but they could all still be led by a nice pair of tits and a plump arse. Once, she had been young and beautiful, able to turn the heads of men, but now those days were long gone.

Just as her man and her sons were gone.

Rowena finished one braid, adeptly tying it off with a short length of wool yarn. She started on the other side. That winter, she had briefly considered marrying Edlyn to one of Lord Beobrand's gesithas, but it would not do. None of the warriors were of noble birth and whilst she would have loved to keep her daughter close, Edlyn deserved better. No, this summer they would travel to Bebbanburg, or perhaps even as far as Eoferwic and seek a suitable husband for the girl.

The children had stopped their screaming and she looked to see what now entertained them. She pressed her lips tightly together as she spotted Reaghan, carrying baby Octa. The Waelisc slave girl was talking to the children in her sing-song tone and they were listening to her with rapt interest on their grimy faces.

"Be careful, mother!" snapped Edlyn.

Rowena had snagged some of the hair in the long plait, tugging painfully at her daughter's scalp. She smoothed the hair with a light touch and continued with the braid.

That slave bitch! Rowena could barely stand the sight of her. Who did she think she was? She paraded around Ubbanford as if she owned all she surveyed. But of course, in a manner of speaking, she did. And she was certainly no longer a slave.

How had Beobrand allowed himself to be bewitched by such a creature? He was a good man; brave, honest and loyal. And yet he was merely a man, like any other. He could no more control his lust than a fish could fly. But to give the slave her freedom! Rowena could scarcely believe it. It was the stuff of madness. When Sunniva had died in childbirth, Beobrand's grief had been awful. Rowena had not been surprised when he had begun to bed Reaghan. The girl was comely enough she admitted grudgingly. A man needed comfort and what were thralls for, if not to serve their masters? But to free her? Make her the lady of the new hall? Sunniva's hall. It was all too much. Seeing Reaghan with Sunniva's child every day, ordering the thralls, living like a queen in the great hall on the hill. Rowena hated it.

"Are you finished, mother," Edlyn asked in a timid tone, as if scared to awaken the anger that simmered just beneath the surface of Rowena's demeanour.

"Yes, my dear," Rowena answered, her mind elsewhere. "Fetch your blue cloak and my green one and we shall go for a walk." She needed to be away from the oppressive hush of the hall. And away from the sight of that Waelisc whore. Edlyn scurried away, perhaps happy to be free from her mother's bitterness. Was it so obvious? Perhaps. Though she never spoke of her thoughts to Edlyn, her daughter was no fool and could surely sense her mother's moods well enough.

As she watched Reaghan conversing with the children, the imposing figure of Bassus strode into view. The huge warrior followed Reaghan everywhere. He looked old after the terrible wound he had suffered the year previously. His hair had greyed and his beard was silver, but despite having lost his left arm from the arrow wound, he was no cripple. He was still a man to be reckoned with. He would never stand in the shieldwall again, but his shoulders still held the memory of the muscle-bulk of the great warrior, and he still wore sword and seax at his belt.

As if sensing her gaze upon him, Bassus turned his scarred face towards Rowena. Their eyes met and she felt her face grow hot. The giant man always made her feel unsure of herself. She turned quickly away, back into the shadows of the old hall.

"Hurry, girl," Rowena called to Edlyn, her voice shriller than she had intended, "bring those cloaks. I wish to walk to the river and the day is cool."

Edlyn returned with the garments and Rowena snatched the green cloak, sweeping it about her form and fixing a clasp at the shoulder. She wished now that she had asked the girl to bring the grey one. It was not as comfortable as the green woollen cloak, but it hung better on her. No matter now.

Without waiting for Edlyn to fasten her own cloak, Rowena stalked away from the hall, leaving the sound of children chattering behind her.

Chapter 8

Beobrand stretched with a grimace, pushing his hands into the small of his back. All this riding made him ache. And the rain had brought with it twinges of pain in the old wounds of his leg and foot. Absently, he rubbed his hand on the left side of his chest where a Mercian shield had cracked his ribs.

"By the gods, why are we kept waiting here like ceorls?" He went to drain the ale from the wooden cup he had been given, but found it empty. He flung it onto the small table in disgust. The cup rolled along the board and then fell with a clatter onto the bare floor.

Wynhelm, frustratingly calm, raised a hand from where he sat.

"Be seated, Beobrand," he said, his voice soothing. "I am sure the king will see us soon."

"Soon?" spat Beobrand. "We have been here since the sun was at its highest, and now it is nearly dusk." He cast a glance out of the open door. The rain had ceased some time ago, and now a thin yellow light cast long shadows on the building work that was underway. Despite being late in the day, men still split wood, chiselled, and hammered pegs into joints. The sound of their labour had been a constant reminder of their own inactivity all of that long afternoon. Beodericsworth was a-bustle with activity while they sat waiting to be attended by the king of the East Angelfolc. Beobrand took a deep breath, forcing himself to relax the tension in his shoulders and back. With a sigh, he sat back down on the bench beside Wynhelm.

"So many strong men working," he said. "and not half a day's ride from here, the fyrd is gathering to meet the might of Penda and his Waelisc allies. We must speak some sense into this Ecgric."

"Hush," said Wynhelm, nervous now at Beobrand's harsh words. "We are strangers in this land and an insult to a king in his own hall will surely bring us nothing but ill."

Beobrand sighed again. Wynhelm was right, but it was infuriating. To ride all the way from Northumbria and then to be made to wait like supplicants at the door of the king's hall. What could be so important that he had not seen them already? They were thegns, not thralls.

"Peace, Beobrand," Coenred spoke up from where he sat flanked by Gothfraidh and Edmonda. He held the intricately-carved casket on his lap, his fidgeting fingers evidence of his own unease. He offered Beobrand a thin smile. "Peace. The king will see us soon enough, I am sure."

As if in reply to his words, the huge doors to the inner hall swung open.

The door wards, who had stood silent and grim-faced while the Northumbrians waited to be seen, now beckoned them to rise and to enter the hall.

Beobrand stood abruptly, only to have the older of the two door wards block his path.

"You cannot bear blades in the hall of the king," said the man, his tone broaching no argument. Beobrand clenched his jaw, but he knew this was no personal slight; to carry weapons inside was reserved for only those thegns who were closest to the lord of a hall.

He unbuckled his sword belt and deposited it, Hrunting and his seax still attached and scabbarded, on the ground. The others did the same and soon there was a sizable pile of weapons in the small chamber.

"Keep good care of my blades and those of my companions," he said, his voice gruff. The door ward nodded, ignoring the rudeness in the younger man's tone.

Beobrand strode into the hall. The first thing that he noted was how dark it was. The shutters were pulled closed, scant light from the setting sun slicing into the gloom through the cracks where the wood met. A few rush lights burnt with small guttering flames that wavered at the breeze from the open doors. The hall was huge, large enough for a king. Longer and higher than Bebbanburg and Ubbanford, most of the hall was in utter darkness, the assorted rush lights not beginning to dispel the gloom from the place. No fire burnt in the great hearth, but Beobrand noticed the embers glowed. The hall had about it more the look of early morning, rather than late afternoon. Compounding the sense of a hall awakening, two slave girls flung open the shutters, making him start. Unbidden, his hand dropped to his side grasping for Hrunting's absent hilt. Embarrassed, at his nervousness, he let his hand relax. Shafts of warm sunlight slanted into the hall like hot knives from the now-opened windows.

"By all that is holy," exclaimed a weak voice from the end of the hall, "my head feels like someone has buried an axe in it while I slept."

Beobrand blinked against the sudden brightness, peering into the shadows at the far end of the room.

A man was slumped on a large chair with a high back. His head rested on one hand, while he shielded his eyes with the other. He was slim and fair, with high cheeks and a square jaw. His green tunic and tight blue breeches were of the finest quality, but looked blotched and stained. Gold and garnets glimmered at his throat and on his fingers.

"God, my head," he said and clicked his fingers. The gold of a ring caught the light with a flash. "Bring wine, ale and mead for my guests. And get the fire lit. They will think I do not know how to welcome visitors."

Thralls and servants scurried to do their lord's bidding.

Beobrand bit back a sharp retort. They had been waiting all this time while the king slept! He gripped his hands into fists at his side and walked forward stiffly.

"My steward tells me you are come all the way from the north, from Oswald's realm," the man Beobrand assumed to be Ecgric said, his voice fraying and slurred. "Why did he send you? If it was to tell me Penda means to invade my lands, your message arrives late." He cast about him, evidently looking for something. When he could not find it, he clicked his fingers again and raised his voice. "Wine, I said. Bring me a cup of wine."

A servant ran from the shadows with an ornate cup and a jug. She filled the cup and handed it to the king, who drained it and held it out to be refilled.

Beobrand stood awkwardly, Wynhelm to his right, their men, dusty and travel-weary some paces behind. To one side, Coenred, Gothfraidh and Edmonda had their heads bowed, as if in silent prayer.

Beobrand clenched his fists at his side. This was the second hall he had visited in this land in the last year and on both occasions the welcome had been sorely lacking. Where was the Waes Hael cup? Why had they not been introduced? He was not even sure that the bleary-eyed man on the throne, who was now well into his second cup of wine, was the king. Tiredness washed over Beobrand. He just wished to be gone from the place. To fulfil his duty by delivering the monks and their gift and then return as quickly as possible to Ubbanford. He was suddenly glad of the poor welcome, it would make it easier to be on their way. The kings of this land were poor lords and war was coming. This land was not safe.

"Lord Ecgric of the East Angelfolc," he said, his voice loud and clear, "we are indeed come from Northumbria, sent by our lord Oswald, King of Bernicia and Deira and Bretwalda of all Albion." Wynhelm gave him a warning glance. It was Oswald's ambition to be called Bretwalda, over-king of the kingdoms of Albion, but to utter the name before the king of another realm was like a slap.

To his surprise, Ecgric did not react to the title, which Beobrand had only spoken to provoke him.

"And you are?" the king asked, holding out his cup for yet another fill of wine. His voice was stronger now, the drink evidently giving him strength.

"I am Beobrand of Ubbanford. This is Wynhelm of Æscendene. We bring with us monks who bear a precious gift for Sigeberht, erstwhile king of this land. We heard from your man, Offa, that Sigeberht was here. Is that so?"

Ecgric ignored the question.

"Monks? I see two and a nun also. Did you forget her?" He laughed at his own jest.

Beobrand did not laugh.

"No, lord. We rescued Edmonda. Her monastery was under attack from a warband of Waelisc. We came to tell you of this. We rode hard to—"

Ecgric raised a hand to silence him.

"You can tell me this and more once you have all slaked your thirst and supped with me at my table. I believe the cooks have prepared swan and pike. You will not have tried finer."

"But, lord," Beobrand said, unsure how to proceed, "we have waited all this afternoon to speak with you."

"Then a while longer will do you no harm," replied Ecgric. The colour had returned to his cheeks now. "And we will all think better on full stomachs."

Beobrand went to speak again, but the king turned away to talk to a man who had approached and now whispered in Ecgric's ear.

All around them servants and thralls prepared the boards. Fires leapt from the logs freshly-placed on the embers. Men, with the aspect of shield-bearers and sword-brothers, the king's comitatus he presumed, Ecgric's hearth-warriors, sat at the benches readying themselves for the fine food their lord promised.

Beobrand looked about him in disbelief.

The land of the East Angelfolc was burning, and their king feasted.

*

"The man is a fool," hissed Beobrand, his hand clutching his cup so tightly that his knuckles showed white.

All around them the hall was a hubbub of heat and sound. The smoke from the fire mingled with the smells of roasting meat, spilt ale and dozens of warriors. It was the fug of a hall in full feast, and normally he would have welcomed it. But a lord does not feast when his people are dying and his land is being raped by enemies.

Wynhelm placed a hand upon his arm.

"Watch your tongue," he said in a voice that barely carried over the din. "Let us hope we can speak to Ecgric soon."

"Why should we bother? The man is clearly not interested in what the sisters of Wyrd are weaving for his people. Oswald sent us to bring the monks safely to Sigeberht, I say we do just that."

For a time Wynhelm did not respond, instead sipping his ale. Then he nodded.

"Very well. But it is late now, and we have not eaten well for more than a sennight, so let us fill our bellies and go to him at dawn."

Despite his anger at the king's treatment of them, Beobrand smiled, lifting a succulent chunk of swan to his mouth on the tip of his small knife.

"At least he spoke true. This swan is the best fowl I have ever tasted."

"And we need to eat," said Wynhelm, chuckling.

Beobrand swallowed the warm meat. It was tender, moist and full of flavour. He washed it down with a quaff of ale. The drink too was exquisite. Ecgric certainly knew how to feed his men and his guests. He had been offered wine and mead, but Beobrand had long since learnt his lesson in that regard. If they were to rise early in the morning, he would need to drink sparingly and nothing stronger than ale. Even so, Beobrand could feel himself relaxing as the drink soaked into him.

The men around him suddenly burst into a storm of laughter. He had not heard the riddle that had caused the reaction, but he could feel the tension seeping out of the hall. But despite the warmth and fine food, Beobrand could not relax. This was all wrong. What had these men to celebrate?

"Attor," he beckoned to the slim warrior, who rose and came to Beobrand's side. "Tell the men we will be leaving at sunrise. They are not to drink heavily."

"What of the monks? And the nun?" Attor nodded in the direction of the three who had sat at the far corner of the hall, away from the raucous noise of the mead-benches.

"We will deliver them and the gift they carry to Sigeberht in the morn, and then we will ride from this place."

Attor frowned and looked set to speak, but merely gave a curt nod and went to deliver the news to the men.

Beobrand took another bite of the swan, chewing absently while watching Coenred. The young monk was leaning in close to Edmonda, speaking to her. Their faces were grave and pale in the firelight.

Oswald had told him to leave Coenred and Gothfraidh with Sigeberht. But had the king known that battle was coming? The monks would not be safe here. And what of Edmonda? He had not rescued her from one burning monastery to leave her in another.

Thoughts and plans flapped inside his mind like the wings of bats trapped in a cave. He did not know what to do, but he was sure that war was coming.

And when war arrived, the gods laughed at the plans of men.

Chapter 9

Dawn barely paled the eastern sky when Beobrand roused Wynhelm, Coenred, Gothfraidh and Edmonda. Ecgric had drunk enough wine and mead to keep him asleep for most of the day. When Beobrand had approached the high table later in the evening to speak to the king, he had been dismissed with an imperious wave of a hand. Beobrand had stood there for a long while, the tumult of the hall echoing around him and stared at Ecgric. The man was clearly a fool. Or perhaps he was moon-struck. But no, he did not rave and jabber and Offa had said Sigeberht had chosen Ecgric to replace him. At that moment, Ecgric had turned away from the conversation he was having. He had looked directly into Beobrand's eyes for a moment, and then lowered his gaze.

Beobrand had returned to his bench, and leant in close to Wynhelm, who had watched the silent exchange.

"Ecgric is not foolish or mad," Beobrand had whispered.

"Indeed?" Wynhelm had said.

"No," Beobrand had said, letting out a long breath, "the king is terrified."

They had left their weapons with the door wardens of the great hall as they stepped out into the cool morning air; they would have no need for them. Attor had joined them, ever alert he had awoken and followed Beobrand out of the hall. They had allowed the others their rest.

It was not difficult to find the location of Sigeberht and his religious brethren. The chanting of their Christ songs drifted over the mist-wrapped settlement. The half-built structures of the buildings loomed in the darkness like the bones of wrecked ships at low tide. All was still and quiet, apart from the singing monks and the footfalls of Beobrand's small band.

"What do they sing of?" asked Beobrand.

"They sing Prime," said Coenred, "the first office of the day."

The sound of the chants was still distant, but clear in the stillness of the dawn. First one voice spoke, then many responded. The words were in the sacred tongue of the Christ followers. Beobrand understood none of it.

"But what do the words mean?" he said.

"The Holy liturgy speaks of many things, young Beobrand," said Gothfraidh. They walked on in silence for a few strides while Gothfraidh listened, mouthing the words to himself as they wafted to them.

"*Dóminus nos benedícat, et ab omni malo deféndat, et ad vitam perdúcat ætérnam.*"

"They are coming to the end now," said Gothfraidh. "They ask that the Lord bless us, and defend us from all evil, and bring us to eternal life."

"*Et fidélium ánimæ per misericórdiam Dei requiéscant in pace.*"

"…and may the souls of the faithful departed, through the mercy of God, rest in peace," Gothfraidh translated.

Beobrand took in a deep breath of the damp, cold air. Did the Christ god really listen to these prayers? He had seen for himself the power of the Christ. But Coenred said he was the god of love and forgiveness. If that were so, why did he allow so many to die? If Christ could defend his faithful from evil, why did he choose not to? Beobrand spat into the mud of the path, as the sounds of the final prayer ended in a loud chant of "Amen". The Christ god wielded power, of that there was no doubt, but would a loving god allow his own to be slaughtered? Beobrand recalled Tata's broken form on the altar at Engelmynster, the fear-filled faces of the Christ worshippers they had left behind to their fate at the hands of Gwalchmei and his warriors. No, the Christ was as fickle and as callous as all the other gods. His priests talked of eternal life and an end of sacrifice, but it seemed to Beobrand the Christ demanded the blood of his own followers as tribute.

They had arrived at a recently dug ditch, with a raised embankment on the far side. The path cut across this ditch over a small timber bridge. The stripped planks still oozed resin, such was their freshness. Gothfraidh, Coenred and Edmonda all paused at the bridge and made the sign of the rood over themselves.

"Once we cross this vallum, we are entering Holy ground," explained Gothfraidh.

Beobrand spat into the ditch and crossed the bridge. The others hurried behind him.

There were many small buildings, but at the centre of the enclosure stood a larger hall. Figures emerged from the hall, leaving in small groups to go about whatever errands the Christ god or his priests demanded of them. Beobrand strode forward.

"You there," he shouted, his voice strident in the dawn-quiet. "Where is Sigeberht?"

The group he addressed were all young men and boys, none more than thirteen or fourteen years of age. They gaped at him with wide eyes and open mouths. He was unarmed, but he was clearly a man of war, broad-shouldered, and as tall as any man they were ever likely to have seen.

"Well?" he asked, his tone hardening, his scarred face pulling into a frown. "Where is he? We bring him tidings."

Still they did not reply, instead they seemed set to run. Fearing that the boys would flee without helping him, he tried to soften his words. "We also bring a gift from afar." He gestured towards Coenred and his ornately-carved wooden casket. The sight of the monk, with his shaved forehead and long robes much like their own appeared to put them at ease somewhat.

The shortest of the novice monks pointed towards the large building they had just left.

"He is in there, with Bishop Felix," he said, his voice squeaking like a field mouse. Beobrand didn't know if that was due to his age or his fear, but he nodded to the boy and made for the hall.

More boys scattered at his determined approach. He was done with waiting. Penda's host might even now be at the great ditch. Beobrand could imagine them swarming up the slope towards Offa's ragged defence. They must be gone from this realm before Penda swept all in his path.

Inside, the hall was dark and cold. The smell of freshly-worked timber hung in the air and on top of that a more pungent scent, one that Beobrand could not place. As his eyes grew accustomed to the darkness within the building, he saw smoke wafting from a small copper bowl that hung by three chains attached to a long rope from the roof beams. He knew not what burnt within that bowl, but the stink of it caught in his throat, making him cough.

At the sound, two men who had been deep in conversation at the end of the building turned towards him. Beobrand recognised one as Sigeberht. The man who had been king wore the same white robe as he had the year before, but now the crown of his head had been shaved, marking him out as one of the Christ's monks. Beobrand knew that Sigeberht had given up his kingdom for the ways of the Christ, but seeing him thus, garbed in simple clothes with his hair shaved into a tonsure, made him start. Why a king would give up his right to rule his people, Beobrand could not comprehend. Sigeberht took in the people who had entered the chapel in a heartbeat. He held up a hand to the man he had been conversing with, warning him to stay behind him, as he squared his shoulders and walked down between the wooden pillars toward Beobrand. He moved with the natural grace of a warrior and Beobrand sensed that he was being appraised even as Sigeberht held out his hands in a sign of welcome and peace.

Sigeberht halted a few paces before Beobrand. He was tall and broad, with the same strong features as Ecgric. Behind him, the other man, shorter and altogether smaller, hesitantly followed.

"I recognise you," said Sigeberht, his voice strong. "You were with the lord Oswald when he came to my hall at Dommoc."

"It is so, Lord Sigeberht," replied Beobrand.

"I am a lord no longer. I am now a servant of God."

"I have heard as much," said Beobrand, his incredulity making his tone sharp.

Sigeberht smiled, as if he was accustomed to men's disbelief at his choices.

"I remember you, but not your name."

"I am Beobrand of Ubbanford."

"Ah, the mighty Beobrand. And why do you come to me here, Beobrand?"

"I am come once more from Northumbria, bearing tidings and a gift from my lord King Oswald."

"Indeed? What tidings do you bring, and what gift?"

Beobrand could not answer. His cheeks reddening, he indicated to Coenred.

"Coenred, who comes from brethren of the isle of Lindisfarena, bears both the gift and the message."

Coenred, pale and timid stepped forward.

"I bear not one, but two gifts of the utmost value. Gifts from King Oswald and Abbot Aidan to help you in your Holy endeavours to teach the Lord's word in these lands." He held out the casket in his trembling hands. "If I may place this casket upon the altar, then I could open it with no fear of dropping the precious contents." His voice shook at finally speaking these words to the intended recipient of the contents of the box.

Sigeberht stared long at the carved oak. It was clearly of exquisite craftsmanship, a thing of great value.

"Only holy sacraments and vestments may be placed on the altar, Coenred," he said.

"Oh, lord," replied Coenred in hushed tones of awe, "these are the holiest of items. Relics from the land of our Lord himself."

The short figure crossed himself, and hurried forward.

"Come, boy," he said, his words carrying the strange lilt of one who did not learn to speak on the isle of Albion. His accent reminded Beobrand of Bishop Birinus of Dorcic. "Come, come," he continued breathlessly, ushering Coenred forward toward the altar at the end of the hall.

Reverently, Coenred carried the box to the cloth-covered table and placed it there. Beobrand and the others followed him, spreading out to better see what the casket contained.

"Go on then, boy," said the short man, "open it."

Coenred ran his slim fingers through his long, unruly hair.

Then, reaching forward with caution, he lifted the lid on delicate silver hinges to expose what lay inside.

*

Beobrand peered forward to see what thing of great value nestled in the box that Coenred had guarded so jealously throughout the long journey south. At first he could see nothing, save a parchment that covered the contents of the box. Coenred gently plucked the vellum from the casket, revealing what lay beneath. Still Beobrand strained to see anything inside. As he stepped closer, leaning over the altar in an attempt to get a better view in the dim light of the chapel, Coenred spoke in a tone that told of having learnt the words to be recited here.

"Behold, a piece of cloth from the very habit that the holy Colm Cille wore on the day of his burial. All the way from the isle of Hii has this come." He paused. The short man exclaimed something in a tongue Beobrand did not understand and clasped his hands together, as if in prayer. He made the sign of the cross over himself. Coenred, Gothfraidh, Edmonda and Sigeberht all did the same. A moment later, to Beobrand's surprise, Attor hesitantly emulated them.

"A precious and holy relic indeed," said Sigeberht. Beobrand glanced at his face. His strong features were filled with awe. What power could a scrap of cloth hold? Perhaps this Colm Cille had imbued it with magic.

"You spoke of two objects," prompted the short man with the strange voice. His words came in rapid gasps of excitement.

"Yes," said Coenred. "Look inside the casket and you will see the most fabulous of relics. From the Holy Land itself, from the very ground where our Lord God walked the earth." Despite himself, Beobrand found he was once again leaning forward to spy what artefact lay within the box. All around him the others crowded and peered with rapt expressions. Beobrand realised with a start that he was not breathing. Coenred paused, surveying all of their faces. Gothfraidh, clearly knowing what the young monk was about to announce, smiled in anticipation.

"See here before you, a pebble from the very slopes of Golgotha."

Edmonda let out a small cry.

Sigeberht exclaimed, "Praise the Lord our God, and may He bring eternal peace to Abbot Aidan and King Oswald for their generosity."

Beobrand leant in close. In the shadowed recesses of the wooden box he saw a frayed shred of dark cloth, woollen it seemed to him. Beside it lay a grey, smooth-edged stone, not half the size of his fist.

"Golgotha?" he asked.

In their excitement both Sigeberht and the short stranger began to speak at once.

With a smile, Sigeberht waved the other man to continue.

"I am sure Bishop Felix can explain better than I," he said.

The smaller man nodded his thanks.

"Golgotha is the hill were our Lord was crucified," Bishop Felix said, his voice echoing in the dark of the chapel as he raised it as if proclaiming to dozens of men. "He was hanged upon a tree until he died in great agony. Jesu's head was wreathed in a crown of vicious thorns and He was mocked and beaten." He was almost shouting now, such was the fervour that had him in its grip. Without warning, he placed his face almost inside the casket, scrutinising the contents. "Perhaps the blood or sweat of our Lord is on the stone!" he exclaimed, raising his face up again.

"I don't see any blood on it," said Beobrand. They all turned to look at him. "So, this stone contains magic?"

Felix frowned.

"No, no! Not magic. Magic is the province of witches."

A crow croaked from one of the windows of the building. Coenred shot him a glance. Beobrand felt the chill of a cave in Muile; a snowstorm in Din Eidyn. They both knew of the magic of witches.

"So what then?" asked Beobrand. "What makes this pebble special? Does it have power?"

"Oh yes," answered Felix.

"To do what?"

"The ways of God are not easy for men to comprehend," said Gothfraidh. "But these holy relics possess great spiritual power."

Beobrand could barely contain his anger. His hands clenched into fists and he had to fight the urge to fling the casket and its contents against the timber wall of the church. By all the gods, was this what they had carried the length of Albion? A stone and a rag? It was madness. This land would soon be plunged into the bloody chaos of war and Beobrand could not fathom why Oswald had sent them here. Surely not merely to bring these useless gifts to a king who had renounced his kingdom.

He took a deep breath and stared up for a moment at the crow perched in the high window, from where it looked down upon them with an implacable gaze.

"You had best pray that they also have power in battle," said Beobrand, his words jagged and harsh, "for war is coming."

Chapter 10

Beobrand strode into the sunlight. His hands shook.

The sun had risen beyond the oak and beech trees that loomed over Beodericsworth. Mist clung to ditches and streams and around the woods, but the sky was clear and brilliant. It would be a hot, bright day. Within the enclosure of the vallum, monks went about their chores. Some glanced at the huge fair-haired warrior, but none approached. Danger and violence came off him like a stench.

The sounds of construction that had filled the previous day once again reverberated around the settlement, but Beobrand hardly noticed. He paced first one way and then the other before the doors of the chapel, breathing hard.

Oswald had known! He had known they were riding towards war.

Sigeberht had asked Coenred to read the message from King Oswald. Coenred had done so in a clear voice. Beobrand saw little value in the scribblings of the monks, but he could hear Oswald's words through the voice of the young man. The king had spoken them many days ago and Coenred had scratched the words into the vellum, but Beobrand could hear the truth in them. There was magic in this, but he cared not for that. He was furious. As Coenred had read the missive, Beobrand had wanted to reach out and shake him into silence. But he knew that would do no good; another would have read the words, if not his friend.

"I, King Oswald of Bernicia and Deira, Lord of Northumbria, son of Æthelfrith, conqueror of Din Eidyn, send greetings to my brother in Christ, Sigeberht, wise king of the East Angelfolc," Coenred had recited. "I trust that this message finds you in good health. As a token of my esteem, I send you a reliquary containing two most holy relics." The message had gone on for some time extolling the virtues of the stone and the cloth, recounting miracles that they had performed. The pebble had cured a babe of palsy when it had been placed next to the child in its crib. The cloth had brought food to a hungry monk who had feared he would die from starvation. He had prayed to the dead abbot of Hii whilst clutching the scrap of Colm Cille's habit and an eagle had flown to the monk, dropping a great salmon at his feet. There were more such stories of miraculous cures, droughts being averted by sudden rain from a cloudless sky, the lame were made to walk and the blind were made to see.

But it was not these tales of relics and miracles that angered Beobrand, it was when the letter turned to tidings of war. "News has come to me that Penda, the great enemy of God, King of Mercia, is even now amassing a powerful warhost. I have been told that he has once more allied with the Waelisc of Gwynedd and they mean to march on your lands."

They had ridden blithely through Mercia, and all the while they had carried a message that informed of imminent war.

"Beobrand," said a timid voice, "will you come back inside? Lord Sigeberht would speak with you."

Beobrand spun round. Coenred stood before him, his face flushed, colour high in his cheeks.

Taking a long breath, Beobrand willed himself to calm.

"You knew the contents of the message," he said, "and yet you said nothing." He shook his head, unsure to whom to direct his impotent ire.

"It was not for me to tell. The message was for Sigeberht, no other."

"We rode into danger. We could have been killed."

"But we were not."

"And now what will you do? Will you return with us? I would ride this very day, before it is too late."

Before Penda's host descend on the land, he thought, bringing fire and death. Before the carrion birds blot out the sun as they wheel above fields stained red with slaughter.

"I will not ride with you," said Coenred. "Aidan has sent us to learn from Bishop Felix and Lord Sigeberht. Both were taught the ways of the Lord in Frankia, following the teaching of the most holy Columbán. We will learn much from them."

"You will learn nothing from them if you are dead," Beobrand snapped.

"Do not fear for us. God will protect us."

"How can you speak so?" Beobrand said. "After what we have seen? Your god allows his own to die just as well as his enemies."

Coenred frowned.

"God will protect us," he repeated, his jaw tensed, the words clipped.

There was nothing more to say. Beobrand pushed past Coenred. "I will speak with Sigeberht now."

He blinked as he walked into the gloom of the chapel from the bright light outside. Again the scent of incense caught in his throat, sweet and cloying. The small group turned to watch him stalk towards them.

"Lord Sigeberht," he said, his voice brittle and sharp, like slivers of iron from a smith's hammer, "you have heard tell of Penda's designs on your kingdom, what will you do?"

"I am no longer king, Beobrand," replied Sigeberht, his steady tone infuriating. "My cousin, Ecgric, is king of these lands now. I serve God."

Beobrand thought of the prayer they had heard when they had walked through the still, fog-filled morning.

"I heard you pray just this morning that your god will deliver you from evil."

"That is true. But—"

"Your cousin is no warrior." Beobrand spoke the words with certainty and he saw the truth of his words reflected in Sigeberht's eyes. "You once were a warrior of renown. A true king. Your men love you. Men like Offa." He saw recognition in Sigeberht's face.

For a long while Sigeberht said nothing. He met Beobrand's ire-laden gaze unflinchingly, as if he weighed up the man he saw. Beobrand felt the force of that gaze, saw the steel in those eyes. This was a man to be reckoned with. He was no soft monk to be cowed by anger or a raised voice. Place a blade in his hand and Sigeberht would be a warlord that warriors would cleave to.

"Perhaps," said Beobrand, breaking the silence, "your god wishes you to lead your people from evil."

"Have you considered," Sigeberht said, a soft smile playing at his lips, "that perhaps it is not I, but you who has been sent by God?"

*

"I am no warlord," said Beobrand. "The men would not listen to me. I am not even from these lands." Did Sigeberht really believe that he should stand in the shieldwall for the East

Angelfolc? That he could help to repel Penda's host? "I am but one man. With my men and Wynhelm's we are but a dozen. I doubt our presence would be noticed."

Sigeberht smiled. He shook his head, as if Beobrand's words were those of a fool.

"Do men not look to you in battle? Do the scops not sing of your battle-fame?"

Beobrand's face grew hot.

"The scops speak of dragons and night-stalkers also. Do not trust all that is sung by bards."

Coenred stepped forward.

"You know it is true, Beobrand," said the young monk. "Oswald says you are God's instrument, even if you do not know it yourself. And the Lord has sent you to my rescue before now. I believe he has done so once more. I have faith in Christ and I have faith that you will protect us from the pagan Penda and his unholy allies."

Beobrand frowned. Coenred had learnt much these past years as he had grown into a man. It seems he could not only write now, but also speak with a persuasive tongue. Beobrand looked at Coenred's open face. The monk returned his gaze. Beobrand felt the weight of Coenred's belief in him. What could he really do here?

He scanned the others. Wynhelm leant calmly on a timber pillar. He gave Beobrand a slight nod of the head. Attor's face was solemn, he seemed to be in awe in the company of the Christ-follower holy men. But he cleared his throat and spoke.

"Lord," he said, voice cracking in his throat, "I know the decision is yours alone to make, but I would be honoured to stand at your side in the shieldwall to defend these lands and these fine people who love the Christ." He closed his mouth and his cheeks reddened. His words spoken, he lowered his gaze now and said no more.

Lastly, he turned to Gothfraidh and Edmonda. Neither spoke. The grey-haired monk seemed disinterested in the conversation, instead he had picked up the vellum that contained the message from King Oswald and was perusing the scratchings there. Edmonda's eyes glittered in the dim light of the building. Again, something about her reminded him of Reaghan.

By Woden, Thunor and Frige, he could not just ride from this place and return north, leaving these people to their wyrd.

Turning back to Sigeberht, Beobrand spoke in an angry rush.

"You must also come. I have seen the men of the fyrd and they are not warriors. They need to be trained. And if they are to stand strong against the Mercian and Waelisc host, they need a true warlord, a king, to look to. Not a young thegn from Bernicia."

Sigeberht's eyes twinkled, but his face grew grave.

"I will not bear weapons ever again," he said. "I have vowed it so before the one true God."

"But you must," said Beobrand. "The men need—"

Sigeberht cut him off with a raised hand.

"But if it is the Lord's will, I will give my guidance to my cousin."

"And you will come to the great dyke where the men await Penda?"

"If my cousin allows it, I will come. But I will not raise a weapon or don armour."

"I believe if you speak to the fyrd, they will take heart. And with strong hearts and courage," said Beobrand, "perhaps we can defeat the Mercians."

"We?" asked Sigeberht, raising an eyebrow. "So, you will stay? You will stand with us against the pagans?"

Beobrand sighed. He would not ride away and leave these people when he could offer his sword and his shield to their defence. And yet, his mind returned to the shambles of the camp where the fyrd had gathered, to the raucous feasting of Ecgric's hall, the king choosing to ignore the peril that approached. He thought of all this and his stomach clenched in fear. What difference would his small band of warriors make? But there was nothing for it now, he had made his decision and there was nothing to be gained from fretting about what might be. He had been told this many times by men older and wiser than him, but that did not prevent his innards coiling like eels.

Beobrand gave a terse nod.

"Aye, I'll stay," he said. "But there is no time to waste. Prepare yourself and have a mount brought for you, for we ride at once."

His mind now made up, he made to leave the hall.

Coenred trotted alongside him to keep up with his long strides.

"I told you God would protect us," Coenred said, face aglow with excitement. "Once more he has sent you to defend his own."

"Pray that you are right, Coenred," Beobrand said. "Pray to your god and see if he listens."

Beobrand stalked out of the gloom of the church and into the warm light of the morning. There was no time to waste.

He had a king to awaken.

Chapter 11

"By Tiw's cock!" hissed Bassus, as the whet stone fell from his grasp. It clattered against the leg of the stool on which he sat and knocked painfully against his ankle. It was the second time he had dropped the thing that morning and he had only been at the task for a short while. He grunted as he reached for the stone, all the while listening for sounds of activity from inside the hall. The sun was up, dawn long past, but he had told the two hall-slaves not to begin preparing food, or airing the hall. Instead, he had sent both the young girls down to the river for water. Reaghan and Octa could sleep a while longer. If he did not wake them with his clumsiness. Octa had cried for much of the night and he knew that Reaghan would be tired.

He had roused the men, those of Beobrand's gesithas who remained in Ubbanford, dragging them out of the hall into the misty wolf-light of the dawn. He had sent them to cut timber down by the river, far from the hall, telling them they could return to break their fast when he sent for them. They had grumbled, but they had done so quietly. Bassus' stern warnings would have been enough to quell their complaints, had they not already loved Reaghan. They all did. Accepting her as their lord's lady and mistress of his hall.

Retrieving the stone, he rested it on his lap while he went about placing the seax blade in just the right position for sharpening. He wedged the antler hilt between his thighs, blade upward, sharp edge towards him. By lifting his left ankle onto his right knee, he could get an angle that allowed him to run the stone over the whole length of the shimmering patterned blade. Careful not to cut his leg on the already-sharp knife, he shifted his position until he was comfortable and recommenced whetting the blade.

Comfortable? He chuckled to himself at the idea. He rarely felt comfort these days. For a moment he paused, closing his eyes. His left arm no longer pained him. Neither did the stump where it had been removed. But he would have sworn the limb and hand were still there, had he not known differently.

He opened his eyes and gazed down into the valley. Smoke drifted up from several buildings and from the old hall where Rowena and her daughter lived. He frowned. He saw the sharp looks they gave to Reaghan when she passed. The ire in their glares was plain. Where the gesithas loved Reaghan, Rowena and Edlyn hated her. He could guess at their reasons, but it pained him. Reaghan was a good girl. It seemed to him she had done nothing wrong but to be born to Waelisc parents, and then to allow herself to be captured and enslaved. That Beobrand had become a widower, and chosen to make the thrall his woman was not through any misdeed of hers. But women held grudges long and heavy in their hearts, just like men. To see a Waelisc thrall girl take her place must have been a bitter draught for Rowena to swallow. She had lost her menfolk and her power. To be surrounded by reminders of what her life used to be, must scratch at her like nettles under the skin.

The seax blade slipped from its precarious position and Bassus shifted quickly to catch it before it fell. He lost neither the stone nor the blade this time, but his hand encumbered and his knuckle caught the wickedly sharp edge of the blade. Cursing silently, he raised his hand to his mouth and sucked the blood away. Thankfully, it was not a deep cut. But it stung. Tiny nicks and scratches always did.

He sighed. By all the gods, he understood how Rowena must feel. He too was getting old, surrounded by young men who were faster and stronger. More able. Whole. Once he had been a champion of a king, now he cowered in this small settlement. He knew what Beobrand and his gesithas must think of him. Pity for the grizzled warrior who had once stood tall and strong in the shieldwall. He would never stand shoulder to shoulder with his spear brothers now. Not since that bastard Torran's arrow pierced his flesh.

Well, Torran was no more. Beobrand had taken the Pict's life, as he had also taken that of his brothers. Bassus was glad, but even the joy of being avenged was sour. He had lain quivering and crying, in the grip of the wound-rot fever, while Beobrand had slain the Pict. There was a time when he would have wreaked his own vengeance on his enemies, not needing to rely on his friends to stand for him.

Perhaps the curse of the witch was also upon him. Bassus shuddered, as if ice had scratched down his spine. There had been no sign of Nelda since she had escaped the siege of Din Eidyn, but could it be that she had woven his wyrd into the warp of her dark magic? He remembered the straw figure they had found dangling by the river, a tiny arrow jutting from its body. And then the searing pain of Torran's arrow as it had plunged into his arm. The arrow that had taken so much from him.

Enough of this! Would he sit here, eyes welling with tears as the sun climbed into the cloud-strewn sky? Was he some greybeard who raved and wept over what had been and what he had lost? No. He was Bassus, son of Nechten, and he yet had power. Awkwardly, he slid the seax into its intricately-worked leather scabbard. To dwell on the past would not bring it back. He still had his strength. He may only have one arm, but he could still wield a blade as well as any man. If any Pictish scum thought to attack Ubbanford while its lord was away, they would discover just how dangerous he could be.

After they had broken their fast he would gather the men and lead them in weapons practice. They must be prepared for anything. Bassus looked down at the silver sheen of the broad water of the Tuidi. The dense forest of the northern bank shadowed the placid waters. Did new enemies lurk there? Let them come. He would lead the men to meet any that sought to attack them. With cold iron and stout boards of linden they would defend this land.

From within the hall, came the wailing cry of Octa. Awake at last. Bassus pushed himself to his feet, stretching. From the valley below the hall came the distant sounds of axe on wood. Squaring his shoulders, he followed the flight of a huge heron with his gaze. The bird languidly flapped its way along the river's still water until it was lost from sight in the shade of the trees.

Octa's cries grew louder. Bassus smiled. He spied the thralls on the path, labouring up the hill with their burden of water.

"Come on!" he bellowed to them. "There is much to do and the day is already old."

They heard his call and he grunted to himself as they picked up their pace.

Turning, he entered the hall. Octa's screams had lessened now, and he could make out the cooing voice of Reaghan, soothing the child. Bassus smiled. No time now for worry and self-pity about the past. There was yet much living to do.

Chapter 12

Beobrand took a firm hold on the thick bear pelt that covered the bed and tugged. The fur was lush and heavy, but it slid away easily from the naked bodies that had nestled beneath its warmth until a moment before.

King Ecgric, flailing at the suddenness of his awakening, let out a roar.

"You sheep-swiving, whoreson!" he shouted. Eyes wide, he cast about him in the gloom to see who would dare assault him thus. Attor and Elmer threw open the shutters, letting the morning sunlight stream into the quarters. A shaft of light illuminated the pale skin of the girl who had been curled at the king's side. Taking in the situation more quickly than Ecgric, the girl leapt up from the bed with a jiggle of ample breasts, snatched up her dress from the floor, and ran for the partition that led to the hall. The men who were gathered around the bed let her pass unhindered.

Ecgric paid her no heed.

"What is the meaning of this?" he asked, his voice high and piercing. His gaze roved around the men, flicking from one to the next. Searching for weapons perhaps, but seeing none. He seemed to will himself to breathe deeply. He blinked at the bright light and rubbed at his eyes. Reaching for his breeches that lay piled by the bed, he finally fixed Beobrand with a cold stare.

"Well? What do you mean by disturbing me in this manner? Are you all drunk?"

Before Beobrand could answer, there was a commotion outside the door to the partition. Shouts. The hollow boom of a bench overturned. Beobrand turned his attention from the noises outside the royal chamber to the king. If he was to avoid bloodshed, there was not a moment to lose. Perhaps this had not been the best of ideas, but his skin had prickled all the while they had waited for the king to rouse himself from his drink-soaked slumber. He had asked to see the king, but had been told once again he would have to wait. Well, he would not sit by wasting another day while Penda's host marched ever closer to the great ditch.

They needed Ecgric to lead his comitatus to battle. They needed Ecgric to act like the king of this land.

Taking advantage of the drowsiness of the warriors in the hall, Beobrand had seized the opportunity to awaken the king himself. He had whispered a quick command to his gesithas, and, with no warning, they had burst through the door that led to Ecgric's quarters.

Wynhelm and his own men remained in the hall. They had been oblivious of Beobrand's plans and were now unarmed and surrounded by Ecgric's hearth-warriors. More yelling emanated from the great hall. A voice raised above all others. Wynhelm.

"Hold! Hold! We are unarmed."

Beobrand sprang to Ecgric, who flinched at his approach.

"Pull on your breeches and come into the hall," said Beobrand. "Now!"

Ecgric jutted his jaw out, defiant now at hearing the clamour of his warriors in the hall.

"Why?"

"For if you do not, innocent men will die."

For a heartbeat, Ecgric held Beobrand's gaze, then he stood and pulled up his breeches.

Beobrand grabbed hold of his arm and propelled him to the door. They stepped into the hall. Light from the shutters glimmered from the blades of swords. A thicket of sharp iron. Each weapon wielded by a grim-faced thegn. Wynhelm had his hands raised, palms outward, showing that he carried no weapons. His gesithas were crowded around him. One had lifted a bench and held it out before him like a monstrous club.

Beobrand swallowed the lump in his throat. No, this had not been the best of ideas.

"Put down your weapons," he shouted in his battle-voice. Everyone turned to look at him, but none of the weapons were lowered.

"I mean no harm to your lord king, Ecgric," he said. "See, he is hale and I have not raised a weapon to him." He kept a firm grip on the king's arm, but all could see Ecgric was unharmed.

"Then what is this madness?" shouted one of Ecgric's thegns, a thickset man with a neck as stout as the bole of an oak.

"It is not I that is mad," answered Beobrand. He raked them all with his gaze, blue eyes glinting. "Is this how a king's comitatus acts in the face of battle? Feasting and drinking and fucking, while Penda rapes your women, burns your farmsteads and kills the freemen who have answered the call to the fyrd?" Some of the men could not meet his icy stare. "You are thegns," he continued, "the finest warriors of this land. You must ride to the great ditch and there you must stand against Penda."

Oak-neck nodded, lowering his sword slightly.

"And who are you, to command me or my men?" asked Ecgric, in a haughty tone. Beobrand turned to him, impressed despite himself at the man's control. Their eyes met.

"I do not seek to command you, Ecgric King. Or to give orders to your trusted thegns. But I sought out your cousin, Sigeberht, at sunrise. The monks who travelled with us brought him holy gifts from the abbot of Lindisfarena and your ally, the lord king Oswald of Northumbria."

Ecgric's eyes narrowed.

"You spoke with my cousin? Took him gifts?"

"We did, lord. Oswald believed him still to rule here. But I found Sigeberht to be touched by the one true God. We prayed together," Beobrand lied, "and Sigeberht received a sign from the Lord." A murmur ran through the gathered warriors. More weapons were lowered. One man made the symbol of the rood. Wynhelm caught his eye. He gave the tiniest shake of his head.

"A sign?"

"Yes," Beobrand said. "He heard the voice of God in the call of a crow." He remembered the croak of the bird at the window of the church.

"And what did the crow say?" asked Ecgric, doubt colouring his words.

"It said I should awaken you and your men. We should make haste to defend this land of Christ's children."

"We? You ride with us?"

"Yes. I, Beobrand, who they call Half-hand, will ride with you. And so will Sigeberht."

"My cousin will ride to battle?" Ecgric sounded eager. "But he has forsworn violence."

Beobrand ignored the king's comment, instead raising his voice so that all would hear his words.

"You know lord Sigeberht to be a strong warrior and a great leader of men. And now he also wields the power of the Christ god. He will ride with us to the great dyke where the fyrd is gathered and there we will make such a stand that Penda will rue the day he set his eyes to the lands of the East Angelfolc."

Woden, All-Father, god of wisdom, let them believe the words and hear the truth in what must be done.

For a heartbeat, there was no reaction. The mood of the hall rested on a seax edge. Beobrand did not breathe.

A clatter at the far end of the hall broke the silence. The doors to the hall swung inward. More light flooded in. For a moment, Beobrand thought that more warriors had somehow been called to their king's defence. All would be lost. The Northumbrians, unarmed and outnumbered, would be cut down. The fate of Ecgric's kingdom would mean nothing to Beobrand then. If only he had ridden north instead of coming here. He could have returned to Ubbanford. To Octa. To Reaghan. No time for regrets now. The die had been cast.

His eyes adjusted quickly to the flare of daylight in the hall. A single man strode into the room. Only one man.

"Lord king," the newcomer exclaimed loudly, his voice cracking with the effort, "Lord king, Ecgric." The man scanned the room, clearly confused and trying to make sense of what his eyes beheld. Ecgric shook Beobrand's grasp from his arm and stepped forward. Once again Beobrand was amazed at his composure. He could understand why Sigeberht had believed him capable of leading his kingdom. Despite holding his breeches up with his left hand, Ecgric managed to portray an air of control and power.

The king pushed out his broad chest and raised himself to his full height.

"I am your king," he said. "What tidings?"

The messenger peered at the bare-chested man for a moment before seeming to accept the speaker's identity. He gave a small bow.

"My lord king," he said, his words coming in a rush of panicked excitement, "I bring word from Offa. You must ride to his aid with your hall-warriors. There is no time to delay. Penda has arrived with a host of many hundreds."

All eyes turned to Ecgric then. The king gave Beobrand a long, appraising look, before raising his voice.

"To arms, my loyal thegns. God has spoken. Penda is a rat that would steal our harvest. He must be slain. Prepare the horses and don your byrnies. We ride to war."

Beobrand let out the breath that had been burning his lungs.

Part Two

Fate of Kings

Chapter 13

Beobrand shielded his eyes as he gazed at the great warhost Penda had brought to the great ditch. The sun was low in the sky, its red fire glinting from countless burnished helms, byrnies and sharpened spear-tips.

Sceadugenga snorted and Beobrand patted his neck. They had ridden hard and the day had been long and hot. The stallion's skin quivered beneath his touch. The horse was tired. Perhaps he was frightened by the great gathering of warriors. The great horse was not one to show fear, but as it tossed its mane and snorted again, Beobrand could not blame the beast.

"I have never seen such a host," said Elmer, awe in his voice.

Dreogan leant from his horse and spat into the mud-churned grass.

"There are not so many that we cannot kill them," he said. "The more bastards that stand against us, the more battle-fame for us."

Beobrand smiled. The words could well have been spoken by Dreogan's old lord and Beobrand's friend, Athelstan. Beobrand wished that the warrior yet lived. He had been worth ten men in a shieldwall.

"How many are they?" Elmer asked.

Dreogan shrugged.

"There must be hundreds," he said.

Beobrand could not count the enemy. Their camp began some distance from the great dyke and disappeared into the evening haze. Standards and banners fluttered and flapped in a building wind that came from the east. Beobrand scanned the standards until his gaze settled on two that he recognised. At the centre of the encampment was raised the wolf-pelt banner of Penda, and beside it stood the grisly totem that had been carried by Cadwallon. He had not been certain of what he saw at first, distance and the smoke from the multitude of campfires blurring the image. Then, a gust of the strengthening wind cleared the smoke and shook the wolf tails that hung from the crossbeam of Penda's standard. The breeze also moved the dark shapes that dangled beneath the other banner. With a shudder, Beobrand recalled what those shapes were. The hair and tattered skin from the heads of the slain. The lighter-coloured shapes at the top of the standard were skulls of the warlord's most famed enemies. It could not be Cadwallon's, of course. Cadwallon was dead. Beobrand remembered the eyes staring up from his severed head as the lifeblood of the king of Gwynedd had soaked the earth at Hefenfelth. No, this must be some other chieftain's. One who had ridden with Cadwallon, no doubt. Suddenly, he was sure whose banner it must be. Gwalchmei ap Gwyar. The Waelisc whoreson who claimed that Sceadugenga was his steed.

Beobrand patted the horse's neck again. Perhaps Sceadugenga could smell his old master. Beobrand leant forward and whispered into the stallion's ear so quietly that none of the others would hear.

"Do not fear. You are mine now."

Sceadugenga whinnied, as if in answer and ceased pawing at the ground.

Wynhelm urged his horse close to Beobrand.

"I hope it is as Oswald believes," the older warrior said, his tone flat and quiet, only meant for Beobrand's ears. "I hope you are truly blessed by God, for I see no way that we can defeat this horde."

Beobrand shot the man a hard look, but did not reply. He too felt the darkness of fear creeping into his heart. There were so many of them. And he had brought the Northumbrians here. And for what? To defend this land so that Coenred and Edmonda would be safe? Was that the true reason or was there something else? Sweat trickled down the back of his neck. He ran his fingers through his hair.

Wynhelm was staring at him, as if expecting a response.

Beobrand looked again at the amassed enemy force. The East Angelfolc would be outnumbered, but it was a strong position, here on this great earthwork with the deep ditch before them that would slow the enemy terribly.

"I am not blessed," he said, sudden anger igniting in him, "but I am a warrior. A thegn of Northumbria. And I would not stand by or ride away leaving friends and allies to face an enemy alone. Is that what you would have had me do? Is it what you would have done, Wynhelm?"

Wynhelm's mount shied away from Beobrand's ire. Wynhelm tugged the reins hard. He gave a shake of his head, his face sombre.

"No," he said, "you speak the truth of it. I am older, my blood is not so quick to burn, but you are right. We had to stand with our allies here. Whatever the cost."

Beobrand nodded. He was glad Wynhelm had finally spoken.

The older thegn had been silent for much of the day. They had waited in tense silence as the king and his comitatus had gathered. Beobrand had made an attempt to speak with Wynhelm, but the older man had stalked away, mumbling under his breath. Beobrand knew Wynhelm was furious. He probably believed Beobrand to be rash and to have endangered them all with his actions, but Beobrand had not the energy to talk of it. Perhaps Wynhelm was right, but there was nothing that could be done now, and besides, the outcome was the same. They had ridden to the ditch and brought the best warriors Ecgric could field, along with Sigeberht, who the men of the East Angelfolc seemed to revere as they would a god.

The erstwhile king still wore his simple white robe and had insisted on riding beneath a cross made of timber. Ecgric's oak-necked thegn had offered to bear the rood standard for Sigeberht and all that day he had carried it whilst riding beside the holy man. Even now, he still held the wooden cross aloft. The wood glowed in the warm evening sun. Beneath the cross, Sigeberht stared out over the vast host that had descended on his land. He had said nothing, but now made the sign of the cross over himself in the way of the Christ followers and mumbled words in the secret tongue of their priests. There was power in the Christ cross, Beobrand had seen it at Hefenfelth. There Oswald had erected a great rood and had them all kneel and pray to the new God before the battle. A battle they should have lost. They had been victorious that night, routing the Waelisc and slaying their king. Beobrand thought of Wynhelm's words. He was not blessed, but perhaps Sigeberht could wield the power of the Christ as Oswald had.

Beobrand looked both left and right at the men they had brought with them from Beodericsworth. The setting sun lit their faces with a ruddy hue as they squinted into the brightness and surveyed the men they would soon face in battle. Their faces were grim, lines of tension etched in their features.

The warband had left Beodericsworth in good spirits. God had given them a sign, they were led by two men of royal blood, and they had powerful allies from Northumbria at their side. All that long afternoon, as they had cantered along the leaf-dappled path, they had been passed by a constant stream of people who fled from the approaching Mercians and Waelisc. Their faces were dirt-smeared, eyes empty of warmth and feeling. Some of the refugees shuffled from the path of the armed riders and watched them pass without a word. Others fled into the forest.

As they had entered one glade, riding suddenly into bright sunlight, they had startled a family at rest. As soon as they had seen the riders, the women had begun screaming, their shrieks unnerving men and horses alike. Snatching up the infants and smaller children they had run as fast as they could into the dense woodland, leaving behind a pitiful collection of belongings strewn about the clearing. They also left an old man who had been too slow to follow them into the cover of the beech and oak trees.

Reining in, Ecgric had called out to the greybeard.

"Why does your family flee from their king?"

Rheumy-eyed, the man had peered at the mounted lord.

"They are frightened, lord king," he had said slowly. His voice was as gnarled and thick as the roots of the oaks that loomed around them. "Men on horseback came. My son, Benoic, tried to stop them…" Tears welled in his eyes and he wiped a twisted, wrinkled hand at his face. "He could not. How could one man stop so many? They burnt our farm. The womenfolk were sorely used, lord. Who is to say whether a mounted warrior is friend or foe-man? Brigand or king?"

"Where do you hail from?" Ecgric had asked.

The old man waved his hand.

"To the south and west of here. You would not know of the place. It is too small to be of interest to kings."

With that, the man had slowly sat back down in the shade of an elm. He had spoken no more.

Ecgric had sat astride his fine horse for a time, staring at the wizened man who was surrounded by all his family's possessions. The king had opened his mouth, as if he planned to speak further, but it was clear to all that the young Ecgric had been dismissed. Eventually, he had closed his mouth and waved the riders on.

There had been less laughter and good cheer after that, and as they passed each new, pathetic, terrified group, the mood of the warband had soured. Their humour had worsened still further when they had reached the great dyke and the encamped fyrd of the East Angelfolc. The shambles of makeshift shelters and small campfires sprawled along a wide expanse of the eastern side of the deep ditch, but it was clear that the number of men who had answered the call to the fyrd was far smaller than those who marched with Penda. Ecgric's eyes had flitted from one group of impoverished men to another. Few bore more weapons than a spear; some carried hoes, scythes and other farm implements. Most had no armour, save for their shields. These were farmers. Ceorls and freemen who had come to the defence of their land and now they watched the thegns and lords who rode by on their fine mounts with dark eyes and drawn faces. The setting sun shone from the riders' byrnies. Shield bosses glittered, helms glimmered and the gold from brooches and sword hilts seemed aflame in the light from the lowering sun. None of the fyrd-men spoke as Ecgric and his warband trotted through the camp. Beobrand wondered what they thought of their king, a man who had chosen to remain in the comfort of his hall until the eve of battle.

Not wishing to lose the chance to see their enemy in the last light of the day, they had ridden straight for the edge of the dyke. Ecgric had seemed shocked by the sea of men they beheld. He stared out into the west, making every effort to appear lordly. His shoulders were pulled back, his spine straight, his hand rested on the hilt of his great sword. Ecgric was the image of a warlord. Yet Beobrand wondered how many others had seen the king's jaw drop open in disbelief. It had taken him a couple of heartbeats to catch himself, closing his mouth and jutting out his chin in a defiant pose, but in that moment Beobrand had seen again the true nature of the king. He may bear the trappings of war and carry himself as one born to lead men into battle, but behind the mask, he was as frightened as any of the ceorls in the fyrd.

Beobrand hoped that the Christ would listen to Sigeberht and bring them victory, for it seemed to him that Ecgric would be of little use once the shieldwalls clashed and the battle-play began in earnest.

Their hushed survey of the Mercian host was interrupted by the approach of a group of riders from the centre of the fyrd encampment. Beobrand swung Sceadugenga's head round to face the riders. As they drew close, his eyes met those of the small band's leader. Above a silver-streaked dark beard, Offa's eyes glittered and smiled warmly. He acknowledged Beobrand with a nod before reining in a few paces from Ecgric and Sigeberht. The other riders halted with a jangle of harness. One of the mounts whickered and was answered by the steed of one of Ecgric's hearth-warriors. It reminded Beobrand of how Sceadugenga and Acennan's mare greeted one another after an absence. Gods, but he wished Acennan were here.

"Well met, lord king," said Offa. "And lord Sigeberht too," he inclined his head to the white-robed monk. "We are blessed by your presence here."

"Where else would I be, Offa?" asked Ecgric.

Offa did not reply for a moment. He glanced at Beobrand and swallowed.

"The men's hearts will be lifted to see you have come to lead them against the Mercians," Offa said at last.

"I will lead them to a great victory here," said Ecgric, once again playing the part of the warrior king. "God is on our side and will guide our spears and blades and confound our enemies. But first," he said with a magnanimous smile, "perhaps we should ride to your tent for refreshment. The day has been long and hot and we would slake our thirst."

Offa shook his head.

"We will drink and eat later, lord," he said.

Ecgric paled, clearly shocked that the older man had contradicted him.

"What is the meaning of this? You dare refuse me? Your rightful king?"

Offa held up a hand.

"I meant no ill, lord king," he said, his voice soft as one who speaks to an upset child.

"What did you mean then?" Colour had risen in Ecgric's cheeks.

"Just that I thought you would first wish to ride and see what they want."

They all turned and looked in the direction of Offa's pointing finger.

Chapter 14

In the russet glow of the setting sun, a group of men had ridden from the ranks of the Mercian warhost. Now they waited beneath their standards on the far, lower side of the deep ditch. Beobrand shielded his eyes from the glare of the low sun to better make them out.

"Penda is there," he said, recognising the king's bulk on a great grey steed.

"You are certain?" asked Ecgric, his voice wavering slightly, just as the wolf tails that hung from the Mercian standard rippled in the wind.

"Aye," said Beobrand. "See there, beneath the wolf-pelt standard. At the centre. That is Penda."

"And the others?" Ecgric asked. His voice was stronger now, as he reclaimed control.

"That other standard, the one with the skulls, is of Gwynedd. It was Cadwallon's."

"Then whose is it now?" asked Ecgric. "Did Cadwallon have brothers?"

"I know not, lord," answered Beobrand, "but I believe one called Gwalchmei now rides under the skulls. He was Cadwallon's man and we saw him on your land, to the north. He was burning a monastery there."

Ecgric frowned. Sigeberht made the sign of the Christ cross.

"And the others?"

There were other standards there. A black raven on a blood-red cloth. The skull of a bull. What looked like the shaggy head of a bear, claws and fur dangling beneath it.

Beobrand could only imagine at the strength of the man needed to hold such a banner aloft. He shook his head.

"The other standards mean nothing to me."

Ecgric sighed as if somehow Beobrand had let him down.

"What do you suppose they want?" Ecgric mused.

"I would say they wish to parley, lord," said Beobrand. "Given that they ride beneath a bough of truce."

"Of course," said Ecgric, but made no sign of moving.

"If we wish to speak to them while there is yet light in the sky, we must ride now," said Beobrand, struggling to keep his annoyance from his tone.

"But what if it's a trap," asked Ecgric.

"Do not fear, lord," answered Beobrand, "Sigeberht will accompany us and God will protect us."

With that, he dug his heels into Sceadugenga's flanks and began the difficult ride down the steep slope of the ditch. He did not ride straight over the edge of the dyke, instead turning Sceadugenga to descend at an angle. This made it less steep but still he feared he might fall from the stallion's back. Sceadugenga's hooves slipped and dug great clods from the grass that grew on the bank. Beobrand hoped the others were following him, but more than that he prayed to all the gods that neither he nor any of the others would be unseated. Such a tumble would be a hard knock to a man's pride, but here, before the enemy leaders, it would be seen as an omen. Morale was surely low enough already, if the men believed the gods had sent a sign of defeat, the battle would be lost before the first blow was struck.

He clung to his reins, gripped tightly with his thighs and wrapped his right fist into Sceadugenga's coarse mane, willing himself and the horse not to fall. He let out his breath in a rush of relief at reaching the muddy bottom of the dyke. Glancing back up the slope, he was pleased to see his gesithas following him. Behind them came the white-robed Sigeberht, closely followed by the cross-bearing thegn. The man must be a fine horseman, for he held the rood straight up while his mount picked its way down the grassy slope. Ecgric and his comitatus came next, and Beobrand recognised Wynhelm and his gesithas bringing up the rear of the band of horsemen who rode to parley.

Beobrand stared up the lower western slope of the dyke. The Mercians and Waelisc gathered there were dark and foreboding against the red-tinged sky. Beobrand shivered. It was cool here in the shadow of the deep ditch. Again, he was struck by the strength of the position of the defenders. To charge up this slope towards a shieldwall would take great bravery. Many would die. But there was nothing else for Penda to do than to attack. To the north lay the great expanse of waterways, marshes and lakes of the fens. To the south, dense forests of beech and oak, dark and tangled with brambles. No warhost could hope to traverse either natural obstacle. The only way to bring a host into the heart of East Angeln was along the old road and over this great dyke. And to cross this great ditch would not be easy. Blood would soak this ground before the next setting sun. But if they just held the shieldwall strong on the earthwork, perhaps the Christ would protect them, even outnumbered as they were.

Beobrand shivered again and waited for his gesithas to reach him.

"Come on, lads," he said, forcing a grin, "let it be doughty Northumbrian warriors that lead the way. Let's show them how it's done." He was not sure whether he wanted to impress the Mercians or the East Angelfolc. Probably both.

He spurred Sceadugenga on and the stallion powered up the slope. Beobrand felt a surge of pride as his gesithas, his oath-sworn men, urged their own mounts to match his. Attor crested the brow of the slope at the same instant as him. Elmer, Dreogan and Ceawlin were a heartbeat later, followed an eye-blink after by Aethelwulf. They all reined in their horses just paces before the gathered Mercian and Waelisc leaders. In a few short moments their spirits had lifted even as the horses had lifted them into the light. Beobrand blinked in the sudden brightness of the fiery sunset. Sceadugenga wheeled on the spot, ready for further racing. Beobrand grinned at Attor, who flashed his teeth in response.

"On the way back we should place a wager," Beobrand said, and his gesithas laughed.

They pulled their now-restless mounts to a halt.

Before them, Mercian and Waelisc warlords, thegns and kings, sat silently on their mounts. They were grim-faced and bedecked in their finest war harness. Sword pommels of gold inlaid with garnets glimmered on hilts jutting from finely-worked and decorated scabbards. Gold and silver torcs and arm rings burnt red in the sunlight. Their shields were newly-painted with sigils and signs in reds, yellows and greens. The byrnies they wore were free of iron-rot and burnished to a shine. Many had war-helms, some with intricately-wrought face-guards that covered the wearer's face completely like a mask, others were simpler with check plates and nose guards. But all of them were fine and polished to a bright sheen that glowed in the sun. Apart from the larger standards and banners they had seen from the other side of the ditch, Beobrand now saw that from many of the spears hung small emblems, trinkets and woven symbols, like miniature standards on chains from short crossbars near the spear-tips.

These were the finest warriors in all of Mercia and whichever Waelisc kingdoms had chosen to ally themselves under Penda's wolf banner. They were rich, powerful and proud. And they had come to these lands in search of plunder. And blood.

Under their gaze, Beobrand felt the excitement of the race ebb away, like ale from a cracked pot.

Sigeberht, Ecgric and the other riders now joined them on the lip of the embankment and Beobrand was glad of the shift of focus from him and his men.

There was some jostling for position. Horses stamped and snorted, but soon enough the newly-arrived riders were aligned before the waiting leaders of the Mercian invaders. Sigeberht, Ecgric and the others squinted into the setting sun, trying to make out the faces of the men who had come here to steal their land and their riches. Beobrand cursed silently at the position they found themselves in. They had lost their place of strength and now appeared weak, breathless from the climb, peering into the sun. He had been wrong to lead them here. They should have remained on the eastern side of the dyke and forced Penda to ride to them.

"Who is king here?" said Penda. Despite the warmth of the evening sun, a huge wolf pelt was draped over his shoulders. His forked beard hid a sneering mouth. He scratched at his chin, and Beobrand saw the tracery of scars on his muscled forearm, the skin-memory of many battles. "Well?" Penda asked, frustration entering his voice.

Ecgric raised his face so that the sun lit him in its glow. His handsome features were wreathed in hair that shone like gold. Once again Beobrand was impressed by the king's poise. He looked every part the noble lord.

"I, Ecgric, son of Rædwald, king of these lands that you have defiled."

Penda fixed him with a hard stare. Ecgric held his gaze for a few heartbeats before looking down at his mount. Penda turned to Sigeberht who stood out in his plain robe amongst so many iron-knit shirts and shining helms.

"You must be Sigeberht," Penda said with a smile. "Finally we meet."

Sigeberht inclined his head.

"Penda, son of Pybba, I presume. I cannot say you are well met on this day."

Penda's smile broadened.

"Indeed," he said. "I would make you an offer, lord Sigeberht. One you would do well to accept."

"What offer?" Ecgric asked, having regained his composure.

Penda ignored him. When it was clear the king of the Mercians would not reply, Sigeberht sighed.

"What is this offer?" he asked.

"You bring us four score pounds of gold and I will lead my host back west."

"Why would we accept this offer from you, pagan?" Ecgric blurted out, his voice shrill. The colour in his cheeks was no longer just from the setting sun. He was furious.

Penda rounded on him.

"You would do well to keep your tongue from flapping, boy," he said. "Were you not taught to remain silent when your betters were talking?" Some of the gathered Mercians chuckled at their king's remarks. Ecgric's face flushed.

But before he could answer, Sigeberht held up his hand.

"Penda, my cousin, Ecgric, is now king of this land and its people. I cannot answer for him or our folk."

Penda, frowned, his face dark and shadowed. Behind him, far beyond the host of warriors he had marched into this land, the red orb of the sun sank to the horizon.

"That is a pity, Sigeberht. I would talk with men, not boys. And you Christ followers at least keep your word." Beobrand was unsure, but it seemed to him that Penda shot him a glance as he spoke the last words.

"Well, boy?" Penda continued, speaking to Ecgric once more. "Do you accept my terms? One way or another, my men will have their plunder. Best to give it to us than have them take it. They have marched a long way and until now I have held their leash tight." Beobrand shook his head at Penda's lies. He thought of Edmonda's monastery and the other fires they had seen to the west. The terrified, tear-streaked faces of the families fleeing Penda's host. "If you refuse me now, boy, I will have no choice but to unleash them. They will make widows of your women, burn your farms and your precious Christ halls. They will enslave your womenfolk and your children and they will still steal your gold. Much more than four score pounds of gold. A wise king would accept my offer."

Ecgric looked as if he might charge at Penda, such was his rage. His hand fell to his sword hilt, his whole body tensed, ready to urge his steed forward. Beobrand liked the king of the Angelfolc then. He remembered vividly his own ire when goaded by the fork-bearded king of the Mercians. The impotent rage that had coursed through him when he had been ordered to take Anhaga's life.

"Easy now, cousin," said Sigeberht, his tone firm. Final. "They ride beneath the bough of peace."

"You listen to Sigeberht," said Penda. "And be a wise king. Accept my deal."

Ecgric took his hand from his sword, but still his body thrummed with pent-up anger. The muscles at his jaw bulged and flexed.

"I will accept nothing from you," he spat the words from between clenched teeth.

Penda shrugged, grinning. He seemed pleased at the reaction he had provoked in the younger man. He turned his attention back to Sigeberht.

"That is the trouble with kin." he said. "They never listen to advice from their elders. Isn't that right, Eowa?"

With a start Beobrand recognised the warrior to Penda's right. Eowa, Penda's brother, wore a helm with large cheek guards which hid the scars Beobrand knew to be on his face. He remembered the savage beating in the dark shed in Din Eidyn. How Oswiu had cut Eowa. How he had given the Mercian atheling his cloak and sent him off into the snow-riven night. Above all else, Beobrand recalled the honour and dignity of the man. Their eyes met and Eowa gave the smallest of nods.

The sun had fallen beyond the edge of the world now, and darkness would be upon them soon. But still they remained, beneath the green bough of truce and Penda appeared to be enjoying himself.

"And I know you," he said, voice loud and brash. "I never forget a bastard!"

Beobrand's heart lurched as he realised the king spoke to him.

"You were at Dor," Penda continued. "There was that terrible business with your man. The cripple." Beobrand felt himself grow cold. "Attacked one of your gesithas, didn't he, Grimbold?" He turned in the saddle and addressed the last words to a large man who rode beneath the bear-head banner.

"Aye, lord," Grimbold replied. "The cripple nearly took the life of Wybert here."

In the gathering gloom Beobrand made out the features of the man who rode with Grimbold. His was a face Beobrand could never forget. It haunted his sleep. Wybert sat astride a large dappled horse. He wore a heavy woollen warrior-coat of blue with an ornate trimming of red and yellow weave. His cloak was the red-brown of old blood. There were rings on his arms and a sword at his side.

Sceadugenga took a step towards the Mercians. Beobrand was not aware of nudging the horse forward.

"Your man is a craven," he shouted, the words leaping from him unbidden. "I have sworn the bloodfeud with Wybert, son of Alric, and I will have my vengeance." His breath came in short gasps. His heartbeat pounded in his ears. His body seethed as if liquid fire ran through his veins. He trembled with the force of emotion that had gripped him. He fixed Wybert with a baleful stare. Sceadugenga took another pace forward, sensing his master's intention. Beobrand judged the distance. With luck, he could kick the stallion through the mass of warriors and reach Wybert. He would surely die, but that was a price he would willingly pay to slay Sunniva's defiler.

Penda kicked his own steed forward to block Beobrand's path to Wybert.

"Perhaps tomorrow you will take your revenge," he said, seemingly amused at Beobrand's outburst, "if the gods smile upon you. Or mayhap it is your wyrd to feed the ravens. We shall see on the morrow." Evidently deciding that the audience was over, Penda swung his mount's head and trotted back towards the Mercian camp. "By the gods, Grimbold," Penda shouted, laughter in his voice, "that half-handed bastard is a noisy one. I'd watch him, or he'll cut his way through to your man tomorrow."

Grimbold replied something to his king, but the words were lost in the sound of the Mercian and Waelisc horsemen turning and riding back to their ranks.

Beobrand cared nothing now for Penda and his taunts. He kept Wybert in his unflinching gaze, just as a hawk does a vole. Though Wybert was no defenceless woodland creature. He was broad and tall and had all the trappings of a wealthy warrior. Still, Beobrand did not fear him. He would kill Wybert or die in the attempt. He watched as Wybert turned his horse and followed his lord, Grimbold. Beside him, the warrior who bore Grimbold's heavy bear-head standard leaned in and said something. Wybert laughed. The standard bearer was a giant of a man, taller even than Bassus. As if his size and the standard wouldn't be enough to find him in the chaos of battle, his shock of fiery red hair and huge, matted beard would make him stand out even in a host of armed gesithas. As they rode away, Beobrand let out a long, shuddering breath.

Woden, All-Father, he prayed silently, let me find Wybert on the field of battle tomorrow. Let me find him and guide my blade that I may make him pay in blood for what he did.

He did not know whether Woden listened to him. Perhaps he listened to no man, but the gods loved mischief and audacity so he promised them a spectacle they would relish, should they allow him to face his blood-sworn foe.

The shadowy shape of a horseman obscured his view of the retreating lords and thegns.

For a moment, Beobrand could not make out the identity of the rider. He had been staring into the afterglow of the sunset for too long. His eyes took time to adjust, but at last the features began to make sense. The dark-bearded chin, the torc gleaming dully at the rider's neck, and the flowing white cloak that was draped over the rump of the man's steed. Gwalchmei ap Gwyar.

"We meet once more, Beobrand the half-handed," the Waelisc lord said. His horse pranced a few steps and Gwalchmei absently slapped its neck hard. Sceadugenga snorted and pawed the earth. "I see you are still riding my horse. By dusk tomorrow, your pitiful fyrd of farmers will be scattered and Taranau will be mine again."

He did not wait for Beobrand to reply. Kicking his heels viciously into his horse's flanks, Gwalchmei galloped after his countrymen and allies.

Chapter 15

Rowena sipped at the cup of warm mead and stretched her feet out to the small fire in the central hearth of the hall. The flickering of the flames was the only light and the dancing shadows of the rafters and beams brought to her mind images and half-forgotten memories from times long past. She remembered sitting by such a fire late into the night with Ubba at her side. His strong arms had encircled her, his hands caressing her under the fur he had draped around them both. They had revelled in each other's closeness, growing increasingly breathless as their hands fumbled in the warm darkness. Heat filled her belly as she recalled how their arousal had grown until he had taken her right there sitting beside the fire. She blushed now to remember how she had hoisted up her skirts and lowered herself onto him, even as his gesithas had snored and slumbered on the floor around them. A tremor ran through her and she sighed. She took another, larger sip of mead, enjoying the way the drink relaxed her into a warm glow where she could almost imagine she was that young woman again, full of lust and love.

A log shifted on the hearth, throwing sparks into the air.

But she was not young. And Ubba was dead. And there were no gesithas wrapped in blankets on the floor of the hall. Rowena was alone. She had sent the thrall girl, Alina, away and even Edlyn was up at Sunniva's hall.

No, not Sunniva's. Reaghan's hall now.

She hadn't wanted Edlyn to go. But the girl had pleaded with her.

"Bassus has said they are going to have goose," she had said. She had been wide-eyed and excited. "Reaghan has asked me to sit beside her at the high table. Oh please, mother, say I can go." Rowena had shaken her head and Edlyn had merely pleaded more loudly, more shrilly. But Rowena had not been refusing to let her go, she had merely been incredulous at the fickleness of youth. Only weeks before Edlyn had joined her in pouring scorn on Reaghan. Edlyn had loved Sunniva and had taken her death almost as hard as Beobrand. And yet here she was now happy to be invited to the Waelisc bitch's hall for a feast.

"You are invited too, mother," Edlyn had said, perhaps mistaking the cause of her mother's mood. "Bassus said you must come. And sit at the high table, as is your rightful place," she'd added quickly.

In the end, Rowena had let her go. She could not bear to see her daughter sad and she had smiled so rarely of late. Life was hard and there were precious few moments of joy, let her have this one. Soon she would be married and Ubbanford would be a memory for her to look back to on long nights. Rowena rubbed at her eyes. Gods, she was not going to weep here like a maid.

She stood and poured more mead into her cup, then sat down, once more enjoying the sensation of the fire on her outstretched feet, and the warmth on her face. Frowning, she worried at a thought that had been scratching at her mind since dusk. What had brought on this sudden change in Edlyn? She had thought it the way of young girls to hate one day and love the next. She had thought Edlyn had mistaken attention from Reaghan as friendship. That thrall whore was a wily one. Surely she had offered her daughter gifts from her new-found wealth, given her trinkets that she'd brought from Aart the peddler, perhaps. Inviting them to the new hall was just a clever way to buy their loyalty. Well, Rowena was no fool. She was not so venal to be controlled by an offer of choice meats and a place at the high table. But something had needled her all that long afternoon and into the cool, dark loneliness of the night. Reaghan sent Bassus to invite them both to the hall at least once every sennight. Every time, Rowena had politely, but firmly, declined. And every time, Edlyn had seemed happy to remain in Ubba's hall with her mother.

Until this afternoon.

What had changed? The fleeting memory of Ubba's touch caressed her thoughts again and as sudden as lightning from a clear sky she knew. What would make a young girl, no, a young woman, change her mind so? A young man, of course. And just like that, she was certain. It was that new warrior, Beircheart. He had not long been a member of Beobrand's retinue, having joined with Dreogan and Renweard the previous autumn, but Rowena was sure it was Beircheart who had given her daughter the urge to visit Reaghan's table, where she had spurned her before.

She even recalled the moment Edlyn's interest must have been sparked in the young gesith. Beircheart had been stripped to the waist, his finely muscled chest glistening with sweat from his exertions in weapon practice. He had offered Rowena and Edlyn a beaming smile as they had passed. Rowena had grumbled and hurried Edlyn along, but now she remembered how her daughter had blushed and had looked back over her shoulder. And Beircheart had waved, grinning.

Rowena took a long draught of the mead and its sweet heat soothed her.

Gods, what should she do? Would they still be feasting? Surely they would. The night was not so old that they would have set aside the food and drink. The hall would still be loud with laughter, talk and riddles. And all the while, Edlyn would be gazing, moon-eyed at Beircheart, the slim-waisted, broad-shouldered warrior who was easily ten years her senior. Rowena had seen him practising with Renweard. He was fast and skilled with a blade, his body lithe and powerful. How had she not seen the danger before? Beircheart was a warrior who had stood in shieldwalls. A killer. Such a man would not be content with lingering looks and perhaps a stolen kiss behind the dairy hut.

But surely he wouldn't dare touch Edlyn. She was a maid, unmarried and untouched. But what if Edlyn offered herself to him? He was only a man, after all, and he would have drunk much ale and mead. Perhaps she should fetch her cloak and hurry up the hill to the hall before it was too late. Edlyn needed to marry well, and no man of worth would want to take her if she was sullied.

But Rowena could not face that Waelisc bitch. She imagined Reaghan's smile, so meek, so timid. Rowena knew Reaghan hated her as much as she loathed the thrall. No amount of smiles could cover the truth. No. Rowena emptied her cup and forced herself to breathe deeply. No. She would wait for Edlyn to return.

Rowena settled herself for what might be a long wait. The fire cracked and popped. A small flame suddenly burst to life from one of the logs with a hiss, as if the wood itself were breathing fire. The tiny gout of flame gushed forth for a few moments, as if a baby wyrm were curled on the hearth. Then, as suddenly as it had appeared, the hissing flame vanished. The shadows of the hall seemed to grow darker. A few paces from the fire, the edges of the hall were cloaked in darkness. Despite the heat from the fire, Rowena shivered.

Perhaps Edlyn and Beircheart were even now in such a dark corner of the new hall. Or had they left the hall in search of somewhere more secluded? If she allowed her mind to wander thus, it was going to be a very long night. Rowena poured herself another drink and was surprised at how light the flask was. She would have to be careful, or she would not be able to keep her eyes open.

Still watching the hearth fire, she listened to the familiar sounds of the hall. She recognised each creak and groan as the building settled into the night. A certain slow cracking sound spoke of the cool night after a clear, warm afternoon. The beams of the roof protested at the change in temperature, like old men complaining as they lowered themselves onto a chair by a fire. Or like an old woman. She smiled to herself. A dull moaning, which had used to frighten the children, Ealdian in particular, was merely the wind blowing from the west under the eaves.

The familiar sounds soothed her. This was her home. Her place on middle earth. It was as if the hall itself was her kin, protecting her in its embrace from the chill and darkness of the night.

She raised her cup to her lips. Just a small sip now. She would have to make this cup last.

What was that?

The cup had barely touched her lip when something made her pause.

There it was again. A scratching. Then nothing save for the crackle of the fire and the settling groans of the cooling hall. She sipped the mead. Rowena strained her ears now, closing her eyes to better focus.

There again. A scratch, scratch, scratch, followed by silence. Could it be an animal? A rat perhaps, or a mouse? She would have to get another cat. Old Pangur had died in the winter, and she had not bothered to replace him. She was not keen on cats, but if there were rats in the hall, she would need one. She would talk to Odelyna about it, her cat had given birth to a litter of six recently. Perhaps some yet lived.

She was sitting on the edge of her stool now. Without realising it, she was leaning in the direction of the scratching, her ears ready to pick up the slightest of sounds. She breathed shallowly through her mouth.

There! Another scratch, this time followed by a sharp knock on the timber of the hall doors. Rowena started. That was no rat. The hairs on her arms and neck prickled. She did not breathe, silently waiting for another sound. She felt very alone. The scraping sound on the timber comes again, then a sharp crack of something hard against the door.

Standing quickly, careful not to upset the flask and cup, Rowena padded through the gloom of the hall to a particular chest where Ubba's seax lay buried beneath an old kirtle and cloak of his that she could not bear to be rid of. As she rummaged under the wool and linen, there was another scratch and knock on the door. Unbidden, she let out a small sound in the back of her throat. Cursing silently at her own foolishness, her hands found the leather scabbard with its studs, buckles and straps. She freed the seax from the grasp of the clothes in the chest and pulled the weapon from the scabbard. The smooth bone handle was surprisingly warm in her hand, but the weight of the blade was more than she had imagined. The blade was thick and easily as long as her forearm. Its heft gave her courage.

Turning to the doors, she walked slowly and stealthily towards them. This time she did not whimper or start when the sounds came once more. She felt foolish. It was probably

Edlyn come back from the new hall sooner than expected. But then why would she not enter?

"Edlyn?" Rowena called out, her voice thin and sharp in the still gloom of the hall. "Edlyn?" she repeated, but again there was no answer.

Another long scraping scratch and then a knock.

"Who's there?" she asked the night, pleased that her voice sounded less fearful now. In her hand, the seax trembled.

No reply came from outside.

Rowena took a long, steadying breath. This is madness. She was the lady of this hall. Wife of a thegn of Bernicia. She was not a maid to be scared by the sounds of the night. There must surely be a simple explanation for these sounds. An animal, or perhaps a branch had fallen from the wych elm that grew close to the hall. That was it. A branch would scratch as it was caught by the wind, and from time to time it might rap against the wood. Yes, it would be a branch, or an animal. Nothing to fear.

And yet her hands shook as she reached for the door. She wished she had finished that last cup of mead.

Her left hand touched the latch just as another scrape and knock echoed in the hall. Her breath caught in her throat, and she pulled her hand away. It will be nothing but a branch, she told herself. You'll see, you foolish woman.

Gripping the bone handle of the seax so tightly that her knuckles popped like pine cones thrown on a fire, she reached once more for the latch. Then, before her mind could conjure up any further terrors lurking in the night, she flung the door wide.

Chapter 16

Beobrand stared out westward at the campfires that dotted the night like so many stars. He rubbed at his eyes. They were prickly, as if he had blinked in grit on the breeze, but he knew it was tiredness. His body craved sleep, but it would not come. For a long while he had lain near the fire with his men, willing himself to fall asleep, but the release of slumber was refused him. Dark thoughts had fluttered around his head as he listened to Dreogan and Attor discussing the best way to gut a man who is wearing a byrnie. As Gram imparted his experience from countless battles to Elmer, worries had clustered and nagged at Beobrand's mind like blowflies on a corpse. Ceawlin and Aethelwulf had remained still and quiet as the night grew chill. The only sound from them came from dragging whetstones along the blades of their seaxes and swords. They had found a flask of mead from somewhere, which they passed between them without a word.

Eventually, Beobrand had left the camp and walked back to the edge of the great ditch, where wardens stood watch. He wished that he too could drink of the mead, to soften the fear and worry that gnawed at him. But his life had taught him that to flee his duty thus was the craven's way. At least for him it was so. He cared not that other men sought the solace of drink before battle, but he would not do so. Bassus had told him years before that often those who drank most were the first to die in battle. Beobrand would never forget that first shieldwall in Elmet. The stench of death, the clamour of metal on metal, the screams of the dying and their killers alike. His stomach churned and he spat. He could not die in the battle. He must lead his gesithas to safety. It would not do if they were drunk. He would return to their fire shortly and make them set aside their drink.

A man to his left coughed and hawked something up, spitting noisily. Sentinels had been placed at regular intervals along the length of the earthwork, watching for any approach from the Mercian host in the darkness. It seemed mad to most that anyone might consider attacking without the light of the sun to guide them, but Beobrand had told Sigeberht and Ecgric of the victorious night assault on the Waelisc at Hefenfelth. The king had appeared doubtful, but Offa had spoken up, lending his voice to Beobrand's and thus the number of night wards had been doubled with instructions to remain vigilant for a surprise attack. Offa had even sent some of the men over to the other side of the dyke, ready to holler in the darkness should Penda decide to bring his host to battle.

Beobrand gazed up at the sky. It was clear of clouds and the half-moon gilded the land with a silver light. They would not attack until daylight. It would be impossible to approach undetected on such a still and well-lit night. But Beobrand had been glad of Offa's support. The king and lord Sigeberht both clearly trusted Offa. He was a good man. One to stand with in the shieldwall. Sigeberht too was a man of honour, who must have been a formidable foe before he set aside the sword and shield for the vellum and the rood. What would happen to the man in the coming battle Beobrand did not know. Had he been wrong to cajole Sigeberht into coming here? He was almost certain that Ecgric would not have ridden to the dyke until it was too late to save his kingdom without his cousin's urging. But had Beobrand's actions condemned Sigeberht to death? The man said he would pray for them, raise a cross as

Oswald had and bless the fyrd. But he would not bear weapons or don battle-harness. If Ecgric and the shieldwall faltered, he would be cut down in a heartbeat.

Beobrand frowned, ran his hands through his hair and massaged the back of his neck. The uneven pressure from the two hands, the whole right and the damaged left, still unsettled him. He wondered whether he would ever be used to it; the feeling of the missing fingers. Years had passed, and yet he still sometimes forgot and fumbled his grasp on something. It was frustrating, but each time it served to remind him of who he was, what he had confronted and what he had overcome. Gods, how he wished Acennan was there. He missed his friend's easy humour and knew he would miss him in the shieldwall. Without Acennan's skill to defend his left, he would rely on Attor. The slim warrior was as deadly as any man in combat, but when Beobrand and Acennan stood shoulder to shoulder, they made music of the sword-song. Besides, he could not confide in Attor. To lead men was lonely and he would not burden his gesithas with his worries. Acennan had seen him in the worst of times, and Beobrand knew he could tell him anything. But his friend was not there.

"You couldn't sleep either, I see," said a voice close behind him, making him start. He had not heard any sound above the murmur of conversations from the men in the encampment, each of whom faced the imminent battle in his own way.

Masking his surprise by turning slowly to face the newcomer, Beobrand saw it was Wynhelm. He grunted in response, not much wanting the older man's company.

"You think they'll attack in the night?" Wynhelm asked.

Beobrand shook his head, then realised Wynhelm could probably not see the movement.

"No," he said, "and I think Penda will wait till the sun is well up in the sky too. I'd wager we'll be standing in the shieldwall waiting for a long while until the Mercians see fit to attack."

"Why do you think that?" asked Wynhelm.

"They are going to have to attack into the east, up a steep slope. The odds are not in Penda's favour. Having the sun in his warriors' eyes is one more thing against them. Also, if the day is warm, the dew will burn off the grass in the ditch, making it easier to climb."

Wynhelm scratched at his beard in the gloom. His eyes glimmered.

"You think the men will stand strong for Ecgric?" Wynhelm asked, his voice low now, so that he could not be overheard by the wardens.

"Hard to say," said Beobrand. "They love Sigeberht. Having him here will help."

"And having the great Beobrand Half-hand," Wynhelm said.

"I have no time for jesting," Beobrand said, anger flaring instantly like fat dripped onto a fire.

"I do not jest, Beobrand. You saw how Offa was when he met you. Do not belittle the impact your presence will have here on the hearts of the men."

For a long while Beobrand said nothing.

"What can I do?" he said at last. "I am but one man, like any other."

Wynhelm chuckled quietly in the darkness. It was cold enough now that his breath steamed briefly.

"Not like any other," he said. "Your battle-fame is already the stuff of songs. The men will take courage from knowing you fight with them."

"I would rather not have the weight of this upon me."

"Ah, but that is the curse of the leader of men, is it not?" asked Wynhelm. Beobrand recalled Acennan saying something very similar. "I am sure that Ecgric feels the terrible weight of the kingdom's fate on his shoulders." He dropped his voice again. "I just hope his shoulders are broad enough to bear that burden. From what we have seen of him, I am not so sure."

Beobrand was silent. For a moment, he wondered at the fear and pressure that must be pressing down on Ecgric. It would be unbearable to carry the lives of so many in your hands. The thought of it made his mouth dry. He felt a terrible pity for the king then. In his place, he would surely have been driven to seek the distractions of wine and women.

"Do you think he knew what I would do?" Beobrand asked.

"Who? Ecgric?" Wynhelm sounded confused.

"No, Oswald," answered Beobrand. "He knew that Penda was marching on the East Angelfolc, who are his allies. But he also swore an oath of truce to Penda." Beobrand's words slowed as he picked his way through the thoughts that he had not voiced aloud before. "So, could it be that knowing my nature, Oswald foresaw that I would bring our small warband to the aid of Sigeberht?"

For a time Wynhelm did not reply as he turned the thought over in his mind.

"You mean that in that way he does not break the truce with Penda, but can feel he has offered some help to his ally?"

"Aye," said Beobrand. "Is such a thing possible?"

"Who knows? Our king is as astute and wise as any man that lives, so I would say it is possible, even probable, that he expected this outcome. But he could never have been certain that you would lead us here."

Beobrand took a deep breath of the cool night air. It was redolent of wood smoke, cooking meat and the acrid stench from one of the midden pits.

Oswald knew him well. The scops told of his rash anger and how he was quick to leap to action. Perhaps, some would say, without giving thought to the outcome. Had he been used as a piece in a great game of tafl that Oswald played with the kingdoms and kings of Albion?

"Have I led us all here to our deaths, Wynhelm?" he asked, his voice not much more than a whisper.

"Who knows what tomorrow brings? None can see the future. But I know this. Your men have sworn their oath to you and follow you gladly. They love you and would happily give their lives for you."

"I know this to be true. But I do not wish them to die because of my rashness." On speaking the words, he realised this is what had most preyed on his mind.

"All you can do," said Wynhelm, reaching out and placing a hand on Beobrand's shoulder, "is try your best to make the right decisions, be just and bring your gesithas fame and glory. That is all they seek from you. Nothing more. They know who they follow. It is too late to worry now. Tomorrow we will stand in the shieldwall and we will kill or be killed. That is our wyrd."

Wynhelm gave Beobrand's shoulder a pat and walked away, back towards the camp. After a few paces he paused.

"And know this, Beobrand," he said from the darkness. "I too have led my men to this place. I have followed you here, and gladly."

Chapter 17

A welter of dark feathers and screeching flapped into Ubba's hall the moment Rowena opened the door. Letting out a yelp of surprise and terror, she stepped back from the creature that flew at her face. She lost her balance and sat down heavily on the rush-strewn floor. The fall rattled her bones and her teeth cracked together with a loud click. The seax fell from her grasp and she scrabbled for it in the rushes. Her hand touched the smooth bone handle and she gripped it with something like relief, as if the iron blade could protect her from whatever had burst into the hall. Surely it must be a nihtgenga, a night creature, come down from the hills and the forests to take her life. Rowena's heart pounded, her blood roaring in her ears. Her breath came in short gasps as she tried to make out where the creature had gone.

A squealing cry came from deep within the gloom at the far end of the hall. *Tchack, tchack, tchack.* The sound was terrifying. Gripping the seax tightly in her shaking fist, Rowena pushed herself to her feet. She would not face this monster sitting down. She was the widow of a thegn and would show she was brave, even in the face of death. Peering into the darkness, she made out the smallest of movements. Straining her eyes against the shadows, she saw it again. A twitch of black feathers. A smudge of grey. She took a tentative step closer. Her heart was slowing now, her breath coming more easily.

Could it be? She shook her head. Just a bird?

She felt suddenly foolish and was glad there was nobody there to see her. On the high-backed chair at the head of the hall sat a dark bird. A jackdaw, nothing more. Not a terrifying night-stalker. Just a bird.

Tchack, tchack, tchack, it called again and she let out a ragged breath. The grey-capped bird tilted its head and stared at her with its white eye. Just a bird. By the gods, she had been terrified. Her hands trembled and she could feel the hairs on her arms bristling, as if with cold.

"You'll not be needing that seax," said a voice, close behind her.

Rowena screamed. Her heart lurched and she feared for a moment she would swoon. She spun around, brandishing the long blade. The dim light from the fire licked its edge with red. The face of the woman who now stood in the doorway to the hall was all shadows and fire-glow.

The woman reached up and pushed the blade to one side with her slender fingers.

"I said you would not need that," she said, her teeth flashing in a smile. "I mean you no harm, Rowena."

Skeletal fingers of dread scratched down Rowena's spine. She took a step backwards. The woman, still smiling, followed her into the hall, pushing the door closed behind her.

"Who are you?" asked Rowena, her voice thin and high. "How do you know my name?"

As the woman stepped further into the hall, the flames from the fire cast more light on her face and the breath caught in Rowena's throat. At first, she had thought this stranger beautiful, her frost-streaked black hair, so much like the jackdaw's feathers, framed a pale face, with high cheek bones and lush lips, but now she saw that the left side of her face was a ruin. Scarred and twisted, the teeth behind those full lips shattered and jagged like grave markers. Rowena shuddered. Perhaps this was no woman, but a nihtgenga after all.

"How I know you is of no concern, Rowena, daughter of Eorl. But what I can do for you is."

Behind Rowena, the bird suddenly called out again in its shrieking harsh voice, making her flinch. *Tchack, tchack.*

"Hush now, Huginn," said the woman with the split face. The jackdaw ceased its calling.

Rowena's head was spinning. What was happening? Who was this woman? But somewhere deep within her mind, she thought she knew. A sudden terrible panic descended on her. Her fear gave her strength.

"If you have hurt my daughter," she said, again raising the seax menacingly, "I shall kill you."

The woman ignored the blade and the threat.

"Now why would I harm the lovely Edlyn? No, she is contentedly making eyes at that handsome gesith in the new hall. Do not fear for her."

To hear her daughter's name on the woman's lips brought another shiver down Rowena's spine. She watched the woman's eyes. They were dark and cold, but she could detect no hint of a lie in her words.

"Who are you?" she repeated. "And why do you come to my hall in the dark of the night, unannounced and uninvited?"

"I think you know my name," the woman smiled and the scars and fire-flicker made her face a savage mask, "and as to why I have come, well, we lonely womenfolk should help one another. Men believe they wield all the power, but what do they know, eh? The world bends to the will of women. Sisters weave the threads of wyrd and it is women who decide the fate of men."

"How can you help me? And why should I help you, Nelda? For that is your name, is it not?"

The woman's smile broadened, twisting her features into something less than human.

"Well, now we are both acquainted," she said. "So perhaps now you would invite me to sit with you? It is cold outside and I would welcome some mead to warm my bones."

So this was the cunning woman who had tormented Beobrand. Cursed him. Joined forces with Torran, son of Nathair, coating the Pict's blade in a deadly venom that had almost slain Beobrand. Rowena was suddenly cold and she had to fight against trembling uncontrollably. She should throw Nelda out of the hall and raise the alarm. Bassus and the other gesithas would come quickly. Perhaps she could hold Nelda until they arrived and could bring vengeance and justice upon the witch.

And yet, something deep within her knew she would not send Nelda away, nor would she call for Beobrand's warriors. No, the lonely old woman who felt powerless in the face of a new lord and his thrall whore wished to know what this cunning woman could offer her. The dark, hidden part of her that feared the day when her one remaining child would leave her all alone in this cold hall, a part of her that she never truly admitted was there at all, was intrigued.

Having come to a decision, she returned to the hearth and pulled another stool up close. She placed the seax by her feet.

Nelda approached with a swishing of her skirts. She sat on the vacant stool. From this position, only the unblemished, beautiful side of her face was in the light. Rowena poured mead into a fresh cup and held it out to Nelda.

Chapter 18

At some point in the night, Beobrand slept. But it was a fitful sleep that brought no comfort and he awoke to the echoes of nightmares, feeling more tired than when he had wrapped himself in his cloak by their small fire. It was still before dawn, cold and murky with mist. Most of the men were already up. Perhaps they had slept even less than him. He stood and stretched, letting out a long groan as his back clicked and cracked. His breath smoked and billowed before him.

Attor looked up from where he was adding twigs to the fire. Dreogan checked the edge of his sword, as he had done countless times the night before.

"No mead this morning," said Beobrand to Ceawlin, who had just unstopped the flask, while Aethelwulf observed him with a rapt expression. Beobrand had ordered them to cease drinking the night before, but evidently now that the sun tinged the eastern sky with the colour of salmon-flesh, they believed the command was no longer valid. "I need you all sharp this day."

Beobrand smiled to see the bulk of Elmer, yet snoring beneath a blanket.

"Where's Gram?" he asked.

Attor pointed with his chin towards the earthwork. The sky to the west was still dark, but Beobrand could just make out Gram's tall form, leaning on a spear.

Beobrand nodded at Attor.

"Get some food ready," he said. "We do not want to fight on empty stomachs." Or die hungry, came the quick thought, as dark as the western sky. His stomach clenched. He spat and walked towards the great ditch.

"Any sign of them readying for battle?" Beobrand asked as he climbed up the incline to where Gram stood watching over the Mercian host.

Gram shook his head. His face was in shadow. Far across the mist-filled ditch, shone the watery glow of dozens of fires.

"No," he said without looking back. "But they'll be coming soon enough."

For a long while they remained in silence. It had been a cloudless night and the land held the memory of winter in its chill. Beobrand wrapped his cloak about him. Like a shroud, he thought, and shuddered.

"Will you stand at my side in the wall, Gram?" Beobrand asked at last.

Gram glanced at him as the sun broke over the edge of the earth to the east. The warm light lent Gram's face a softness that belied his prowess in battle. His eyes were dark-ringed. Lines pulled at the corners of his mouth.

"Of course I'll stand by you, lord," he answered, as if Beobrand were moon-touched. "You have my oath."

"I know that," Beobrand smiled grimly. "It is just that I am accustomed to having Acennan at my side, but the gods alone know where he has got himself to. You are used to standing with Bassus, are you not?"

Gram's lips pressed tightly together and he nodded.

"I miss him too," said Beobrand, thinking of Bassus' gruff voice and easy laugh. "Gods, I miss them both."

"I'll stand by your side, Beobrand," Gram said. "And with your luck we'll slay all of those Mercian and Waelisc bastards and be home in Ubbanford before the next full moon."

Beobrand clapped him on the shoulder.

"I hope so. I truly do." His eye caught movement further along the raised earthwork. "But first let us break our fast and don our battle-harness. It seems we are not the only ones to rise early, and I would hear what the king and his cousin have to say to the fyrd."

*

"Gods, I need help with this," said Beobrand.

He had managed to thread the straps into the buckles, but he could not pull them tight enough and hold them secure for long enough to fasten them in place. It would have been difficult with a whole hand, but with his damaged left hand it was nigh impossible. Perhaps if they had more time, but he could see the fyrd gathering and he did not wish to miss what the leaders of the East Angelfolc had to say.

Around him all of his gesithas were ready for war. Swords and seaxes had been checked again for a keen edge. If they were made to wait for battle, Beobrand knew they would all be checked many times more. Helms were polished and laced tight under chins. It was always so before battle. Warriors donned all of their war gear even if later they would remove helms, or set aside gloves while they waited for the enemy. The ritual of pulling the heavy byrnies on somehow set the warrior's mind to the task at hand. Slipping the byrnie over head and shoulders, jumping up and down with arms reaching for the sky until the iron-knit shirt fell comfortingly bulky on the shoulders, felt like sliding into the skin of a warrior. There was comfort in the heft of weapons pulling at the belt that was cinched tight about the waist to hold some of the weight of the byrnie.

Byrnie, great helm, seax and sword, even his shield, with the straps fashioned to prevent him losing his grip on the boss-handle, all these things were familiar to Beobrand and he welcomed the feel of them against his body. It was only these damned splints of metal that did not feel right. He had first seen such splints of iron attached to leather and then fastened to the forearm on some of Eowa's men the year before. He had described them to the smith at Berewic who had forged them for him for a price. He had carried them in his saddlebags until now. Now was the moment, with the fyrd gathered and preparing for battle, when a lord must be bedecked with all the armour he possessed. The splints were well-made, and would stop a slash at his arm during battle, if only he could fasten the accursed buckles.

Gram came to his aid. Pulling the straps as tightly as possible over the wrappings Beobrand had wound around his arm, he buckled the straps with dexterous fingers.

"I like it," Gram said. "How does it feel? Can you move your arm freely?"

Beobrand clenched his fist and swung his arm around. He twisted his wrist, feeling the wrapping and straps grip his forearm. He nodded.

"I can move it well enough," he said.

"Good. I don't want to be at your side if you cannot move your sword." Gram grinned, his teeth bright in the glare of the early-morning sun. He wore a helmet similar to Beobrand's, with cheek guards and a strip of iron to protect the nose.

Beobrand clapped Gram on the shoulder in thanks and glanced about him. All the men were ready. These were fine men, hale and strong. They were well-armed with blade and shield. They were good, brave gesithas. They had fought in the shieldwall before and proven themselves many times over. His heart leapt with pride.

"My brave gesithas," he said, raising his voice enough so that they would all hear him, "Before this day is over there will be war. Do not ask yourselves whether this is your war. It is our war. The enemy of our friend is also our enemy. And so I have brought us here to stand beside our king's allies and I know you will stand in the wall beside me for you are my oath-sworn men. There are no better men in all of middle earth, and I am honoured to hold your oaths."

He looked at each man in turn. Attor's eyes burnt with the prospect of battle. Beobrand could feel it too. Excitement was burning away the fear of the shieldwall. Dreogan nodded his approval of Beobrand's words, the soot-darkened lines on his face adding to his grim aspect. Dreogan had given his oath less than a year before, but Beobrand trusted him completely. Ceawlin and Aethelwulf stood close together, their faces mostly hidden under helms and behind thick beards. They appeared to be relaxed, almost slouching, but Beobrand knew they would be formidable when the time came. Lastly came Elmer. The burly warrior's cheeks were flushed and his eyes glittered. He rocked from side to side, unable to be still. Elmer had bemoaned being left behind at Ubbanford in the past, Beobrand hoped he would not regret having been brought on this journey. But it was too late to change their course now.

Off to one side, Beobrand saw that Wynhelm's men were ready. Wynhelm nodded at him. Beobrand turned back to his gesithas.

"So, my brave warriors," he said in a clear voice that rang with pride, "are you ready to fight beside me?"

The small group let out a cheer. Men who were making their way to the earthwork turned to stare. Beobrand ignored them. Soon they would stare at the dead heaped before his warband.

"Are you ready to soak the earth with the blood of Mercian and Waelisc scum?"

Again they cheered, this time more loudly. Dreogan raised his fist in the air and shouted the loudest.

Beobrand nodded to Wynhelm.

"Come then, let us hear what the lords of the East Angelfolc would say to us."

*

Beobrand was already hot in his battle-harness and the day was hardly begun. The sun was yet low in the sky, casting long shadows before the warriors who stood on the earthwork on the eastern side of the great ditch. The ditch was dark with shadow. Tendrils of mist still clung to the marshy earth at the bottom. Gazing across the dyke to the west, Beobrand could see that Penda's host was preparing for war. But they would not be ready for some time. To cross the great dyke towards a shieldwall would take great courage, and that would mean time. And ale. Few sober men would wish to be the first to run up that steep embankment towards a forest of spears and a wall of shields. They would have a long wait he feared. The waiting was the worst. His scalp prickled with sweat under his great helm and he longed to remove it. But he would keep it on for a while longer.

The fyrd-men had all but finished gathering. They stood along the top of the earthwork and also in a great mass of men to the west, looking up at the symbol that Sigeberht had ordered to be raised. A wooden rood, the symbol of the Christ god, stood on the earthwork for all to see. It was not huge like the cross that Oswald had erected at Hefenfelth, but it was visible enough from its raised position on the bank of earth. The sun glinted from iron on its crossbar and Beobrand realised it had been fashioned by strapping together several spears and then driving the base into the earth.

Beobrand, Wynhelm and their warband had pushed and bullied their way close to the rood, near to where Sigeberht stood. Still wearing the simplest of white robes, he seemed to glow in the warm morning light. He raised his hands and the murmur of voices slowly subsided until all the men were quiet, straining to hear the words from this man who had been their king. Beobrand was reminded of Oswald in Sigeberht's gesture; in the calm power he commanded without bluster.

Somewhere off to the south a woodpigeon called into the silence.

"Today, we stand before a terrible foe," said Sigeberht, his voice clear and loud. "Penda of Mercia seeks to take what is rightfully ours. Like a plague on the distant kingdom of Ægypte, he has descended on our lands, stealing, slaying and destroying. But like God's children in Ægypte, we shall be set free. For the Lord is the true King, and if we pray to Him, He will grant us victory this day over the heathen plague."

Beobrand glanced at Wynhelm. He knew nothing of this Ægypte. The older man's brow was furrowed.

"So kneel," continued Sigeberht. "Kneel before the rood of the one true King and let us pray to Him for deliverance from the infidel horde."

Offa was the first to kneel, followed quickly by his gesithas. Then slowly, uncertainly, all of the men bent their knee. The ground was damp with dew and soaked into Beobrand's breeches.

Sigeberht prayed loud and long. And he did it in the sacred tongue of the Christ priests. Beobrand wondered if any there understood the words. He did not, and to judge from the fidgeting, and the whispers that began shortly after the tonsured lord began, none of the men of the fyrd did either.

"Gods," he hissed to Gram, "if he continues like this, the men will wish to be killed to rid them of this boredom."

It seemed that Ecgric must have come to the same conclusion, for he now stepped close to his cousin and whispered something. Sigeberht frowned, but came to an abrupt halt.

"Amen," he said.

A handful of the warriors replied with the same word. Sigeberht looked perplexed at the lack of response to his prayers. Beobrand wiped the sweat from his brow. Perhaps he had been wrong to bring Sigeberht here. The men loved the man, but his words and actions had done nothing to instil the fyrd with the courage to fight. Maybe Sigeberht truly had the ear of his god. Beobrand hoped so.

Ecgric now raised his hands to the host of East Angelfolc. He was resplendent in his battle gear. He looked every bit the great warlord. The sun picked out every detail of his fine sword hilt, with its gold and garnet pommel. The intricately-tooled leather of the scabbard shone, as did the finely-wrought links of his byrnie. His fair hair was brushed back from his striking features. The man certainly knew how to play the part of king. Perhaps, thought Beobrand, that was all any man ever did.

The men of the fyrd, uncomfortable to be kneeling for so long, began to rise to their feet, until at last they all stood in silence, eyes turned to their king. A frown darkened Ecgric's face for a moment, as if a cloud had flitted before the sun.

"Men," he said, raising his voice for all to hear, "countrymen. You have come from all corners of our land, from the fens in the north, the great forests of the south, and the low lands of the coast. For that, I thank you. As you know, I called you here to defend our land and you have answered that call. You are the bravest and the strongest of the warriors of our folk and those arrayed against us should feel fear. For we will not break."

He paused, as if expecting a response, but none came.

"Yestereve, Penda asked me to buy our peace. As if I would part with gold and treasures to be free of him and his rabble of Waelisc and Mercians."

A murmur of whispered exclamations ran though the men. They had not known of this offer. Beobrand looked at some of the faces nearest him and saw anger there. Perhaps they thought losing some gold a better prospect than that of spilling their lifeblood into the soil.

"No," shouted Ecgric, trying to hold the host's attention, "I told Penda we East Angelfolc would face him with shield, spear and sword. We have God on our side and we would rather shed our blood than to give our land and our riches to him. If he wants our gold, let him try and take it from us by force."

Again he paused and again there was no cheer of acclamation. A sinking feeling came over Beobrand. If the spirit of the fyrd could not be fired with the belief they could win, all would be lost before it began. And if they faltered, what then of Coenred and Edmonda? Despite the warmth of the day a chill ran through him, making him shiver. And what of Wybert? The East Angelfolc must hold firm if he was to be able to face him and bring an end of their bloodfeud. More than the safety of the land and those who could not defend themselves against the Mercians, the thought of facing Wybert in battle consumed him.

Without further thought he pushed forward towards Ecgric. He shouldered his way through Offa's warband, ignoring the curses and pushing aside men who tried to shove him back. Ecgric's eyes widened as Beobrand strode towards him.

"What madness has gripped you?" Ecgric hissed.

For a heartbeat, Beobrand thought of explaining himself to the king, but just as quickly he knew it would lead to naught but trouble and confusion. Well, if he was to have trouble, best he make good use of it. He turned to the gathered men. The sun was hot on his face.

"What are you about?" whispered Ecgric with urgency.

Beobrand ignored him.

"Many of you know me," he shouted in the tone he used for battle. Not one of the men there would be able to ignore his words. "I am Beobrand, son of Grimgundi. Lord of Ubbanford and sworn thegn of King Oswald of Northumbria, who is Bretwalda of Albion." Sweat trickled from underneath his great helm, stinging his eyes. But he did not wipe at them now. He could show no weakness before these men. "I stand here because I believe we can win. I have brought my men to this place not only to help friends in their time of need, but because I see there is much plunder to be taken from those Mercian whoresons. And what do all men want if not good land and plunder? You have the land already. And now Penda brings you a whole host of warriors wearing metal-knit shirts and fine swords. Think not of them as enemies to be feared. Look at them as men bearing you gifts of armour and weapons."

A smattering of laughter from the men.

"Look at where we stand," Beobrand continued. "This great ditch is a place of great strength. If we stand firm in the shieldwall at the top of this earthwork, we can hold this place until the end of time. We will rain death down upon our enemies as they seek to bring their gifts to us, and they will fill the ditch with their bounty. All we must do, is to remain steadfast and strong here. We do not need to chase them should they run, for the ditch gives us the greatest protection. Let them come to us. We will give them death in return for the treasure they bring."

He paused for breath. The sun was blinding in its brightness. Blinking away the sweat that sheeted down his forehead, he tried to make out the faces of the men looking up at him, but they were blurred and in shadow.

"What will we give them?" he bellowed.

"Death!" came the reply from the fyrd.

"What will we give them?"

"Death!" they roared.

Beobrand joined in the cry.

"Death! Death! Death!" they chanted. The sound washed over him and with each shout, Beobrand pictured finding the bear-head banner and ripping the life from Wybert.

Chapter 19

The attack finally came as the sun reached its zenith.

By mid-morning the men on the earthwork had tired of hurling abuse at the invading force. There had been a brief moment of excitement when one young warrior had thrown a javelin across the great ditch, skewering a long-haired Waelisc man through the throat. The man had fallen over onto his back, clawing at the shaft of the spear, his feet scraping and kicking the ground briefly, as if trying to regain his footing. The defenders had let out a cheer and the jeers had intensified for a time. The Mercians and Waelisc had pulled back from the lip of the ditch and continued drinking and eyeing the East Angelfolc balefully. A few others launched spears at Penda's host after that, but no more came close to striking an enemy. Eventually Offa had yelled at them to save their weapons for when they could not miss.

The morning had worn on, and as Beobrand had known would happen, men had begun to shed helmets and, in some cases, even armour. They sat slumped in groups on the raised earthwork, using their shields for shade. Women and boys came up from the camp with water skins, but there was never enough for all the men and by midday the warriors' tongues were swollen; their mouths dry.

When the attackers suddenly charged towards the ditch, it took Beobrand a heartbeat to react. The first of the screaming warriors were already hurtling down the western slope when he leapt to his feet. He shoved his helm onto his head, cursing

144

at having removed it. There was no time to tie the cord beneath the cheek guards.

"Spears! Spears!" he bellowed, pushing his arm through the straps of his shield and grasping the warm iron of the boss-handle.

With horror, he saw that the enemy had reached the bottom of the ditch. They were slowed by the sodden ground there, but they would be starting up the longer eastern slope in a matter of moments.

"Spears!" he yelled again, snatching up his own.

Something hard clanged off his helmet, deafening him. His head was thrown back by the force of the blow and his great helm tumbled off and down the earthwork bank behind him. Beobrand staggered a pace backwards. His ears were ringing and his vision blurred. He shook his head to clear it, unsure what had happened. Dazed and scarcely thinking, he stepped into the gap he had left in the rapidly forming shieldwall. The first of the enemy host were now labouring up the slope beneath him. On the far side of the ditch and some way back from its edge stood a ragged line of men. For an eye-blink he could not focus on what they were at, then in an instant he understood what had hit him.

"Slingers and archers!" he yelled into the din, though whether any heard him, he knew not. Arrows streaked across the ditch towards the shieldwall and more stones clattered from shields and helms. Beobrand ducked behind his shield, cursing again the loss of his helm. He felt naked without it.

Off to his left one of Wynhelm's men let out a scream as an arrow pierced his thigh. To the right an unarmoured fyrd-man tumbled down into the ditch without a sound. Perhaps stunned by a stone, or already dead. The man's body rolled into the path of the attackers and one stumbled, falling to his knees on the grassy slope.

All around Beobrand men were launching short throwing-spears down at the Mercians and Waelisc who came in a ragged wall of men, slowly but inexorably up the side of the dyke. Something thunked hard into the linden-board of his shield. Beobrand winced as the blur of an arrow flew a hand's breadth above his head. Gripping his spear firmly, he ignored the men on the other side of the ditch and their deadly rain of projectiles. Peering under his shield rim, he fixed his gaze on a squat, broad-bellied man who wore no byrnie. The man's nose was an ugly mess of scars from a previous fight and his eyes were white-rimmed like those of a frightened horse. He struggled to run up the hill, his feet slipping, and with no hand free to help steady him, he came on slowly. The sound of battle seemed to lessen around him as Beobrand focused fully on the oncoming man. The man who would be the first he would kill this day. The ringing in his ears subsided and the calm madness of battle washed through him like the rush of strong mead on an empty stomach.

He watched as the man came ever closer, wide-eyed and winded, with no strength left to yell his defiance. To the left and right of them spears were thrusting into shields and flesh. Men screamed and the blood-piss-shit stench of battle filled the air. But Beobrand was only vaguely aware. For that moment, his world was reduced to him and the scar-nosed warrior. Beobrand lowered the point of his spear, awaiting the perfect moment to strike. He saw easily the moment when the attacker would lash out his own spear at Beobrand's unarmoured legs, leaving himself open to attack. Beobrand skipped to the side and the spear met only air. At the same instant, he plunged his spear down hard. The thrust was true and found the man's chest. The steel point pierced flesh and drove deep.

Scar-nose dropped his spear and shield and his eyes opened even wider until Beobrand thought they might fall from the man's head. The dying man grasped the haft of Beobrand's spear, perhaps meaning to pull Beobrand with him into the ditch. For a moment, all his weight hung on the spear-tip and Beobrand feared he would indeed be pulled from the earthwork or have to drop his spear. With a roar of rage, he twisted the spear savagely and the man relinquished his grip and fell away. Dark blood spouted and then he was lost behind the next attacker.

Beobrand let out a barking laugh.

"Death!" he screamed and thrust his spear down once more, this time into the face of a beardless boy. The point slammed into the boy's mouth, smashing teeth, cutting sinews and crushing bone. Another twist of the spear haft and the boy fell in a whimpering heap into the ditch where the wound-sea was already running thick.

For a moment there was no enemy to slay, though many more were trudging through the quagmire at the lowest point of the ditch. To the left and right the line of defenders was mainly intact, the elevation of their position and the reach of their spears enough to hold off the first wave of attackers. Arrows still flicked across the ditch. Some thudded into the earthen bank below the defenders, and some flew harmlessly overhead. But a few struck home and a handful of the East Angelfolc had retreated back toward the encampment, nursing their wounds. Beobrand saw Wynhelm's man, arrow still jutting from his thigh, skewer a Waelisc warrior in the gut. The attacker fell back and the injured Northumbrian spat down the slope at him, seemingly unheeding now of the pain in his leg or the blood that soaked his breeches and leg bindings.

Before the next Mercians and Waelisc could come within spear-reach, Beobrand risked the arrows and stones and glanced over his shield. He quickly scanned the thronged host on the far side of the great ditch. There was Penda's banner, the grey wolf fur looking almost white against the blue sky. Further off was the grisly Waelisc standard of skulls and scalps. Spears and banners waved above the invading host like a wind-blown forest. But where was the standard he sought?

He could look no longer. The new attackers had climbed within range of the defenders' spears. Beobrand feinted the gore-slick tip of his spear at the legs of a warrior who wore a heavy coat of leather over a long byrnie. The man lowered his shield slightly to deflect the spear, and as quick as a striking viper, Beobrand raised the spear-point to the warrior's exposed chest. The ash haft of the spear jarred and jolted in Beobrand's hand at the impact. And yet it was not the man's wyrd to die thus. The steel sliced into the leathern warrior-coat but did not penetrate the man's byrnie. He was halted in his tracks and Beobrand pushed his weight onto the spear, hoping to drive it between the metal links of the armour. But still the iron-knit shirt held and the warrior released his hold on his shield and, gripping Beobrand's spear, he twisted his body and tugged it towards him. Beobrand staggered forward, off balance for a moment, before relinquishing the spear.

The man must have been in pain from the force of the blow to his chest, but his face broke into a wide smile at having won this small battle with the huge fair-haired thegn atop the earthwork. He slipped a few paces back down the slope before fully recovering his footing. Then he tossed the spear aside and stooped to pick up his shield. He raised his sword and pointed it at Beobrand. He shouted something, a challenge perhaps, but his words were lost in the tumult of the battle.

Then he resumed his climb towards Beobrand, who now pulled Hrunting from its scabbard. He would accept the man's challenge. He had escaped Beobrand's spear, he would not live to tell the tale of facing Beobrand with a sword.

The man's eyes bored into Beobrand as he clambered up the blood-streaked grass.

"Come and meet death!" yelled Beobrand, lost now to the savage glee of blood-letting. Hrunting thrummed in his hand, ready for the sword-song to begin. Standing on the balls of his feet, Beobrand quivered with excitement. Hrunting was light in his grasp. The man shouted something again and strode the last few steps up the slope. Beobrand beckoned him on. He would allow him to reach the top of the slope and there slay him for all to see. He grinned.

"Come and die!" he bellowed, banging the flat of Hrunting's blade against his shield.

The man let out his own scream and closed the distance with Beobrand in a last burst of speed.

But before their blades or shields clashed, Beobrand's opponent stopped short, a look of confusion on his face. As Beobrand watched, the man's throat opened into a broad gash and blood sheeted down his chest over his fine leather coat. A gush of hot blood fountained bright in the sunlight, splattering Beobrand's face, chest and arms.

The man's eyes rolled back into his head and he toppled backwards down the slope. Attor lowered his spear.

"Did you see that?" he asked. "He didn't even know his throat had been cut until he was dead. He was too intent on fighting the great Beobrand Half-hand to see Attor the quick nearly take his head from his shoulders." He laughed.

Beobrand blinked the sting of blood from his eyes. The broad-leafed head of Attor's spear was painted red with the man's battle-sweat. Attor grinned at the look on his lord's face.

"Well, you told him to come and die," he said.

They stepped forward and looked down into the ditch. Dead and dying men were strewn on the slope and in the mud at the bottom. An arrow buried itself into the earth at Beobrand's feet. He did not flinch.

"Look," said Gram, stepping close to Beobrand and Attor, "they retreat."

It was true. All along the ditch, Mercians and Waelisc warriors were running back towards their host. Some stopped to help injured comrades out of the corpse-strewn mud, but most jumped over the fallen warriors and ran up the far bank. The East Angelfolc host grew still. The sound of their panting was loud. A man screamed somewhere with the ululating wailing of an infant and, unbidden, the face of Octa came to Beobrand. Now was not the time to think of his son. Now was the time to deal death.

"Men of the East Angelfolc," he shouted in a voice loud enough to rip his throat. "Behold the treasures that Penda and his band of thieves have brought us." He gestured into the ditch and all who heard him looked at the tangled mass of bodies. Swords, seaxes, spears and shields were scattered amongst the dead. The midday sun glinted on the fresh crimson of blood and the gold of brooches, hilts and arm rings. There was treasure indeed. Riches in a charnel pit.

"They bring us gifts and what do we give them?" he bellowed.

"Death!" replied his gesithas and a few other men of the fyrd.

"What do we give them?" he repeated.

"Death!" the cry was picked up by more of the men.

The chat grew in volume until it was a wall of noise that rolled over the ditch to reach the retreating men and those other warriors who had yet to be blooded in the battle.

Around him the men continued to shout their defiance at the invaders. But Beobrand fell quiet. He stared intently across the great dyke. Sweat streamed down his face, mingling with the sticky blood and stinging his eyes. He wiped at them with the back of his hand.

There, almost directly before his position, swayed Grimbold's bear-head banner. Beneath it he could see the giant warrior's shock of flame-red beard. And beside him, the smaller form of Wybert. Beobrand glowered across the distance at the man, willing him to be the next to climb the slope, to be the next warrior to come to accept the payment for the gifts he brought.

Beobrand hawked blood and spit from his mouth, and once more lent his voice to the chant that he had started.

"Death! Death! Death!"

Chapter 20

"By Tiw's cock!"

Gram's scream reached Beobrand even over the clamour of hundreds of men shouting their loathing and fear at one another; despite the smithy-crash of metal on metal and the muting of sound that came from his helmet's cheek guards. He had retrieved the helm after that first assault and it was now firmly tied in place. There was a dent in the metal where the sling stone had hit. It would need hammering out. If they survived. For now, the bent metal made the helmet uncomfortable, pressing as it did into the tender place where the stone had impacted. But better the pain than an unprotected head. The helm had saved his life once already this day, and he would not set it aside now.

Beobrand glanced at Gram. He was yet standing, but his face was pallid beneath his helm.

"What is it, Gram?" asked Beobrand, looking back at the balding Waelisc man who screamed at him in his impossible tongue. Spittle flecked the man's lips as he yelled and thrust forward with a short stabbing sword. Beobrand deflected the blow with his shield, sending a counter at the man's groin. Hrunting was sheathed now, and Beobrand had taken up the seax that had been his brother's. Its blade was shorter; good for the butcher's work of the shieldwall. The Waelisc avoided the seax blade, stepping back slightly. Though he could not step far without the risk of slipping down the slope into the ditch.

"My leg," Gram shouted, his voice clipped and tight. "Spear." The words came with difficulty, his teeth clenched against the pain. He needed all his strength to hold off the warrior who menaced him with a short hand axe.

Beobrand glanced down and saw fresh blood soaking Gram's breeches and leg bindings. He had taken a blow high up on his thigh, probably from one of the men behind and lower down the slope than the first line of the shieldwall that faced them. There was much blood. He would die if it was not bound. Beobrand would not allow that.

With a bellow, Beobrand shoved forward with all his might against the balding Waelisc warrior. As their shields clashed, Beobrand dropped to his knee, holding his linden-board high. He felt the Waelisc warrior's sword clatter against his shield boss. At the same moment Beobrand slashed under his shield. The heavy seax blade bit deeply into the man's right foot. He screamed piteously. Beobrand wrenched the blade free and rose to his feet in one fluid motion, shoving forward as he stood. The Waelisc, face the colour of whey, fell away from him, colliding with the men who came behind up the embankment.

Without pause, Beobrand swung to the left, to Gram's attacker. The warrior was intent on killing Gram and so was oblivious of Beobrand at his flank where moments before a comrade-in-arms had stood. The man never knew who killed him. Beobrand swung his gore-spattered seax into the back of the man's neck. The blade hacked into the flesh and severed bone and sinew. The warrior fell like a slaughtered bull at Blotmonath.

A man with a red-tipped spear, perhaps the spear that had wounded Gram, came fast to fill the breach. Beobrand swung his shield round to parry the attack. The shock of the spear-blow brought a pang of pain from old wounds, but his arm was healed now; strong. The spear-point dug into the scarred

153

hide of the shield and scraped across the boards. Beobrand pushed forward, hoping to unbalance the spearman. But the man did not falter, instead he flicked the wicked point of the spear at Beobrand's face.

Beobrand was exposed here. The defenders' shieldwall would crumble quickly if left broken for long. But a seax was no match for a spear. The man would be able to hold him off for long enough to allow others to swarm up the slope and into the gap Beobrand had opened up. The spear came at him again, and once more Beobrand caught it on his shield. He must finish this. But how? All the while he fought here, Gram's lifeblood was pumping from him.

Then, without warning, the spear ceased its probing. Beobrand feared a feint; a trick of some kind. But the splash of scarlet on the spearman's throat told him quickly of the truth of it. Attor had sprung forward and once more plunged his spear into the throat of an enemy.

Attor cackled, drunk on the killing.

"I will eat your fucking entrails, you curs!" he screamed. "I will bathe in your blood."

Around them, Penda's men fell back from the two battle-crazed, blood-drenched warriors.

Beobrand resisted the urge to throw himself down the slope at them. His blood pumped hot in his veins. He could rush them now, hewing through their ranks to find Wybert. But in his mind, he heard Scand's voice yelling at him that to do so would bring destruction and death. They must hold the shieldwall. He stepped back.

"Attor," he snapped, "to me."

Attor, savage and blood-spattered shook his head like a dog stepping from a river. For an instant, Beobrand thought he would ignore him and run at the Mercians, but then, Attor moved back to take his place beside his lord.

"Get one of the women to bind your wound," Beobrand said to Gram.

"My place is here," Gram replied, his voice as jagged as pine splinters.

"Your place is to do your lord's bidding," Beobrand snapped. "You are no use to me dead. Now go."

Gram nodded and half-walked, half-fell down the slope towards where the camp womenfolk were congregated in a huddled group. There was much blood on his leg and he was as pale as ewe's milk. Beobrand hoped he would live.

"To me," he shouted, his voice now cracking from the strain. Attor and the rest of his gesithas closed ranks with him, filling the void left by Gram. Dreogan, as grim-faced and menacing as a monster from a scop's tale now stood to his left. His eyes glared out at the enemy line that still had not resumed the fight.

Beobrand took in a great gulp of air. His throat was dry and his body drenched in sweat and the cloying stickiness of blood. This was the third time that Penda's host had attacked since that first brutal onslaught and the day was still far from over. Clouds had begun to form in the north and west, but they gave no respite from the heat of the sun. The pauses in between attacks had been too short to allow the defenders to fully rest. The camp women and children ran up the slope to them with water and what food they could carry when the fighting ceased for a moment, but the slumped warriors could scarcely dampen their mouths or swallow more than a mouthful of bread before the Mercians and Waelisc came on again. If the East Angelfolc had hoped that the great ditch would prove too much of an obstacle for the invaders, none now believed it. No matter the number of warriors they killed, more took their place.

The shieldwall was yet intact. But many defenders had fallen. With each attack, the wall became more ragged, buckling in places, before men rallied and pushed the attackers back. It still held, but for how long?

In the ditch before them, the men who had retreated seemed to have lost their appetite for battle. They stepped back cautiously. The bottom of the ditch was clogged with the dead and some of the retreating men had to step on the pallid corpses of their fallen. Beobrand let out a sigh. He desperately needed something to drink. He rammed his seax blade into the earth and was just preparing to lower himself to the ground when a great cheer rose from the centre of the shieldwall. Beobrand raised himself to his full height and peered over the line of men who stood atop the earthwork. But the line was thinning. His stomach twisted as he understood what he saw.

The East Angelfolc were charging down the slope in pursuit of the retreating attackers. At their head he recognised the shining great helm of Ecgric. The king seemed to have found his bravery, but his recklessness would likely lead to the doom of his people.

"No!" Beobrand screamed. "Hold the shieldwall!" His voice was lost in the tumult of voices now raised in an ecstasy of anger as defenders became attackers.

"No!" he shouted again, and his men faltered. Wynhelm too held his men in check. Any warrior knew that holding the high ground was their best and only hope of victory.

But all along the dyke, men rushed down the slope, where they fell upon Penda's warriors, hacking and hewing them in the blood-churned quagmire there.

Beobrand stopped shouting. Nobody was listening. The warriors had followed their king, perhaps believing that victory was certain. He shook his head, looking over the ditch to where a mass of Penda's host now gathered, ready to throw themselves upon Ecgric and his fyrd.

With horror, he watched as the Mercians and Waelisc surged over the lip of the lower, western edge of the ditch. Ecgric and the East Angelfolc would be destroyed.

"What should we do?" Wynhelm asked, his voice hollow from fatigue and shock. He had come close to Beobrand to make himself heard over the din of the battle. "We should flee this place while we have the chance."

Beobrand nodded absently. He knew that the older thegn was right. They owed nothing to this land or its foolhardy king. And yet, Beobrand did not turn to seek out Sceadugenga and the other horses where they had been corralled. Instead, he tugged his seax from the earth, wiped it on a corpse's kirtle, and sheathed it.

For, entering the fray directly below them, he saw a huge red-bearded warrior, who had stood beneath Grimbold's bear-head standard. And beside the giant came a smaller, darker warrior. A warrior who was in fact a walking corpse and had been these past two years.

Without a word, Beobrand dragged Hrunting from its scabbard. The fine sword caught the rays of the sun with a flash. It had been his brother's blade before him and it was right that it should be the one to taste the blood-price of vengeance.

"What are you doing?" asked Wynhelm, incredulity in his voice.

"What I must," replied Beobrand, and ran down the blood-slick slope, into the morass of the slaughter.

Chapter 21

"Careful, girl," snapped Maida, her voice shrill, "nobody wants yarn full of dust and ants."

Reaghan had never been good with spindle and whorl, but she had offered to help Maida nonetheless. She enjoyed spending time with the goodwife and her children. On a day like today, warm and sultry, with midges hazing the air, it was pleasing to be outside of Elmer's hut, watching little Octa play with the other children. Reaghan had been smiling to see him crawling after Maida's youngest, Bysen, a girl of four years, when she had inadvertently allowed the yarn to break and the spindle had fallen to the dirt. The girl was teasing Octa, dangling a small carved wooden horse just out of his reach. Each time she did this, Octa would stop and reach up a pudgy hand, only to have her snatch the toy away with a laugh and scurry away. He did not cry. He merely frowned and started after the girl once more, a look of serious determination on his baby features.

"Sorry," Reaghan said, "I'm not being much help to you." She hated feeling she was a burden on Maida, who was one of the few people in the settlement who had been kind to her.

"It is I who should be sorry," replied Maida, smoothing her dress nervously with her hands.

It was always thus with Maida. Reaghan's heart clenched.

"You have nothing to be sorry for," said Reaghan. "I am in the wrong, and it is right you should tell me."

Maida mumbled something, but looked unhappy.

Reaghan quickly gathered up the wool from the ground and continued spinning, taking more care this time on what she was about. If only Maida would treat her as her equal, just another woman waiting for her man to return. Were they so different? But Reaghan knew the answer to that question all too well. This woman had always been kindly to her when she was a thrall, and she was not unkind to her now. But could they ever be friends? It seemed not. They were separated by too much perhaps.

Maida bustled into the hut, from where the comforting smell of pottage wafted. The older woman felt as uncomfortable as Reaghan no doubt. Neither knew how to behave with the other, and yet Maida could not send her away. Reaghan was the woman of the lord of Ubbanford now. She longed for just one friend. Someone with whom she could speak her inner thoughts. But the women despised her for having been a thrall, and the thralls loathed her for the same reason. It seemed there was nothing worse in their eyes than a freed slave.

She gazed absently up at the hall on the hill. Wisps of cloud were forming in the sky, but there was no sign that rain would come anytime soon to clear the air.

It had been a surprise to see Edlyn the night before. When the girl had entered the hall, all those seated at the boards had fallen silent. It was the first time Rowena's daughter had accepted one of the weekly invitations and at first Reaghan had feared Edlyn came to make mischief. She had treated her so despicably since the death of Sunniva that merely seeing her had made Reaghan sweat. And yet they had been as friends once and part of Reaghan still yearned for the whispered conversations about everything and nothing that they had shared whenever she had been able to sneak away from her chores.

Her heart had leapt to see Edlyn, and Reaghan had welcomed her into the hall. Edlyn had accepted the Waes Hael bowl from Reaghan and joined her at the high table. For a time, it had seemed all the bitterness had been forgotten. Perhaps she had grown tired of blaming Reaghan for things that were in no way hers to control. But soon, Reaghan had seen Edlyn's frequent glances to Beircheart and she had known the true reason for the girl's sudden change of heart.

She sighed. She could not blame Edlyn for being interested in the young gesith. He was handsome and strong, quick to smile and popular with all. But she had worried when the two had left the hall together when the night was still young. The riddling had scarcely begun when the couple slipped from the hall into the night. She hoped Edlyn was clever enough to control Beircheart. Reaghan frowned as she recalled the terrible pain of the year before when she had rid herself of the child that grew within her. She would not wish that suffering on Edlyn, however much the girl had tormented her of late. Edlyn was really a girl no longer, she mused, but a young woman. Perhaps she would soften now in her approach to Reaghan. Perhaps they could even be friends once more.

She hoped so. She would love to be able to confide in someone. She knew she could never speak openly with Maida or the other women. And if not with the women, who then? Bassus? She smiled at the thought. The gruff warrior was a constant presence in the hall and often walked with her. He was clearly protective and tried his best to be good company, she knew. But he was a man, and an old one at that. She was thankful for his loyalty to her, and he made her feel safe. Despite the loss of his arm, he was yet formidable, huge of stature and grim of face. A good man. But he could never be a true friend to her any more than Maida could.

Octa, who had continued to crawl after Maida's daughter, suddenly stopped beside the tree stump that Elmer used for chopping firewood. He reached out his tiny hands, his face a mask of grim concentration, and heaved himself to his feet. He stood like that for a moment, unmoving, watching the little girl with a keen intent. His feather-like fair hair drifted around his ears. Bysen slowly stepped towards him, holding the horse outstretched before her.

"Do you want this, Octa?" she asked, her giggle of excitement bubbling in her words.

Octa did not move.

The girl stepped closer, tempting him with the toy. Still, the infant did not respond, instead staring at her with a frown.

"Come on, little man," she said, "you can get it."

Reaghan could see the girl was going to snatch it out of his reach as soon as he moved. She hated to see him teased thus, but he must learn. So, she watched, wondering where Bassus was. Just the previous day they had been talking together about when Octa would take his first steps and now it looked as if the moment may have come.

The girl edged even closer, so that the wooden horse was a mere hand's breadth from Octa's face. Then, without warning, Octa jumped forward. The girl made to move the horse up and away from him, but he ignored the prize. Instead, he wrapped his stubby fingers into the girl's peplos, flinging his whole body weight into her. He was not a small boy, having inherited his father's bulk and height, and the girl tumbled to the grass with a shriek. As soon as they hit the earth, Octa climbed over her and, taking the carved horse in both of his hands, he seized her

161

wrist in his teeth and bit down hard. She screamed again, but let go of the toy.

Without a second glance, Octa rolled away from the weeping girl and sat up to examine the spoils of his victory.

Despite herself, Reaghan smiled broadly. Gods, but he was Beobrand's son alright. She could imagine how Bassus would receive the news of Octa's conquest. It would bring a smirk to his face, she was sure. The giant was still sombre for much of the time, but since the weather had improved, he had seemed more content. He more frequently drilled the warriors in the ways of combat, and she had on occasion caught him humming to himself when he thought there was nobody to see his happiness. He would be overjoyed with the tale of Octa besting a girl four times his age. He doted on the boy.

Maida shuffled out of the hut, wiping her hands on a rag.

"What is it now, child?" she asked, her tone tired.

The girl sobbed and spluttered her way through the story of how Octa had knocked her from her feet and then bitten her. Her face was streaked in tears and snot. Maida turned to Reaghan to see if she had understood. Reaghan confirmed the child's story, careful not to smile now.

Maida looked down at where Octa now played quietly with the horse. She scooped up her daughter, setting her on her feet and wiping her face with the rag that was still in her hand.

"Well, Bysen," she said in a firm tone, "it seems to me you got what you deserved. You have been teasing Octa with that horse for an age. You don't like it when your brothers tease you, do you?"

Incensed at the truth of her mother's words, Bysen let out a piercing scream of defiance and anger and fled behind the hut, hiding her misery from the world. Maida shook her head and sighed.

On the ground, Octa ignored the screaming and continued studying the slender curve of the wooden horse's neck and legs.

"So like his father, isn't he?" Maida said, not looking at Reaghan.

Reaghan felt a pang in her belly, the memory of her pain and loss still there. Much as Bassus said he yet felt the arm that had been removed.

"Aye, he is. Scared of nothing and always ready to fight."

Maida sighed and shook her head again.

"Only a fool fears nothing and Beobrand is no fool. But he does not shy from a fight. That is true." She frowned then and peered up at the slowly gathering clouds in the hot sky. "I wonder where they are. They have been gone a long while."

"Yes," Reaghan said, unsure what to say. Maida's anxiety was plain. "I hope they return soon."

They stood in silence then, each lost in her own thoughts. Reaghan thought of Beobrand as she had seen him when he had come to rescue her from Nathair's hall. He was fearsome in battle, huge and terrifying. Danger and death seemed to stalk him.

"I have prayed to Danu and her children," she said at last. "I left some good cheese and mead for them in the glade in the forest. Odelyna says spirits dwell there."

Maida turned to stare at her.

"And what did you wish for?"

"That the men would come back to us."

Maida nodded. Was there really anything else to pray for?

"That is a good wish, Reaghan," said the older woman, her voice soft. "A good wish."

Reaghan said nothing, content to relish the closeness to Maida and the warmth in the older woman's tone.

Again she looked up at the sky. A raven flapped slowly overhead, flying southward. She followed the bird's path with her gaze. Where would it fly? Would it see Beobrand, Elmer and the others on its travels? She hoped that if it spied them as it looked down at middle earth it would find them hale and safe.

Reaghan felt the scratch of fear run claws down her back and she shivered.

Hale and safe. And heading homeward.

Chapter 22

Beobrand's eyes stung and he could barely see. But he could not pause even for a heartbeat to wipe away the blood and sweat that mingled on his face and ran into his eyes. The fighting was as fierce as any he had ever encountered. His heartbeat roared in his ears as he hacked Hrunting down into a man's head. The blade sang as it cut through the man's leather cap, his hair, scalp and skull. More slaughter-sweat sprayed in the hot air, as Beobrand wrenched the sword free of the man's brains and turned to the larger, grey-haired man who took the dead man's place. The man made to step over the twitching form of his fallen comrade, but before he could find his footing Beobrand rammed Hrunting into his mouth. Teeth shattered around the man's choking scream. He too collapsed before the onslaught of Beobrand's sword.

Beobrand's muscles screamed, but he ignored them and continued the butcher's work of slaughter. He no longer thought of what he was at. His instincts kept him alive and his savage sword-play added to the harvest of man-flesh that was heaped before him and his gesithas. All the long days of practice, coupled with his natural speed, strength and ability with a blade, made him seem to those who watched as mighty as Tiw himself. If the god of war had stepped onto the field of battle, surely he would be such as this: a giant of a man, in fine war harness, great helm gleaming, the serpent-skin patterned blade of his sword drinking deeply of his enemies' blood.

Dreogan and Attor at his sides were no less fearsome to behold. All three of them were blood-drenched, their blades deadly, their shields strong. Men cowered away from them, as they pushed further into the ditch. The ground was a swamp of blood, piss and spilt guts, the stink of it catching in their throats. Their feet squelched, the mud sucking at their shoes. But that was better than when they trampled over the pliant, uneven, mottled corpse-flesh of those already slain.

The battle-din was terrible. The crash and thump of linden-boards, the screams of the dying, the anvil-clang of blade on blade. This was the true music of the sword-song. It was a thing to fill men with fear and awe. Here in the churning clamour of the battle's maw, men found their true worth. Many were frozen with a terror so strong that they were scythed down like barley. Others fought with grim determination to survive; kill or be slain.

A few found they were born to the bloody blade-work.

Beobrand felt his heart swell with pride as Dreogan and Attor stepped forward with him, slaying all who stood before them. There was no shieldwall now, just confusion and death. He had lost sight of Elmer, Ceawlin and Aethelwulf soon after they had slipped and slid down the slope into the ditch. They had followed him, of that he was certain. He had seen them coming down just behind Dreogan and Attor. Wynhelm and his men had followed too, but now he had no idea where any of them were in this chaos.

He stumbled as the chest of the corpse he stood on shifted. For a moment he was off balance, and Dreogan and Attor leapt forward to ensure his flanks were not left exposed. He hoped he had not led them all to their deaths, but he could no more contain the desire for vengeance that burnt within him, than he could put out a forge fire by spitting. It burnt too hot. Nothing would extinguish this fire except for Wybert's lifeblood.

A young man, wispy moustaches dark against his fish-belly pallid face, came toward Beobrand then with a short axe held high. The blade was newly sharpened and it glimmered in the bright light of the sun. The axe looked new, as if it had never been used. The battle lust was upon Beobrand now, and it felt to him that all his opponents moved as if underwater. Too slowly the man brought down the axe. Beobrand caught it on his shield with ease, so that the blade snagged on the board's rim. Beobrand stepped back, yanking his shield hard, pulling the man's axe and extending his arm as he clung to the haft. Then, with a twist of his body, Beobrand swung Hrunting down into the outstretched arm. The blade bit deeply. The man yelped and released the axe, which fell to be lost in the corpse-mire beneath them. Without pause, Beobrand pushed forward, and once again Hrunting came down on the man's bleeding arm. His enemy was lost now to the pain and the fear, lowering his shield, his face slack with dismay and disbelief. Beobrand drove Hrunting's point into his armpit, lifted the hilt and shoved the blade fully into the man's body. The man juddered and slid from the steel and was quickly indistinguishable from the other bodies that littered the great dyke's floor.

Through the thronging mass of Penda's host before him Beobrand glimpsed the flame-red beard of Grimbold's giant. He was not thirty paces away and Wybert was sure to be by his side. He must reach him.

"There," he yelled, "Wybert is there. He is mine!"

His mind was full of blood and death now, and nothing else mattered to him. He made to strike forward, trusting that Dreogan and Attor would lend their skill and weight to his attack, helping their lord to fight through the amassed ranks to the subject of his vengeance. But before he moved, a tremor ran through the fighting men. It was almost as if they had all sighed at the same moment. A strange hush and stillness fell on them, and men stood blinking in the hot sun, battered and confused.

Battles are strange things. It is almost as if they take on a life of their own, quite separate from the individual lives of those men who fight and die in them. Sometimes battles seem to pause, or shift in some unexplained way. Beobrand thought this was the case now. He took the opportunity presented by the lull to wipe the sweat-blood mix from his forehead, wincing as his fingers grazed the swollen bruise where the stone had struck and the helm now pressed. He was suddenly aware of the dull ache that throbbed in his skull.

Men all around him panted, dragging in great gulps of the foetid air, glad of any pause in the fray that allowed them a moment's respite from the continued hammering of blade and shield. But this was no lull in combat without explanation. A moaning rumbled through the East Angelfolc and Beobrand watched as faces turned to stare back up to the top of the earthwork where their shieldwall had held strong until King Ecgric had led them down into this bloody brawl.

Beobrand took a step back and followed their gaze.

He clenched his teeth and a groan escaped him at what he beheld there.

Against the pale sky, the rood that Sigeberht had erected before the battle was surrounded by Mercian warriors who had somehow found their way up the steep slope of the ditch. Beside the cross, they held aloft the wolf standard of Penda. The sight of Penda's battle banner on the eastern side of the great ditch would be enough to sow seeds of despair into the hearts of the East Angelfolc. And yet it was not the wolf tails dangling in the soft breeze that brought the prickle of tears to Beobrand's eyes or that made his heart twist in his chest.

No, it was the sight of what now adorned the Christ rood. On the crossbeams there now hung a red-splashed white robe that could only belong to the erstwhile king of this land. And atop the cross, skewered upon the spear-tip there, was the fine-featured head of Sigeberht, tongue lolling, gore dripping from the neck.

*

A great roar rose up from Penda's host when they saw the grisly spectacle of Sigeberht's head and robe mimicking the tale of the Christ who was nailed to a tree. The Christ was said to have risen from the dead three days after his murder. Beobrand gave a last look at the blind, staring eyes of Sigeberht, and turned back to face the Mercians and Waelisc. He was unsure whether he would live to see the sun rise tomorrow. The gods alone knew what would transpire in three days hence. But he was quite sure that it was not Sigeberht's wyrd to rise and place his royal head once more upon his lordly shoulders. No. Sigeberht was gone and Beobrand felt a wrenching pang at his part in bringing him to this place.

But there was no time for regrets. Penda's host surged forward with a renewed energy and Beobrand found himself pushed back, once more on the defensive. And now without the benefit of the stronger position on higher ground. Attor and Dreogan locked shields with his and together they shuffled back, forced back towards the foot of the eastern slope by the reinvigorated Mercian host. They stumbled and slipped as they retreated, the bodies beneath them a squelching mass of meat, blood and bones. The Mercians came on with new-found strength now. Even over the blood-shit stench of death they could scent victory and they came with mouths agape like wolves.

So this was how it would end. They would be overrun here by Penda's wolves and this ditch would become their grave. Beobrand let out a scream of rage. He would not die before he saw the life leave Wybert's eyes. By all the gods, he would not be slain here, so close to the object of his vengeance.

Woden, All-Father, do not allow death to take me now. I must have my revenge!

Without warning, Elmer, Ceawlin and Aethelwulf were once more at his side. Wynhelm and his men drew close too and together they quickly formed a shieldwall. Beobrand laughed to see the Northumbrians. Woden had heard his plea. Perhaps he too wished to see blood spilt in vengeance. Yet surely there was enough blood shed here to slake the thirst of Woden and all the gods.

The laughter died on his lips as Penda's host engulfed them, like a great wave crashing over a boulder. All was chaos then. A tumult of screaming, biting blades and shoving shields. Relying on his strength and speed, Beobrand ducked beneath his shield and lashed out with Hrunting beneath the shield rim. He felt the blade connect with flesh, but whether of a living foe-man or one of the countless corpses, he could not tell. He leaned on his shield with all his weight, digging his toes into the blood-marsh. His mouth was full of the salty tang of blood. The taste of death.

And they were pushed back. Step by step they were moving further from the giant and Wybert. Further from the object of his hatred. He screamed again, dropping his shoulder into the shield and shoving hard, but the weight of the enemy host was too much. To his left, one of Wynhelm's gesithas fell in a welter of blood, his shield shattered by a great axe.

Closer to him, a spear slipped between the shields and pierced Ceawlin's belly. The steel spear-head buried in the short man's flesh and his eyes widened in pain. Beobrand watched in dismay as his gesith, dour, mead-loving Ceawlin, threw aside his shield and pushed towards the spearman who would soon be his killer, for none could survive such a thrust. The spear drove further into Ceawlin's body and still he went on. The face of the Mercian who gripped the spear was full of awe, as his enemy refused to die and instead pulled himself with his left hand along the spear's length. Ceawlin shuddered then, and blood bubbled between his clenched teeth. The back of his byrnie bulged and Beobrand knew that the spear had broken through Ceawlin's back and was now held fast by the rings of his battle-shirt. With a roar loud enough to be heard over the battle-din, Ceawlin pushed himself forward, using his legs for power. His enemy watched in disbelief as the Northumbrian, who should now be dead, forced the haft of the spear to slip backward through his sweat-slick grasp. The Mercian's face still wore the expression of amazement as Ceawlin, all the while bellowing like a bull, chopped his sword's blade into the man's neck. Blood fountained and both Ceawlin and the Mercian fell to the ground, gasping their last breaths.

None who saw the feat of Ceawlin's final death blow would forget it. It was the stuff of legends. But for the story to reach the scops, to be heard on the mead-benches of great halls, someone who witnessed the hero's act must live. But the Mercian host pressed forward.

Beobrand spat the blood from his mouth. Damn the gods. They cared nothing for mortal men. The gods laughed to see such chaos. To see hope torn into shreds of despair like mist in a wind.

Another step backward. Another. The sea of Mercians and Waelisc rolled on, pushing them ever back.

A spear-tip scraped along his forearm, and Beobrand was glad of the metal plates he wore there.

Without the gods' favour, they would not escape death this day. Beobrand's men were dying. Sigeberht had been slain and now watched with sightless eyes as his folk's fyrd was destroyed. He had led them here. Would they all perish now? Had Beobrand brought them to their doom?

What a fool he had been. Death surrounded them, and now it was coming for them. Mayhap he deserved it. He was not worthy of the gesithas who had sworn their oath to him. But they would not fall timidly. If he could not reach Wybert, he would at least give the gods a death worthy of song.

"Come, my brave Bernicians," he screamed in his battle-voice, pointing Hrunting's gore-slick blade at the sky. "If we are to die here today, let us each take a dozen of these whoresons with us to be our thralls in Woden's corpse hall."

Dreogan grinned savagely, his teeth white in a face painted red and black with his soot markings and the blood of his enemies.

Beobrand nodded to the man, but could not return his smile. He had failed to take the blood-price for Sunniva's defiling. A sudden stabbing pain made him gasp. For a heartbeat, he thought he too had been pierced by a spear, but he was uninjured still. With a start, he realised that what he felt was the anguished agony that he would never see Octa again. He felt his dismay replaced with ire.

"Ceawlin has claimed the man to bring him mead in the afterlife," Beobrand shouted. "Let us fill Woden's hall with dead to serve us!"

With a cry, Beobrand pushed his shield forward, stamping down as he stepped with purpose. To his surprise the wall of Mercian and Waelisc shields had retreated somewhat. The weight he had expected from the press of their boards had gone. Beobrand's remaining gesithas and Wynhelm and his retinue moved forward as one. Could it be that his words had frightened their opponents? Or had Ceawlin's bravery shocked them into retreating?

But then he heard it. The unmistakable wailing call of a horn. The thin sound cut through the tumult of fighting. All along the line, men once again faltered, as the battle seemed to take a breath. Again the horn's cry over the embattled men. Then another horn lent its voice to the first. Then another.

What was this? Were the Mercians bringing reinforcements?

On the low ridge of the western side of the ditch there suddenly loomed a row of horsemen. The sun glimmered and shone from their battle gear. They rode beneath a banner of red cloth with a golden emblem stitched upon it. The long red cloth fluttered in the soft breeze and Beobrand saw that the emblem was a great wyrm. The golden dragon glittered as brightly as the war harness of the riders. The flapping crimson banner was a grim reflection of Sigeberht's bloodied robes that hung on the road to the east.

"That is the sigil of the Gewisse," shouted Wynhelm. "The men of Wessex have ridden to war."

And as the warriors of Wessex leapt from their horses and rushed down the slope to fall upon Penda's thronged host, Beobrand's heart leapt. For with the new threat, the shieldwall before them had fallen away and parted. And there, directly before him, where moments before there had been a mass of enemies, stood the red-bearded giant.

And beside him, eyes glaring from under the brows of a great helm, was Wybert.

Chapter 23

Hope flared within Beobrand at the sight of Wybert. Perhaps it was his wyrd after all to avenge Sunniva. He rolled the tension from his shoulders and neck and prepared to rush at his enemy. The tide of battle could shift in a heartbeat once more; he must not waste the chance that the Wyrd sisters had spun for him.

To his surprise, Attor and Elmer both leapt forward before him.

"For our lady Sunniva!" screamed Attor. The words goaded Beobrand into action. He had thought this vengeance was his alone. How had he not remembered the sorrow of his men at having failed to protect Sunniva?

Around Wybert, men were already forming ranks, bringing their shields into a wall.

With a scream devoid of words, Beobrand unleashed all of his anger in a torrent. He ran at Wybert, shield and blade light in his hands. Vengeance would be his.

The red-bearded giant and another warrior had intercepted Attor and Elmer and the four of them were now engaged in a vicious exchange of blows. The fighting men moved quickly between Wybert and Beobrand, impeding his progress. For an instant, Beobrand could see Wybert's eyes staring at him from the eye guard of his helm.

Between them, Attor pushed his opponent back, but Elmer was struggling against the giant. Splinters flew from Elmer's shield as the giant smashed a great axe into the board like a smith beating at an anvil. Around Wybert, the Mercians were recovering from the shock of the West Seaxon attack. Soon, he would once more be protected from Beobrand behind a solid defence of wood and iron.

"I will kill you, Wybert!" Beobrand shouted, spit and blood flying from his lips. "By all the gods, I swear it."

He must reach Wybert, but the giant's bulk was in the way. The man's axe was a whirring blur of destruction and it was all Elmer could do to keep his shield high. Beobrand stepped closer. He could take the red-bearded bear of a man in the flank while he concentrated on Elmer. But as Beobrand watched, Elmer's shield shattered. For a moment, Elmer stood as a hare when seen by a hawk, eyes and mouth wide, body still, as if a lack of movement might turn death away. Beobrand bellowed and lunged forward with Hrunting, but he knew he was too far from the giant. He could not prevent the axe blow from connecting.

The giant must have heard Beobrand's approach, for he half-turned towards him. Then, as quick as an eye-blink, he sliced downward with the huge axe and Elmer slumped into the pile of corpses in the ditch.

"No!" Beobrand yelled, his voice ripping in his throat.

With a speed that belied his size, the giant spun towards him and caught his sword-thrust on his shield. Beobrand could sense the gathering press of men around them, but he cared for naught in that moment save the giant who had killed Elmer. The giant who had slain the husband of Maida and father of four children. Elmer, son of Eldred, most-trusted of warriors.

The giant who stood between him and Wybert.

Beobrand rained blows down on the man's shield. The giant soaked them up as if they were nothing. The crashing, roar of battle flared around them, reaching a new intensity that seemed to echo Beobrand's savage attack on the red-bearded warrior. Beobrand caught a fleeting glimpse of Wybert mere paces from where he battled. The sight of Sunniva's tormentor taunted him. So close, and yet the giant was as immovable as a boulder. How the gods must be laughing.

Beobrand swiped at the huge axe-man's legs, but again he anticipated the strike and skipped out of reach, as lithe as a stoat. The man was as skilled as he was massive. Beobrand's arms were aflame from standing in the shieldwall and his head throbbed from the sling stone's blow. His strength was waning and he could sense the wind of battle changing its direction. He must take the red-bearded whoreson down if he wanted to get to Wybert before it was too late.

With a scream, he rushed at the giant, raising his sword to attract him to do the same with his shield. The Mercian's shield went up, and Beobrand twisted Hrunting, aiming a vicious slicing cut at the man's belly. But the red-bearded giant had known full well what Beobrand planned. Seemingly without effort, he parried the blade with the haft of his axe. Beobrand's shield clattered into the Mercian's and the old wound in his arm screamed. The shock of the collision rattled his teeth. It was as if he had run into a cliff. Beobrand was a large man, strong, tall and fast. He was not used to standing before those larger or stronger than he. He shook his head now. He had barely moved the man, and the giant warrior was his match in weapon-skill. He knew he would be able to slay that worm, Wybert, but he was not so sure about this wall of a man. He could almost hear the gods cackling over the death-screams of battle.

Beobrand and the giant stood like that for a moment, shield to shield. Over the rims of their boards Beobrand stared into the other man's eyes. They were pale blue and shot through with bloody veins. And they were empty. It was like looking into the eyes of a fish, or staring into icy winter ponds. There was no emotion there.

With a great shove against the shield, the Mercian pushed Beobrand back. Beobrand knew he could not best the man with strength, so he leapt backwards, trying to connect with Hrunting even as he retreated. But the man saw the attack as if it had been that of a child. He swung his heavy axe and it clanged into the sword blade. The tremor from the blow ran up the sword and into Beobrand's arm, numbing his hand and wrist. It was all he could do not to drop the sword. Again he retreated. Too late he saw the giant had changed the direction of the axe. The iron head glinted as it sped towards his neck. With nothing more than instinct, Beobrand threw his shield up. But he was too slow. The shield would never reach high enough to intercept the axe. And yet, the sharp iron did not bite into his flesh. For Beobrand had stepped upon one of the many corpses that littered the marshy ground, and his foot had plunged into the bloody cave of the body where the fyrd-man had been opened from navel to breast. Beobrand lost his footing and was falling, even as the giant's axe skittered through the foetid air towards him.

The blade did not connect with his neck as the giant had intended, but, as Beobrand fell, it did strike. With a great clangour the axe smacked hard into Beobrand's helm, in the same spot where the sling's stone had already dented the metal.

For a moment, all was black. Beobrand could not make sense of what was happening. He was lying on something soft. His hand was warm and sticky. There was something stinging his eyes. A roaring in his ears, but he could not hear. Pain in his head. The clouds above him were wisps of white against the pale blue of flax flowers. Darkness seeped into his vision then.

Beobrand shook his head. He knew he must not succumb to the darkness. His skull felt as though it had been cracked open like an egg. Perhaps it had, he thought grimly.

A shadow loomed over him. The giant. The huge man's bulk blotted out the sun.

With a start Beobrand found that Hrunting was still in his grasp. He tried to lift his arm, but it was numb.

The giant raised his axe.

Beobrand's arm refused to do his bidding. He would die now.

But the blow did not fall. A dark shape, even larger than the giant, flew across Beobrand's vision. A horse cannoned into the giant, sending him tumbling away.

Scarcely believing what he had witnessed, Beobrand tried to pull himself up, out of the quagmire of death in which he lay. But still his limbs would not respond. Nothing made sense. His head span and the pain cut into him with each movement.

A rider leaned down from the saddle of the mount. Beobrand squinted up, willing his eyes to focus. This was a face he recognised. And yet he must surely be dead, or dying. For the face that swam above him belonged to one who was not here in this death-churned ditch.

"Acennan?" he croaked. "Is that really you?"

Part Three

Old Friends and New Enemies

Chapter 24

Beobrand closed his eyes and drew in a deep breath. The scent of the roasted boar was rich and heady above the other smells in the great hall. Ale, mead, woodsmoke, the dogs gnawing bones in the rushes and the dozens of men at the benches all added their aromas. All around, men talked cheerily, laughing and recounting tales. None now attempted to speak with Beobrand. At first they had made some effort, but the fair-haired warrior had been taciturn and sour company.

The hall was familiar to Beobrand in the way an old dream might be. He had been here before, but not for several years. And he had never seen the hall from his current position at the high table of the lord and his guests. When he had been here before he had been a child. He had marvelled at the girth of the stout roof pillars and the height of the beams that supported the great thatched roof. It had always been a place of celebration when he had visited. Feasts of Thrimilci and Blotmonath had been held here and everyone from the surrounding area had flocked to Folca's hall. He remembered the awe he had felt to see thegns, warrior rings upon their arms and fine brooches clasping their long woollen cloaks. How Beobrand had longed to bear a sword and shield in the service of a lord then. To be like his brother, Octa, and their uncle, Selwyn.

Now his own hall was grander than this. Its beams were higher, its stout pillars cunningly carved and broader. He had rich land. Treasure. And the ear of a king.

But would he have wanted the life of a thegn, if he had known what awaited him in Northumbria? Death and sorrow seemed to walk in his shadow, but what else would he have done? Tended the land like his father? He snorted and took a sip of the ale in his drinking horn. Even the taste of the drink was familiar to him, bringing with it fleeting memories of his mother's hearth. His sisters.

No, he could not stay in this place then, any more than he wished to now. The thread of his wyrd had pulled him north, to Bernicia. To think of what could have been was madness. He could never go back and unpick the weft and warp of his life.

He looked into the flames of the great hearth fire for a moment. Unbidden, the image of his father's face came to him. The fire consuming the man and his home, smoke billowing into the sky like an offering to the gods.

He took another draught of ale. No, he could never go back.

And yet, here he was. A shiver ran down his spine.

When he had left Hithe, he had merely been the son of a ceorl. What was he now? A lord who left his oath-sworn men to die in battle, while he fled like a woman.

"This boar is wonderful," said Acennan, breaking into his reverie. The stocky warrior sat to his left chewing on a great hunk of meat, oily juices trickling into his beard. "You really should try it."

Beobrand shook his head, lifting his horn and draining it of ale. Usually his favourite meat, he had no taste for boar now.

Acennan frowned, then continued to eat in silence.

Beobrand knew he hurt his friend. And yet, he had not forgiven Acennan for what he had done. Perhaps he never would.

He gazed back into the hearth fire, but his mind was far away.

He recalled the galloping chaos from the great ditch. His head had been swimming and it had been all he could do to stay in the saddle of the horse Acennan had brought for him. All had been confused. Like a dream.

Or a nightmare.

The battle had turned. The East Angelfolc had been routed. As Acennan and Beobrand's wild-eyed mounts had carried them along the floor of the boggy ditch, images had seared themselves into his memory. A man pushing another's face into a puddle of blood, drowning him in the bubbling slaughter-sweat of the fallen. A pale-faced warrior standing alone, swinging his sword in great arcs, oblivious of the arrow jutting from his neck and that there were no enemies left for him to fight. A boy, sitting calmly in a pool of his own blood, singing a harvest song with the sweetest of voices. He had nodded to Beobrand as they'd galloped past, his face blood-spattered but serene. Who he had been singing to, Beobrand had no idea.

All the while Beobrand's head had throbbed, his vision blurring at times. His stomach had churned and he had swayed, clinging to the horse's saddle. He had followed Acennan, not truly knowing what they were doing or where they were going, so addled was his mind from the blow to his head.

The mounts had clambered out of the dyke and Acennan had led them into the forest. As the tumult of the battle had fallen away behind them, Beobrand's head had begun to clear. He had remembered Elmer falling beneath the giant's axe; saw anew Ceawlin's heroic death blow. But what of Aethelwulf? He was as close to Ceawlin as a brother. And what of brave Attor and Dreogan? He had left Gram being tended by the camp women. How had Wynhelm and his gesithas fared?

As they had cantered along the path beneath the thick canopy of branches, Beobrand's head had pounded. His stomach clenching, he had vomited as they rode, retching hot bile down his leg and across his steed's back. For a time, Acennan seemed not to notice, until Beobrand dragged hard on the reins, halting his headlong rush into the shadowed cool of the woods. Acennan wheeled his horse around then, returning quickly to where Beobrand spat ropes of spit and puke into the dust.

"We must ride," Acennan said, his voice urgent. "I will tell you how I came to be here to save you when we are sure not to be caught by Penda and his wolves."

"Save me?" Beobrand spat. His head felt too large for his neck. Sweat streaked from beneath his helm. He fumbled with the cords that held the cheek guards close together. Loosening them with a curse, he let the fine helmet fall to the earth. The rush of cool forest air to his head and face made him woozy. For a moment he believed he would pass out. He leaned forward and rested his head against the horse's mane. It was dark brown and coarse. Comforting somehow. But it was not Sceadugenga's mane. He had abandoned the stallion as he had abandoned his men.

"Save me?" he repeated, anger seeping into his tone as blood colours water. "From what? From defeat? From the shame of running from battle and leaving my sworn-men behind?" He felt as though his head would shatter with the force of his ire.

"Beobrand—," Acennan said.

"No," Beobrand cut his words off. "I do not need saving from this." A sudden sobbing gripped him. Oh gods, were they all dead? "We must return," he shouted. Tears pricked his eyes, their salt smearing with the blood and sweat that caked his face. A wave of dizziness washed over him. His skull felt twice its normal size. "They gave me their oath," Beobrand said, swiping the tears from his face. "I must be with them. Even if that means death."

He tugged on the reins, turning his horse's head back towards the slaughter in the ditch. Faintly, the noises of battle came to them on the breeze. But before he could ride back, Acennan urged his own mount forward and grabbed Beobrand's horse's bridle.

"They would not wish you to perish, Beobrand," he said. "Attor, Aethelwulf and the others would want you to live." Beobrand kicked his heels into the flanks of his horse. The beast whinnied and strained against Acennan's grip, but the short warrior pulled hard on the leather. The horse rolled its eyes, its ears lying flat against its head. "As do I," Acennan said. "Do not forget that I too swore an oath to you. I will not have you die for nothing."

Beobrand feared he would vomit again, as once more dizziness swirled in his head.

"Wybert was there…" he said, his voice trailing off.

"And if he yet lives, we will take the blood-price from him as we swore it at Dor. But to ride back now to the ditch will gain us nothing. King Ecgric is slain. I saw him struck down. King Sigeberht too is gone. The men of Wessex were too few. They could not turn the tide. Besides," he added, allowing a shadow of a smile to play over his lips, "even the great Beobrand could not defeat scores of men when his brains have been scrambled in his skull like a smashed egg."

Beobrand did not smile in return. There was no mirth to be found in him. After a long pause, he had nodded, instantly regretting the movement as his head shrieked in protest.

"We must go to Beodericsworth. I left Coenred there. And a girl we found on our journey south."

"A girl?" Acennan had raised an eyebrow. He'd dismounted and retrieved Beobrand's dented helm, tying it to his own saddle.

Beobrand had no time for his friend's humour.

"A holy woman of the Christ god. We cannot leave them to Penda and his whoreson horde. There is a rich hall there. Penda will seek it out like a weasel sniffing out duck eggs."

They had ridden hard through the forest, passing those who had fled on foot from Penda's force. Men shouted out to them, asking for news of the battle. But one look at Beobrand's face, grim and dark with dried gore, told them the only tale they needed.

When they eventually arrived at Beodericsworth, it was long after dark. Beobrand's head still pounded, but his vision was steady, and he had not puked again, managing to hold down some water from a leather flask Acennan had handed him as they rode.

All was quiet in the settlement and Beobrand wondered when the Christ followers would next be singing their strange prayers to their nailed god, for there never seemed to be long intervals between the services.

They had made straight for the monastery, clattering their horses over the small timber bridge that crossed the vallum. They had found the new buildings deserted. All save an old man, whose wispy white hair floated around his face like a wreath of mist in the darkness. He had come from one of the smaller buildings, carrying a rush light that he shielded from the night breeze.

"I remember you," he'd said to Beobrand. "The Northumbrian."

"Where has everyone gone?" Beobrand asked.

"That way." The old monk pointed off to the south and east. "Bishop Felix led them. He said it would be better to move everyone to safety. The relics too."

"Why did you not go with them?" Acennan asked.

"I believed God would protect us and see that the pagan Penda would be turned back from our lands. The bishop ordered me to go with him, but I thought I knew better. I thought they'd be back in a few days and I'd be spared the journey." He laughed then, his rasping cackle unnerving in the silent gloom of the half-built buildings. "It seems the Lord wishes to teach me a lesson in obedience."

They had urged the old man to seek shelter away from Beodericsworth's buildings, but he had shaken his head, muttering something about God knowing best, and returned to his hut.

Leaving Beodericsworth behind, they had rested some way off the path for a short while. Acennan woke Beobrand at the first glimmer of dawn and they rode on. Beobrand's head still throbbed and ached, but his thoughts were less confused and he no longer felt he would either faint or retch. Acennan told him of how he had been in Wessex when news had arrived of Penda's warhost marching on the East Angelfolc.

"Well, Eadgyth's father is a tough old goat," he said over his shoulder as they rode. "He had kept me waiting for weeks for his answer. I think it was so that I would increase the brýdgifu and it worked." He laughed. Beobrand had not replied, merely gritting his teeth against the pain in his head. "I'd already ended up agreeing to twice what I'd thought I'd have to pay. Not that Eadgyth's not worth it, of course. I just wanted him to agree the damned price and be done with it, so that I could return north. Eadgyth will be worried." For a moment, he looked wistfully into the distance, perhaps imagining Eadgyth's raven-black hair. "Anyway," Acennan shook his head, bringing himself back to the present, "then Wulfgar comes to his father's hall and says he is riding to the aid of their East Angelfolc allies and the old bastard says, 'I trust you will ride with my son too. Your king is also an ally of the folk in the east, is he not? And it is right for kinsmen to ride together.'"

"And so you rode with the West Seaxons," Beobrand managed.

"Couldn't say no, could I? Not without looking craven."

"You say Wulfgar rode with you?" asked Beobrand, wishing he had been able to see Eadgyth's brother. He was a good man, one he considered a friend. "Did you see him in the battle?" A sudden pang of fear gripped him, twisting his stomach. Please, not Wulfgar too.

"When we left, he was unharmed. It was he who saw you in the ditch. And it was his idea for me to ride to your rescue."

Beobrand frowned at the reminder of fleeing the battlefield and they rode on in silence. After some time, they crested a slight rise and scanned the horizon behind them. Several smudges of smoke rose to be lost in the rain clouds that now gathered, grey and heavy in the west. The heat of the previous day was gone, and a cool breeze tugged at their cloaks.

"Penda has unleashed his wolves," Acennan said, staring at the smoke in the distance.

Beobrand did not answer. Instead, he dug his heels into his horse's sides and cantered down the shallow hill towards the east. Towards the sea. There was no time to waste. He hoped that Bishop Felix had a plan, for he did not relish the idea of being trapped between the Whale Road and Penda's host of marauding warriors.

That afternoon, they had caught up with the straggling group of monks, priests and nuns. It was raining a drizzle that was cooled on the skin by blustery gusts of wind that came from the nearby sea. He could smell salt on the air and white sea birds were plentiful in the darkening sky.

The weight that had pulled on him since the battle was lessened somewhat at seeing Coenred, Gothfraidh and Edmonda, walking in a small group towards the rear of the column of some two dozen men and women. Coenred was pushing a hand cart which was laden with chests and sacks. It was hard work to move it over the rutted track they followed and Coenred only paused to look up when Edmonda called out to him.

"I am pleased to see you well, lord," Edmonda said, lowering her eyes.

"What happened?" asked Coenred, breathless from his exertions and perhaps excited to hear of the battle. "Where are your gesithas?"

Acennan shook his head by way of answer.

"Acennan!" Coenred exclaimed, breaking the awkward stillness that smothered Beobrand like a great cloak. "How are you come to this place?"

"You know me, Coenred," said Acennan. "I don't like to miss a fight. Besides, it seems my lord Beobrand needed saving."

Beobrand had spat then and without a word he had ridden off towards Felix.

That had been over a week ago. Acennan had long ceased mentioning having saved Beobrand. In fact, they had spoken of little of consequence.

Beobrand pushed himself to his feet. The ale was strong, he could feel its effects dulling the edges of the pain that was so sharp within him. Acennan made to stand too, but Beobrand waved him back.

"I don't need your help to piss," he growled, and stalked out of Folca's hall.

*

Beobrand was glad to be rid of the heat and noise of the hall. The sharp edges of his memories were smoothed by the drink, but not yet obliterated. He was tempted to continue drinking, until the world ceased to have meaning and he would fall into a deep stupor. But he knew that the memories would always return. He could flee from a battle, fail to protect his gesithas, allow those he loved to be defiled and killed, but there was no escape from his own thoughts.

He relieved himself at the midden, the noise from Folca's hall merging with the sounds of the night. The distant thump and grumble of waves came to him and he set off towards the beach. They had arrived in the late afternoon and there had been no time to reacquaint himself with the familiar settlement of Hithe. King Eadbald's men had led them directly to meet Folca, and the thegn had welcomed Beobrand as if he were a returning son. Beobrand was surprised the lord of Hithe even remembered him.

"Who would have thought it?" the grizzle-haired man had said, clapping him on the back and ushering him to a chair at his high table. "A son of old Grimgundi becoming a great warrior."

At the mention of his father, Beobrand had tensed. It had been a risk to come here, but after what he had heard in Cantwareburh, he could not turn away without visiting.

"So sad," Folca had continued, "your father's death in that fire." Beobrand had watched him warily for any sign of accusation in his words, but Folca continued without pause. "What a terrible year that was. So many died."

Beobrand had merely nodded, clenching his jaw. Folca spoke true. So many had died, then and since.

"But come," Folca had smiled, "let us not talk of sorrowful times. There are too many of those. Let us eat and drink and you can recount tales of your battle-prowess that is now legendary."

Beobrand had made a poor guest. Glowering into his ale horn, he answered requests for tales with a grunt or a couple of brusque words and, after some time, Folca and his retinue had grown tired of trying to draw him into conversation.

Leaving the looming shadows of the buildings behind, Beobrand walked down towards the sea. The night was not warm, and as his feet crunched onto the shingle of the beach, he regretted not bringing his cloak. The cool wind from the Narrow Sea was helping to clear his head, but nothing was able to free him from the dark thoughts that tumbled in his mind.

Folca had reminded him of the year when he had left this place. The year he left behind all he had known. He had buried his mother and sisters, before seeing his father taken by the flames.

He sat down and watched the pale foam on the waves roll up the beach towards his feet, before fading and disappearing once more into the darkness with a sigh. In the years since leaving Cantware, people had entered his life and drifted away again as easily as the tide. He had gained much, but lost so much more.

A night bird shrieked and Beobrand shivered.

It seemed Nelda's curse would come to pass. He would die alone. No tidings had reached him of those he had left at the great dyke. Tales of Penda's host's destruction of the land were rife in Cantware, brought by merchants who had fled by boat, just as Beobrand had. But nobody brought news of survivors from the great battle. Bitter bile filled his mouth as he thought again of his betrayal of his gesithas.

When the group of monks and nuns, led by Bishop Felix, had finally arrived at Gipeswic, the harbour was in uproar. Households of wealthy men thronged the port, all eager for passage away from Penda's advance. Some had retinues of spear-men, who guarded them and their possessions. Those fighting men, clean and unbloodied as they were, Beobrand had glared at. They had not answered their king's call. Instead they had run.

Running from an enemy was not the way of a warrior. Not the way of a man. And then the realisation of his own actions had come to him and he had turned his dirty and blood-streaked face away.

He had allowed Felix to barter and haggle with the masters of the ships and boats that were huddled in the harbour. His head had ached terribly and his body felt weak. He had slid from his horse, and slumped down with his back to the wall of a building; a shed or storehouse. The rain had continued to fall and he had been glad of the shelter from the wind. All that afternoon and into the evening he had watched the people coming from the west. He had grasped at the small hope that

Attor, Gram or Aethelwulf might have escaped the slaughter and would somehow find their way here.

But nobody he knew had come.

He dug his fingers into the beach beside him now, lifting a fist-sized pebble. For a heartbeat he weighed it in his hand, before throwing it out into the darkness of the sea. He did not hear its splash.

A crunching step on the pebbles behind him made Beobrand turn suddenly. A bulky figure stood close by. His face was hidden by the gloom of the night. Beobrand jumped to his feet, his hand reaching for Hrunting's hilt. But his sword was not here; it hung in its scabbard in Folca's hall. Pulling himself up to his full height, Beobrand squared his shoulders and took a deep breath.

"Who are you, that you would creep up on a man in the night, like a thief?" Beobrand's words were as hard as the flint he had just tossed into the waves.

"Well that is some way to greet me, I'm sure," replied the stranger, a smile in his voice.

"I cannot greet you, for I know not who you are."

For a moment, the man did not reply. The waves rolled and sighed on the beach. The wind tugged at Beobrand's pale hair.

"Well, it would seem that becoming a thegn has made you even more of a disagreeable bastard than you were before. I heard you had come back, but couldn't believe it."

Beobrand's ear finally made sense of the voice it was hearing, and he felt his mouth pull into a smile. Moments before he had been caught in the darkest of moods, now he felt as though he could laugh.

"Alwin?" Beobrand asked.

"Well, I'm not King Eadbald, am I?" the man replied with a laugh. "I can hardly believe you are alive. It is good to see you." The man opened his arms then and stepped closer.

Beobrand only hesitated for an instant and then he embraced him. He had almost forgotten the friends he had left behind.

"By the gods," he whispered, "it is good to see you too."

Chapter 25

Gods, how could the girl be so stupid?

Rowena shook her head, swatting at the midges that flitted around her face. The last house of Ubbanford was some way behind her now, the settlement quiet, getting ready for the night that would soon fall. She hoped nobody had seen her walking away. To leave so soon before night, and alone, would be hard to explain. But she could not remain in the hall alone tonight. Edlyn's words still rung in her ears. Her hand still smarted where she had struck her daughter's face.

Rowena needed wise counsel. It had been several days since Nelda's night-time visit and she had pondered what they had talked about as much as she had thought about anything in her life. She wanted what was best for Edlyn. Didn't every mother seek the best for her children? Rowena had fretted over the problem of her daughter until her thoughts had jumbled together in a mess like so many skeins of yarn. She had picked and tugged at the tangle of thoughts so, that now she could make no sense of them.

But she was clear about one thing. Edlyn would not marry beneath her.

Rowena raised a hand to her tightly braided hair. Beads of sweat pricked her neck. The day had been hot and the evening was stifling. It would not be dark for quite some time yet, but Rowena knew that the darkness would not bring much in the way of welcome relief from the heat. A thick haze of clouds hung over the world like a blanket. A storm might be coming. Rain would wash some of the cloying heat away. Rowena looked up at the red sky. A storm might come, but not soon. She would be back in Ubbanford before then, she was sure.

She pressed on towards the place that Nelda had spoken of.

Again, her mind returned to Edlyn's words. Rowena had confronted her daughter as she prepared to leave. Once again Edlyn was to be a guest of Reaghan in the new hall.

"Do not get too fond of Beircheart," Rowena had said, as she had finished brushing her daughter's long hair. Edlyn had pulled away, rounding on her with sudden fury. It seemed she had been waiting for her mother to voice her opinion.

"I will grow fond of whom I like, mother," she had said. "Why should I not? Things are not the way they were when you were young."

Rowena had stood there, mouth agape. Speechless. Edlyn had never spoken to her like this before. What devil had possessed her?

"I will not live like you did," the girl had continued, warming to her subject. "I will not marry a man I do not love, just to manage his household and provide him with sons. Look at what that life has done to you. You are old and alone. I will not have your life."

Rowena had slapped her then. Hard. She had not known she would until the crack of her palm striking the girl's cheek had resounded in the hall. She had hit her hard enough for her hand to sting.

Edlyn had stared at her, pure hatred in her glare, eyes brimming with tears.

"Hitting me will not make me love you!" she had screamed. And then she had gone.

Into the warm evening. Off to Sunniva's hall. To share drink and meat with Reaghan, the erstwhile slave. And maybe to share her body with Beircheart…

By all the gods, who did the girl think she was? Did she truly believe life would be different for her? That she would not grow old as the years passed like an eye-blink? Her beauty too would fade along with her self-belief. How many girls had believed they were special before now? That they would marry for love and that they would not need to live within the confines of the world of their parents?

Rowena had reached the clearing Nelda had told her of. West of Ubbanford, some distance from the path, there was a glade. A huge alder had fallen in some long-forgotten storm, leaving an area where willow saplings now grew. A stream trickled at the edge of the clearing, from the hills to the south to flow into the Tuidi to the north.

It was dark under the trees and a shiver of fear ran along Rowena's back.

There was no sign of the cunning woman. What had she thought, coming here as the sun set? It would be full night soon and she would need to make her way back through the snagging brambles without the aid of sun or torchlight.

Perhaps Nelda had not even remained in the vicinity of Ubbanford. It was possible. Who could understand the ways of such women? Rowena shuddered again, now growing angry at herself for her foolish belief that the strange woman would indeed help her. Mayhap she was as stupid as her daughter.

Away in the forest gloom, an animal shrieked, and then was suddenly silent. The leaves above her sighed as a breeze caressed the treetops.

Rowena's hand fell to the hilt of her husband's seax. She had hung it from her belt before leaving Ubbanford and was glad of its solid reassurance now.

"I told you before," said a voice from directly behind her, "you will not be needing your blade against me."

Rowena barely stifled a scream. She spun around to see Nelda, standing in the centre of the glade. She had made no sound as she approached. Rowena again felt the fingers of fear trace a line down her spine.

Like a dark forest spirit, the jackdaw, Huginn, flapped from the tree-gloom to land on Nelda's shoulder. Nelda reached up a long-fingered hand and stroked the bird's black feathers. It cocked its head and glowered at Rowena with one white-rimmed eye.

The unblinking eye unnerved Rowena, almost as much as Nelda's silent appearance. The bird had a malevolent look about it. Rowena pulled her gaze from the jackdaw to look at Nelda. The woman's hair shaded her face in the gloaming, but her scars were still visible, distorting the shadows, twisting and pulling at her mouth and cheek. Rowena willed herself not to shudder. Was she mad to come here, alone into the forest?

No. She had made up her mind about this. She had accepted Nelda into her hall, and had sought out her counsel now. For good or ill, the die was cast.

Nelda looked at her appraisingly, as if she could peer into her very soul.

"I see the time has come for action," she said, her voice sensuous and sibilant in the gathering dark. "What has happened?"

Rowena swallowed. Her decision had been made.

In an angry rush, she told of Edlyn's words to her, how she had slapped the girl and her fears that her daughter would ruin herself with Beircheart.

"Ah, the rashness of youth," whispered Nelda, running her finger the length of Huginn's back, "would that we could bottle it up, for it would be a heady brew."

"What should I do?" asked Rowena. "I cannot bear the thought of losing her." The fear that her daughter might go away, leaving her all alone coiled and twisted deep within her. "But she must marry well. Not some lowly gesith, without hall or gift-stool. She must marry a thegn."

Nelda nodded, and the jackdaw mirrored her movement, bobbing its head from its perch on her shoulder.

"Of course, you are right," she said. "You want what is best for your remaining child, what mother would not?" For an instant the darkness seemed to gather about Nelda, her face was hidden but for the flash of white from her teeth and eyes. "You could take her away. To Bebbanburg or Eoferwic. There you might find a suitable thegn or ealdorman…" Rowena said nothing. She knew as much, but was fearful of the day when she would need to make the trip.

"And yet," continued Nelda, "perhaps there is a thegn closer to home who could marry Edlyn. A young man. A man of renown."

The cunning woman's words settled on Rowena like a cool drizzle.

"You speak of Beobrand?"

"He is a lord. He has wealth. Men flock to his warband."

Rowena weighed Nelda's words. They had the heft of truth to them. And yet something snagged at her thoughts.

"You would help Beobrand? He is your enemy."

"I would help you, Rowena. And your daughter. Besides," she said, finally tiring of Huginn and shooing him from her shoulder in a sudden flap of wings, "a lady married to a lord inherits from him, does she not? Beobrand will not live forever."

Darkness engulfed them now and the clearing felt colder than it had only moments before. Despite herself, Rowena shivered.

"But Beobrand is with Reaghan," she said, surprised at how small her voice sounded in the dark.

"So he is. The freed thrall. But they are not hand-fasted, are they?" Rowena shook her head in the gloom. She could barely make out Nelda's form now. The witch would not be able to see her movements. And yet Nelda continued as if she had seen the shake of Rowena's head. "No. They are not wed. And your daughter is smitten with a gesith. So, there are two things we must do, if we are to ensure Edlyn and Beobrand will marry."

"What things?" asked Rowena, scared to hear the words Nelda would speak in the black of the night. Far away, an owl screeched in the forest.

"You must put an end to this thing with Edlyn and Beircheart. Your daughter must not beget a child of the warrior, for no man would take such a girl to wife. You must watch her, Rowena. Like a hawk."

Anger bubbled up inside Rowena. How dare this witch speak thus of her daughter? She was no common slut to flatten the hay in a barn with a handsome man with a spear and a smile. And then she recalled how Edlyn had talked to her this very evening. Perhaps the girl was mad, but she would not be the first woman to open her legs and live to regret it nine months later. Rowena swallowed her angry retorts.

"And the second thing?"

"Why, nobody enjoys being lonely. Beobrand less than most. And he is but a man. He needs a woman at his side."

Far away, the owl screeched again. Rowena wished she had stayed in her hall with her anger and her loneliness. She had come too far now to flee, but she feared the words Nelda would say next.

When Nelda remained silent, Rowena prompted her.

"The second thing?"

It seemed to Rowena that Nelda had become lost in a reverie of her own, for now she appeared to start, as if disturbed from deep thought.

"Oh, that is simple," she said, and despite the all-enveloping darkness of the forest that hid her features, the twisted smile in her voice was plain to hear. "Reaghan the thrall will have to die, of course."

Chapter 26

"Tales of your battle-fame have reached us even here in Hithe," said Alwin, before emptying his cup of ale. He refilled his cup and offered the jug to Beobrand, who shook his head. Alwin's ale was good, strong with just the right hint of bitterness, but Beobrand had drunk enough already at Folca's hall. He sipped from the drinking horn that Alwin had pushed into his hand shortly after they had entered the small house. The hut was warm; the fire on the hearth nothing more than embers that winked in the darkness, but the night was not cold.

"The scops like to spin the longest tales from the thinnest of threads," Beobrand said.

From the furthest corner of the hut came a snort. Alwin's father lay there. They had thought him sleeping, but now he croaked from the dark.

"Any fool can kill. Why do all tales speak of feeding the ravens and soaking the land in slaughter-sweat?" He coughed. "Tending the land, growing good crops to feed your folk, that is what tales should be about."

"Nobody wants to hear about the life of a farmer," snapped Alwin.

The old man hoomed in the back of his throat and then was quiet again.

"There is honour in farming," said Beobrand. "Your father speaks true."

"Then why did you not stay here?" asked Alwin.

Beobrand pursed his lips in the darkness. Alwin had always been direct and honest and he had speared Beobrand squarely with his question.

"You know why," Beobrand answered, and they both fell silent, each lost in his thoughts.

Beobrand took another sip of ale and pondered how his life had changed so much since the last time he had spoken to Alwin. As boys, they had both dreamt of joining a lord's gesithas. They had played at fighting with sticks, imagining the glory of the shieldwall. Now Beobrand's memories were full of blood and death.

And ghosts.

"Listen to Beobrand," said another voice from the darkness, "there is nothing wrong with being a farmer." This was Andswaru, Alwin's wife. A comely enough girl. She'd always liked Alwin, but had never so much as smiled in Beobrand's direction when they had all played together. When they had come in from the night, she had fussed for a while, pouring the ale and bringing stools near the fire so that the old friends could talk. Then, with a scowl at Beobrand and a warning to her husband to not get drunk and wake the baby, she had retired to the rear of the house. Beobrand had wondered if she'd fallen asleep behind the partition that hung there, but it appeared she was listening intently to their conversation.

"Hush, woman," Alwin said with a shake of his head at Beobrand and a comical raising of his eyebrows. In the expression Beobrand recalled Alwin's sense of mischief. He was never far from a jest and together with their friend Scrydan, the three of them had wreaked havoc on the people of Hithe as youngsters. Only a few short years had passed, but it was hard to imagine them as they had once been, so serious and grown had they become, heavy with responsibility.

"So, you are now the master of the farm?" asked Beobrand.

From the gloom, Alwin's father snorted with derision.

"Aye," said Alwin, pouring himself yet more ale. "Father's back ails him sorely, especially on cold days, but he yet comes with me to the field."

"I know every stone and clod of earth in that parcel of land," his father said.

Alwin ignored him.

"And you and Andswaru have a child?"

"A son. Swithun. He'll sleep through anything, praise the Lord. Even my old man's jabbering," he said, directing this last into the darkness. "He'll be two years old this midwinter."

"I give you joy of him," said Beobrand. "Children are a blessing." He took a draught of ale, his mind summoning the round face of Octa.

"Do you have children, Beobrand?" asked Andswaru.

"A boy. Not much younger than yours."

"You are wed then?" an eagerness had crept into her voice now, as is the way with womenfolk when they talk of kin; of births and weddings.

Beobrand let out a long breath.

"I was," he said, his tone hollow. "She died."

Silence then. They all knew how closely death walked in the shadow of men and women alike.

"You said you had come from Cantwareburh," said Alwin, breaking the awkwardness that had fallen over them. "How came you to that place?"

"I travelled with some men of the Christ. Bishop Felix and his brethren." He chose not to talk of the battle at the ditch. Instead, he told of how they had travelled by boat from

Gipeswic to Sandwic and then inland to Cantwareburh. He did not wish to recount how he had fled from battle, leaving his men to their fate.

"I had forgotten how grand Cantwareburh is," Beobrand said. He preferred the open hills, forests and cliffs of Bernicia, but Cantwareburh had always excited him with its ancient walls and the constant bustle of the countless people who dwelt in the shadow of the newly-erected church building and King Eadbald's great hall. Of course, when he had visited as a boy with his father or Uncle Selwyn, he had never set foot in the lord king's hall. Arriving now as a thegn of Northumbria and escort of Bishop Felix, Beobrand had been welcomed as if he were royalty himself.

He looked around the gloomy confines of the small, single-roomed house in which he now sat. He had visited Alwin's house so many times throughout his childhood. It was almost as familiar to him as his own family home had been. Again, he was struck by the strangeness of his life. Not two days before he had been dining with the king of Cantware. Just earlier this evening he had been drinking the ale of the lord of Hithe. And now he sat on a worn stool in a cramped hut on the edge of the settlement.

He knew where he felt most at home.

"What is he like?" Alwin interrupted his tale.

"Who?"

"The king. Eadbald." There was awe in Alwin's voice.

"Oh, much like any other king," answered Beobrand.

Alwin guffawed at that, thinking that Beobrand jested, as they had when they were both boys.

"It was in Eadbald's hall that I heard tell of my uncle," Beobrand continued.

He still could scarce believe who had borne the tidings of his uncle's sickness. He had all but forgotten the girl, but when she had spoken his name from the darkness, the memories of his first night in Bernicia had enveloped him, bringing back the raw sorrow he had felt at the loss of his brother. All his kin had gone. He had been so alone.

Years later, standing in the shadows of Eadbald's hall, having fled to escape the difficult questions about the battle of the East Angelfolc against Penda, he wondered whether anything had truly changed. He had felt cursed when this girl had found him crying in the stables of Bebbanburg. That curse still hung over him. Or maybe it was a new curse, screamed in the darkness of a cave on Muile, or from the windswept ramparts of Din Eidyn.

Mayhap something had changed.

She had found him sobbing in Bebbanburg. He was dry-eyed now, despite the pain that ravaged him at the loss of his men.

"Eanflæd," he had said, and turned to look at the princess.

She was yet a child, but had grown willowy. Her eyes had gleamed in the light of the torches and her long hair had caught the flickering flames like burnished gold. She had been like an apparition of a young Sunniva standing before him. At the sight of her, his heart had clenched and tears had pricked his eyes. The flood of dark memories had threatened to unman him, but he had blinked back the tears and swallowed hard.

"Edwin's daughter, we are well met."

"I knew we would meet again one day," she had said in her soft voice. Sounds of conversation and laughter had drifted from the great hall and again Beobrand had been reminded of that night in Bebbanburg.

"You did?" he had asked, feeling foolish before this wisp of a girl.

She'd offered him a radiant smile.

"Yes. I remembered what father had said about you. That you would one day be a great warrior. It seems he was right."

Beobrand had felt himself flush in the darkness.

"I am no great warrior," he had said, remorse jagged within him. Great warriors do not run from battle.

"You are yet alive," she had said, and her words cut him like a seax blade. She had the right of it; he should have died in that bloody quagmire of the great dyke. "Many are those who lie dead in the path behind us." It was true. He had killed countless enemies, and lost many kin and friends. Yet perhaps she'd referred to her own dead, for she too had known much sorrow in her short life; her father, uncle and brothers killed at the battle of Elmet. And more recently, the news had come of the death of her younger brother and nephew in the court of King Dagobert of Frankia. "You live, so I say you are great, or perhaps blessed by God. I have heard tell of your exploits. The scops sing tales in which you are the hero."

"I truly am no hero."

"That is not for you to decide, Beobrand."

For a time they had stood there in silence, each studying the other as if trying to understand what they saw before them.

"I heard your name mentioned just the other day," she'd said at last.

Beobrand had frowned, wondering what saga the tale-tellers had spun.

"It was not in a song or a tale," she had said, as if she could hear his very thoughts. "They spoke of your kinsman. I was at Liminge, where my mother now resides. On the coast. She has built a monastery there for the glory of God."

"My kinsman?" Beobrand cared nothing for Ethelburga's monastery.

"Your uncle. He is taken ill and is not long for this world."

"Selwyn is the last of my kin here."

"Then it would seem the Lord God has brought you here with a purpose. You can go bid your kin farewell from this earth. I think that might make the parting less painful." Her tone had grown wistful. She had been far from all her kinsmen when they had died.

They had talked no further, for the girl's gemæcce sought her out then. The young woman had cast Beobrand a killing glower and shooed the princess away.

Eanflæd had turned, her golden locks glimmering in the gloom.

"Godspeed," she had said. "Until we meet again, Beobrand."

But he had not seen her again. And the next morning he had asked Eadbald's leave to travel to Hithe, to visit his ailing uncle.

"Your uncle is much changed," Alwin said, his voice suddenly sombre.

"I have heard his remaining days on middle earth are few now."

Alwin nodded in the gloom.

"You will find much has changed here," Alwin said, his face clouding in the ember-licked darkness.

"What do you mean by that?"

But before Alwin could answer, Andswaru pulled back the partition.

"Come, husband," she said. "It is late and we must all sleep. The babe will awake when God wills it, whether you are drink-soaked or not. I would have you able to work tomorrow. Now, put aside your cup and come to bed." Her tone broached no argument and with a raised eyebrow to Beobrand, Alwin stood.

"You are welcome to sleep here," Andswaru said to Beobrand, her voice clipped and unwelcoming. "There is space enough by the fire."

Beobrand's head was full of memories and questions, but he could see there would be no answers this night.

"Thank you, Andswaru, you are kind. I will rest here, and, come the dawn, I will go to my father's house and seek out my uncle."

Alwin and Andswaru shared a glance then, but said nothing and soon the dwelling was quiet and still, save for the rasping snores of Alwin's father.

Beobrand lay gazing into the embers. He breathed deeply and blew gently into the fire. Ripples of red ran over the few pieces of wood that yet smouldered there.

He wondered if Reaghan was looking into the fire back in Ubbanford. Or perhaps Acennan, in Folca's hall, was even now lying beside the hearth wondering where his lord had gone and if he would return that night.

Beobrand closed his eyes. He longed for the release of sleep. But his mind brimmed, and though his eyes were shut, he saw again the rain-slick buildings of Gipeswic where he had sat all that long afternoon while Felix and Acennan had arranged passage for them to Cantware. His head had ached and he had fleetingly wondered whether his skull had been cracked. All the while he had sat there in the wind-shadow of the hut and looked to the west. He had prayed to Woden All-Father and all the gods that somehow his gesithas would come, that they had escaped the slaughter at the ditch and followed eastward. Beobrand had even offered up a prayer to the Christ god before Acennan had come to lead him down to the vessel they had finally secured through a mixture of the offer of riches and threats.

But it seemed that no gods listened. For none of his men came to Gipeswic.

Acennan had sold their mounts, and once again Beobrand had felt the pang of losing Sceadugenga as sharply as if the stallion had been another of his warriors.

Though he was no sailor and the motion of the Whale Road often made him sick to his stomach, on this occasion he had found the roll of the waves soothing. He recalled now the feeling of the keel juddering over the waves and the spray from the surf as the merchant ship pulled out of the harbour on the evening tide. The memory of the strangely calming movement of the boat pulled him slowly down towards the oblivion of sleep.

He had sat in the stern of the small, crowded craft and stared back to the land they were leaving behind. He had not spoken when Acennan or Coenred had approached him. There had been nothing to say. He had brooded sullenly, his anger doused by his failures and the terrible realisation that he had lost his men. His friends.

The low sun had hazed through the rain, and it had not taken long for the land to be lost in the distance. Just before the land had been cloaked by the rain and distance, a movement on the strand had caught his eye. Peering into the misty distance, Beobrand spied a rider galloping south, following the direction of the boat. The man was astride a huge black horse that carried its rider effortlessly at great speed so that the man's white cloak billowed behind him with the wind of their passing. As he watched, the rider reined the horse in and it reared, hooves pawing the air.

Beobrand could not be certain, but he thought the white-cloaked rider had raised a hand, as if in salute. Could it have been Gwalchmei ap Gwyar? Was it possible that the Waelisc warrior had done that which he had threatened and taken back the horse he said was his?

The rain had swallowed horse and rider into the gathering dusk and Beobrand had been left pondering what he had seen.

Now, his mind went to that image again and he tried to unpick the truth of it, but before he could, sleep finally came, and with it, blessed peace from earthly worries.

Chapter 27

"Come on, you maggots," Bassus bellowed. "Put your weight into it! You're like maids trying to shove kine through a gate."

The men renewed their pushing and Bassus grunted with the effort to hold them back. Sweat trickled into his eyes and he cursed silently. He had no other hand to wipe the stinging sweat from his face. He gripped the shield in his right hand, leaning his bulk behind it and heaved. It was yet early, the sun barely in the sky, but the day would be hot and he had decided it was time to show the newcomers what it meant to be part of a lord's retinue.

"Is that the best you can do?" he screamed through teeth that were clenched in a savage grin. He knew he would never stand again in the battle-din, but by the gods it felt good to hold a shield, to be surrounded by spear-brothers. To his left stood Garr, almost as tall as Bassus himself, but willow-thin. To look at him you would think him weak, but he had proven himself in many battles. He may not have the bulk that would help push back a shieldwall, but when the time for blood-letting came, his speed and spear-skill made him a deadly adversary.

"You can do better than that, you turd-eating pig-swivers," yelled Beircheart from his position to Bassus' right. Broad-shouldered and long-legged, Beircheart was a natural warrior; strong, yet light of foot. Bassus knew that the younger of the men who had arrived over the past weeks admired the man. Bassus liked him well enough, but Beircheart's preening and vanity prickled him. He was a good man to have at your side in a fight, Bassus was sure, but Beircheart was as likely to have a comb in his hand as a seax.

The last man in their small shieldwall was Renweard. Like Beircheart, Renweard had been Athelstan's man before joining Beobrand's gesithas. The two were close friends, often sharing some joke that only they understood, but they could not have been less alike. Where Beircheart was vain and quick to speak, Renweard was slovenly and rarely offered an opinion. He was stocky with a great black rook's nest of a beard. Looking at the three men in the line with him, Bassus, was pleased with what he saw. There was iron and determination in them all, as they dug their toes into the grass and leaned into the shields.

Before them, the line of four young men slowly slipped backward.

"Would you give up so easily if we were your lord's enemies?" Bassus screamed at them over the rim of his shield. "We will fuck your mothers and sisters if you let us pass. Will you let us get to them without a fight?"

A young man glared into Bassus' eyes over the shields. The boy was called Fraomar. He barely had a beard on his chin, but there was a depth to him that singled him out. In some ways, he reminded Bassus of Beobrand. Fraomar was shorter and his hair was dark, but he had the same intensity in his stare. A glint of steel that spoke of death-dealing.

"No!" Fraomar shouted. "Come on, men. Heave!"

The men with Fraomar pushed with renewed strength. Grunting with the effort, they halted Bassus' shieldwall.

Bassus hid his smile behind his shield rim. Fraomar showed courage and the others turned to him to make decisions, despite his youth. A natural leader, he had come to Ubbanford a couple of weeks before with nothing to his name but an old spear, an eating knife and the threadbare clothes he wore. He had come before Bassus to offer his service to the lord of Ubbanford. Bassus had been tempted to send the youth away. He had no heregeat, no horse, and no reputation. In fact, Bassus knew nothing of the boy's past. But when Fraomar had knelt in the great hall, Bassus had recalled Beobrand standing proudly before King Edwin in Bebbanburg. Beobrand had been a farmhand, with no weapons to his name, but Edwin had liked the boy's mettle and so had allowed him to join his warband. Watching the young man rallying the others now, Bassus was pleased with his decision to allow him to stay.

The three other men with Fraomar were all older, but still young to Bassus' eyes. Eadgard was thickset, with a brawler's face. His broad nose was crooked from a break and when he smiled there were many gaps between his teeth. Eadgard's arms were gnarled and strong and bore the scars of numerous fights. His older brother was Grindan. Slimmer than Eadgard and he either fought less, or was more skilled, for his face was unmarked, all his teeth were still in his mouth and his arms carried fewer scars. The pair had arrived a few days before Fraomar. They told of having served a lord south of the Wall who had died at Hefenfelth. Each carried his own spear, shield and seax, and Eadgard also had a long-handled axe.

"We wish to serve the mighty Beobrand," Grindan had said, speaking for them both as was his custom. Tales of Beobrand's battle-fame and the gifts he had received from King Oswald and the atheling Oswiu had travelled far and Bassus had thought these would not be the last seeking to swear an oath to him.

Bearn was the oldest of the newcomers to Beobrand's hall. Perhaps five or six years Beobrand's senior. He was quiet, never speaking unless asked a direct question. A compact man, he rarely seemed to hurry, but was always the fastest in foot races. Bassus wondered how he would fare against Attor, who ran as fast as a wolf.

Bassus looked over at Bearn now. Despite the warmth of the morning, where the others' faces were all sheened with sweat, Bearn appeared not to have exerted himself. When asked where he came from, Bearn had waved a hand vaguely.

"I have no lord now," he had said. Of all the men, he was the only one who rode his own horse, and wore a sword at his hip. He was a dangerous man, that was clear, and Bassus would know more of his past. Secrets unnerved him and in Bassus' experience they always led to trouble. But when pressed, neither Bearn nor Fraomar would speak of whence they had come.

He would ensure Beobrand got the truth from them before countenancing hearing their oaths.

For now, he had told them they could remain in Ubbanford until Beobrand's return. Strong arms were always needed and he had set all the men to chores around the settlement.

But today they would spend the day playing at war.

The two shieldwalls were unmoving now, every man leaning his weight behind the linden-board and iron boss of his shield.

Bassus' line shifted slightly, taking a hesitant step back as the unsworn men gave a great heave.

Fraomar seemed to scent victory, his eyes gleaming in the early-morning sunlight.

"We have them now!" he screamed. "Push! Push! Let us show these old men what we can do!"

With a great roar, the four men gave an almighty shove on their shields.

"Now!" shouted Bassus, his voice cutting through the din.

As one, Bassus and the others in his line stepped back and to the side, angling their shields as they did so, allowing the would-be gesithas to surge forward. Fraomar tried to catch his balance as the shield that had been as immovable as a boulder, now slid past. But before he could halt his forward rush, Bassus lifted his shield high in his strong right hand and brought it down on Fraomar's back. The young man sprawled onto the mud-churned grass.

Similarly, Beircheart sent Eadgard to the earth with an outstretched foot and a well-timed push of his free hand.

Bearn and Grindan both managed to stay on their feet, jumping back from the trap and avoiding the embarrassment of being laid low before Beobrand's hearth-warriors.

"Old men are we?" laughed Bassus. "At least we do not need to lie down to regain our strength." Garr, Beircheart and Renweard laughed.

The younger men did not smile.

Eadgard leapt to his feet and lumbered towards Beircheart bellowing with rage. He had discarded his shield but raised his meaty fists to pummel the man who had tricked him into falling in the mud.

Beircheart skipped back, holding his shield before him to ward off the burly man.

"Easy now, Eadgard," Beircheart said, a broad grin on his face, "we are but playing today. Besides, you are unarmed and I would not wish to hurt you."

Eadgard seemed not to hear Beircheart, instead with a great scream, he rushed on swinging his great fists into the hide-covered wood of Beircheart's shield. It was as if he felt no pain. He rained hammer blows down on the board, forcing Beircheart back. Eadgard's knuckles split, blood splattering the shield and Beircheart's face.

"Hey," shouted Beircheart, "enough! I do not wish you harm, but so help me, if you do not back away now, I will spill your guts on the grass."

He reached a hand to the long seax scabbarded at his belt.

Bassus had watched for a moment, believing the young brawler would come to his senses, but now the morning air was suddenly filled with the menace of bloodshed and death.

"Enough of this!" he shouted, but still Eadgard stormed on.

Beircheart slid his wicked-looking blade from its sheath and crouched behind his shield, ready to pounce when he saw an opening. This was no game now. Eadgard would die here.

There was no time to think and it was clear that words meant nothing to Eadgard. Bassus dropped his shield and leapt at the young man from behind. Eadgard was completely unaware of the huge warrior's approach and the first inkling he had was when Bassus' muscular arm wrapped around his throat. Eadgard raged and screamed, trying to claw at the man who had him in his iron-like grip. But Bassus was a giant amongst men and his arm was as strong as any man's. He clung to Eadgard's throat, using his weight to bring him down, as one might wrestle a calf to the ground for slaughter.

They fell together to the dew-damp earth and Bassus could feel the fight draining from Eadgard. The young man was gasping like a fish and his face was crimson. Bassus relaxed his grip on the man's throat, letting him draw in a great shuddering breath.

At that moment, they were both drenched in water that felt as cold as ice-melt. Grindan had fetched a bucket of water from the great barrel by the hall. Eadgard spat and spluttered. Bassus sensed that his madness had passed. Rolling away, he heaved himself up from the ground. Water dripped from his hair and beard. He cuffed the worst of it from his eyes.

Grindan let the bucket fall and crouched beside his brother.

"Eadgard, it is I, Grindan. We are with friends, brother. You need not fight them."

Eadgard shook his head, as if awakening from a dream. He looked about him, blinking in the bright light.

"Gods, your brother has a temper to rival Tiw's," Bassus said, unable to keep a grin from his face. Gods, but he'd missed a good fight. He felt more alive than he had in months.

Grindan rose, ashen-faced.

"Eadgard is a good lad," he said, his voice full of anguish. Bassus thought Grindan must have been in this situation before, having to speak in his brother's defence. "There is nobody better in a scrap." Bassus wondered at that, for what use would an untamed bear be in a shieldwall. He knew what the brothers were thinking, it was clear in the abject sorrow on Eadgard's scarred face and in Grindan's slumped shoulders and down-turned gaze. The fear in them was as obvious as Eadgard's great broken nose. But the brothers were too proud to beg.

"Do not fear, boys," Bassus said, "I will not send you away." Grindan looked up, hope in his eyes. Eadgard still looked like a hound that has been caught eating its master's best meat. "We can use your strength and ire in battle, Eadgard, but we'll need to make sure you direct that anger of yours at our enemies." If they could control the lad, he would make a terrifying addition to Beobrand's warband.

"You have our thanks, Bassus," said Grindan, face still sombre. "I would ask for your pardon for the cold bath, but I think you can consider that payment for the low cunning trick you played on us with the shieldwall." His eyes twinkled then, and his mouth twitched into a smile.

Bassus returned the smirk.

"Cunning is a better weapon than a sharp blade," he replied. "Do not forget that."

Before Grindan could reply, a shrill voice cut through the calm that had descended on the gathered warriors.

"Beircheart!"

Turning, Bassus saw the Lady Rowena, fine dress pressed against the contours of her body as she strode rapidly up the hill towards them. By Frige, she was a handsome woman, that one. Proud and bitter too. He would not wish to be Beircheart. All the warriors turned to the man, whose face had grown milk-white. Bassus suppressed a snort of laughter. The vain warrior could stand in a shieldwall and fight against the brute Eadgard without losing his smile or ruffling his hair, but in the face of a girl's angry mother, he was unmanned.

The men parted at Rowena's approach. They all knew what this was about, and there was no man there who would seek to prevent a mother from defending her daughter's virtue. She halted before Beircheart, ignoring the others. She placed her hands on her hips, planted her feet and glared at him. Beircheart withered under that stare, looking at his feet, unable to return Rowena's gaze.

"Beircheart," she said, voice clipped and cold as shards of ice, "look at me."

With an effort, he raised his head and their eyes met. He flushed red, but said nothing.

"I will not waste my breath or spit on long words," she said, eyes blazing. "I know you have been spending time with my daughter, Edlyn." One of the younger men sniggered. Bassus cast them a warning look, but he was not sure who it was who had laughed. Rowena ignored the sound, her eyes fixed on Beircheart's, who seemed trapped there. Again, Bassus wondered at how a stern word and look from a woman could render a killer of men such as Beircheart as meek as a scolded child.

"Know this," she continued, "Edlyn is meant for a better man than you. She will be wed to a thegn, or even an ealdorman, and not some poor house-warrior. Do you understand?"

Beircheart nodded. Bassus almost felt sorry for the man. Almost.

"And know this," Rowena said, spitting the words at Beircheart now, such was her fury. "If I find you have taken my daughter's maidenhead, I will seek weregild for the act." Another suppressed giggle from one of the onlookers. This time Rowena spun to rake the men with her fiery glower.

"And the same goes for any of you men who think they might wish to bed my daughter." None of them laughed now. "If I find that any of you has touched her, I will come for payment. But I will not come to your lord asking for silver or gold. No, I will come in the night while you are sleeping. Like a nihtgenga I will stalk into the hall in the shadows of the night and I will take that which you value most." She stared at each man in turn then, letting her words settle in their ears like stones dropped into deep ponds. "I will come in the darkest march of the night, when not even the owls are abroad, and I will take my sharp seax," she pulled a big knife from where it had hung sheathed at her back. The blade caught the morning sun with a flash. It was a large seax, a man's killing blade, meant for the shieldwall, for ripping the guts from enemies. For feeding the ravens. It looked huge in Rowena's small hands. Huge, and sharp and deadly. "I will take my husband's seax and I will take that which can never be returned, just as a girl's maidenhead can only be taken once." The men stared at her now; mouths agape, faces pallid. "I will take the blood-price, for my daughter's maidenhead. Your manhood." She mimicked holding something in her left hand and brought the seax across and under her hand in a savage slicing motion.

Bassus swallowed hard. He was sure he heard all the other men do likewise in the silence.

"Do not think I would hesitate in this," she said, turning back to Beircheart. "Mark my words the next time you have an itch, scratch it with a house thrall, but not with my daughter."

She spun on her heel then, not waiting for an answer. Bassus let out a slow breath. Indeed, what answer could any of them give? There was nothing more to be said. By the gods, but the woman was spirited.

As she stalked away, making her way back down the hill towards Ubba's hall, the men began to chatter, jesting and laughing. Renweard slapped Beircheart on the back.

"Looks as though you will not be ploughing that furrow any time soon."

Laughter rippled through the warriors, the tension of the fight and Rowena's outburst blowing away like chaff on a stiff breeze.

But Bassus did not join them in their jesting. He stood frowning and scratching his wet beard. He watched the sway of Rowena's hips as she walked away and did not move until she was lost to sight behind a stand of ash trees that shielded the path.

Chapter 28

Beobrand awoke feeling refreshed despite the ale of the previous night. Alwin and his father yet slept, their snores rumbling in the small house. Andswaru was up with Swithun. She sat in the gloom with the infant content at her breast. Her gaze was upon Beobrand as he rose from the fireside and stretched. Beobrand felt suddenly awkward. Again, he was struck by how familiar the hut was to him. He had known Alwin and Andswaru all his life and yet their paths were so very distant now that they were almost like strangers.

He stooped to pick up his shoes, and then made his way to the stool he had sat on the night before. With a thud, his head connected hard with one of the roof beams.

"Thunor's balls!" he exclaimed. Gods, he had forgotten how low the roof was. Rubbing his mutilated left hand gingerly over his forehead, he sat and pulled on his shoes. This was no place for him. He wished he had not returned to Hithe. Nothing good would come of it.

"Would you break your fast with us?" Andswaru asked. Then, with a smile, "Or are you content to break your head and our roof?"

Beobrand forced a smile. His head had not hurt these past days, but the crack against the timber had reminded him of the wound he had suffered at the great ditch.

"I am not hungry," he said. "I thank you for your hospitality, Andswaru."

"Will you not wait for Alwin to awaken?" she asked, frowning in the darkness.

Beobrand felt a pang of guilt. But he did not wish to tarry any longer in this dark, cramped hut that was full of the shadows of memories from a past he hardly recognised as his.

"No, let him sleep. He drank more than I. I will see him again before I leave Hithe."

He finished tying his leg bindings and, with a final nod of thanks to Andswaru, he was out into the open air, carefully bending to avoid the door's low lintel. Dawn had barely caressed the east with light. It was cool, but still. A thin morning mist embraced the trees and buildings. Taking a deep breath of the chill air, he tasted the salt from the sea. He was tempted to walk back down to the strand, but being alone with his thoughts was not what he needed. Instead, he made his way towards Folca's hall. He would find Acennan there, and then together they would seek out Selwyn.

He knew not what to expect when he found his uncle. Would the old man recognise him? Or had has mind slipped beyond this world, as oftentimes happened to those who reached such a great age? He would know soon enough, though the thought of what he might find unnerved him. He had never thought to return here. He had thought he had buried his memories along with his kin, but now those memories shadowed his mind the way Folca's hall loomed on the hill in the mist.

There was one thing that Beobrand was certain of. Facing the fears of his past would be easier with a friend at his side.

*

Beobrand found Acennan before he reached the hall. The stocky warrior came down the hill, cloak wrapped about his shoulders against the early-morning cold.

"I wondered where you had gone," Acennan said. "I thought perhaps you had taken a horse and ridden north. Or boarded a ship and left on the tide to return to Bernicia."

"I would not do such a thing," Beobrand said.

"Well, the way you have been these last days, I was not so sure." Acennan scratched at his beard and gave him a twisted grin. "And truth be told, I do not think I would have missed your company."

Beobrand nodded, feeling his face grow warm. Acennan was right. He had been poor company indeed.

"I would not leave here without you," he said.

"I know you would not," replied Acennan, suddenly serious. "And you must know that I could not leave you to die in that shit-filled ditch."

"I do know it," Beobrand raked his hand through his hair, wincing as his fingers brushed the growing lump on his forehead where he had collided with Alwin's roof timber. It was in just the spot where he had been hit by Wybert's giant. "I know you did what you thought best."

Acennan gave a short barking laugh.

"No, Beobrand. I did not do what I thought best. I did what was best."

"I wish I could be so sure."

"Well, I am not sure why, given what a poor companion you have been, but I am certain that I would rather you lived than died."

Beobrand's face clouded. The thought of those who had fallen against Penda's force was never far beneath the surface of his thoughts.

"And I know," Acennan said, clasping Beobrand's shoulder, "that Attor, Elmer, Ceawlin, Aethelwulf and Dreogan would all agree with me."

Beobrand wished to speak more of the hollow he felt within him. How he felt as though he had betrayed his gesithas, as though he had slain them as surely as if he had plunged Hrunting's blade into them himself. But he could not talk of such things. He held Acennan's gaze for a long while before reaching out and clasping his friends forearm.

"I am sorry," he said at last.

"I know you are," said Acennan, and Beobrand felt a weight lifted from him, as if he had shrugged off an iron byrnie. "Now," Acennan continued, "if we are friends once more, let us do what we came here for. I would return to Northumbria as quickly as we are able. Much as I enjoy your cheery company, it is the promise of taking Eadgyth the tidings of our betrothal that sustains me."

"Very well," said Beobrand, "let us find my uncle. I would see him one last time and ensure that he is cared for. He has no kin here to tend to his needs."

"And then we head for Eoferwic?"

"Eventually, yes," said Beobrand, flashing a grin at Acennan. His head throbbed from the fresh blow, but his spirit was lighter than it had been for many days. He led the way through the settlement with a determined stride. Acennan jogged to keep up.

"Eventually?" asked Acennan.

"Yes. Before we return home, there is something I must do."

"What?"

"As Bassus would say, someone needs killing."

*

The sun had risen well beyond the trees to the east by the time they reached their destination. Around them, Hithe was now fully awake. They had passed men digging drainage ditches, already mud-caked and sweating. A broad-hipped woman had waddled past, straining under the weight of buckets full of fresh, warm milk. A thickset man with a grey beard had called out to them, raising his hand. Beobrand recognised him. It was Immin, one of the men who had been aboard the ship that had taken him to Bebbanburg after his father's death. Beobrand lifted his hand in greeting, but did not stop. Immin had been good to him, even giving him the small bone-handled knife he still used for eating. The sailor deserved more. Beobrand knew he should pause and talk to the man for a moment, but he did not wish to delay. His mind was set now. He pressed on, leaving Immin staring after him with a disgruntled expression. Beobrand recalled the faces and names of many of those they passed, but he did not speak with any of them.

As the sun climbed into the sky and painted the land with golden light, Beobrand felt as though he walked in a dream. He had helped his father and brother to pollard those ash trees on the hill. He remembered cutting the timber for those fence posts. The rows of peas already sprouting in that field, grew in rich earth he had ploughed many times. He was from this land; had grown into the man he now was in this place. He gripped his half-hand into a fist, then, reaching up, he traced the scar on his face.

No, he had been a frightened boy when he left here.

As they rounded the bend in the path, past the pollarded ash trees, Beobrand for a moment imagined it had all been a dream, that his mother and sisters yet lived and would come to greet him from the house. But if they had not died, it would mean that neither had his father. His skin prickled at the memory of the last time he had seen Grimgundi. He could almost smell the smoke from the blazing house.

His nostrils were full of woodsmoke, but it did not billow from the inferno of his burning home. It wafted on the breeze from an earthen bread oven that a woman tended.

Beobrand had not known what to expect. Had he thought the blackened timbers of his father's house would yet jut from the earth like accusing fingers? Had he imagined that Grimgundi's bones would lie in the rubble, charred and cracked by the intense heat that had consumed the house?

What he found was a well-proportioned house, built on the site of his old home. It was larger than Grimgundi's house had been, with fresh thatch on the roof and whitewashed walls of daub.

The woman who fussed over the bread oven, looked up as Acennan and Beobrand walked along the path towards her. She squinted into the rising sun. She wiped tears from her face where the smoke had stung her eyes and peered at the two men as they drew nearer. She was a plump woman, with good broad hips and meaty breasts. Her face, though partly in shadow, was pink and round. She was young and not unattractive. A memory of her face tugged at Beobrand's mind. Who was this woman?

With a sudden squeal the woman clapped her hands to her face, her mouth round with astonishment.

"Beobrand?" she said. "Is that really you?"

Instantly, Beobrand remembered her name, though he could not comprehend why she was here.

"Udela," he said. "Well met."

Udela nervously wiped her hands on her apron. She opened her mouth, and then she snapped it shut again. Now they were closer, Beobrand saw that what he had thought was a shadow was in fact a large bruise around her eye and cheek. She must have noticed his gaze, or perhaps she just remembered the black eye, for her hand fluttered up to her face. After a moment, she let it fall back again to wipe on her apron. There was no hiding those bruises now.

"Should I bring the dough, mother? I can carry it."

They all turned towards the door of the hut, out of which tottered a small girl of three or four years. In her tiny hands she grasped a wooden board on which lay a round loaf ready for the oven. The board and the bread were much too large and heavy for such a small child to carry, but the fair-haired girl bit her lip with great determination.

Udela seemed to awaken from a daze. She rushed to the girl and snatched the board from her.

"I have told you before, Ardith. You are to wait for me. What would father say if you dropped the bread in the mud?"

The girl frowned and her lower lip trembled at her mother's harsh words. Her eyes glistened, but she did not cry.

"Sorry, mother," she said. She brightened then and turned to Beobrand and Acennan. "Who are you?"

"My name is Beobrand, and this is Acennan."

"You're very tall," Ardith said, gazing up at him.

"Hush now," Udela said, placing a hand on her daughter's shoulder. "Go inside and prepare a cup of ale for our guests." Ardith puffed out her chest, clearly pleased to have been given such an important task. She ran back into the house.

"What brings you back here?" Udela asked. "It has been a long time since you went away."

"I might ask the same of you," Beobrand replied. "How do you come to be living in a house on my father's land?"

Udela's jaw clenched and for a moment her eyes blazed, but then she dropped her gaze.

"You will have to speak to my husband about that, Beobrand." She looked back at him then, her eyes imploring. "But he is away at Teothic's farm. My husband is the reeve here and there is a dispute about Teothic's pigs. Lilla says they've been foraging for mast on his land." Beobrand said nothing. So, Udela had married the reeve. Surely she could not mean old Cyneheard. There was something amiss here. Beobrand's father had been a freeman and his land should have gone to his remaining kin. His uncle, Selwyn, had not been a wealthy man, and Beobrand had thought to find him here.

"Where is my uncle?" he asked, an edge of ice entering his tone. He did not think of this place as home; had not done so for many years. But to see it in someone else's possession rankled.

"He is in a house at the end of the path, by the meadow. My husband built it for him there. Selwyn said he would prefer to live alone." Beobrand stared at her, his eyes the colour of sea-ice. "But I care for him," Udela continued in a rush, "as if he were my own kin. I prepare him food and drink and wash his clothes." A sudden anger flared in her face. "It was not I who abandoned him and everybody he knew, Beobrand, son of Grimgundi," she snapped.

Beobrand sighed. She spoke the truth.

Ardith came slowly out of the house, stepping carefully to avoid tripping, her brow wrinkled in concentration. She held a large cup of ale in both her tiny hands before her. She proffered the cup to Beobrand.

"I bid you well come to our home," she said, as formally as a princess in a great hall.

Beobrand could not help smiling.

"I thank you, young mistress Ardith," he replied, taking the vessel and drinking deeply of the contents.

Ardith beamed. Udela smiled too, her sudden outburst forgotten, it seemed.

Beobrand passed the cup to Acennan, who inclined his head solemnly and drained the rest of the ale. He handed the cup back to the girl.

"That is the finest ale I have drunk in a long while," he said. "Is it brewed by the gods themselves?" Ardith looked up at him with wide eyes.

"No," she said, "mother makes it."

Acennan laughed.

"Well, it tasted good enough for the gods."

Beobrand was done with pleasantries.

"I would see my uncle now, Udela," he said. "How is he?"

Udela had placed the board with the unbaked loaf on a block of wood by the oven. Smoke was roiling from the oven's mouth. No bread could bake in there until the fire had died back. She smoothed her apron over her thighs.

"He is old, Beobrand," she said, her voice tender. "He drifts… Like flotsam on the sea… If it is a good day, he will be pleased to see you." Beobrand did not ask what would happen if it were a bad day.

"Thank you for your care of him," he said, but it didn't seem enough. She was right to be angry with him. He had fled from the horror of the pestilence, from the death of his loved ones and the memories of his father's spite. He had run without a thought for those he left behind. She was staring at him now with an expression he could not fathom. The bruise on her face was dark and brooding.

He set off down the track towards the meadow. Acennan ruffled Ardith's hair and fell into step beside Beobrand.

They had only gone a few paces when Beobrand halted.

"When we return, we will talk of how your husband came to own my father's land." Her face paled under the bruises.

"Who is your husband?" Beobrand asked. "Do I know him?"

"Aye, you know him," she replied, absently pulling Ardith close to her. "My husband is Scrydan."

*

Beobrand and Acennan left Udela and Ardith at the house and walked along the path that led to the meadow. A horse in a fenced-off enclosure stopped cropping grass and raised its large head to gaze at them quizzically as they passed. Suddenly Beobrand was overcome with a wave of sorrow at the loss of Sceadugenga. It was stupid to think that way. It was only an animal. And yet the pain was real. He paused, stepping off the bare earth track to lean on the fence. The wood was freshly cut and yet to be aged by rain and the harsh winter frosts. The horse was curious, and trotted over to where Beobrand stood. It was a fine beast, strong-backed with long legs that would carry it fast over the land. It was a horse for riding, not for work in the fields. Oxen or mules were better suited to the work of pulling the plough. Beobrand reached out and stroked the horse's soft nose. It snorted and shook its head.

In the far field, down by the wood that marked the edge of his father's land, Beobrand saw a man ploughing with two oxen. A thrall, he supposed. Scrydan was doing well for himself. Better than his father had, that was for certain. But perhaps Scrydan was sober most of the time. Perhaps he worked hard.

"This Scrydan," said Acennan, "he is a good man?" He unclasped his cloak pin and draped the cloth over his arm. The sun had burnt away the mist now and the day was already warm.

"He was," answered Beobrand, thinking of the bruises on Udela's face. "We were friends. Alwin, Scrydan and me."

"And now he is the reeve here," Acennan said. The reeve was a man of great influence, settling disputes and managing the collection of tribute for the lord of the land. "And he married your girl."

Beobrand looked at him sharply.

"Udela was not my girl," he said, feeling his cheeks grow hot.

"So you didn't swive her then?" Acennan grinned, raising his eyebrows. When Beobrand hesitated, Acennan laughed. "I knew it, you dog. Well, she looks like she'd have plenty to hold on to while flattening the hay."

Beobrand looked away. Down the hill the thrall was turning the oxen around a large oak. He knew the tree well and had often sat in its shade when helping plough the field. Gulls fluttered and wheeled in the air behind the plough like fine linen skirts blowing on the wind. For a fleeting moment, he remembered the scent of Udela's skin as they had coupled. His face was burning now. He could feel beads of sweat forming on his brow. Certain that Acennan knew what he was thinking about, Beobrand wiped at his forehead, careful of the lump there, and resumed walking along the path.

"Do you suppose he beats her?" Beobrand asked suddenly.

Acennan shrugged.

"They are married. He can do what he wants."

Beobrand brooded on this as they walked on.

Acennan placed a hand on his shoulder, halting him.

"I know how you feel about such things, my friend," Acennan said. "A man should not raise his fist to a woman. But Udela is his wife. She is his to hit. And, who knows? Perhaps she deserved it. It is not your problem to solve."

Beobrand nodded absently. Acennan was right. It was not his problem.

The feeling of walking in some half-remembered dream was stronger than ever now that he was on the land where he had grown up. He knew every tree, every rock beside the path, and yet everything had changed. They passed the bend in the track and before them stood a small hut where before there had been a stand of hornbeams. One great tree remained, as if standing guard over the tiny dwelling. The tall hornbeam's branches were thick with foliage. It reached upward to the clear sky, the only reminder now of the copse that had once shaded the ground here.

The sight of the tree filled Beobrand with a sudden loneliness.

He paused outside the small building.

"Ready?" Acennan asked him.

He had no desire to see Selwyn brought down with age. He had always loved the man and admired him. Would that he had heard his uncle had already passed on to the afterlife. Then he could have grieved for the memory he had of the old warrior. But he had come too far to turn away now.

"As ready as I'll ever be," he said, and opened the door.

Chapter 29

The air inside the hut was stale and sour. Light from the open door sliced through the gloom, but for a long moment Beobrand could see nothing save darkness. And then his eyes began to adjust to the shadowed interior and he made out shapes beyond the motes of dust swirling in the shaft of sunlight. There was a pallet at the rear of the small room. A stool beside it. A wooden chest. All was still, the only movement the cold ash that swirled in the air, disturbed from the hearth stone by the breeze from the opened door.

Silence inside.

Far off in the distance, Beobrand heard the cries of the thrall as he goaded the oxen. The gulls that fluttered behind shrieked thinly as they fought each other over worms thrown up by the ploughshare. Closer, from the tall hornbeam that grew where once many had lifted their branches to the sky, came the wittering of sparrows and chaffinches. It was a cheery sound, at odds with the dark stillness of the hut.

Had his uncle already died? Despite his wish for just such an outcome moments before, Beobrand's heart twisted at the thought.

"Is that you, you bastard son of a turd?"

The thin voice spoke from the far side of the hut. It rasped with age, and trembled as if the speaker shook with the ague, but Beobrand recognised it as that of his uncle, Selwyn. As sudden as a flash of sunlight from a blade, Beobrand was glad he had come. The thought of returning here, of raking over the embers of memories best left forgotten, had unnerved him.

But now his heart soared at the sound of a familiar voice. Apart from his son, Octa, this was his last kin. And he was now overjoyed that he would have the chance to speak with Selwyn one last time.

"I may be a son of a turd, uncle," he said, "but not the one you expected, I'd wager." Motioning for Acennan to wait outside, Beobrand went into the rank-smelling hut and crossed to the stool beside the bed.

"Octa?" Selwyn said, raising himself up weakly on an elbow to peer at the tall, broad-shouldered young man who had entered his house. As Beobrand drew closer, the old man's rheumy eyes widened. "By the gods, no, not Octa," he said. "Beobrand. Well, well…" The effort of lifting himself from the thin mattress where he lay seemed to have exhausted him and he fell back, breathing heavily, with long scratchy breaths.

A cup, half-full of liquid, stood on the coffer by the bed. Beobrand picked it up and sniffed the contents. Mead. He offered it to his uncle, who nodded and allowed Beobrand to support his head and shoulders while he drank. When Selwyn had drunk enough, Beobrand lowered him down gently onto the mattress.

"Thank you, my boy," Selwyn said, his voice firmer. It seemed the mead had revived him somewhat. He had ever liked a drink. "You were always a good boy." Beobrand thought of all he had done. He was not good. And no boy. But he said nothing.

"Ah, but I am gladdened to see you," Selwyn continued, his beard cracking open in a gap-toothed smile. "That Udela girl cares for me well enough, but it is not the same as having kin around you. By all the gods, it has been years. I have heard tell of your deeds. It seems you are a great warrior. I always told your mother that you were born to wield a blade. Just like me… though I think that's what worried her." His voice drifted into silence and his gaze focused on some point beyond the walls of this hut. Beobrand did not want to lose him to the snare of distant memories so soon, so he tried to pull him back to the present.

"How is it you are living here, uncle?" Beobrand gestured to encompass the mean hut. "My father's land should have fallen to you. I thought you would be comfortable."

Selwyn's gaze came slowly back to Beobrand from wherever it had roamed in his memories.

"It was not so simple," he said. "There was some doubt as to how my brother had died." Was there some reproach there? Beobrand detected none. "And," Selwyn went on, "you left before a moot could be held. In the end, the land was given to the reeve. But that is of no import now. I will be gone from this earth soon and would talk of happier times."

Beobrand's jaw clenched. His uncle had lived like the poorest ceorl these past years while Scrydan had grown rich on Grimgundi's land. Beobrand choked back his ire, forcing himself to remain calm.

"I hear you serve Oswald now," Selwyn said, his voice bubbling with phlegm in his throat. He coughed and swallowed. "Wyrd, it is a strange thing."

"How so, uncle?"

"Remember how I used to tell you tales of my travels in the north?" Beobrand remembered well how Octa and he had listened enthralled to his uncle's stories of shieldwalls and sieges, thegns and kings, sword-song and spear-din. It was with those tales that the seeds had been sown that led to Octa and Beobrand travelling north in search of their own battle-fame. Sometimes, when he had thought back on those boyhood tales from his grizzled uncle, Beobrand had wondered at the truth of them. Perhaps Selwyn had merely been an old drunk who liked to see the sparkle of awe in his nephews' eyes.

Beobrand nodded. If his uncle wished to tell him one more tale, then he would listen, and gladly.

"It seems," said Selwyn, "that the wyrd of the father is also woven into the weft and warp of the son's life." He hesitated then, as if considering whether to continue. Beobrand waited patiently. At last, Selwyn seemed to make up his mind and continued. "I served Oswald's father, Æthelfrith."

Beobrand started. Could this be true? Was it possible that his uncle had stood in the shieldwall with Æthelfrith? Oswald's father had known great glory in his lifetime. He had ruled all of Northumbria before Edwin had slain him. That was more than twenty years ago now.

"He was a great man," Selwyn continued. His voice cracked and he stifled a cough. Beobrand held out the cup for him to drink. "I don't believe there was ever a finer warrior."

"You told us you served a lord in Bernicia. You never said it was the king of that land." Beobrand's head was reeling. A sudden thought came to him. "Why did you not follow his sons into exile?"

Selwyn sighed.

"Perhaps I should have, but they were just boys then and I had had my fill of blood-letting." Again, Selwyn went silent as his mind took him to those distant times and places; when he was a young man, proud and strong in the service of a king. From outside, Beobrand could hear the finches and sparrows chittering and chirping in the branches of the hornbeam. After a long moment, Selwyn looked once more into Beobrand's eyes. "Besides," he said, "there was always something pulling me back to Cantware. To Hithe."

"Your kin?" Beobrand had never thought Selwyn put much stock in his family. The old man had never taken a wife, which had always been a subject of gossip amongst the womenfolk of Hithe.

Selwyn seemed not to have heard Beobrand's question.

"You have a wife?" he asked.

Beobrand's face clouded. He took a long breath. The air was redolent of old sweat, stale breath and the sickly sweetness of ill health. He wished he were out in the warm light of day, with the smell of green things growing and the warbling of the birds on the breeze. But he would not flee from his uncle's question, much as it pained him to think of it.

"I did," he answered, his words clipped, "for a time." He swallowed the lump that had suddenly filled his throat. "She died."

"Ah, I am sorry to hear that, Beobrand. Every man needs the love of a good woman."

"But you never married, uncle."

"True. True." Selwyn sighed and stared up at the darkness of the thatch above them. "But there was one I loved in Hithe. I had travelled far, seeking battle-glory or perhaps a warrior's death, rather than see her with another. But in the end, the memory of her beckoned me back. I could not bear to be parted from her."

Beobrand frowned, uneasy at the path the tale was taking. He could not recall ever having heard his uncle speak thus; of his feelings for a woman, or his love of family.

"I have done much in my life that does not fill me with pride, Beobrand," said Selwyn. "I sought death in battle, hoping to be rid of the anguish of a desire for a woman I could never have. And yet, I returned home whole. And now, I will have a straw death it seems." He laughed then, a short bark that changed to a cough. At last, the coughing abated. "All of the fighting, all the killing and I will die in my bed, old and feeble. Well, perhaps this is my wyrd. Mayhap I am being punished for my sins, as the Christ priests would have us believe. Well, it seems to me that one more sin, one more broken oath, won't make much of a difference now."

Selwyn reached out and gripped Beobrand's half-hand. His hand was cold, his bones jutting from underneath taut, thin skin. Beobrand fought not to shudder at the touch.

"I promised your mother I would never speak of this to you, or anyone. But she is now long gone, and I will be joining her soon." He drew a shuddering breath. "And I do not wish to carry this secret with me."

Beobrand knew then, as he watched Selwyn's eyes brim with tears. He knew what secret he was about to be told. His stomach twisted and he suddenly felt sick. It was as if some power had drawn him back here just for this moment. He did not wish to hear Selwyn's words, and yet he did not pull away, instead he remained motionless, the old man's bony grip cool on his hand. For a long moment they looked into each other's eyes. There was no reason now for the words to be spoken. Beobrand remembered his mother's dying words to him, "You are not your father's son...", and their mystery was gone, burnt away like the summer morning mist outside the hut.

Beobrand squeezed Selwyn's hand.

"I loved her, Beobrand," the old man said, his voice catching. "And my brother was a brute..." Beobrand remembered all too well Grimgundi's terrible anger; the violence that had often seen Octa and himself beaten and bloody. For a long time, Beobrand had been terrified that his own violent nature stemmed from the shared blood with that monster. But if Grimgundi was not his father...

He gazed down at Selwyn as if seeing him for the first time. The old man's hair was unkempt, ragged and thin like tattered cobwebs. When he had been a young man, had it been the same fair hue as his own? Both Grimgundi and Selwyn had been tall men, each heavily-muscled and broad chested, but Selwyn, like Beobrand, was slightly shorter, his muscles bulkier. Had Grimgundi looked at Beobrand and seen his own brother? Had Beobrand been a constant reminder of his cuckolding? But if anything, Grimgundi had singled out Octa more frequently than Beobrand. Surely this secret had never been known to him.

Beobrand became aware of Selwyn's eyes upon him. They glistened in the gloom. The old man seemed to be holding his breath and had grown very still. For a sickening moment Beobrand thought that the old man's spirit had left him. But then he realised that Selwyn was silently awaiting his reaction to the momentous tidings. After holding a secret for so long, his uncle must have been fearful of what Beobrand might do.

No, not his uncle. His father. The thought felt strange to him. In the same way that he had fumbled with his missing fingers, so now his mind fumbled with the new knowledge about his kin. He let out a long breath. Looking down, he saw that he still held Selwyn's hand. The man had been more of a father to him than Grimgundi ever had. He had taught him to use sword and spear, had always had time for a word of advice. And he had never struck him in anger.

Beobrand stared down at the frail form of the old man.

Father.

He smiled and squeezed Selwyn's hand again.

Selwyn pulled his hand away and swiped tears from his cheeks. He turned his face away, sniffing and rubbing at his eyes.

"Why did you never wed?" Beobrand asked. Selwyn's life would have been easier with a woman to tend to his needs.

Selwyn coughed and turned back to Beobrand.

"I could not face living without your mother. That's the truth of it." He waved a hand towards the rush-covered ground. "There should be a flask down there with some more mead. I have not talked so long for months and my throat is as dry as a Christ nun's cunny."

Beobrand squinted into the dim light and found the flask. He shook it, and some liquid sloshed in its depths, though it was far from full. He emptied it into Selwyn's cup, then helped him to sit up. Selwyn took a great swig with as much pleasure as a man who has travelled all day in glaring sun with no water.

"At least that bastard, Scrydan, gives me good mead," he said, smacking his lips. "There were other women, of course," he continued, finding new strength for talking from the mead. His eyes hazed for a moment, staring back into the mists of time. He grinned, his eyes twinkling at his memories. "There was one real vixen in Bernicia. I shacked up with her for a while. I was young then and for a time I could think of little else but ploughing that woman's field. By the gods, she was a beauty. Hair as black as raven wings and curves as fine as the best fighting ship. Oh, those hips…" His gaze again pulled away into the unseen past. The smile faded on his lips.

"What happened?" asked Beobrand.

"Hmmm?" Selwyn's focus came back to the present but for a few heartbeats Beobrand wondered whether he knew where he was, or what they were talking about. "Oh," Selwyn said at last, "she frightened me in the end, with her potions and spells. She wanted to do things… dark things…" The old man shuddered. "A cunning woman, she was, you see? I would do many things to keep her happy, for she really was a beauty. Like one of the goddesses she prayed to. But she asked too much… I left one morning and never saw her again."

Beobrand was suddenly cold, as if a thunderhead had smothered the sun. And yet the hut was warm, the sun outside warming the interior. Fingers of dread scratched down his spine.

"Do you recall her name?" he asked.

"Oh, I would never forget it," said Selwyn with a toothy grin. "Such a beauty is never forgotten. Even now, sometimes, if the gods smile on me, I see her in my dreams. There was a darkness to her, but oh, her skin… I loved your mother, but I was bewitched for a time by Nelda."

Beobrand recoiled as if struck. He pulled his hand away from Selwyn and stood, the stool clattering to the ground behind him.

To hear the witch's name here, in this small hut in Hithe, filled him with a terrible dread. Could it be that the woman Selwyn spoke of was the same Nelda who had cursed Beobrand from within that echoing maw in the earth on Muile? Was it truly possible that all of their wyrds were so intertwined and tangled? But somehow, he knew that it must be so. His uncle, no, his father, had for a time lived with the very woman who had repeatedly sought to kill him in revenge for his killing of her son, Hengist.

He was shaking now, and breathing hard as though he had run a great distance. This could not be. It was too much. Had all of his life been a great riddle of the gods that he was only now beginning to unravel?

Selwyn looked up at him, his face a mask of shocked fear. He cowered upon the straw-filled mattress, as if he expected

Beobrand to rain down blows upon him. Beobrand took a steadying breath, unclenching his fists with difficulty.

"Selwyn," he said, unable to utter the word 'father', "did this Nelda have a son?" The words fell heavily from his mouth, like hunks of granite falling into a frozen lake.

Selwyn frowned, confused.

"Did she have a son?" Beobrand snapped.

"No," Selwyn replied, his voice once again the tremulous, fearful thing of the ancient greybeard awaiting death.

Beobrand let out a sigh of relief.

"But I have always felt ashamed of leaving her when I did," Selwyn continued. "She was with child, you see? I have oft wondered what became of her and our child."

Beobrand did not need to wonder. He knew. She had borne a son. And he had been named Hengist.

Beobrand turned from his father and staggered from the noisome hut, out into the bright sunlight of the summer's morn. He blinked, hoping the light would burn away the darkness that swirled in his mind.

Acennan turned to him from where he leaned against the bole of the hornbeam, his expression concerned and questioning. Beobrand shook his head. He could scarcely comprehend that which Selwyn had revealed to him, speaking of it aloud to Acennan was more than he could bear to contemplate. For a long moment Acennan searched Beobrand's face, clearly seeing that something was amiss, but he did not press him for an explanation.

Movement down the path, towards Udela's house, drew their gaze.

"We have company," said Acennan.

Four horsemen cantered along the track, the sun glinting on the horses' harness. The crump of their hooves was loud in the still morning.

Beobrand said nothing, his head still swam with what he had just learnt.

"I don't know why," said Acennan, with a half-smile on his lips, "but I would swear they don't look pleased to see you."

Chapter 30

Reaghan liked being in the forest. The dappled shade under the canopy of trees was cool and soothing on a hot day such as today. She enjoyed the peace and solitude within the woodland that rose up on the northern bank of the Tuidi. She knew the path well, having visited the secluded glade regularly over the summer. Each time she left a gift for Danu and the other spirits and prayed for Beobrand's safe return. And after each visit, when she returned to Ubbanford she half-expected to see Beobrand already there, or hear the pounding of the hooves of his warband as they galloped into the settlement. She would berate herself then. It was stupid to think Danu would answer her wishes so quickly. And then the days would drift by, each without tidings of Beobrand, and her faith would twist and squirm. At least they had not received news of Beobrand's death, she would tell herself. Perhaps even now the goddess is guiding him homeward, but it takes time to travel the length of Albion. The lack of news weighed on her, and she would think that Danu needed just one more offering and then her man would be returned to her.

She patted the sack she carried. With each visit the gifts she brought became more valuable, in the hope that the voracious appetite of the old gods of the forest would be sated and they would heed her pleas.

A sudden blast of noise and movement made her start. A magpie, startled by her approach, flapped noisily away from the safety of the undergrowth.

Bassus placed his hand on her shoulder.

She offered him a thin smile. She would rather be alone with her thoughts, but Bassus would not hear of it.

"If anything happened to you," he had said, "Beobrand would never forgive me."

She had blushed at his words, warmed by the reminder that she was important to Beobrand.

And so it was that Bassus always accompanied her on these trips. She was accustomed to his presence now and he seemed to understand her moods well, seldom speaking on these treks into the wood. Truth be told, there were moments when she was glad of his silent bulk. There were parts of the forest that were unduly cold, where even on the warmest of summer days, their breath steamed before them and their skin prickled as if countless eyes roved over them from the gloom. They hurried past such areas of chill, both glad to be away from them.

All manner of spirits dwelt here. Some did not welcome the intrusion into their realm.

Reaghan felt the sack squirm and she clutched the cloth more tightly, scared that she might drop the bag and lose its precious contents. She hoped this offering would appease the gods, for it seemed they had not yet heeded her calls.

"Perhaps the old ones are angered," Odelyna had said when Reaghan had asked her why they did not grant her wish and have the men return. "If they are angry, the only thing that might satisfy them is blood."

Reaghan pressed on towards the glade, gripping the sack tightly enough to make her fingers ache. Grim-faced, Bassus lumbered behind her, his one hand resting on the hilt of his great seax.

The spirits were not alone in their ire. Rowena had yet to set foot in the new hall on the hill, even though Edlyn was now a frequent guest. Reaghan thought of Ubba's widow's loathing for her. Rowena hated her for what she had been and was filled with envy at what she had become. The bitterness had grown within the old woman the way bruises will rot away an apple. With each day that passed her hatred for Reaghan seemed to blossom and flourish like some poisonous fruit. She understood that Rowena had never liked her. Why should she? Reaghan had been her husband's thrall. She was Waelisc. Nothing to Rowena. Perhaps she had known that old Ubba and his sons bedded Reaghan whenever they felt the urge, but if so, she had never hinted at it. In fact, the flames of her hate seemed to have flowered from the spark of Sunniva's death. Before then, Reaghan had been invisible to Rowena. Since, Rowena appeared to blame all of her ills on the slave who had become the lady of the new hall.

The latest blame she laid at Reaghan's feet was for Edlyn spending time with Beircheart. Reaghan had heard of Rowena's outburst at the warrior while Bassus trained the men. Everyone in Ubbanford had heard of Rowena's anger, and her threats to the men. Word of her fury at Beircheart had probably reached as far as Berewic and perhaps even Bebbanburg, such was the fiery nature of Rowena's encounter with the warrior. Reaghan understood Rowena's worries for her daughter, but Edlyn was headstrong. Like her mother, Odelyna said, and Rowena's confrontation had only served to make Edlyn more brazen. The girl flirted with Beircheart openly when she attended the hall and they would always slip away from the benches long before the gathering dispersed. It was worrying, but why Rowena thought it her fault, Reaghan could not fathom.

Reaghan and Bassus passed a huge fallen tree with great skirts of fungus. Looking down at the powdery, rotting wood, she saw that it was crawling with insects. It was as if the tree itself was moving, its bark a writhing mass of black beetles, ants and woodlice. The sight unnerved her and she shivered. Was it colder here? She breathed out of her mouth, but her breath did not steam. No, it was yet warm, but the wriggling surface of the dead tree unsettled her.

She rushed past, keen to leave the tree and its insect denizens behind. They were almost at the glade now.

Perhaps she should also wish for Rowena to cease her petty hatred; to come to the hall. She doubted they would ever be friends, but she would be glad of a respite from her neighbour's enmity. But why should she waste her energies or any small amount of influence she might have with the goddess of the forest? Rowena had shown her nothing but disdain and open loathing and before Beobrand had freed her she had seemed to relish beating Reaghan for any infraction, real or otherwise. No, Rowena could rot in her husband's old hall, with her sour memories and the ghosts of her dead menfolk for company.

Before them, the woodland path opened into a small clearing. It was still and hushed here, as if the forest itself held its breath. Reaghan paused on the edge of the glade. The burble of a stream was the only sound, the air redolent of ancient green decay.

"I come with gifts, Danu, Mother of all," she said in her own tongue, as she always did.

She stepped into the open area, and, as usual, Bassus awaited her at the entrance to the glade. This was her ritual, and he wanted no part in it.

Reaghan looked around the clearing. Despite the warm day and the sun being high in the sky, it was dim and cool here. The water seeped up from some deep, secret place in the bowels of the earth and ran fresh and clear through the forest to the Tuidi. Wellsprings brought forth the power of the earth and Odelyna had told her of this place a long time ago. Gifts and totems dangled from the branches of the bushes. At the base of the old alder she could make out several small mounds of earth where offerings had been buried. Some of the items she remembered bringing to the goddess, some had been left here by others; women from Ubbanford or other nearby settlements probably.

Now that she was here, she was suddenly unsure of herself. She had never brought a blood sacrifice before, but death carried power and the goddess would surely not ignore her. Reaghan cast a look over at Bassus. He stood in the shade of the trees, as immobile as if he had been carved from the wood itself. He nodded to her in curt encouragement. She knew he did not like to be at this place of power. He was a brave man, a king's champion once, but the thought of goddesses and sacrifice filled him with dread.

She took a steadying breath and went to the foot of the alder. There she knelt, placing her sack on the ground before her. The earth was moss-covered and damp, cold on her flesh as the moisture seeped through her dress. Before opening the sack, she pulled from her belt the sharp knife she had brought from the hall. She placed this on the ground and reached for the bag. It had ceased moving now, as if the creature inside was resigned to its fate. Or dead already. She shivered and pushed her hand into the darkness. She half-expected the bird to fight back, to peck at her in a bid to escape, but the hen was docile now, as if it had fallen asleep in the bag. Perhaps it had. It came easily enough, she drew it out of the warm darkness of the sack and it blinked in the pale forest gloaming. One of its clawed feet snagged on the sack rim and she had to prize the talon free. But even then, the hen remained calm and still.

She placed it on the ground before her knees, making sure it did not run away, and picked up the knife. Its blade gleamed, the edge as sharp as she could make it. That morning she had taken Bassus' whetstone and worked at the thing until he had told her she would wear the blade clean away if she did not stop. He had looked as the edge, testing it with his thumb and nodded.

"You will not be making that any sharper, girl," he had said.

Placing a hand firmly on the hen's back to hold it still, Reaghan began to recite the words that Odelyna had taught her.

"In the eye of the Mother who gave me birth. In the eye of the Maiden who loves me. In the eye of the Crone who guides me in wisdom. Through your gift of nature, O Goddess, bestow upon me fullness in my need. Danu, Mother of all, I bring you blood. Danu, Mother of all, I bring you life. Danu, Mother of all, I offer you this blood that you may hear my plea."

She repeated the words again and again. The words began to blur and merge into each other, to lose their meaning. Around her the air felt heavy, laden with energy as before a thunderstorm.

Reaghan could hear nothing now apart from her own words, running together into a gibberish of ancient lore.

"Danu, Mother of all, I bring you blood. Danu, Mother of all, I bring you life. Danu, Mother of all, I offer you this blood that you may hear my plea."

There was nothing now apart from the words, the hen and the knife. She chanted the words until they lost all meaning, but then, as if at some unheard command from the forest spirits themselves the hen stretched out its neck, offering itself for her need. Proffering its life and its blood for Danu, mother of all the gods. Its feathers were warm, dusty and soft under her hand. The bird trembled and pushed its neck out further.

Then, without realising what she had done, she brought down the knife. It was sharp and her aim was true. The head parted cleanly from the neck and a small spurt of blood soaked the earth.

Reaghan gasped. She had not known that she was going to act. It was as if she had killed the bird in a dream.

"I offer you this blood that you may hear my plea, Danu, Mother of all," she said, her voice sounding distant to her own ears.

She gazed down at the hen, but where it had lain so peacefully before its death, now it flapped and shook. Reaghan's stomach clenched and she choked back bile as the hen jerkily rose to its feet and then, without warning, ran away from her into the clearing. Drops of blood spattered from its ragged neck. On the moss by her knees the bird's head lay, beak open as if in disbelief, eye staring accusingly up at her.

With horror and amazement, she watched as the hen crossed the clearing towards Bassus.

"Woden protect us," he shouted, terror in his voice.

He looked set to flee from the approaching bird, when the hen turned and clattered into something. It toppled to the loam and there scratched at the forest mould a moment with its hook-like talons before finally coming to rest.

Bassus spat and drew his seax.

"By Woden and all the gods," he said, his voice still trembling.

He stepped into the clearing, moving cautiously towards the hen, as if he expected it to leap up and attack him with its sharp claws. Reaghan rose on shaky legs. Her body shook and her head span, as if she had drunk strong mead.

She was only halfway across the glade when Bassus turned to her. His face was pallid above his beard, he was as pale as the night the monks had sawed off his arm. Reaghan swallowed.

"What is it?" she croaked, her mouth dry.

"We must be gone from this place," Bassus replied, his voice urgent, jagged. "There is evil here."

The hen had been unnerving, it was true, but it was not unheard of for the birds to run about for a few moments even though they had been separated from their heads. Her heart yet raced and she could hear her blood pumping in her ears, but surely that was just from the shock of it, and the power of the blood-incantation.

"No, Bassus," she said, trying to reassure him, "all is well. I must finish what I came to do here. Danu is listening now."

"No," replied Bassus, his voice as hard as iron, "we leave here now. This place is evil." He was staring at the ground. She followed his gaze and realised he was not looking at the dead hen. He was staring aghast at the object the hen had collided with. It was a large, long pale thing, a stone she thought at first. Then she saw it was no stone, it was a horse's skull, part buried and stained brown in places, perhaps with mud, or maybe with some other substance. Atop the brow of the skull, between the dark cavities of the eye sockets, rested a small pile of twig-like bones and a tiny beaked skull. The skeleton of a bird. Another sacrifice of blood perhaps.

Then she saw the object that had unsettled Bassus so. She was certain it was this thing and not the bones that had filled him with such fear.

On the crown of the great skull sat a small figure. It was crudely fashioned from straw and scraps of cloth, but it was clearly meant to represent a man. Around its neck was tied a miniature noose of cord.

And then she knew what had terrified Bassus. The straw man had no left arm.

Chapter 31

"I never thought you'd have the nerve to come back here," the leader of the riders said in a brash tone. The four horses threw up dust from the path as they were reined in before Selwyn's hut.

Beobrand recognised the man instantly. He wore fine clothes, a dark red tunic, girdled with a tooled leather belt. His shoes were made from supple calfskin and his cloak was held with a silver clasp at his shoulder. The man had gained weight since Beobrand had last seen him, but there could be no mistaking that toothy grin and those bushy brows beneath the shock of dark, wavy hair. Beobrand took in the other men with a quick sweep of his gaze. One he had never seen before, the other two he recalled as brawlers; the kind of men who were always eager for a fight. They would have no qualms doing whatever was asked of them, for a price. They were older than Beobrand by maybe half a dozen years, and when he had been growing up, these bullies would often cause him and his friends mischief. It seemed now at least one of his childhood friends had found a way to make use of their particular talents, such as they were. All of them remained mounted, their horses snorting and stamping.

Beobrand was forced to look up at them, squinting into the bright sky. The words of his uncle – no, his father – yet rang in his mind. Was it truly possible that Hengist had been his kin? Could it be that Selwyn, who he now knew to be his father, had also sired the man who had taken the fingers from his left hand? The man who had committed such awful deeds?

Around him the mounted men jostled, allowing their steeds to pace around in an attempt to intimidate Beobrand and Acennan.

Acennan stepped out from the shade of the hornbeam. Beobrand, having now sized up his adversaries, ignored the riders, instead addressing their leader.

"And I never thought you would steal from my family," Beobrand said, his tone light, but his eyes glowing with a cold fire. "Or beat your wife, Scrydan, son of Scryda."

Scrydan bristled.

"This land ceased to be yours the moment you boarded Hrothgar's ship. You were lucky old Cyneheard allowed you to leave. You should have been questioned. I would never have allowed such a thing."

"Questioned me about what?" Beobrand could feel his focus narrowing. His words came out clipped and sharp as shards of slate. The pain and anguish over the loss of his men had been burning just beneath the surface these past days, the way an ember can burn beneath a peat bog, to later burst free when disturbed. Selwyn's tidings had shaken him terribly. Scrydan would soon regret upsetting the simmering fire that roiled within him.

"You know full well what, Beobrand," Scrydan said, blustering in the face of Beobrand's calm. "There were those who wondered how it was your father came to be inside the house when it burnt. How it was that his one remaining son survived and did not seek to rescue his father from the flames."

Beobrand could stomach no more of Scrydan's words. He took a couple of quick paces towards Scrydan. The reeve's horse tossed its head. Scrydan tugged hard on the reins, sawing the bit into the animal's mouth.

"Ride away from here, Scrydan," Beobrand said, his voice low and yet still carrying easily over the sounds of the horsemen and the horses' hooves. "I did not come back to Hithe for this. I came to see my uncle and that I have now done. I do not want to fight, but do not provoke me. I warn you, as we were once friends. I will not warn you again."

"Perhaps you will kill me as you killed your father?" Scrydan sneered.

Beobrand went very still.

"Grimgundi was never a father to me. He beat his woman and children too." He fixed Scrydan with his ice-blue stare. "Perhaps it is the way such men end their lives. Consumed alive by flames with nobody to care whether they live or die."

"You heard that, men. He admits to murder. Seize him and we shall take him before the moot."

On hearing those words, Beobrand moved. The flames of his ire burst into savage, searing life and he grinned with the joy of action. Without seeming to look at any of the riders, Beobrand took three quick steps towards the nearest as he passed. The horse shied away and the man made to kick out at Beobrand. Beobrand grabbed the man's foot in both his hands and twisted. The man yelped as the bones and sinews of his ankle ground together. Beobrand pulled hard and the man tumbled to the earth, his horse leaping away, keen to be away from the commotion. The man, one of the heavyset bullies, made an attempt to rise, but Beobrand moved in rapidly and drove his knee into his face. There was a sickening crunch as his nose was crushed. Blood and snot splattered his lips and chin and the man fell back, eyes glazed.

Over by the hornbeam, Acennan had also snapped into action.

Belying his short height and brawny shoulders, Acennan moved with the easy speed of a wolf chasing down a stag. The sun winked with a flash from the blade of a small knife he had drawn from somewhere. The closest horseman's eyes widened in fright. He was ready to fight with fists or even a cudgel, but blade-work was the thing of tales, he was no killer of men. But he saw death coming for him then. Acennan grinned as he leapt towards the man.

But Acennan did not mean to kill him. As fast as a striking adder, he grabbed a handful of the man's kirtle and without pause, jabbed his knife savagely into the horse's rump. It was nothing more than a flesh wound, but the beast screamed and reared, it hooves raking the air. Acennan tugged against the horse's motion and yanked the man from the saddle. The man fell onto his back upon the packed dirt. He fell hard and before he could rise, Acennan followed up with a kick to the man's jaw. They all heard the crack as bone broke. The man mewled like a newborn babe, clutching his face in his hands.

Beobrand left Acennan to deal with the last of the reeve's men. He turned back to Scrydan. Now the bastard would see what happened to those who stole from him. To those who betrayed his friendship and threatened him. To those who raised their fists to womenfolk.

But before he could reach Scrydan, the reeve, wild-eyed at the chaos that had descended so suddenly on the hitherto still morning, tugged his steed's head around and kicked hard at its flanks. The animal bunched its muscles and launched itself back down the path, speeding Scrydan away from the two warriors who had so easily defeated the men tasked to protect him.

The man was as much of a coward as Beobrand had feared. It was perhaps easy to strike a woman, a child or a greybeard.

It was quite different to stand toe-to-toe against a killer who had made the ravens fat with his slaughter.

For a moment, Beobrand watched Scrydan gallop away. A small voice within him cried out. There was no reason to pursue him. They should be gone from Hithe, from Cantware. To linger now would only bring further trouble. But the fire raged within him now, drowning out the voice of reason. The flames roared in his mind and his ire bellowed. He could not allow Scrydan to flee.

The man he had unseated from his horse was groaning, making an effort to rise. Some way beyond him stood the horse, eyes white-rimmed, ears pressed against its head. The reins had fallen over the animal's head and now dangled to the dusty earth. Beobrand looked at Scrydan's retreating form, gauging the distance. He had grown up on this land; knew every tree and each rock. With luck, he could catch him.

Beobrand stepped quickly towards the horse. He did not run, for the beast was likely to bolt with fear. He glanced quickly at the blood-smeared face of the man he had felled. He considered delivering another blow to the man, even though he didn't look like he would be giving Acennan any trouble, but Beobrand was concerned that he would frighten the horse even more. So he left him spitting and gagging into the dust and closed on the horse.

"Easy. Easy," he said, using the voice he had so often employed to calm frightened beasts. He had his hands out, showing the horse they were empty. He was close now. He reached out to take hold of the swinging reins when Acennan and the third man clashed with a grunt and a yell. The horse shied away from the noise, blowing hard and trembling, jerking the reins out of Beobrand's reach. In his mind's eye, he could picture Scrydan galloping along the path to the house.

But he would not stop there. He would ride on to find help, to raise the alarm that the reeve and his men were under attack. If he was to have any chance of catching him before he did so, Beobrand needed to capture this gods' accursed horse.

"Easy there, girl," he said, in that soothing voice, struggling to keep the edge of anger from his tone. "Easy there."

And he lunged.

The horse tried to flee, but Beobrand's fingers brushed the reins and he gripped the leather tight. The steed panicked, pulling away. But rather than try to wrestle with the brute, Beobrand ran after it. He matched its pace, grasped for the saddle and leapt, swinging his leg up and over. The instant he was astride the horse, it tensed, ceasing its onward rush, instead turning in a quick circle. Beobrand thrust his hands into the animal's coarse mane, gripping that as well as the reins. He felt the muscles bunch beneath him and the horse bucked, trying to throw him from the saddle, to be rid of this cumbersome rider. Beobrand clung on, but as the creature bucked again, he could feel his balance slipping. He had no time for this, it might already be too late to reach Scrydan.

Before the horse could buck a third time, Beobrand kicked its ribs. Hard. With a whinny of anger, the mare chose not to fight this large man any longer. The horse galloped forward and Beobrand tugged at the reins to follow Scrydan down the path.

The dust thrown up by Scrydan's horse hung in a haze over the path, stinging Beobrand's eyes and throat. He blinked away the tears, looking for something as they careened down the track. There it was. The old elm that had been split in a storm long ago. There was nothing but a jagged stump now, but it was a clear enough marker. Beobrand yanked on the mare's reins, turning the animal's head towards the bracken growing on the slope just past the elm stump. The bank was steep and verdant with thick vegetation. Bushes and trees grew in a seemingly impassable tangle. The mare snorted, terrified at what she was being asked to do. But Beobrand dug his heels in harder and urged the beast on.

He hoped he had not made a mistake. There should be a track that ran over the hill, a shortcut between the two sides of the loop in the path. He remembered it well, had often run along it as dusk descended, glad to be able to reduce his journey home by a few moments, knowing that if he was late, Grimgundi, the man he had thought was his father, would make his disapproval known to him as only he could. But as the mare's hooves hit the steep incline and her pace slowed, he could see no sign of a path. Had he misremembered? Could it be that his mind had tricked him? If so, they would never be able to push through the foliage on this hill. But then he saw other trees – a holly, leaves shining darkly; a birch with a strangely twisted trunk – that told him where the track had passed. It seemed nobody used it now, and it was overgrown, but if the gods smiled on him, there would be nothing to block their progress. The steed wished to slow down. It could not see a clear path and the ground was strewn with a thick carpet of bracken. But they could not spare the time finding a safe route, Beobrand slapped the horse's rump and kicked its sides savagely. Rolling its eyes, the steed clambered up the hill. Through dappled flashes of sunlight, they crested the rise and skittered and skidded down the other side.

Beobrand could hear the beat of Scrydan's horse's hooves approaching someway off to the right, but he could not see him, the branches and leaves of the trees were too thick. Praying to Woden that no saplings now blocked their path, Beobrand gave the mare a final slap. The horse sped down the hill in a welter of ripped leaves and churned loam. Beobrand lowered himself behind the animal's neck. Branches whipped his face. He could see nothing. Scrydan's horse's hooves were thunder now, loud and close.

And then they were out of the woodland, into eye-watering bright sunlight.

Scrydan cried out as Beobrand and the mare crashed into his horse. Both mounts went down, Beobrand and Scrydan with them, in a thrashing of hooves and screams.

Chapter 32

Beobrand landed hard in the dust. The air was driven from his lungs and he could not draw breath. All around him was chaos. The mare whinnied and kicked, trying to right itself. Scrydan's steed screamed pitifully. Hooves thrashed close to Beobrand's face, threatening to crush his skull, so he rolled away quickly. A searing pain engulfed his left leg as the mare's frantic kicking landed a glancing blow on his shin.

Grimacing against the pain, Beobrand, clear from the carnage now, staggered to his feet. His vision was darkening, he could still not breathe. Then, just as panic swelled up to smother him, air rushed into his lungs in a shuddering gulp. He tested his leg. It was agony, but it held. Thank Woden it was not broken.

The mare was upright now, and it gave him a reproachful look before cantering away down the path. Scrydan's mount still whinnied and screamed. One of its forelegs was snapped, bent at an impossible angle, and every time the creature tried to rise, it caused itself more pain. Beobrand felt a pang of regret that the horse would need to be killed. That voice again attempted to be heard, to tell him that this had been foolhardy; he could have been killed.

But the voice of his rage was louder. His blood coursed hot in his veins, as Scrydan rose to his feet and faced him.

"You mad fool," Scrydan shouted over the horse's din. He was dust-covered, and his face flushed. "What will you do now? Slay me?"

And Beobrand thought on this for an eye-blink. Perhaps death would not be so bad for this man who had once been his friend. This man who now bullied others for his own gain and terrified his wife and child.

Beobrand stepped towards him and he saw fear in Scrydan's eyes.

"Do not dare to raise a hand against me," Scrydan said, trying to make his voice firm. "I will take you before a moot of freemen and there you will be found guilty of the murder of your father, Beobrand, son of Grimgundi."

"Grimgundi was not my father," Beobrand shouted, his fury ripping at his dust-choked throat.

And with that shout, the quiet voice of reason within him was silenced. Beobrand leapt forward, swinging his right fist at Scrydan's face.

Scrydan was not a small man, and they had wrestled and fought many times over the years as they grew up. Scrydan had never been a natural fighter, but he was fast and strong. And clever. He had surely known where this would end. He had seen Beobrand bring down his man moments before; knew that violence came easily to him. And so, he had scraped up grit and dust in his hand even as he had climbed to his feet, in readiness of the attack he was certain would come. Now he flung the contents of his fist into Beobrand's face and, not waiting to see the results of his action, Scrydan fled along the path.

Beobrand had not expected Scrydan's guile and the gravel and grit spattered against his face. But the sand did not enter his eyes as Scrydan had hoped. Beobrand was faster than most men, and the instincts that had kept him alive in so many battles now served to snap his eyes shut. His punch missed

Scrydan, but the reeve had only run a few paces when Beobrand sprang after him with a bellow.

Beobrand was taller and faster and he quickly reached Scrydan, barging into him with his shoulder and sending him sprawling to the ground.

"Get up," snarled Beobrand. Behind them, the injured horse still writhed and whinnied piteously. "Stand and fight me like a man."

Scrydan climbed unsteadily to his feet. He opened his mouth to speak, but Beobrand had no desire for words now. He hammered a punch into Scrydan's jaw that sent him flailing onto the earth again. Scrydan shook his head. Drops of blood spattered the dry earth.

"Get up," Beobrand repeated.

Scrydan, on all fours, spat, but made no move to stand.

Beobrand reached for him then. He took hold of Scrydan's belt and the cloth of his kirtle and he lifted him bodily, standing him before him. Beobrand shifted his grip, moving both his hands to the front of Scrydan's kirtle. Blood dribbled from Scrydan's lip, painting a scarlet line down his chin. The reeve's eyes were dazed. He was defeated, barely able to stand without Beobrand's support. And yet Beobrand could no longer contain the fire he had unleashed. The flames burnt within him, searing away thought and reason. He pulled Scrydan toward him and snapped his head forward at the same moment. His forehead smacked into Scrydan's nose. The shock of the collision sent a jolt of pain into Beobrand's head where he had walked into the beam at Alwin's hut. But if it was painful to Beobrand, it was devastating to Scrydan. Blood gushed from his nose and his eyes rolled back. Scrydan was suddenly heavy in Beobrand's grasp, and he let him slide to the ground.

Looking down, there was no doubt that Scrydan would not rise. Blood drenched his kirtle and ran from his nose and mouth in dark rivulets to soak into the dust. Somebody was adding their shrieks to the injured horse's, but the voice sounded very far away. Scrydan was no longer a threat, but Beobrand reached for him once more. This bully thought he could drag him before Lord Folca and a moot? The idea that this man would question Beobrand's involvement in Grimgundi's death filled him with an incandescent rage he could no longer control. Scrydan, who so easily raised his own hands to his woman, would never understand. Grimgundi had been a monster. A rabid dog must be killed. That was justice.

Beobrand grabbed Scrydan's collar in his half-hand, pulling him up into a sitting position. Scrydan's head lolled, blood dribbling from his slack mouth. Beobrand's forehead throbbed. He pulled back his hand and slapped Scrydan hard. Scrydan's head snapped to the side, but he did not rouse. The screaming was louder now, but still Beobrand ignored it. He would show this miserable dog what justice was. He slapped him again. Blood, spit and snot slicked Scrydan's face, chin and neck. Hot droplets fell onto Beobrand hand and forearm. He looked as if he had butchered an animal at Blotmonath. The reeve's eyes were blank. Gods, but the man was pathetic.

Beobrand swung his hand back again, but someone grasped at his arm, preventing him from hitting Scrydan. The screaming continued. Beobrand released the reeve, who slumped motionless to the earth. Then, face twisted with ire, Beobrand stood quickly, twisting his arm from the grip of his unknown assailant. He spun around, lashing out with a backhanded blow that caught this new enemy and sent them tumbling to the ground. He stepped over the prostrate form, fists clenched menacingly. Whoever this was, they would regret intervening.

But there was something about the figure on the dusty path. He recalled the hair. The curve of the hip. The dress. His stomach clenched. He staggered backward, dropping his hands to his sides. By all the gods, what had he done?

"Mother!" The thin scream pierced the fog in his mind. He turned, suddenly terribly ashamed. Ardith was running towards the scene of carnage, her fair braids bouncing, her eyes wide with uncertain fear.

Beobrand looked down at his blood-spattered hands. What had he become? On the ground, Udela was pushing herself upright, brushing dust from her dress. There were no tears in her eyes. She reached up gingerly to touch her face and then glanced at her hand. She was checking for blood, but there was none. She shot Beobrand a hate-filled glower, and then quickly moved to intercept her daughter so that she would be spared from seeing the worst of what had befallen her father.

Udela stooped and swept the child up in her arms, turning to face Beobrand so that the girl's back was to the struggling horse and Scrydan's unmoving form.

"I am alright, dear one," Udela said, her voice falsely full of cheer.

"But father—" sobbed Ardith.

"Your father has taken a fall from his horse."

"Is the horse hurt?" she asked, twisting in her mother's grasp to better catch a glimpse of the animal that was still crying out in pain.

"Yes, Ardith," Udela said. "It is hurt. Now, I need you to be a big girl for me. Can you do that?"

Ardith sniffed, but nodded, her face serious.

"We will need to clean and tend to your father's wounds, so I need you to run back home and place the large pot over the fire, and then fill it with water. Do not fill it first, or you will not be able to lift it. Understand?"

"Yes, mother."

"Good girl," said Udela and placed the girl on the ground. Ardith looked back pale-faced at the horse and her father. "Run now, Ardith," said Udela, "and we will be home presently."

Ardith gave Beobrand a fearful glance, and then turned and ran as fast as she was able back towards the house.

When she was gone beyond the bend in the path, Beobrand took a hesitant step towards Udela. She recoiled from him.

"I am so sorry, Udela," he said, aghast at the look in her eyes. She was not scared of him, she was disappointed.

"For what, Beobrand?" she asked, her tone curt and angry. "For beating my husband senseless? Or for killing his favourite horse? Or for terrifying my daughter? Or," she reached up, wincing as her fingers caressed her cheek, "for striking me?" He stared at the earth. All of the anger had gone now. It had burnt through him leaving behind only the bitter ash of regret and remorse.

"I am sorry," he said again, but the words sounded hollow, meaningless. "I did not mean to hit you."

She let out a mirthless laugh. "No man ever means to hit a woman."

Beobrand could see the red welt on her face where he his knuckles had made contact.

"You once said only cowards hit women and children," she said. "It seems there are many cowards on middle earth."

He did not know what to say. She spoke true. He was no better than the man he had thought to be his father. He knew now that he shared blood with Hengist, who had been a man to whom the worst savagery came as easily as breathing. Death and misery had followed him wherever he walked, as they now followed Beobrand. It seemed it was his wyrd to become that which he most despised.

The horse's crying had abated somewhat now. It had ceased struggling against its fate and now lay panting, its great chest heaving and it eyes rolling in fear and agony. Beobrand strode towards the beast, pulling his seax from its tooled leather scabbard. He placed a hand on the shaking horse's neck, and whispered to it in his soothing voice.

"There now. Easy. Hush." Its ears twitched at the sound of his voice, the skin quivering at his touch. He stroked the warm neck, feeling the life there, the firm muscles and the pulsing arteries. The animal was calmer now. Beobrand ran his half-hand gently along the neck. He wondered whether Sceadugenga yet lived, or perhaps the stallion had also been injured by a foolhardy rider. Beobrand sighed, drew in a deep breath, and plunged his seax into the horse's throat.

Hot blood spurted in a great arc, washing over Beobrand's hands and spreading across the path. The horse made a strange sound, almost like the whimper of a child, and kicked out, once more trying to stand. Beobrand leaned his weight on the beast's neck and shoulders and soon the strength had ebbed from the animal. He watched as its chest heaved for the last time, and then it was still.

Filled with a great sadness, he pushed himself up.

Udela was helping Scrydan to his feet. The reeve stood shakily, blood dripping bright from his nose and mouth. The tang of slaughter was sharp in the air. A movement from the direction of Selwyn's house caught Beobrand's attention.

Acennan walked towards them, raising an arm as he saw Beobrand. He was alone.

Beobrand turned to Scrydan.

"You will not be taking me to any moot, Scrydan. We were friends once, and I am sorry it has to end thus."

Scrydan spat a great gobbet of bloody phlegm into the dust.

Beobrand reached for the silver arm-ring he wore, one of the spoils from the siege of Din Eidyn. Scrydan flinched. Beobrand tugged the silver band free of his arm and proffered it to Udela. It was finely wrought, with cunning carvings like intertwining serpents, or the threads of men's wyrd. It glimmered in the sun. Udela made no move to take it.

"This is for you, Udela," Beobrand said, knowing the words and the gesture would never be enough. "For the wrongs I have done you, and as thanks for your kindness to..." He was going to say, 'my uncle', but after a hesitation, he said, "Selwyn."

Udela did not move. Her eyes looked as sad as he felt.

"Take it," he said, and at last, she accepted the glittering metal ring.

"And know this, Scrydan, son of Scryda. That silver is Udela's and not yours. It is as much hers as her brýdgifu. You have stolen my kin's land but I hereby renounce it. It is yours. But if I hear you have stolen from Udela, or raised a hand against her, Ardith or Selwyn, I will return to this place. And I will kill you. Do you doubt my words?"

Scrydan glared at him sullenly.

"Do you?" asked Beobrand, an edge of anger creeping back into his tone. He fixed Scrydan with his stare and after a few heartbeats, the reeve shook his head.

"By all the gods," said Acennan as he sauntered up, "what a terrible mess you have made here."

Beobrand took in the horse's corpse where already flies had begun to gather. Scrydan glowered at them from his deep-set eyes. Dark bruises had begun to mottle his cheeks. The swelling would start soon. Lastly, he looked at Udela, who had always been kind to him; had maybe even loved him once. Acennan was right. He had made a terrible mess of everything.

He wiped the blade of his seax on the dead horse's saddle blanket.

"Yes," he said to Acennan, "I fear we will not be so welcome here now. It is time for us to leave Hithe and head north."

Acennan smiled broadly. Beobrand noted that there was a smear of blood on his friend's chin. Other than that, there was no sign Acennan had been involved in a skirmish.

"At last," Acennan said, "I would see Eadgyth. We have been apart for too long."

"Sorry, my friend. But there is something we must do before we return to Bernicia."

Acennan frowned.

"What?"

Beobrand turned and strode away from Scrydan and Udela without looking back. His head ached and dark thoughts battered his thought-cage. Acennan caught up with him, matching his stride.

"What must we do?" he repeated.

Beobrand did not slow his pace.

"We must kill someone who long since should have been a corpse."

Part Four

Blood-Price

Chapter 33

"What are you doing?" hissed Acennan, trying to pull Beobrand back as his lord rose to his feet.

They had been watching the hall for three days and they were both short-tempered. They had not brought much in the way of provisions, having left Cantware in a hurry and they could not light a fire for fear of being spotted. And whilst it was summer, the nights were cold. A light drizzle had fallen the night before, chilling them both and making them fear the weapon-rot would soon begin to gnaw at their blades and armour. But it was more than the discomfort that made them irritable. Both Beobrand and Acennan were men of action, not thieves who skulked in the shadows, and although they knew they must employ some guile if they were to succeed in their endeavour, the inactivity did not sit well with either of them.

It seemed Beobrand's patience had finally snapped.

They were hidden amongst a dense copse of beech. From their vantage point, they could see the hall and its outbuildings, but so far no opportunity had presented itself. They had spotted their quarry once on the first day when he had beaten a thrall mercilessly. The slave, a skinny boy, had fallen to the ground and the man they hunted had kicked and stamped on him until one of the other warriors had pulled him away. The men had returned to the hall, the raucous sound of their laughter drifting to the two watchers in the damp copse. The slave boy had lain still on the earth for a long while and Beobrand had begun to think that perhaps he had been slain. But eventually the boy had struggled to his feet and carefully made his way to the stables. They had not seen him again that day or the next.

"Perhaps he died from his wounds," Acennan had offered. Such things did happen, as if the body continues to bleed inside after a fight. The beating the boy had taken had been savage, and Beobrand had cringed to watch it. For grown men – warriors – to hit and kick a defenceless boy turned his stomach. It reminded him of the blood that ran in his own veins. The blood of cravens who would torture and kill for pleasure. He had shuddered, watching from the shadow of the trees, gripping Hrunting's hilt with such strength that his fingers ached. He had wished to rush down the hill and smite the thrall's tormentor. But Acennan had placed a hand on his shoulder, as if he could hear Beobrand's thoughts. If they attacked now, so close to the hall, where strong hearth-warriors sat at the benches, they would both be killed. Worse, they might not manage to kill the object of their hate first.

But the thrall had not succumbed to his wounds, for now, as the dawn's fingers just began to caress the darkness in the sky, they saw him. He carried two heavy buckets. They had watched him for a moment until they were sure where he was heading and then Beobrand had made a decision. At this early time of the day, few people were abroad in the settlement. And fewer still would approach the boy's destination, which was one of the reasons Beobrand and Acennan had chosen their hiding place.

The boy walked stiffly, holding the buckets as far from his body as possible, lest they splash upon him. They were brimming full of slops and night-soil ready to be tossed into the midden. When the wind shifted, the stench of the place reached them in the copse, making them gag. Thankfully the cool and the drizzle of the previous night had softened the acrid smell somewhat.

Now Beobrand seized the only opportunity that might come to them. He stepped from the gloom beneath the trees just as the boy poured the contents of the first bucket into the stinking pit of refuse. Cursing quietly, Acennan struggled up and followed a few paces behind Beobrand.

The boy did not see them at first. It was yet the time of wolf-light, when men can appear as wraiths and sounds seem louder than they are when heard in the bright light of day. They were still several paces from him when the thrall saw them. His eyes grew wide and his face became as white as curds. He dropped the bucket he held, oblivious now of its offensive contents and whether it might splatter him. He turned, ready to run back to the safety of the hall and its buildings.

"Wait," said Beobrand in that soothing tone he used on horses and nervous animals. "We mean you no harm."

He could tell from the boy's expression he did not believe him. And yet the boy was curious. And brave. For he halted and turned to inspect these men who approached him from the forest's gloaming. Beobrand tried to imagine what the thrall saw – two killers, scarred, grim-faced, bedecked as for war, stepping menacingly from the cover of the woods. He must have thought they were come to attack his lord's hall. Beobrand stared into the eyes of the grime-smeared boy for a long while, weighing him up, thinking what his life must be like.

"We do not come with a warband," Beobrand said. The stench from the midden caught in his throat, threatening to make him retch. "We are not seeking to burn the hall, or to attack the lord here." The boy stared at him. Beobrand noticed he was poised on the balls of his feet, ready to run at the slightest sign the warriors might give that they meant him ill. The thrall said nothing.

"We seek one man who serves Grimbold."

"What man?" the boy spoke at last.

"Wybert, son of Alric."

The slave spat into the midden. He absently raised a hand to his side, to the ribs that must have been cracked when Wybert kicked him while they had watched from the trees.

"I know him," the boy said. "What do you want with him?"

Beobrand hesitated. He fixed the boy with his pale blue gaze. He hoped he had the measure of this thrall. If he was mistaken, the boy could raise the alarm and all would be lost. Every heartbeat they remained here in the open, the more chance they would be discovered. The sky was lightening. Somewhere down by the huts and the hall, a cockerel crowed loudly.

Beobrand took a steadying breath, immediately regretting it as he tasted the midden-stink anew.

"I mean to slay him. I have sworn the bloodfeud with him."

The boy spat again. His gaze flicked down to Beobrand's half-hand.

"You are Beobrand," he said. It was not a question.

"Yes," Beobrand replied. He could see no reason to deny it.

"He speaks of you when he's drunk," the boy said. "He hates you."

Beobrand said nothing.

"What do you want from me?" the boy asked. His eyes sparkled then, with a keen intelligence.

"I seek a place where I can face him, sword against sword, shield against shield. I do not bring a warband, so I must separate him from Grimbold's retinue if I am to have my revenge on him."

The boy nodded. He closed his eyes for a moment and scratched his head, as if that would help thoughts come to him. He clicked his fingers and grinned. He looked very pleased with himself. Beobrand found himself liking this strange thrall.

"You can help?" he asked.

"What's in it for me?" asked the boy.

Beobrand had thought of this already. He pulled a seax from his belt. Acennan had taken it from one of Scrydan's men. It was a fine weapon, sharp-edged with no spots of iron-rot. Its hilt was polished antler and the scabbard was tooled with intricate patterns. It was the weapon of a warrior, not a thrall. Slaves were forbidden to bear arms, but Beobrand noted how the boy's eyes lit up at the sight of the seax.

"If you give me that blade," the boy said, "I will see to it that you meet Wybert away from the hall. Somewhere where you may make him pay his debt to you in blood." Again, his hand touched gently to his side and he winced.

"How?" asked Beobrand, looking up impatiently at the brightening sky.

And the boy told him.

Chapter 34

"Odelyna tells me you have been leaving gifts for the forest spirits these last weeks," Rowena said, reaching for another honey-cake.

The shift in conversation came unexpectedly and Reaghan blinked. She was still reeling from having Rowena sitting at the high table with her, alongside Edlyn and Bassus. The night was warm and muggy, the doors and shutters of the hall thrown open in an attempt to draw a cooling breeze through the great building. But despite the flutter of a draught now that the sun had set, Reaghan could feel sweat prickling her neck. Rowena unnerved her. The older woman had been silent to her for so long, and before that, she had shown her nothing but spite, so it had been with shock that Reaghan had welcomed her to Beobrand's hall that evening.

Of course, Rowena's presence almost certainly had nothing to do with Reaghan, but more to do with her wayward daughter. Since Rowena's now infamous confrontation with Beircheart, Edlyn had become more brazen in her displays of affection. Rowena had probably decided that coming to the new hall was the only way she could seek to prevent her daughter from spending time alone with the young gesith. Reaghan couldn't blame her for trying, though she wondered how much a mother could change the course of her daughter's will when that daughter was already a woman, and a headstrong one at that.

Still, Edlyn had been the perfect daughter all evening, scarcely making eye contact with Beircheart where he sat with the hearth-warriors on the benches. The young woman had sat, straight-backed and serious at her mother's side, sipping her mead and listening intently to the scop, a young man, by the name of Cædmon, who had never been to Ubbanford before. The mood in the hall was buoyant, for it was not often that a tale-teller would come to their small settlement on the Tuidi. And Cædmon was talented. "As fine-voiced as Leofwine," Bassus had said. Reaghan had nodded, but had not thought to ask who Leofwine was. She had been too preoccupied with Rowena.

"Well," Rowena asked, raising her eyebrows inquisitively, "is it so, or does Odelyna lie?"

Reaghan shook her head. Beneath the table, she dug her nails into her palms.

"No, she speaks true," she said, her voice as meek as if she were still Rowena's thrall. "I have been leaving tokens and praying for the return of the men."

Rowena frowned, her face dark for a moment, as if a cloud had passed before the sun. Reaghan cursed silently. To remind the woman of her lost husband and sons was stupid. Rowena would think she did so with the intention of wounding her.

But Rowena assented slowly with a nod of her head.

"It is as it should be. We need the men to return. The harvest will be hard without them."

Now it was Reaghan's turn to frown. The harvest was months away.

"Surely the men will return before then," she said, trying to keep the tremble out of her voice.

"I am sure of it," said Bassus, his bluff tone blowing away the tension as a strong wind disperses fog. "Beobrand will be back soon. More mead, lady?" He proffered the flask to Rowena, who offered him a bright smile and lifted her cup.

"Thank you, Bassus."

When he had poured enough for her liking she placed a hand upon his wrist. Reaghan was surprised to see Bassus' face flush. After a moment, Rowena lowered her gaze and pulled her hand back.

"What tidings from the south, Cædmon," Bassus called out. The scop had just finished part of a tale about a nihtgenga who came to a lord's hall, killing thegns as if they were nothing more than children. The creature was slain in the end by a great warrior, who pulled off its arm and hung it from the beams of the hall. Bassus had grumbled at the tale, often interrupting the bard, who had forged ahead manfully, drawing most of his audience into his tale of stagnant meres, night-walkers and heroes. The scop had paused to drink ale and take a morsel from the board, but his story was not complete.

"Lord," he said, perhaps seeking to flatter Bassus by elevating his status to that of hlaford of the hall, "I have yet much to tell of the saga of Beowulf."

But Bassus seemed to have had enough of the tale.

"I know that story," he said, in a tone that would broach no argument. "I would hear tidings of the lands to the south. Has word come to you of Wessex, Mercia, the lands of the East Angelfolc and Cantware?" Some of the gesithas groaned. They would hear more of the saga Cædmon had been recounting, but a glance at Bassus told them not to push the matter.

Cædmon did not seem flustered to be interrupted. He ran his long fingers through his hair and set down his cup.

"For the great hospitality shown to me here in Ubbanford, I will of course tell you all I know of the southern kingdoms." He bowed, sweeping his right hand low to brush the rushes in an extravagant gesture. "In fact, I had intended to give you tidings of great import. Tidings that I heard not two days hence from the lips of a sea-travelling trader who had put in at Berewic."

Men settled down, taking up their drinking horns and cups, leaning forward to hear the words of the scop. Tales of monsters and bawdy riddles were entertaining, but news of the shifting tides of power amongst the kingdoms of Albion could give them an inkling into what their wyrds might hold in store. There had been no campaigning this summer and they had only been required to defend the land from small bands of ruffians, Picts mostly, who stole the odd sheep. The thieves would never stand and fight, instead slipping away into the mountains and forests before the warriors of Bernicia could close with them. Perhaps they could glean from Cædmon whether they would be called to battle soon.

Reaghan ignored Rowena now, instead offering her full attention to the smooth-faced bard. He stood tall, puffing out his chest and speaking with a clear, ringing tone that all could hear.

"I have heard tell of a great battle in the land of the East Angelfolc. Penda, son of Pybba, that fame-hungry king of Mercia, amassed a great host of his folk along with a horde of Waelisc and descended on the peace-loving Angelfolc. There, at a place called the great ditch, the Angelfolc, arrayed in all their battle-glory, stood strong before the dread king of the Mercians. The East Angelfolc had not one, but two good kings to lead them. Ecgric, the new king, and he who came before him, Sigeberht, that most holy of rulers who had given himself to the service of the Christ God.

"And other brave men had ridden to the aid of these Christian kings. Wulfgar, son of Ethelbert, led a warband of doughty Wessexmen into the fray. And there were even some of our own Bernician warriors who stood strong in the shieldwall there."

He raked them all with his gaze, his eyes blazing in the shadowed darkness of the hall. Sweat beaded on his forehead. Silence fell on the hall. Two dogs growled over a scrap of meat that had fallen from the board. Bearn silenced them with a kick. Reaghan felt suddenly sick. She was certain now which men of Bernicia had lent their shields and spears to the defence of that realm so far to the south.

"Yes," Cædmon continued, raising his voice almost to a shout, "the lord of Ubbanford himself stood in that thicket of spears and wall of linden-boards. Half-handed and yet they say blessed in the battle-skill by the gods themselves."

"What foolishness is this?" shouted Bassus. "You have tidings of our lord and you did not think to tell us before now?" Bassus' brows bristled and his chin jutted. Reaghan could see that he gripped his wooden cup so tightly that his knuckles were pale and his hand shook. Others of the gesithas shouted out their own displeasure at the scop.

Cædmon raised his hands, motioning for calm.

"Every tale has its time," he said. His smile was less charming now. He was young, talented and attractive, Reaghan thought, but he was inexperienced. It seemed he had badly misjudged his audience. "And every story has its order."

"Well, we would hear tell of our lord," snapped Bassus.

"All in good time, mighty Bassus," Cædmon smirked. "The tale must not be rushed or spoilt."

Bassus surged to his feet, upsetting his cup. The hounds leapt up and started barking.

"I care nothing for your tale-craft, boy," he thundered. "Tell me what befell Beobrand and his gesithas."

Now, at last, Cædmon's smile slipped. But only for a moment. He nodded and brushed invisible dust from his kirtle. He was silent for a few heartbeats, eyes closed as if he was remembering his story, or reminding himself of where he had left off.

Bassus' face was thunder and Reaghan marvelled at how completely this youthful scop had failed to sense the mood in the hall.

At last he spoke again, and to his credit, his voice was clear, without a tremble of doubt.

"With such an amount of royalty, and the divine blessing of the Christ, you would think that the battle would be easily won by the East Angelfolc." He paused for tension. Bassus growled and Reaghan thought he might launch himself over the boards and throttle the tale-spinner. But perhaps the young man was learning, for he quickly continued.

"But alas, it was not to be. The East Angelfolc were crushed, their fyrd-men and their allies slaughtered in a great blood-letting that turned the ditch into a marsh of gore and fed the foxes and crows of that land for many days."

Reaghan heard someone let out a cry of anguish. Then, with a start, she realised it was her own voice. Without warning she felt tears on her cheeks.

No. No. It need not be such dark news. Perhaps Beobrand would yet return. Perhaps he had escaped from that awful battlefield where the birds gorged themselves on the flesh of the fallen. She wanted to speak, but she could not form words.

Instead, Bassus asked the question they all wanted the scop to answer.

"What tidings of our lord Beobrand? Did he fall in the battle?"

All eyes turned to Cædmon, who seemed to puff up with pride, revelling in the rapt attention.

"Well, that I cannot tell," he said, a half-smile twisting his mouth.

Bassus growled again at the man's response, but Beircheart was closer and had also run out of patience. Leaping to his feet, he sprang forward and grasped the scop by his kirtle's collar. The slight bard cowered. Beircheart shook him like a dog worrying a river rat.

"You will tell us, worm-tongue," Beircheart said, "and you will tell us now. What of our lord and his hearth-men? Did they fall? Speak all you know, or I swear you will never tell another tale."

Cædmon's eyes bulged in fear. He was not so pleased to be the centre of attention in the hall now, Reaghan thought. Beircheart shook him hard.

"Speak!" he shouted.

"I cannot tell what happened to your lord," Cædmon said, his voice now feeble and tremulous. "I cannot, for I know not. Many fell that day, so the merchant said. Both the kings of the East Angelfolc were slain and the host scattered. But he did not speak of Beobrand of Ubbanford. I asked him, but he did not know."

Beircheart shook him again. His other hand was balled into a fist and he looked set to strike the scop. He looked to Bassus, who shook his head. Beircheart released the bard, who staggered away, breathless with fear.

"You have outstayed your welcome in this hall, scop," snarled Bassus. Outside, through the open doors, Reaghan saw that it was now night. Moths flitted around the rush lights and oil lamps, causing the light to flicker.

"But, lord," whimpered Cædmon, all semblance of control now lost, "it is dark and I have sung you songs and told you tales, surely this is enough for me to enjoy the shelter of this fine hall?"

Bassus was grim-faced.

"You have made light of the fate of our lord. Our friends. Now begone. I do not wish to see your face any further. To look on you reminds me that brave men die while cravens often live." Bassus raised his one arm and pointed towards the doors and to the gloom of the night beyond. "Now get out."

"Wait," Reaghan said. Her stomach churned, but she rose to her feet for all to look upon her. Could it be that Beobrand was truly dead? Slain in some bloody battle far away? Tears ran down her cheeks. She cuffed them away. To speak out before all did not come easily to Reaghan. She had been a slave too long, more used to being shouted at or beaten, than giving orders to others. And yet, there was something about the young scop that spoke to her. He was young and foolish, but he was not evil.

Bassus raised his eyebrows, awaiting further words from her. She was the lady of the hall, after all. Yes, she was. She placed her hands upon the linen cloth that covered the high table, smoothing it, feeling crumbs of bread like grit beneath her fingers.

"Wait," she repeated. Her mouth was dry as all those gathered stared at her. She cleared her throat. "Do not turn him into the night."

"But, my lady," protested Bassus.

"No," she said, her voice firmer now. "He has made a mistake, but I do not believe he meant any malice by it. Did you?"

"Not at all, my lady," Cædmon said. "I wished nobody ill. It is just that the sagas speak to me, they whisper how they must be best told, and who am I not to listen?"

Bassus tensed and made a guttural sound deep in his throat.

"Hush, Cædmon," Reaghan said, "ere I change my mind and have you thrown out into the dark." Cædmon stopped talking and lowered his gaze. "You may sleep in the hall this night and then you will leave."

Bassus stared at her with a strange expression. She could not tell whether he was angry at her, or something else. After a long moment, he nodded and the outrage leeched away from the hall, to be replaced by a dark, brooding melancholy.

Reaghan sat back on her stool. She reached for the flask of mead, but her hand shook, so she placed it on her lap beneath the board. She thought she might vomit. She trembled with the tension of having spoken out before all of those men, but that is not what made her truly sick. Her stomach turned and soured with the fear of what might have happened to Beobrand. All these long weeks she had prayed and dreamt of his return. What if he never came back? What then?

A light touch on her arm startled her from her reverie. It was Rowena. The older woman took up the flask of mead and filled Reaghan's cup. Rowena handed her the cup, taking care that her hands were steady enough not to spill the contents. A tremor ran through Reaghan at Rowena's touch. She could not recall the lady of Ubba's hall ever having touched her without the intent to harm or chastise. She suppressed a shudder and raised the cup to her lips. The sweet liquid soothed her as well as moistening her parched throat.

"Thank you," she whispered.

"Perhaps the news is not so bad," Rowena said, and Reaghan shot her a sharp look. How could these tidings not be bad? "The scop himself said that Beobrand is blessed in battle-skill, did he not?" Rowena continued. "And he could not say that Beobrand had fallen in the battle. So, it may not be as bad as we fear now, in the darkness of night. Everything is less grim in the light of day."

Reaghan took another sip of the mead, but said nothing.

"But," said Rowena, "it cannot hurt to ask the gods for their aid. Tomorrow I will travel with you to the sacred glade and together we will leave tribute. Perhaps the gods will hear when the voices of two ladies are combined."

Chapter 35

"You really think that Waelisc boy can be trusted?" asked Acennan. Absently, he fingered the silver rood amulet he wore around his neck. It was similar in shape to the hammer of Thunor that Beobrand himself wore. Acennan had told Beobrand it had been a gift from Eadgyth when they had last met at Eoferwic. He wore it close to his heart, beneath his clothes, but Beobrand had noticed how he often pulled the thing free from his clothing and fiddled with it.

Beobrand shrugged.

"If he was going to betray us, we would have found out by now," he said. A day, a night and part of another day had passed since they had approached the boy at Grimbold's hall. Standing there, enveloped in the miasma of the midden-stench, they had listened to the slave's idea and it had seemed sound. Or at least they had no better alternative. They had found the place he had told them of quite easily and although they were still uncomfortable and wished they could light a fire, they had set up camp in a dip in the earth that was sheltered by a large overhang of mossy rock. It kept them out of the worst of the wind and even offered some protection from the rain that had fallen from time to time the day before.

The boy seemed to have been speaking true about the place, for they found many signs of boar spoor and the path they had followed was studded with the beasts' distinctive tracks of sharp cloven-hooves with trailing imprints of dew claws.

Beobrand looked up at the sky through the canopy of leaves. It was a warm day and the white clouds that scudded across the sky did not carry rain.

"They might come today," he said. "It is a good day for hunting."

Acennan grunted. He was irritable, and Beobrand could not blame him. He had been a poor companion these past weeks and now they crouched in a Mercian forest with only the prospect of death ahead of them. The plan seemed foolish now. How did they expect to escape after confronting Wybert? If the gods did not smile upon them, they would surely be caught and slain. Beobrand thought back to Hithe, to his meeting with Selwyn, and the fight with Scrydan. The loathing and fear in Udela's eyes.

It seemed unlikely that the gods favoured him.

He wondered how much longer they could wait here before deciding Wybert would not come. A day? Two? They had already been lucky not to have been stumbled upon by some local ceorl or thrall. The day before, Acennan had been watching the path when he gave the signal for someone approaching. They alternated the positions, one in the shadow of the rock, looking down the track, while the other waited below, ready to circle round and come at their quarry from behind. Beobrand had seen the signal and snatched up Hrunting and his shield. But before he had headed for the path, Acennan signalled again that he was not to move. It turned out to be a swineherd, with six snuffling pigs rooting for pannage amongst the tree roots. Acennan had crept down the slope to Beobrand and the two of them had hidden behind a great oak. The man and his pigs had wandered off, but Beobrand didn't know how much longer they could remain here without being discovered.

It was Beobrand's turn to watch the path now, but before he clambered up the incline to the rock that had already become familiar to him, he placed a hand on Acennan's shoulder.

"Thank you for coming for me," he said. "Thank you for my life."

Acennan nodded.

"You are my friend, lord," he said, and his eyes twinkled in the green-tinged forest light. "You think we will kill that bastard now, once and for all?"

Beobrand held his gaze for a long while.

"We will," he said, hoping it was true, "or we will die in the attempt. I feel this is where the threads of this story end."

Acennan nodded again. He did not seem overly concerned.

"We could have ridden here with your warband. You still have men in Ubbanford. Though it might have started a war."

Beobrand thought of the great ditch; of Ceawlin's sacrifice. Elmer, Gram and the rest of them lost in the bloody-mire. Dead because of his decision to fight.

"No," Beobrand said, his voice hollow, "this is not their fight. I could not lead them here to their certain death."

"If we live, they will not thank you for this. Sunniva was dear to them and all who knew her would like to be part in the collection of her blood-price."

"They will have to be content with the tale we will tell."

Acennan looked grim. Beobrand wondered whether he believed they would escape this place with their lives.

"Or the tale they hear sung in halls by others."

Beobrand squeezed Acennan's arm and climbed up to the lookout spot by the rock that provided a good view of the path. Acennan was probably right. It was more likely others would recount their tale. Mayhap a scop of Mercia would hear tell of the events here and spin a saga worthy of the gods themselves. Beobrand smiled thinly. Songs and tales always grew in the telling.

He remembered Alwin's bright eyes when he talked of the stories he had heard concerning Beobrand's battle-skill. They had been friends since childhood, but it was as if he believed Beobrand was somehow truly a hero of legend. It was true that he had stood in shieldwalls and killed many men, but Beobrand could scarcely remember how those things came to pass. Before a battle he was all jangly nerves and a need to piss, then came the blood, crash and screaming of combat. He dealt death easily, of that there could be no doubt, but when a battle was over, the thrill of the blood-letting drained away as quickly as mead from a cracked pot, leaving only a hollow emptiness of trembling hands and nightmares. The faces of men he had slain often came to him in his dreams and he would awaken trembling, as if he had just stepped from a shieldwall. He thought he cried out at times, but if he did, none ever spoke of it.

Scops sang of battle-fame and glory. The truth of whimpering boys holding their gut-ropes and the sickly stench of shit, piss and blood would be less exciting. And yet, Beobrand could not deny there was something inside him that thrilled at the approach of a fight. He was certain his true father had felt the same. And he shuddered to recall the glimmer in Hengist's eyes when he scented suffering and a chance for blade-play.

Gods, but the man had been savage. Did he too have such a beast within him? He pushed the thought away, all too certain of the answer.

Beobrand leaned his head against the cool moss on the rock and gazed down the path. There was no movement in the dappled sunlight that lanced through the trees. His mind wandered even while his eyes watched.

Alwin had been so disappointed when he had come to Beobrand and Acennan on that last day in Hithe. They had made their way quickly to Folca's hall, eager to be gone from the place before news of their fight with Scrydan and his men reached the lord. Beobrand thought that Scrydan would not dare to cross him again, but he could make it difficult for them to leave. There were too many questions that could be asked about Grimgundi's death.

Alwin had come upon them as they were mounting their steeds, a gift from King Eadbald's stable. His face was aglow in the warm sunshine.

"Take me with you," he had blurted out, flushing with embarrassment as soon as the words were spoken.

Beobrand's hands had ceased shaking, but he'd still felt as though his body were taut, humming like a bow string. He had looked at Alwin for a long while.

"Take me with you," Alwin had repeated. "You know I can fight and I am loyal. I would swear my oath to you, Beobrand."

Beobrand had looked down at his old friend's open face. He'd swallowed against the thickness in his throat and dismounted, handing the reins to Acennan.

Placing his hands upon Alwin's shoulders, he'd looked him in the eye. He'd seen nothing but honesty there. For a heartbeat he'd imagined the blood he had seen spilt, the men he had sent wailing to the afterlife, the loved ones he had lost. He'd shaken his head.

"No, Alwin. You are a good man, and any lord would be honoured to have your oath. But you are sworn to others. You have a wife, a child, and a parcel of land. Your father's land must be tended to, and you are the man to do it." Alwin had been crestfallen. "You are a good man," Beobrand had repeated. "Stay here. See your children grow. Tend the land, plant seeds and watch them bear fruit. Bring life to the world, Alwin. You are not a killer."

With that, he had embraced his friend, then vaulted into the saddle and ridden away from Hithe. He had not looked back.

A slight, silent movement brought his mind back to the present. Beobrand peered down the path. There it was again. A slow movement, a stealthy movement. And then he raised his hand behind the rock, so that Acennan would see. For men were moving slowly through the forest towards them and the time had come to claim the blood-price for Sunniva.

And despite himself, Beobrand felt once more the thrill of death's approach.

Chapter 36

The day was much cooler than the night had been. Clouds had boiled in the dark morning sky and a heavy rain had fallen, washing away the oppressive heat of the past days. A drizzle yet fell, but here under the dense canopy of the forest, little water reached Reaghan and Rowena as they made their way in silence towards the sacred glade. A strong wind had picked up, filling the often-silent woodland with the rustling murmur and rattle of leaves and branches high above. Reaghan pulled her cloak about her, pausing to allow the older woman to catch up. Rowena nodded an acknowledgement, but did not offer a smile. Reaghan pressed her lips together and turned once more in the direction of the clearing. She could not feel at ease in the presence of her erstwhile mistress. They had spoken briefly when they had set out together, but the conversation had dried and shrivelled quickly. They had little to speak about and neither, it seemed, knew how to bridge the gap between them.

As she turned her back on Rowena, Reaghan felt her muscles and skin twitch, as if they remembered the beatings; the sting of the hazel switch. She knew her body still bore the marks of Rowena's punishments. No, they would likely never be friends, but she was glad of the change in Rowena that now saw her treat Reaghan with something like respect. Edlyn's mother had even seemed content when they had met that morning. Reaghan had been surprised by the lightness of her mood that was in stark contrast to the grey turmoil of clouds in the sky and the tidings of battle and death that Cædmon had imparted. Despite all that, Rowena appeared to have found some source of secret pleasure. She walked with a bounce in her stride and Reaghan had caught her smiling quietly to herself.

They each carried a small sack with their offerings for the forest gods. Reaghan had wondered whether she should bring another animal, more blood for the goddess, but in the end she could not bear the thought of a repeat of the terrifying sacrifice when the hen had careened headless across the glade. Instead she had brought a finely-wrought cup. It was a treasure indeed, heavy with gold and gems, taken from Beobrand's chest that was hidden beneath the floor of the hall. She had worried that he would be angry with her at losing the cup, but then she thought that if he was angry, it would mean he had returned, so she had stuffed the chalice into the sack, pushing aside the thought that she was somehow a thief. She prayed that the spirits would accept her offering and bring Beobrand back to her. She would happily face his ire, if only he would return. She did not know what Rowena brought for her own sacrifice.

A tremor of fear rippled down Reaghan's back. What if Beobrand was dead? Since Cædmon's words of the night before, her dread had grown inside her, dark and brooding. The sense of sadness and loss had fallen over Ubbanford, as cold and all-encompassing as the rain. She did not know what would happen should he not return. She was no longer a thrall, but what would happen to her? She had no brýdgifu, there had been no real declaration of what she was to Beobrand. He had freed her from thralldom and she had slept in his bed and shared his board and hall. The men and women of Ubbanford had slowly become accustomed to this new reality, even Rowena it seemed, and Reaghan flicked a gaze at the lady of Ubba's hall where she laboured along the path behind her, but what if Beobrand were dead? What then?

The wind gusted, making the trees creak and crack. The rustle of the leaves grew louder, as if a warhost whispered words of doom. Reaghan shuddered, suddenly wishing she had made Bassus come with them. It was Rowena who had suggested that Bassus remain in Ubbanford.

"No ill will befall us," Rowena had said, her voice soft and calm. "We do not need a man there, do we Reaghan? This is work for women."

Reaghan had felt her face grow hot, despite the cool breeze and the rain. She was so accustomed to obeying the woman that she had merely nodded.

"There," Rowena had said, with a smile, "it is decided. Bassus, you can take Octa to Maida, and Reaghan and I will go to the glade and return by midday or shortly after." Reaghan had noticed how Rowena reached out and placed her hand on Bassus' arm.

The huge warrior had put up a brief struggle, protesting that he should watch over them, but at Rowena's soothing voice and the soft caress of her fingers on his hand, he had quickly backed down.

Now, with the wind making the trees talk above them and the damp, cool gloom of the forest all around them, Reaghan felt foolish. She should have insisted that Bassus accompany them. There were brigands and bandits in these woods; Picts who hated Beobrand and the Angelfolc of Ubbanford. What would two women be able to do should they stumble across a band of such men? Why had Rowena insisted on going alone?

The wind seemed to hold its breath, a sudden silence falling on the forest. Reaghan shivered. They were close now. Reaghan's skin crawled as she scurried past the rotting, insect-writing tree trunk. Were they being watched? She spun around, but the only movement was Rowena. Ubba's widow was pale-faced, her pace no longer sprightly across the forest loam.

"Do you feel it too?" Reaghan asked, as Rowena drew close.

"Feel what?" Rowena replied. "All I feel is cold and damp. I wish I had worn a thicker cloak." She offered a thin smile, but there was no warmth in it. Her words sounded hollow. False.

"You feel it, don't you? The eyes of the forest. We are being watched."

Rowena cast her gaze around them, peering into shadows beneath the trees.

"Nonsense," she said, but her words lacked conviction. "Come, girl, let us get to this place and leave our offering. Perhaps we might be back to Ubbanford before the rains fall again in earnest." She glanced about them again before setting out once more on the overgrown path towards the glade.

Reaghan watched her pass. The hair on her arms and neck bristled. There was somebody out there. Or something. They should not have come alone. She clutched the sack tightly and wondered again whether the sacrifice she brought would be enough for the dark spirits of the forest.

The heavy stillness that had engulfed the forest was pierced by a shrill, cackling cry somewhere up ahead. A bird, surely. As if awoken by the shriek, the wind began to moan through the tree limbs again. Reaghan pulled her cloak close to her body with a trembling hand. To think she often wished to come here alone, with nothing but her thoughts for company. Never before had the woods seemed so full of malice. The twisted shapes of the moss-clad boles seemed to loom towards her.

Rowena was well ahead of her now. Reaghan had thought she had not known the way to the clearing. Another gust of wind shook the trees. The trees were waiting for her, she could hear it in the sibilant susurrus of their leafy voice. Again she heard the shrieking call. Whether bird or spirit, she knew she did not wish to face it alone. She ran after Rowena.

"Wait for me," she cried out, but her words were pulled from her mouth by the wind so that Rowena did not hear. Terrified now, frightened beyond all reason, Reaghan sprinted forward, her feet slipping in the leaf mould. "Wait," she panted, "wait." But still Rowena did not appear to hear her, for she did not turn or pause. And then Rowena was at the opening to the sacred glade. She did not pause, but vanished from Reaghan's sight for a moment. Panicked at being left alone, Reaghan ran on and followed the older woman into the clearing.

Reaghan skidded to a halt, her terrified mind trying to make sense of what she saw before her.

Amidst the totems and offerings, the ribbons and straw dolls that danced and dangled from the branches of the sacred alder stood not the single figure of Rowena, as Reaghan had expected. Before Rowena there stood another woman, her white-streaked black hair wind-tossed and flowing about her face as her long dress billowed and flapped around her lithesome body. For a heartbeat, Reaghan was certain that this was the goddess herself, Danu, stepped from the gloom of the forest to listen to the two women who had come to offer her sacrifice. But then, with a stabbing of terror and confusion she realised this was no goddess.

She knew this woman.

The woman turned her face towards Reaghan and grinned. Her face twisted into a mask of beauty and disfigurement, half untouched smooth skin, the other side broken and scarred from some terrible blow, teeth gleaming white from behind split lips.

"Oh, you have done well, Rowena," Nelda said.

Reaghan flinched as a jackdaw flapped past her and landed upon the cunning woman's shoulder. The bird glowered at Reaghan with its pallid eye and let out a cry.

Tchack. Tchack.

Nelda reached up and stroked its feathers.

"Yes," Nelda said, her smile broadening, grotesque and savage, "you have done very well."

Rowena did not speak, but her hand reached into the sack she carried. Reaghan watched, transfixed like a mouse before a swooping hawk, powerless to move. Rowena brought forth from the sack a large scabbarded seax. A warrior's blade, as long as Reaghan's thin forearm.

And, as sudden as lightning from a summer storm, it was clear what offering Rowena had brought to the glade for sacrifice.

The goddess would have blood after all.

Chapter 37

Beobrand smiled grimly. Oswald said he was lucky above all things. Such talk always angered Beobrand. His life had seen so much misery, how could anyone consider him lucky? But now, looking down the sun-dappled path at the men who approached he had to admit it. This was luck indeed.

There were only three of them, and one of the men who walked stealthily along the track was the object of his hatred.

Wybert.

The plan they had laid out with the thrall back at the midden had been simple. So simple in fact that both he and Acennan had fretted. Would it work? Would Wybert take the bait that the thrall would set before him? And would he come with few enough men that Beobrand and Acennan would be able to defeat them?

There were many things that might have gone wrong. The boy could have betrayed them, or perhaps he might fail to entice Wybert with his tales of a great boar in these parts. But for once, it seemed the gods smiled on Beobrand. His wyrd was to kill Wybert here. For Acennan and he could defeat three men. Especially as they would take them by surprise.

A light breeze sighed in the treetops. It was a soothing sound, but Beobrand's blood thrilled in his veins. He heard its rush in his ears. He had awaited this moment for so long. Now he must only wait a few more heartbeats until the men were at the place Acennan and he had decided upon. He took a calming breath, reaching his hand to grip Hrunting's hilt. Soon the great blade, his brother's sword, would once more drink the blood of an enemy. Beobrand felt his lips peel back from his teeth in a feral grin. A small voice within him whispered that he was no different from his half-brother. He too revelled in maiming and killing. He pushed the dark thought away. He was not like Hengist. Wybert deserved to die. It was justice for what he had done.

Beobrand cautiously peered around the rock, hoping that the sun would not glint from his helm. The men were almost at the designated spot for the ambush. They each carried a stout boar spear, with a forged crossbar to prevent an injured beast doing that which Ceawlin had done at the battle of the great ditch. For such was the bravery and strength of boars that they were known to push themselves down a spear haft and gore a careless hunter; killing their killer whilst taking their dying breath.

They were walking slowly, cautiously, placing each foot down carefully to avoid making a sound in the forest mould. They must believe there to be a boar nearby. None of the men were armoured, but they did carry shields upon their backs. They advanced. A few more steps and they would be ready for the trap to be sprung.

Beobrand closed his eyes and drew a long breath of the rich woodland air into his lungs.

This is for you, Sunniva.

Beobrand stepped onto the path and dragged Hrunting from its scabbard.

The men, alert to the hunt, saw him instantly and halted.

For a moment, all was silent save for the breath of the wind through the trees. The three men looked about them for sign of others around Beobrand, but, seeing none, they stared up the path at him. He was arrayed in all his battle gear. He knew what they saw before them. A great warrior, tall and broad in heavy byrnie and helm. His linden shield was strapped to his left arm, the splints of metal and rings on his right arm caught the light that sliced through the forest gloom. And, finally there was the snake-skinned patterned blade of Hrunting. The sword seemed to shine with its own light, such was the quality of the metal.

For such a warrior as this, three unarmoured opponents might not prove too much of a challenge, and yet, Wybert and his companions did not appear nervous. They each shifted their stance slightly, gripping their spears, ready to fight. There was no trace of panic in their eyes. Beobrand quickly appraised the men. They looked competent enough, young, strong and fit. But with no armour, they would stand little chance against Acennan and him.

His gaze finally rested on Wybert. When he had last seen him, they had both been in the tumult of battle, but now he had time to see the man that Wybert had become. Wybert had broadened and had the shoulders and strong hands of a fighter. At his belt hung a fine ring-hilted sword, such as would be gifted by a lord to his trusted gesithas. Their eyes met and Wybert smiled. How confident he had become! Gone was the angry youth filled with petty hatred. This was a man to be reckoned with.

"I have awaited this moment for a long time, Wybert, son of Alric," said Beobrand. "Too long have you walked this earth. I swore the bloodfeud with you and now I mean to reclaim the blood-price you owe me."

"Indeed?" said Wybert with a sneer. "And what price would that be? I did not think I needed to pay for your whore, I thought she was a house thrall, free for any man who visited your hall."

Beobrand felt his face grow hot. The torrent of hatred that flooded him was shocking in its intensity. His fingers clutched tightly about Hrunting's grip. He would not be able to control his ire for long in the face of Wybert's jibes and taunts. But he must not listen to Wybert's words. He must allow Acennan time to get into position. Despite the urge to leap forward and lay about him with Hrunting, Beobrand held himself as still as one of the great oaks that surrounded them.

"Do not speak of her," Beobrand said. "You will pay for what you did with your life." Each word fell from his mouth like a shard of ice.

Wybert held out his arms in mock innocence and cast a glance at his friends to either side.

"I had thought we came to hunt a fine Mercian boar and all we find is this Cantware pig."

One of the men laughed; a harsh, too-quick braying cackle that hinted at his hidden nervousness.

The man was still laughing when Acennan stepped silently from behind a thicket of brambles, took four quick steps and swung the blade of his sword into his shoulder, at the point where it met the neck. The steel-edged iron blade shattered the collarbone and ribs below and carried on into the man's flesh, ripping and tearing until it came to rest halfway down his chest.

His laughter died at the same moment he did. Wide-eyed, he stared down at the gore-smirched blade that protruded from his body. Then Acennan gave it a savage twist, pulling it free with a sucking sound and a gush of blood, as he jumped back from the two remaining men, out of the range of a spear thrust.

"This is no time for laughing, you horse-turds," Acennan said, his teeth gleaming white from his beard. "You are going to die here, Wybert, and if your friend stands with you, he too will soon feed the wolves like you and this one here."

Wybert gawped at the twitching corpse of his companion. The man who had been laughing until a few heartbeats before lay slumped and broken on the mud of the forest floor. His lifeblood pumped silently into the dark earth. After a time, Wybert sucked in a deep breath and drew himself up, squaring his shoulders. His face was pale, but his jaw was set in defiance. His smile had vanished. He raised his spear and pointed the iron tip at Acennan.

"I will kill you for that," he said, his voice clipped, as if his throat was tight.

Acennan smirked.

"So you mean to fight, do you? Good."

"Aye, we'll fight you, and willingly."

Wybert and his friend crouched into the warrior stance, poised, ready for the death-dealing. Gone was the time for talk.

Beobrand glared at Wybert, allowing all his pain and anger to fill him. Wybert became the focus not only for his vengeance for Sunniva's defilement, but also for her death, for the loss of the love he had found so fleetingly. And for lost friendships. If not for Wybert, Anhaga, that poor faithful cripple, would yet live. He had died trying to avenge Sunniva, and Beobrand had given Anhaga his oath that he would slay Wybert.

Now was the time to make good his oath.

Beobrand's head had started to throb. He could feel a presence here in this forest; the eyes of the gods upon him perhaps. Could it be that they watched this woodland path? Acennan had spilt first blood, and the gods would see more.

For a merest moment, Beobrand saw in Wybert's dark features a semblance of his fair brother, Leofwine, the scop.

Leofwine, who had fallen in the battle at Gefrin's ford. The wrong brother lay dead these past years. He felt a pang at the thought. Leofwine had been his friend, as had his father, Alric. How could those good men have been kin to one such as Wybert?

Then, as Beobrand stepped towards his enemy, Wybert's shock of black hair reminded him of Hengist. Leofwine could no more choose his brother than could Beobrand. How the gods must be laughing. Beobrand could feel the beast of his rage straining within him. Was it the same beast that had driven Hengist? Did a similar dark animal gnaw at Wybert's insides? Perhaps they were all the same.

Beobrand shook his aching head to free it of these thoughts. This was not the time to ponder. Enough of this. It ends now.

He unleashed the beast, leaping forward with a sudden savage glee.

"Now you die!" he screamed.

He had barely taken two strides, when a flick of Wybert's gaze alerted him to something amiss.

A movement to his right. A sound. And before he could react, a snarling, grey weight hammered into Beobrand. He staggered, agony searing into his leg. For a moment, Beobrand was lost in confusion. What was this thing that had rushed from the tree-shade? Could it be a wolf? He struggled to maintain his footing, as the growling beast savaged his thigh. Looking down he saw that it was a great hound, bearing a thick leather collar. A hunting dog. Of course. How could he have been so stupid? He had been so blinded by the vision of his enemy that he had already tasted the victory before he had even dealt a single strike.

And now, as sudden as the wind changes direction in a storm, the luck Oswald often spoke of had vanished.

What a fool he had been.

Behind the hound, loping between the boles of the trees, came the red-bearded warrior he had faced at the great ditch. The throbbing of his head reminded him of that day, and of the speed and skill of this huge man who would be upon him in an eye-blink. He must rid himself of the dog that had sunk its teeth into the meat of his leg.

Beobrand hammered Hrunting's pommel into the animal's head. Once. Twice. But its snarls just grew angrier, and it tightened its jaws yet further. The pain was excruciating. The red-bearded warrior was raising his hunting spear. He would spit Beobrand like the boar he had been stalking.

The hound shook its head, attempting to rend and rip his flesh. Beobrand swung Hrunting down in a desperate arc, slicing into the dog's back. Dark blood spattered and the animal's growls changed in pitch.

Red-beard pulled back his arm for an overarm lunge with his spear. He was no more than ten paces from Beobrand.

The first cut had hacked the hound almost in two, but it seemed not to know that it was dying. Beobrand chopped down again with all his strength and hewed the dog's body in two. The jaws were yet clamped onto his leg, but he was suddenly free of the bulk of the animal.

The giant came on, thrusting the spear forward in a blow that would have burst through his byrnie and pierced his chest had not Beobrand managed to spin towards his attacker and raise his linden-board. The spear-tip gouged a great splintered furrow across the board and clanged from the shield boss.

Beobrand staggered back, his leg a burning agony. A quick glance showed him the dog's head was yet attached to him by its maw, the beast's fore legs and gore-dripping chest flopping, almost tripping Beobrand, as the red-bearded warrior advanced towards him.

Chapter 38

The cool weight of the seax grounded Rowena. Somehow it seemed like the only solid thing in that accursed glade. Everything else felt like a dream. Nelda was smiling her terrifying grin at her, clearly overjoyed at the delivery of Beobrand's woman for her bloody vengeance. Rowena shuddered.

She glanced at Reaghan. The girl's face was the colour of whey. Her mouth was open in shocked realisation at what awaited her here, beneath the creaking, moss-clad trees. The trickle of the stream was loud in the cloying stillness of the clearing.

"How? Why?" Reaghan asked.

Gods, the girl was stupid. She had never even been a good thrall. How Beobrand could have made her his lady was something Rowena could not comprehend. The wind swirled in a sudden gust, shaking the spirit-gifts hanging from the branches. Reaghan's long, auburn hair was thrown back from her face. Her dress pressed against her slender form, accentuating her breasts and the swell of her hips. Rowena snorted. Of course she knew what Beobrand saw in the girl.

Men. Idiots one and all. But oh, how she had missed the warmth of a man in her bed. She forced herself to breathe slowly, to calm herself.

Nelda took a step forward. The jackdaw on her shoulder let out a single cry.

Reaghan shivered, but she did not retreat. The girl had some steel in her, thought Rowena. Good.

"It is simple, child," said Nelda, her voice soft, as one who speaks to a sick child. Or to someone on the verge of death. "I have sworn to destroy Beobrand, and to heap upon him such suffering as I am able before his death."

Reaghan spun to face Rowena.

"But why? Do you hate me so much?"

Rowena did not answer. The seax in her hand was heavy. She had hated Reaghan, it was true, but part of her knew it was not of the girl's doing. The Waelisc thrall had ever been subject to the men in her life. As all women were.

"Rowena here has a more practical reason for seeing you dead," Nelda said. "With you gone, her daughter can marry Beobrand and become the lady of Ubbanford. We mothers must always do what is best for our children. Isn't that so, Rowena?"

She gave Rowena her lopsided, horrific smile, as if they were the best of friends.

Rowena hated herself for her own weakness. By Frige, what had she been thinking? She gripped the bone handle of the seax as tightly as she could. Her hand trembled.

The wind shook the boughs of the birch and beech trees all around them. Nelda raised her voice to be heard over the forest-hiss of the trees.

"But you are no mother, are you Reaghan? You sought to be rid of the burden of a child. You should already be dead. Isn't that so?"

Nelda had told Rowena of how she had almost succeeded in taking Reaghan's life the summer before. But somehow the girl had survived. Helped by Maida and Odelyna most likely. Rowena recalled the days when they had said Reaghan was unwell. She had not given it any thought until Nelda had told her of Reaghan's plight and the poisoned gift she had given the thrall.

Reaghan squared her shoulders. Colour had risen high in her cheeks.

"But I yet live, witch," she spat. Her voice shook, but with defiance or fear, or both, Rowena could not tell.

"Well, child," Nelda said with a savage-looking smirk, "now you will die. It is your wyrd."

Nelda turned to Rowena.

"It is time," she said, glancing down at the seax in her trembling hands.

Rowena swallowed. She slowly drew the sharp blade from its leathern sheath. She dropped the scabbard and the sack to the mossy earth. Now was the moment she must act. Her heart thundered in her breast, her blood roaring in her veins. To think she had come so very close. How had it come to this? She loved Edlyn. More than anything. She was all she had left. But this was not the way to help her daughter. She knew that now. As she had many times already this morning, she offered up thanks to Woden, Frige, Danu, even the Christ, that Bassus had come to her the night before. She had so craved a man's touch again, to feel the heat and strength of a warrior beside her in her bed. But more than that, she had longed for a strong man's counsel. Was she truly so weak that she needed a man to make her decisions for her?

Reaghan stood, white-faced and transfixed at the sight of the polished seax in Rowena's hand.

"No, Nelda," Rowena snapped, "it is you who will die here this day. I had been blinded by my love for Edlyn, but you are no friend of mine. You bring death and pain with you. You have caused too much harm. Now, like a moon-touched dog, you must be killed so that you can hurt no more."

Rowena raised the seax. The time had come to put this right. Bassus had the truth of it. She must end this here. Now. She advanced towards Nelda.

As if a cloud had passed before the moon, Nelda's expression changed instantly, pulled into a nightmare scowl of anger and hatred.

"I curse you, Rowena, wife of Ubba. I curse you and your daughter." Above them, the sky grew dark. The wind picked up, shaking the trees, tugging at their clothes. Nelda's hair billowed about her face. The jackdaw flapped into the air, adding its own angered cries to those of its mistress. "You will die terrible deaths," screamed Nelda. "Your flesh will melt from your bones, your eyes will be blinded, your tongues will shrivel. You will choke on your own blood."

Rowena was suddenly filled with a great strength.

"I am the bride of Ubba, thegn of Bernicia," she shouted, her voice firm and loud in the windswept forest glade. "I will not be cursed by the likes of you, Nelda, Hengist-mother. I am old and my remaining days may well be few, but Edlyn will live long and happily. I swear this on your blood, which I offer to the gods and the spirits of the forest."

Rowena moved forward, gripping her dead husband's seax firmly.

But Nelda did not wait for her to close the distance between them. With snake-like speed, she produced a wicked knife from the folds of her dress.

"We shall see whose blood is spilt here today," she screamed, and with an ululating shriek she rushed at Rowena, the knife blade lambent in the woodland gloom.

Rowena tried to gauge where Nelda's knife would strike. She was sure she would be able to slay the witch, but she was no warrior. She had no blade-skill. It would be all she could do to ensure that her seax found its mark. Nelda would almost certainly wound her too. Perhaps mortally. So be it. She must hold on to life long enough to kill the cunning woman. For Edlyn.

She braced herself for the collision.

But Nelda never reached her. With a speed belying his huge bulk, Bassus crashed from the undergrowth into the clearing. He shouldered past Reaghan, who watched, aghast and unmoving. In his right hand Bassus held aloft his great sword. It flashed once in the dim dappled light of the forest, bringing Nelda to a crashing halt. She crumpled under the force of the blow. Bassus stepped quickly over her prone form. He kicked the blade from her hand and glowered down at her.

Nelda panted, gasping for air. Her dress was plastered to her body, dark and blood-drenched. Blood bubbled at the edge of her twisted mouth.

"The giant..." she said, loathing in her eyes. "I should have foreseen this." She coughed weakly, dribbling blood. "Bassus, son of Nechten, I curse—" Her words were cut off as Bassus rammed the point of his sword into her mouth, pinning her head to the loamy earth. Nelda fixed him with her glaring eyes, her mouth yet working against the steel of his sword's blade.

"Your days of cursing anyone are over," Bassus said, returning her gaze. He waited for a long while until the light of life departed her eyes. Then he pulled his sword free with a grunt.

The wind calmed and the forest was suddenly silent around them. Without a thought, Rowena dropped the seax to the ground and rushed to Bassus. She flung her arms around his neck. He stood there, solid and stiff, unable to return her embrace due to the sword in his grasp.

Like one who is woken from a nightmare, Reaghan was dazed and confused. She took a tentative step forward, shaking her head as if to clear it of what she had just witnessed.

From the branches of the alder, the jackdaw looked down, twitching its head this way and that, its white-rimmed eyes bright against its charcoal feathers. The sound of its call made Rowena's skin prickle. Her trembling increased and, at last, hot tears began to flow down her cheeks.

Chapter 39

The red-bearded giant advanced, the stout boar spear fast and deadly in his meaty hands.

Beobrand watched in dismay as another hunter ran from the forest, making the number Acennan now faced three. Without help, Beobrand was unsure how long Acennan could hold out.

Mayhap it was their wyrd to die here this day after all.

But there was no way Beobrand could help Acennan whilst this monster of a man stood before him. He took three quick steps back, giving himself a moment to reach down and use the edge of Hrunting's blade to lever the dog's jaws from his thigh. The weight fell away and the pain doubled, blurring his vision. His breeches and leg bindings were soaked, drenched with his own blood.

The huge Mercian rolled his shoulders, loosening muscles.

"That was a good hound," he said with a frown. "Now I will finish what I started back in that shit-filled ditch in East Angeln."

As fast as a snake, the point of his spear lanced towards Beobrand's stomach. Beobrand caught the blow on his shield, but before he could counter, the spear flickered at his exposed neck. He twisted his body and the blade missed him by a finger's breadth.

Gods, but he had forgotten how quick this giant was.

The Mercian pushed him back with a flurry of blows that Beobrand was barely able to deflect or dodge. Cursing his own stupidity at not having thought there might be more hunters with Wybert, Beobrand stepped back, keeping out of reach of the spear.

The crash of weapons on a shield and the jeers of defiance from Wybert and his companions spoke of Acennan's struggle some way down the path. Beobrand could not spare a moment to see how his friend fared, but he knew it must only be a matter of time before Acennan would be overrun by his three opponents.

Beobrand parried another spear jab with Hrunting and then slid the blade along the haft in an effort to sever the giant's fingers. But the spear was long, and his adversary was nimble and quick, despite his bulk. He skipped back out of range, smiling broadly.

"You'll not get me with your shiny sword, Bernician," the massive man said with a grin. "I'll have your head on this spear-tip before the day is through."

Beobrand's mind raced. The big man was right. With his long-hafted spear, speed and skill, there was little chance of Beobrand landing a blow. Especially not with the wound in his thigh, which pulsed hotly as more blood oozed into his breeches.

Another fierce attack from the red-bearded warrior left Beobrand panting, his shield-arm numb. He would not hold out much longer. His head ached terribly now, and he recalled how he had narrowly avoided death at the hands of this monster at the great ditch. He jumped back again, using his agility to allow the spear to slip harmlessly past him. His foot caught on a tree root and he stumbled, almost falling. To fall now would be certain death.

And just like that, an idea crept into his head.

The man was sneering at him now, scenting the kill. Beobrand may have byrnie, helm and shield, but he was also dripping blood from the savage bites from the hound, and his shorter weapon and reach made him only able to retreat.

Beobrand lowered his shield and sword almost imperceptibly and allowed the next strikes from the massive Mercian to come even closer. He continued to parry and deflect the blows on his shield, but he shifted the direction he was retreating, side-stepping, only half-pretending to stagger. The huge warrior's smile widened as he pushed forward. It was all Beobrand could do prevent the spear from hitting its mark and to keep his retreat angling back the way they had come.

Sweat poured from beneath his helmet, stinging his eyes. His arms screamed from the efforts of defending against the powerful attacks. His leg was a throbbing, heart-beating agony.

He heard a scream of pain from down the path, but he dared not look away from the bearded giant before him and his whirring spear. He could wait no longer. Offering up a silent prayer to Woden, Tiw and Thunor that his plan would work, he suddenly crouched low and sprang at the giant. He did not attempt to strike with Hrunting, instead all he sought was to deflect the spear and then barge into the huge man with his shield. The bearded warrior was a bear of a man, hugely muscled, with great tree-trunk legs; he would not be easily toppled. But Beobrand, whilst not as massive, was tall and broad, and he had timed his rush perfectly. For a heartbeat, his opponent was caught off guard, having expected Beobrand to continue his backward motion. But just as quickly, he regained his composure, changing the angle of his spear and stepping back to gain a better position. If the ground had been flat – the lathed and sawed boards of a hall perhaps – he would have taken control of the fight once more. But this was no hall, and Beobrand had manoeuvred him with his own retreat so that his foot stepped in the steaming entrails of the rear half of the hunting dog. The man's eyes widened as he began to lose his footing, and Beobrand surged forward, shoving with his shield to send the huge man sprawling onto the carcass of his own hound.

There was no time to waste. This was his chance to be done with the fiery-headed brute and to aid Acennan.

Beobrand carried on forward, stepping on the spear haft, and swinging Hrunting down. He meant to take the man in the throat, but the giant was too quick. He twisted and raised his arm and, instead of ripping out his gullet, Beobrand's sword hacked into the man's upper arm, shattering bone and sinew. The giant screamed and blood spurted hot and bright in the cool forest air.

Beobrand did not pause. He kicked the giant in the face, snapping his head back and silencing his screams. Then Beobrand limped down the slope as fast as he was able. With each step, pain engulfed his leg. He clenched his jaw and pushed on to his friend's aid.

Acennan had his back to the trunk of a great oak. Before him lay one of the hunters, unmoving, skin as pallid as whey. By the position of his body Beobrand saw that he was dead. Wybert and the newcomer to the fight were jabbing at Acennan, but like Beobrand he too suffered against the range of the long boar spears the Mercians wielded. Acennan was quick and skilled, but he could not reach his opponents. Nor could he shield himself from two spears with one linden-board.

As Beobrand staggered down the slope, his vision blurring with the sweat-sting and pain from the dog bite, he saw Wybert flick his spear-tip at Acennan's face. Acennan raised his shield, catching the metal blade on the rim and deflecting it away from him. But at the same moment, the other Mercian lunged at his midriff. Beobrand, yet too distant to attack, watched in horror as the spear slid beneath the shield.

"No!" screamed Beobrand, willing his injured leg to carry him forward more quickly.

Chapter 40

Acennan grunted and chopped down with his sword into the ash haft of the spear. The wood splintered and Acennan, face pale with rage and pain, surged forward. The severed spear fell to the earth and both Wybert and the other hunter took a step back, shocked at the sudden attack from the stocky warrior who should have been pinned to the oak by the stout spear.

Beobrand did not stop to think.

"Wybert, you shit-eating whoreson," he bellowed. "Now you die!"

Wybert, eyes wide and mouth agape, spun to face Beobrand as he stumbled down the path towards him.

Acennan rushed the other Mercian, pushing him back. The hunter pulled a langseax from a scabbard at his belt. There was a loud clang of metal on metal as the Mercian parried Acennan's wild sword thrust, and then the two moved out of Beobrand's sight and he focused fully upon Wybert.

Dully, as if from a great distance, he was aware that his head yet ached and his leg still burnt with pain. But these were worries for another time. Now, all that mattered was that finally the object of his bloodfeud stood before him. Beobrand no longer cared whether he would live to return to his hall. All that was important was that Wybert was before him.

And Wybert must die.

Wybert raised his spear, lunging at Beobrand. Wybert had learnt much battle-skill and the steel point flicked out at Beobrand's eyes. He was strong and fast, but Beobrand had reached that state of battle-ire where he no longer thought as a man. The beast that strained within him was truly free now, snarling and savage, lusting for blood and vengeance. Beobrand saw the spear-point moving as if it were travelling through honey. He did not stop his forward motion. Lifting his shield, he halted the spear, allowing the point to strike and bury itself in the hide-covered wood. For the briefest of moments the spear was lodged in the wood, but that eye-blink of time was all Beobrand needed. He levered the point away from him and stepped inside the spear's reach. Before Wybert could free the weapon or think to pull his sword from its scabbard, Beobrand swung Hrunting across his body and into Wybert's right forearm. The blade was partly deflected by the spear haft, so the arm was not severed. But blood blossomed, red and bright in the shade of the trees and the spear clattered to the gnarled roots that grew in a tangle across the path.

Wybert let out a pitiful scream and clutched his wounded arm. Blood flowed between his fingers, quickly covering his hand in gore.

Beobrand's heart swelled at the sight. Baring his teeth in a wolfish grin, he swung Hrunting back, pommel-first into Wybert's face. Wybert sagged and fell to his knees.

For a moment, Beobrand looked down at him. Wybert's chest heaved from the exertion of the fight and blood dribbled from his arm, where his grip was unable to staunch the bleeding.

Wybert gazed up at Beobrand. His eyes were white-rimmed in terror. Blood and spittle ran down his chin from split lips. Leaning forward, he hawked and spat blood into the earth.

As quickly as Beobrand's fury had come, so it vanished.

"You are a nithing," he said. "Less than a man."

Behind Wybert's kneeling form he watched as Acennan parried the hunter's langseax with his shield and then opened the man's throat with a backhanded slice of his sword. Blood spurted in a great arc. The man looked surprised. He did not yet believe death was upon him and he vainly attempted to press his attack. But Acennan took a step back and smashed the rim of his shield into the dying man's wrist. The Mercian dropped the blade and tried to scream at the pain in his shattered arm. All that came was a gurgling groan. He reached up and placed his fingers into the gaping wound at his neck. Looking down at his blood-drenched hand he seemed to finally understand that the Wyrd sisters had already cut the thread of his tale. He crumpled forward and Beobrand was surprised to see Acennan pick up the man's weapon and place it in his bloodied left hand. The Mercian gave a final convulsive moan and lay still.

Acennan straightened and walked stiffly towards Beobrand and Wybert.

"I thought you dead for sure," said Beobrand.

"Aye, and so I would have been, if not for Eadgyth's cross and my good byrnie." Acennan pulled the silver rood amulet from beneath his byrnie and held it up to the light. It was bent and twisted now; distorted. "I am sure the Christ followers will call it a miracle, but I still feel as if I have been used by Thunor to test the heft of his hammer." He grimaced and rubbed his midriff where the spear had hit him. "So," he looked down at Wybert, "this is the pig's turd we have sought all this time? He hardly seems worth the effort."

Beobrand flushed. Perhaps Acennan was right. Had it truly been worth it? The blood soaking his breeches was growing cold, the pain returning with alarming intensity now that the fighting had ceased. Wybert had lowered his gaze, seeming to accept his fate.

"Look at me," said Beobrand.

Wybert ignored him, unmoving.

Beobrand shrugged off his shield straps, allowing the scarred board to fall to the earth. Then he delivered a vicious slap to Wybert's face with the knuckles of his left half-hand.

"Look at me!" he shouted, feeling the anger rekindling, like a fire that has been allowed to burn down overnight, only to have breath and new fuel added at dawn.

Wybert raised his gaze.

"Wybert, son of Alric, you are a disgrace to your father's memory," said Beobrand, his words as sharp and cold as Hrunting's blade. "I am glad that Alric has not lived to see the man you have become."

Wybert said nothing, but a spark of defiance flared in his gaze.

"You defiled what was mine," continued Beobrand. "Because of you, my faithful servant, Anhaga, a better man than you, was slain. By my own hand." Beobrand shuddered, remembering the anguish as he had driven his seax into Anhaga's flesh. "I swore the bloodfeud against you then, and now you will pay with your blood and your life." He could think of no more words. Nothing would bring Sunniva back to him. Anhaga was gone, as were so many others. Killing Wybert would accomplish nothing. He knew that. But perhaps it would bring some peace to his spirit. Mayhap Anhaga and Sunniva even now watched from the afterlife. He would give them what they desired. What they deserved.

He raised Hrunting high above his head. The patterned blade caught the rays of sunlight that speared through the forest. And then, the instant before he brought the blade slicing down into his enemy's neck, Wybert cried out.

"You cannot kill me!" he screamed. "You cannot. We serve the same lord, you and I."

The words made no sense to Beobrand, but something in Wybert's tone tugged at his interest. He stayed his hand and lowered the sword slowly to his side.

"What do you mean? I am a thegn of Bernicia. My lord is Oswald. You are Grimbold's man now. And he a Mercian who serves Penda. We share no lord."

"He just wishes to delay his death," said Acennan. "He is even a craven now, when he is defeated. Kill him and be done with it. Then we can go home."

Beobrand made to raise Hrunting once more, but Wybert spoke out again.

"It is true that I am Grimbold's man," he said, his voice breathless, quavering with pain and fear, "but he is not my lord."

Beobrand spat. His leg throbbed with each heartbeat. His head ached terribly.

"Speak plainly, or I will take your life so as not to hear your voice again."

Wybert looked up at him for a long moment. The trees rustled. A magpie chattered loudly way off in the wood. After a long silence, Beobrand lifted his sword once again.

"Enough of this. We need to be gone from here, and you need to die. I have no time for your games."

"I serve King Oswald of Bernicia, Lord of Northumbria," Wybert blurted out.

The words seemed nonsensical, and yet, there was something in Wybert's voice. Did he believe what he said?

Again, Beobrand lowered his weapon.

"Explain your words. I will not tell you again. Tell us clearly your meaning, or die now."

He caught Acennan's gaze. His stocky friend frowned and shook his head.

"Before I left Bernicia, I was approached by one close to Oswald." Wybert grimaced, clutching his bleeding arm closer to his chest. His fist was gloved in gore. "He offered me riches and land in the future, if I would inform Oswald of what occurred in Mercia. I have been faithful. I have done that which has been asked of me. I have given tidings, and when asked to perform other tasks, I have done so."

"What other tasks?" asked Acennan.

Wybert cast a glance at Beobrand's trusted gesith, suddenly unsure of himself.

"What other tasks?" Acennan repeated. "No time to be shy now, little man."

Wybert swallowed.

"A secret message came for me. I was to travel to Frankia and seek out the athelings, Wuscfrea and Yffi."

"The son and nephew of Edwin?"

"The same."

"And when you found them," asked Beobrand, "what were you to do?" He had a sinking feeling that he already knew.

Wybert looked furtively first at Acennan and then at Beobrand, but it was too late to halt his story now.

"I was to slay them, that they could no longer lay claim to the throne of Northumbria."

"And," asked Acennan, his brow creasing in consternation, "did you fulfil your... quest?"

"Yes," replied Wybert, "I told you, I have served our lord well."

Acennan suddenly stepped forward, grabbing Wybert's dark hair in his grip, pulling his head back to expose his throat.

"I will hear no more of this venom from this serpent's tongue," Acennan shouted, his fury shocking, "I will kill him myself."

He raised his blood-smeared sword.

"No, Acennan," shouted Beobrand. He could not bear the thought that he would not be the one to claim the blood-price after all this time. "He's mine!"

For an instant, they stood there, eyes locked. Then a new voice spoke from the forest, causing them all to start and look round.

"No," the voice said, "he is mine."

Chapter 41

Beobrand stared in shocked silence at the ring of men who surrounded them. There must have been close to a score of them; warriors all, spear-men, sword-men. Byrnies glimmered dully in the sunlight that filtered through the branches of oak and beech. Gold and garnets glittered on many sword pommels. How such a warband had gathered about them without Acennan or him detecting their presence was a mystery.

He shuddered. Could there be some magic here? Had these gesithas sprung from the wood itself; spirits come to take the lives of these hapless mortals within their domain?

It was Wybert who broke the silence, shattering the strange feeling of being in the presence of something otherworldly.

"Lord, thanks be to all the gods."

Instantly, Beobrand saw the man who Wybert addressed, and who had spoken moments before. Grimbold. Wybert's hlaford. And Beobrand realised at the same moment that his luck had finally, truly, run out.

The large man had his hands on his hips, feet apart. His grey-streaked beard jutted and his eyes flashed from beneath dark brows. These were his lands. Here, his voice was justice; life and death. For a long moment, he did not speak. He raked Wybert with his gaze before focusing on Beobrand.

"Lord?" Wybert offered, uncertainty in his voice.

"Silence," Grimbold snapped, not looking at him. He took a step closer to Beobrand, looking him up and down, taking in his battle-harness, his weapons and his wounds. "So, you finally decided to seek the blood-price that had escaped you at Dor and at the great ditch." He cast a glance at the corpses strewn on the path of the glade. He frowned, tensing when he saw the red-bearded giant sprawled in the dirt. "You are a dangerous one it seems."

It was not a question, so Beobrand said nothing.

"Lord," Wybert said, "these men have murdered your sworn-men. They would have slain me too, if you had not come to this place."

Grimbold turned back to Wybert.

"I had bidden you be silent," he said, his tone as cold as the Whale Road at Geola.

"I am sorry, lord…" Wybert stammered.

"You call me lord, but who do you serve, Wybert, son of Alric?" Grimbold's gaze did not waver.

Wybert, already pallid from the loss of blood oozing from his shattered forearm, grew paler still.

"I serve you, lord. Grimbold, son of Grim, thegn of Mercia. You are the best of lords. I am sworn to you, have served you in battle, and I would give my life for you."

"Why do you lie, worm? Tell me who you serve."

Wybert swallowed hard.

"You, lord. I serve you. You have my oath."

"Your oath!" shouted Grimbold. "Your oath is not worth a fart in a storm!"

Wybert flinched in the face of his master's fury.

"You would surely not believe those things I said to Beobrand?" he said, looking about him in desperation for an ally. The warriors, his shield-brothers, men with whom he had oftentimes shared the Waes Hael cup, were grim-faced. It seemed they had all heard Wybert's confession of service to an enemy king. "But lord, I merely spoke to save my life. They were going to kill me."

"So, you are a craven, or a nithing liar and a breaker of oaths," spat Grimbold. "Which is it?"

"Lord…"

"Which is it?" screamed Grimbold. "Coward or oath-breaker?" A crow, startled at the noise, fluttered and flapped in the tree canopy far above their heads.

Acennan edged closer to Beobrand.

"I think Sunniva will be avenged this day," he whispered. "But I do not think it will be you doing the killing."

Beobrand shot him a glance. His head throbbed and he was still trying to make sense of Wybert's words. Grimbold's sudden appearance had thrown all his plans into disarray, but given the man's ire at discovering Wybert's duplicity, he thought Acennan had the right of it. Wybert would surely die this day. Beobrand looked at the hard faces of Grimbold's hearth-warriors. These were killers, men of many battles. Beobrand drew in a deep breath and clenched his fists against the trembling that always beset him as the rush of battle lust drained from his body. He would not wish these warriors to see him shake and to believe him scared at the prospect of his death. For surely, that would be his fate. And Acennan's.

"Well, worm?" said Grimbold, when Wybert failed to reply. "You seemed happy to tell all to these Northumbrians, why not speak to me?"

Wybert glowered, but still did not speak.

"Lord Grimbold," said Beobrand.

The large man turned to him.

"We are on your land and have shed the blood of your men, and for this we will surrender to your justice. But I,

Beobrand of Ubbanford, thegn of Bernicia, hearth-warrior of Oswald, King of Northumbria, would ask one thing of you."

Again the raised eyebrow.

"And what would that be?"

"That before we answer for the slaying of your men, you would allow me to watch as you take the life of this nithing, Wybert."

Grimbold appraised him for a long while.

"You have sworn the bloodfeud with Wybert, isn't that so? Some matter of honour regarding a woman."

"My wife," Beobrand said, in clipped tones.

Grimbold nodded slowly.

"Your crippled man failed to kill him at Dor, and you clearly did not slay him at the great ditch. Perhaps it is not your wyrd to take Wybert's life."

"It seems that may be. But the man is worse than a cur. He has betrayed you. You heard his words with your own ears. As a man of honour, I beseech you, let me see him die."

"You would watch me slay him?"

"It would bring me some peace, I believe." Beobrand thought of other men he had killed. For an instant he recalled Hengist as he lay on the earth before Bebbanburg, his lifeblood soaking into the mud. Had his death brought him peace? Beobrand clenched his half-hand more tightly and pressed his arm into his side. His vision blurred. They would not see him tremble.

"I will do better than let you watch his death," Grimbold said. "Revenge is a noble pursuit. You may slay the wretch yourself. He has forsaken his oath to me and his life is forfeit. Let his blood sate your thirst for vengeance."

Wybert cried out.

"Lord! Do not do this! I am your servant. This man is your enemy…"

His voice rose in pitch as he first begged and then, when he saw that Grimbold was unmoved, hurled abuse at his erstwhile lord.

"Shut him up," said Grimbold, turning away from Wybert's ravings. Three of his men grabbed the doomed man. He struggled, but he was easily overpowered. Quickly and roughly, they tied his wrists, making Wybert cry out in agony as his wounded arm was handled. All the while he spat and screamed until his voice cracked.

Beobrand stared in disbelief as the men ripped off Wybert's belt and gagged him with it, pulling it so tight that it ripped into his mouth, causing more blood to run down his chin. Beobrand could scarcely understand what was happening. He looked to Acennan, who gave the slightest of shrugs as Wybert's screams became muffled grunts and moans. One of the men gave Wybert a kick, and then they stepped back, leaving him huddled and trussed on the path before Beobrand.

This must be some trick. Beobrand turned to Grimbold, but the old thegn simply nodded.

"It is your wyrd to have your revenge this day," he said. "Take it."

Beobrand held Grimbold's gaze for a long time. The older man's face bore no expression, but there was something there. Some secret thought behind his dark eyes. At last Beobrand nodded. He did not understand this lord of Mercia, why he was being granted his wish and more when by all rights Acennan and he should be tied and ready for slaughter alongside Wybert. But he would not question his luck. He might yet die this day, but by Woden and all the gods, he would see Wybert breathe his last before Grimbold changed his mind.

Wybert had fallen onto his side when the warrior had kicked him. He lay there still, shaking and moaning from behind the gag.

"Pull him to his knees, Acennan," Beobrand said, hefting Hrunting. The sword felt at once light and heavy in his grip. It seemed to him that the blade thrummed with a life of its own, as if the serpent within the metal hungered for more blood.

Acennan grabbed Wybert's bindings and pulled him up. Wybert whimpered around the leather wedged into his mouth. Tears streaked through the blood and grime on his cheeks. Beobrand stepped forward, raising his sword. Wybert's eyes grew wide with terror. Death was in this vale. They could all sense its presence. A silence fell upon them.

"You will die now," said Beobrand. Wybert's eyes were locked on his. Fear rolled off him like the stench from a rotting carcass.

Beobrand lifted Hrunting above Wybert. Its shadow fell upon Alric's son and again Beobrand was reminded of Wybert's father and brother, both good men. Both true friends.

"If I kill you now," Beobrand said, "with no weapon in your hand, what will happen when your spirit departs middle earth? Woden will not take you into his corpse hall. You will be lost. A nithing in this life and in the next." Wybert shook and moaned, his eyes rolling with his anguish. Beobrand leaned down close to Wybert's face. "But what if I were to allow you to clasp the hilt of your sword at the time of your death? Would you wish that?"

Wybert's eyes burnt with a loathing almost as great as his terror. For several heartbeats he scowled at Beobrand, and then, with the smallest of movements, he nodded.

Beobrand picked up Wybert's sword from the earth with his left hand.

"Very well," he said, "I will let you hold your blade. But I would hear something from you first."

"Gods, man," said Grimbold, "I do not wish to hear more of the worm-tongue's jabberings."

Beobrand ignored Grimbold.

"Ungag him," he said to Acennan. Acennan frowned, but after a moment's hesitation began fumbling with the belt.

"Scream again, and I will kill you before the sound reaches Lord Grimbold's ears."

Acennan removed the belt. Wybert groaned, and spat a great gobbet of bloody spittle into the earth. He stared up at Beobrand, a flicker of defiance in his eye now, at the end.

"All I want from you in exchange for your sword is the name," said Beobrand, his voice hushed. Gone was the battle-fury. Fled was the fear of being caught here in Mercia. All that remained now was a bitter calm.

The men gathered around that forest path seemed to hold their breaths. The wind ceased its rustling in the leaves, as if the gods themselves listened.

"What name?" asked Wybert. His voice cracked and he spat again.

"The name of the one who offered you riches to betray your oath and," Beobrand hesitated. It was all he could do not to strike the man dead at the thought of the things he had done. "And," he continued, "to murder children in the name of my king, Oswald of Northumbria."

Wybert glowered. Beobrand lifted his sword, showing it to him, reminding him of what was at stake.

"I will tell you," Wybert said at last.

Beobrand leaned close. Wybert whispered a name. Acennan might have been close enough to hear, but none of the other warriors would have been able to discern the word Wybert uttered. Beobrand let out a long breath. He shoved the hilt of Wybert's sword into the man's hand and stood tall once more, wincing at the stabbing pain in his thigh. Without pause he turned Hrunting's point downwards and instantly plunged the blade into Wybert's chest, beneath his upturned face. The sword slid down, between bones, piercing organs and slicing veins and arteries. Wybert's eyes widened with the terrible shock of staring at death. Beobrand pushed the sword deeper and Wybert shuddered. For a moment, Beobrand held the sword still, watching as the light faded from Wybert's eyes. Wybert's sword fell from his grasp, and his head lolled back. Beobrand pulled Hrunting free from Wybert's corpse, which slumped over and lay still atop his fallen blade. Blood welled from the wound and pumped into the mud.

Beobrand took a long deep breath. The air carried the sharp tang of death. He closed his eyes for a moment, searching his feelings. Apart from the aching in his head and the throb of the bite on his leg, he felt nothing but an overwhelming tiredness. What had he expected? He smiled grimly to himself. It was said that revenge was best served cold, but it seemed to him vengeance was never a satisfying dish. But just as a drunkard is drawn to drink, despite knowing it will do him no good, so the call of vengeance was ever loud and Beobrand was powerless to ignore it. He hoped that the spirits of Sunniva and Anhaga at least found some peace from Wybert's death.

He opened his eyes, turning from Wybert's still, crumpled form. Acennan stepped close, slapping him on the shoulder.

"It was well done, Beobrand," he said.

Beobrand nodded his thanks to his friend before addressing Grimbold, who yet stood in silence with his men, respectful of the sombre moment they had witnessed.

"I thank you, Lord Grimbold. I have long sought vengeance. Even if it meant my own death." He indicated around him. "Surrounded as we are by your men, I fear that has come to pass. But again, I offer you thanks for allowing me to claim the blood-price from one oath-sworn to you."

Before Grimbold could reply, a groan from one of the fallen drew their attention. It was the red-bearded giant. He moaned twice and then sprang to his feet with a roar. Blinking, he looked about him, dazed and surprised at the mass of men in the forest clearing.

"Easy there, Halga," Grimbold said. "There is no fighting left to do here." The huge man glowered at Beobrand and Acennan, taking in the corpses that lay strewn along the path. Grimbold turned to one of his men. "See to Halga's wounds," he said.

"Until this moment, I was unsure what to do with you, Beobrand of Ubbanford. But now my way is easier."

"Lord?"

"I had thought that Halga here was slain. It is not an easy thing to forgive the death of one's son."

By all the gods, the red-haired beast was Grimbold's son!

Grimbold glanced over at where the huge man now sat, leaning against a beech tree whilst one of Grimbold's gesithas bound his arm. Halga was pale, but he looked full of life yet.

"Now that I see he yet lives, my decision is easier." He paused, seeming to relish the anticipation of his audience. "You may ride free from this place."

"Lord?" Beobrand said again, his tone incredulous. Was Grimbold toying with them, as a cat will play with a mouse?

"I am Grimbold, son of Grim, and I take care of those who protect my kin."

Beobrand was speechless. He opened his mouth, then shut it again. It was true the man's son yet breathed, but his arm was gravely wounded. To say he had protected him was madness. He would have killed him if his aim had been true. Seeing the bemused look on Beobrand's face, Grimbold laughed.

"I do not speak of my foolish son. He can take care of himself. I speak of my daughter."

"Your daughter, lord?" Beobrand had no inkling of who Grimbold spoke of.

"Yes. Word has reached me that you saved her life."

"I did?" Beobrand felt stupid hearing his own words. He did not even know this man had a daughter.

Grimbold laughed again.

"Yes, she was always a wayward one, but I love her dearly. What father doesn't love his daughters? Still, she has always been so headstrong. Just like her mother. I couldn't stop her following that new god, the Christ."

Beobrand frowned. At last Grimbold's words sparked recognition in his mind. Could it be?

"Who is your daughter, Lord Grimbold?"

Grimbold beamed, pleased with himself, like a scop at the conclusion of a fine riddle.

"My youngest daughter is named Edmonda."

Chapter 42

"Gods, but I will be glad to reach Ubbanford," Beobrand said. "This mount's back is as sharp as a seax blade." The horse flattened its ears and snorted as if it understood his words. It was not a bad steed, carrying him all the way from the coast of the Narrow Sea at Hithe to the river Tuidi in Bernicia, but it was not a pleasant creature. On more than one occasion it had taken a bite at him when he had been distracted. He was now wary not to turn his back on the mare. He missed Sceadugenga. The anger at the stallion's loss still simmered within him. From time to time he would find his mind turning to the black horse's fate, the way one might pick at a scab that itched, only to crack the skin and cause more pain and bleeding. Still, it was a less painful thought than when he remembered the men he had lost at the great ditch. That was a scab he would have been best to leave alone altogether he told himself. But of course, he could not. He had forgiven Acennan for his part in dragging him from the battle. He well understood his friend's reasons and they were sound. But he had not forgiven himself. Perhaps he never would.

Instead he worried at the aching memories, picking and probing them with his mind. And, as with a scab, so this constant scratching of his thoughts would leave its own scar.

The wounds on his body were easier to deal with. After the fight, Grimbold had ordered one of his men to tend to Beobrand. The warrior had been gruff and none too gentle, but he had known his craft. He had cleaned the puncture marks on Beobrand's thigh, then he had daubed them with thick honey, that he carried in a small clay pot, before binding the leg tightly. Beobrand reached down and pressed his hand against the wounds. There was still pain, but not much now and when he had replaced the bandage three days before there had been no sign or smell of the wound-rot.

His head also felt better. When he grew tired it still ached, but the headaches were ever less frequent and severe.

Beside him, Acennan looked up at the sky. The sun was low, but they were close to Ubbanford now. They would reach their destination well before nightfall. The day was dull with low, leaden clouds and a smirr of drizzle that seemed to hang in the air rather than fall from above.

"It will be good to share a cup of ale with the men," Acennan said. Seeing Beobrand's scowl, he continued quickly, "And of course, you will see Octa. And Reaghan."

Beobrand grunted. He was unsure how he felt at the prospect of seeing either. He had long been far from his hall. Would Octa remember him? The boy must have grown in the months since he had last seen him. The thought of Reaghan often came to him as he lay wrapped in his blanket at night. Yes, he was looking forward to sharing his bed with her once more, but after that? He had freed her. Now he must learn to live with her. He pushed the worries from his mind. Could he never allow himself to be content?

"With your leave," said Acennan, "I will go on to old Nathair's hall in the morning. I would see how it fairs. There is much to do if I am to be wed before Blotmonath." Acennan grinned broadly and Beobrand could not help but return his smile. Happiness was not so elusive for his friend.

Acennan had been in ebullient spirits ever since they had visited Eoferwic. Beobrand had wished to head straight for Ubbanford. He had no desire to see Oswald, or his brother,

Oswiu. He had been as tired as he had ever been and the thought of the hustle and bustle of the walled town made him irritable and short-tempered. All he had wanted was to return to his hall and be able to rest and allow his wounds to fully heal. And perhaps even to know peace for a few months. But they had instead gone to the royal hall at Eoferwic. He had owed it to Acennan.

As they had entered the busy hall, grime-smeared and travel-sore from their long journey, Beobrand had a sudden chilling sense of foreboding, as if something terrible was about to occur. He had swallowed the lump in his throat as they had strode towards the hearth fire where the queen and her ladies sat weaving. He was certain that they were going to hear the worst tidings, news of death or sickness. And yet he said nothing of his fears, and nothing untoward came to pass. Eadgyth had welcomed them with a curtsy and the queen had offered them mead. It was not long before Acennan had given the joyful news of Eadgyth's father's agreement to their betrothal. Beobrand frowned at the memory of the sudden raucous twittering of the ladies at hearing the tidings. Eadgyth had glowed with happiness and Acennan had beamed with pleasure.

That night, Queen Cyneburg had arranged a celebration feast, and there had been choice cuts of beef accompanied by cunningly decorated loaves and pastries, the like of which Beobrand had never seen before. The queen's cooks further showed off their skills by serving a thick fish paste which they had sculpted into the form of a great sea creature. As the tray was carried to the high table, the guests had broken into applause and Cyneburg had beamed at the reaction. There were riddles and tales told by a talented young scop called Cædmon. He reminded Beobrand of Leofwine.

Beobrand had been happy for Acennan, and yet he found no joy in the feast. The mead and ale dulled his senses as the night went on, but he had been as an island of rock surrounded by a sea of swirling merriment.

Since Wybert's death he had found no contentment. Perhaps peace was this hollow emptiness he felt, but he did not believe so. His nights were yet filled with dreams of blood and death, leaving him sweat-drenched and shaking. Wybert's face now joined those of the others he had killed. For how long would these wraiths plague his slumber?

Although he did not enjoy the feasting, he had been pleased not to have to confront his fear of facing the king or his brother. Oswald and Oswiu were far to the north, meeting with Bridei, the new king of the Picts. Beobrand was glad not to see them. He did not know how he would react when he did, with the knowledge he now held following Wybert's last words.

Once, on the journey from Mercia, before they had reached Eoferwic, Beobrand had tried to broach the subject with Acennan, but his friend had brushed it away with a sweep of his hand.

"These are the problems of kings and athelings. And lords," he had said, continuing to whittle a stick he intended to use to skewer a piece of hare meat over their campfire. "I am none of those things, Beobrand. I am but a warrior, nothing more."

Beobrand had nodded. He had no right to burden his friend with his concerns.

"You may not be a lord, but you will be needing a hall and land if you are to keep your fine lady happy."

"Aye, I suppose that is true." Acennan had ceased cutting at his twig for a moment and gazed into the flames, perhaps imagining his meeting with Eadgyth and what her reaction would be to his news.

"I know of a hall that was destroyed by fire," Beobrand had said. Acennan had glanced over at him, his eyes twinkling in the firelight. Beobrand had grinned at the look on his friend's face. "I would give you Nathair's lands to tend. You can build a new hall. I would like to have you as my oath-sworn man and my neighbour."

"I will accept and gladly, lord. And I will always be your oath-sworn man."

"And friend too?" Beobrand had said, feeling foolish for asking.

"Of course," replied Acennan. "Always."

Beobrand smiled at the memory. He had known the answer before it had been spoken. Acennan had proven his friendship and loyalty time and again.

Looking over now at where the stocky warrior trotted beside him, Beobrand felt a surge of gratitude for Acennan's friendship. Beobrand trusted few men, but of Acennan he had no doubts. He was not so certain of the third rider in their band. Reining in his saw-backed steed, Beobrand twisted in the saddle to watch as the skinny youth kicked his pony's flanks in an effort to keep up. The boy was not a good rider, never having learnt the skill prior to Beobrand buying him a mount at Eoferwic. Before that, he had jogged along behind them as they had ridden. Despite riding until the sun was dipping low in the sky, the boy had seemed not to tire and had still helped each night with the usual chores around the camp. Watching him now, bouncing and gangling on his mount like a sack of parsnips, Beobrand wondered whether he should have saved the silver he had parted with for the pony.

Neither Acennan nor Beobrand had expected to ride out of Mercia with their lives, they certainly did not think they would bring a new companion with them in their wake. But as they had prepared to strike camp on the day after Wybert's death, the boy had stepped from the shadow of the trees.

He was the slave from Grimbold's hall.

Beobrand had started, noting the fine seax he had given the thrall now hanging openly at his belt. The boy had come upon them as silent as thought and if he had meant mischief, he would have had the advantage of surprise. For his part Acennan had acted as though he'd expected the youth. But Beobrand could not believe he had heard the boy's approach any more than he had.

"So," Acennan had said, tightening his horse's girth and scarcely glancing at the Waelisc boy, "what would you be wanting?"

"I would travel north with you, lord," the boy had said, addressing himself to Beobrand.

"I have thralls already. And you are another man's." Beobrand had rubbed gently at the bandage on his leg. The dog bites had throbbed. "I am no thief."

The boy had raised himself to his full height.

"And I am no man's property. And I am no thrall."

Acennan had snorted, picking up a bag to tie it behind his saddle.

"Is that right? So you chose to carry shit for Grimbold and to allow Wybert to beat you like a cur?"

The boy bristled, his eyes flashing with hot anger.

"I said I am no thrall and no man's property. I do not lie." He took a deep breath and his hand moved absently to his side. His ribs must still have troubled him. "Wybert was my master." He spat onto the leaf-strewn earth. "Now he is food for the ravens."

"And just like that, Grimbold freed you?" Beobrand had asked.

The boy's dirt-smeared face cracked into a wide grin. If he were clean and fattened up with good food, he would be a handsome youth.

"I did not wait to ask."

Acennan had laughed.

"Well, I can't say I blame you. So why come with us?"

"I would be a warrior, a hearth-warrior of the great Beobrand."

Beobrand had raised his eyebrows, giving the youth another look up and down. He was slim, but strong, and clearly quick-witted.

"Indeed? What know you of fighting?"

"I know little, it is true, but," he had grinned again, "I have a good seax and I would be taught by the best warrior in all of Albion."

Acennan had not been able to contain his mirth.

"For the best warrior in the land, he often seems to leave battle limping or carried."

"And yet he lives and his enemies no longer walk this middle earth," replied the boy, as quickly as a whip-crack.

Beobrand had stared at him for a long while, before finally pushing himself to his feet with a grunt at the pain in his thigh. Watching this boy puffing out his chest like a cockerel and hearing the confidence in his tone, Beobrand saw a reflection of himself, heard the echo of his own voice as he had stood before Edwin and Eanfrith.

"Well, if you are to be my oath-sworn man," he'd said, keeping his expression stern, "I would know your name."

The boy's grin had grown even wider.

"I am Cynan."

And so it was that Cynan swore his oath to Beobrand in a forest glade in Mercia. Acennan had later said to Beobrand that it was madness. The boy was surely fled from Grimbold. Why accept his oath? He knew nothing of war, he would slow them down. All of this was true, but Beobrand liked the lad. And so, it seemed, did Acennan, for he did not protest for long or with much passion.

The very next morning, Beobrand had smiled to see Acennan begin to train Cynan in the correct stances for shield and spear. And each day had been the same. Acennan would train Cynan for a while before they continued their journey north. Cynan was a fast learner, and again Beobrand was reminded of his early days in Bernicia, when Bassus had worked with him in a desperate attempt to give him enough weapon-skill to survive his first battle. With luck, Cynan would have longer than he had been allowed to hone his skill before he was called upon to take up shield and spear for his lord.

Cynan finally caught up to where Acennan and Beobrand waited astride their mounts. He trotted up, jolting and ungainly upon his small horse.

"I do not believe I have ever witnessed a worse rider," said Acennan. "I am sure you were faster when we made you run."

Cynan grinned.

"I can't be good at everything," he said. "It wouldn't be fair to everybody else."

They were approaching the path that led up through the wooded slopes to Ubbanford now. For a moment, Beobrand thought of galloping up the last hills, as he had done many times on Sceadugenga, but his foul-tempered mare would just as likely unseat him if he tried to push it now, after a long day of riding. Besides, he feared its blade-like spine would cause him more injury than the hound in Mercia. Nevertheless, he did kick the beast into a trot. The scent of woodsmoke was in the air. The sound of logs being chopped drifted to them on the breeze. They were so close. Beobrand was suddenly struck by the strength of his desire to be back at Ubbanford. He thought back to Hithe, to Selwyn, Udela, Alwin and Scrydan. Cantware was like a bad dream to him. There was nothing for him there. This was his home now.

They emerged from a stand of birch, out of the dry gloom and into the watery light of the afternoon. Some way ahead he could see a small group of men. The dull sun brushed the head of an axe as it fell. A heartbeat later, the thud of the cut reached him.

There were four of them. Beobrand squinted. Who were they? A chill of dread prickled his neck. He did not recognise any of these men.

"They look like fighters," Acennan said, his tone low. "But they wear no metal shirts. They have no shields."

Beobrand scanned the men who had clearly seen them riding towards them. They stepped away from their work and formed a line across the path. The meaning was clear. One of them was a beast of a man, perhaps as tall as Halga. The axe in his hands seemed tiny. Who were these men?

"How is your leg?" Acennan asked. "Do you think the two of us can take them?"

"The three of us," said Cynan, his words shrill, nervous.

Acennan flashed him a scornful look. Beobrand frowned. His leg was not yet strong. They could probably kill these woodsmen, whoever they were, but he did not wish to see Cynan die in some forest brawl.

"Let us speak with them first," he said.

Acennan nodded. They rode on.

One of the waiting group raised a horn to his lips and blew three long, piercing blasts. The sound echoed through the trees. Several crows flapped into the slate sky croaking angrily, disturbed by the sudden noise.

Beobrand glanced at Acennan. There could be only one reason to sound a horn. Four men they might be able to defeat; if more came to the aid of these, their chances of victory would be slim.

"If I give the word," Beobrand whispered, "we flee. Understood?"

Cynan was pale, but nodded without dissent. He had learnt the value of obedience as a thrall it seemed.

Beobrand halted his horse a spear's throw from the line of men.

One of them, a dark-haired young man with a confident air, took a pace forward and yelled in a clear voice.

"Who are you that ride in these lands?"

Beobrand frowned.

"Can you tell us whose land's we are travelling through?" he asked.

"These are the lands of our lord, Beobrand."

"Your lord, eh?" he said, looking askance at Acennan, who shrugged. "And where is this Beobrand?"

"That is none of your concern," the man shouted back. "Now state your business and your name or turn away from here."

Beobrand kicked his mare's flanks, so that it bounded forward with a shake of its head and a snort. He pulled at its reins savagely, causing it to sidestep and prance.

"I will tell you my business and my name," he said, raking the men with a gaze as cold as the first meltwater of spring. "I have been abroad these many weeks, far to the south. I have stood in the shieldwall with the East Angelfolc against the might of Penda of Mercia and a horde of Waelisc from Gwynedd. I have waded through the guts of my enemies to be here and I would now go to my hall. To warm myself by my hearth. To drink my mead." He paused, allowing the men time to comprehend his words. "I am Beobrand of Ubbanford, thegn of Bernicia, servant of Oswald, King of Northumbria. Now," he said, meeting the wide-eyed stare of each man in turn, "who are you?"

Chapter 43

Reaghan watched Beobrand raise another horn of ale, the flame-flicker from the hearth fire lighting his hard, scarred face. His teeth flashed in a wide grin and he shouted something to the gathered gesithas. His words were drowned out by their raucous laughter. Acennan looked to where she sat at the high table and caught her eye. He nodded to her, as if he could hear her thoughts. I have brought him home alive, he seemed to be saying to her. She offered him a small smile, then quickly dropped her gaze.

Emotions buffeted her the way winter storms hammer at a hut, making it creak and shake.

The goddess had finally heard her plea. Her man had returned. She reached for her cup, but found it empty. Rowena, smiling, lifted the jug of mead and refilled it for her. Reaghan nodded her thanks. Perhaps they would never be friends, but so much had changed, who could say? To think that Rowena would sit with her willingly in the new hall would have struck her as impossible only days before. Sometimes, at night, she saw Nelda's snarling face in the instant of her death. The memory of that afternoon in the sacred glade would never leave her. Rowena had clung to Bassus for a long while, but the warrior had soon turned to what they must do next.

"We must ensure that the witch can cause us no more harm," he'd said. He had been pale, shaken by Nelda's words perhaps, or at having struck dead a woman. Or mayhap he had been frightened by how close the cunning woman had come to slaying Rowena.

Bassus had decapitated the body with one mighty hack of his sword, and then he had gone about the grisly task of disposing of the witch's body. Reaghan shuddered when she recalled how he had chopped off Nelda's legs, so that she might not rise from death and walk in the night. The sound had reminded Reaghan of when the pigs were butchered at Blotmonath. She had helped Rowena dig a shallow grave in the glade for Nelda's torso and arms, scratching with sticks in the loam. It had taken a long time and when they had finished they were both slick with sweat and streaked with dirt. Bassus had rolled the head into the sack that had contained Rowena's seax. He had thrown the sack into the stream, so that the flowing water would carry away any ill magic. The witch's legs, he dragged into the forest in opposite directions and left them there, for the wolves and foxes. They had returned late in the afternoon to Ubbanford, exhausted and shaken. They had been silent as they'd walked back and none of them had spoken of what had occurred since. But from that day, it had felt as though the cloud of a curse had been lifted from Ubbanford.

The following day, the remnants of the warband who had ridden south with Beobrand had trudged into Ubbanford. They were sombre and sorrowful, but the women and children of the settlement rejoiced at their return. The men did not wish to celebrate with a feast, feeling keenly the loss of their lord, but there had been no refusing the womenfolk, who had slaughtered a sheep and prepared fine ale with a heather gruit.

Attor had told of Ceawlin's heroic death in the savage steel-storm of the great ditch, while Aethelwulf had wept into his horn of mead for his lost friend. Dreogan and Gram had been subdued, drinking deeply of the ale and mead, but never smiling. Gram limped and had aged years in only a few weeks, but he did offer some hope, when he told of seeing a horseman riding from the battlefield leading another steed that seemed to carry a wounded warrior. He had thought the injured man might have been Beobrand, but he could not be certain. They had clung to that hope all through their long journey northward. They had wondered who might have rescued their lord from the fray, or if perhaps Gram had been mistaken. Or worse, that he had seen true, but their lord had not been injured, but slain.

The first thing Gram had asked when they had walked into Ubbanford had been, "Is our lord Beobrand returned?"

At seeing the response in the faces of the women, children and old folk who had gathered to welcome them, Gram had spat and trudged away, limping down to the river's edge. Bassus had gone after him later and brought him back to the hall, but there had been no gaiety in the men's mood, just a resignation that they had failed to protect their hlaford and they were now lordless men. And worse, men who had survived their lord, for such are not respected.

One who had brimmed with delight at the returning men had been Maida. Reaghan suspected that Maida had long given up hope of being reunited with her husband. Her moods had grown sour, her tone terse, and she seemed to find no happiness in her children. But at the sight of Elmer, gingerly stepping towards her, Maida had let out a shriek of pure joy and had flung her arms around his neck, almost knocking him to the ground. He had winced.

"Easy, woman," he had laughed, "would you finish the job of that bastard Mercian who near split me in twain?" With care, he had prised her arms from his neck. They had heard then how a giant of a man had broken several of Elmer's ribs with a great axe, leaving him for dead.

On the way northward, the Northumbrians, who included in their number Wynhelm and two of his gesithas, had sheltered in the fens, at the steading of a man named Offa. He had led them from the battle by paths few would know of, and the marauding Mercians and Waelisc had passed them by, either not caring to hunt for treasure in the fens, or having no idea of how to find firm trails through the meres, streams and lakes.

Maida had fussed over her man, tending to his wounds, cleaning and mending his clothes, and serving him the choicest slices of mutton at the feast. All the while with a glowing happiness about her that had given her the look of a young maid. Reaghan had been pleased for her, but she had been unable to enjoy the feast.

Another who had shared Reaghan's sorrow was Ceawlin's wife. She was a small woman, quiet and dour like her husband, but she had always seemed strong and determined to Reaghan's eyes. Sombre and steadfast, like a rock in a storm. Yet when she had seen that Ceawlin had not returned to her, she had sagged as if all her strength had fled. Aethelwulf had tried to console her, recounting her husband's bravery, but she had shrugged him off and staggered away as one in a dream. Or a nightmare. Reaghan, uncomfortable to be surrounded by so much joy, would have liked her company at the feast, but Ceawlin's wife did not come. She had wished to be alone with her grief. Reaghan had not begrudged her that. She too would have preferred to have been left to weep for her loss alone.

But now, not five days later, the goddess had responded to the blood sacrifice and sent Beobrand back to her. Reaghan felt as though a weight had been removed from her shoulders. She was lighter, free of the sadness that had clung to her like a sodden cloak, heavy and cold.

And Beobrand had been overjoyed to find that his men had lived through the battle of the ditch. He heard how, after he had disappeared in the confusion of the rout, the Northumbrians had managed to hold together under Wynhelm's command. Finding Elmer, blood-soaked and staggering across the corpse-strewn ditch, they had formed a small shieldwall, and had hacked and sliced their way from the killing ground. Penda's victorious warriors had soon left them alone; there were far easier pickings than the snarling, deadly Northumbrian warband once the East Angeln army had fallen apart. It was then that they had fallen in with Offa, who had led them into the sanctuary of the fens.

When Beobrand had seen the warriors in his hall, he had gazed upon them for a long while before smiling broadly. His pale blue eyes had glimmered in the firelight.

"My brave, loyal, gesithas," he had said, his voice catching in his throat, "I had thought I had lost you all. I had cursed myself for living when you lay slain in the mud of that gods' forsaken ditch. I berated Acennan here for pulling me from the ground where I would surely have perished. And, as I know you all, I know you too will have been full of sorrow, fearing you had left me for dead. Well, my friends, it seems the gods have had their fun with us these last few weeks, all believing the others slain. But it is our wyrd to stand together again. And I see the ranks of my warband are swelling. I think I have oaths to hear," he had swept his gaze across Fraomar, Eadgard, Grindan and Bearn, "and I would share meat and drink with these fine men who claim they are my warriors to unsuspecting travellers when they have never met me." He had laughed then, and the men had laughed with him.

"We will eat and drink tonight," Beobrand had said. "And tell the tales of how we came to be here, for I would hear those stories. Mayhap we will tell riddles and sing songs. But tomorrow we will be up with the dawn and we will practise with blade and shield." He had looked then to Bassus, who had grinned and nodded. "For I would see that my warband is the most feared in the whole of Albion. I have drunk too deeply from the bitter cup of defeat and I do not mean to lose a battle again."

The men had cheered.

Happiness filled the hall like the heat and smoke from the hearth.

Beobrand had sat with them, choosing not to come to the high table. Reaghan sat, content to watch him as he laughed and drank with his men, for a time with little Octa, red-cheeked and beaming, sitting upon his father's knee. She felt Rowena's eyes upon her. Judging her perhaps. But she cared not. Beobrand was safe and all was well.

The night drew on. She carried tired Octa to his cot. Other children were taken away to their beds. The men grew drunker and the tales bawdier. Reaghan sipped at her mead and watched. Ever more frequently Beobrand's eyes turned to her and she felt the thrill of anticipation as their gaze met over the crackling, dancing flames of the hearth. At last, Beobrand pushed himself to his feet and drained his horn of ale. With jeering shouts from his men, he walked purposefully towards her.

She watched his approach, a welcome warmth flooding her body. He reached out a hand to her. She took it, shivering at his touch after so long. He pulled her to her feet.

"I have spent the evening hearing tell of my gesithas' exploits," he said, his words slightly blurred by drink. "Now I would hear your tale, Reaghan. Let us go to our chamber and you can tell me of your summer."

She allowed him to lead her from the main hall. His hand was large, callused and hot against her skin. She thought of the hot days of the last months. Of the fear. The pain. The ever-present terror he would never return. The sacrifices and Nelda's savage, bloody death.

They reached the bed chamber, where she had lain alone these past months. He began to fumble at his belt, but she pushed his hands away.

"Let me, lord," she whispered in the darkness. She undressed him with her small hands. He groaned with pleasure as her fingers caressed his body. With growing eagerness, she pulled off her peplos, letting the dress fall to the rushes on the floor. Her mouth found his in the gloom and they both moaned.

Perhaps she would tell him her tale tomorrow, in the light of day. Now was not the time to speak of those smothering, fear-filled days of summer.

They lay upon the bed, stroking, kissing, panting. And in moments, all thoughts of speaking had fled from her mind.

We hope you enjoyed this book!

The fifth novel in the Bernicia Chronicles, *Warrior of Woden*, will be released in summer 2018

More addictive fiction from Aria:

Find out more
http://headofzeus.com/books/isbn/9781784978952

Find out more
http://headofzeus.com/books/isbn/9781784977511

Find out more
http://headofzeus.com/books/isbn/9781784978938

Historical Note

The idea for this book came while I was researching *Blood and Blade*. When reading about King Sigeberht of East Anglia (also known later as Saint Sigeberht, following his martyrdom), I discovered the tale of how he renounced warfare and abdicated his throne to be able to focus the rest of his days on prayer and the teachings of Christ. He was largely responsible for bringing Christianity to the East Angles, inviting Bishop Felix to found churches and a school for the education of boys there. This was interesting enough to include in the story, but when I then read in Bede's 'History of the English Church and People' that East Anglia was later attacked by that most successful of pagan warlords of the age, Penda of Mercia, and that Sigeberht refused to fight, but was forced onto the battlefield unarmed and unarmoured to lead his people, I could not resist telling that story. And, as ever, Beobrand is at the thick of it.

The date and location of Penda's attack on East Anglia is not known, but there is evidence that the great ditch (known now as The Devil's Dyke, or St Edmund's Dyke) was constructed during the fifth and sixth centuries and was clearly built for defensive purposes, so I chose to situate the battle there. There are other dykes that cut across the Icknield Way (the ancient, pre-Roman track that runs from Wiltshire in the west to Norfolk in the east), and any approaching army would need to cross each great ditch, probably facing staunch defence at each. However, I chose to ignore the other dykes – Bran Ditch, Brent Ditch, Fleam Dyke and Black Ditches – and focus the battle in one location for the sake of simplicity.

There is no evidence of a Welsh or Wessex presence in the battle between the East Anglians and the Mercians. The emblem of a golden dragon, or wyvern, on the banner of the West Saxons was first mentioned by the historian Henry of Huntingdon, when he wrote of King Cuthred bearing a golden-dragon standard at the battle of Burford in 752. It is later referred to again when King Edmund Ironside bears it in the Battle of Ashingdon against Canute in 1016. Such golden-dragon standards are also seen lifted by the English on the Bayeux tapestry.

Details of Penda's attack on East Anglia are extremely scant, and all we really know is that Sigeberht and Ecgric were killed. Penda was a pagan king, but did not ban Christianity from his lands, it seems to be hypocrisy that he really disliked, not any specific religion. So it is feasible that on the far reaches of his land, perhaps in disputed marches along the frontiers with other kingdoms, such as East Anglia, there may have been Christian monasteries. At this time, it was common for men and women to share the same monastery. I have taken some liberties with the location of the monastery where Edmonda is found, situating it on the edge of the Fens, near Peterborough. A monastery was founded nearby in 655, but it is unlikely that any monastery existed there twenty years previously. It is also dubious that its inhabitants would have considered themselves to be part of East Anglia and not Mercia, but I have chosen to have the land in dispute between the two kings, which, given the constant warfare that raged across Britain at the time, is hardly inconceivable.

The old path that Edmonda finds to lead them into the Fens is the Roman road known as The Fen Causeway. It provided a link from the major Roman north–south route of Ermine Street into East Anglia, running from Peterborough to

Denver, Norfolk. It is possible it continued east of Denver to meet Peddars Way at Castle Acre, but evidence of this is less clear. The road is thought to have been raised above the marshy fens with gravel. It is believed that, by the seventh century, it had already fallen into disrepair and disuse, but I thought that locals would know of it and perhaps it was still used as a shortcut to avoid the much longer route needed to go around the fens to the south.

The exact relationships between kings and royal heirs during this period is often confusing and open for debate. Scholars cannot decide whether Ecgric was the son of Eni or Rædwald. I have chosen the latter, as it is plausible and I like the link to Sutton Hoo, which is most likely the burial place of King Rædwald.

The death of the two young athelings, Wuscfrea and Yffi, in Frankia is almost a footnote in Bede's 'History', but when I read it, I couldn't shake the feeling that there had been foul play. Ethelburga had sent the boys to the court of Dagobert to be safe from the sons of Æthelfrith who had killed her husband Edwin and reclaimed the land of their father. Yet despite Ethelburga's efforts at safeguarding, both boys from Edwin's line still died before reaching maturity. There were many ways to die in the seventh century, but I cannot help but think that kings will do whatever is necessary to cling onto their power, even kings who are later revered as saints.

The relics that Oswald and Aidan send to their Christian brothers in the south are fictitious, but based on many such items in medieval Europe. The belief that inanimate objects can be imbued with religious power is an old one and not limited to Christianity, but the number of relics, often stored in priceless bejewelled reliquaries, would become a huge business in Europe in later centuries. The miracles recounted by the monks are all derived from early medieval accounts. The story of the salmon being dropped by an eagle at the feet of a hungry monk is said to have happened to Saint Cuthbert on the banks of the Tweed some decades after the events in this novel.

Much of Beobrand's story is concerned with the idea of the bloodfeud. Honour and kin were all important and a murder could legally be avenged by a family member killing the murderer. The price of compensation for each wrongdoing was laid down in law, and a law-breaker could pay the family of someone they had killed the agreed amount to avoid a bloodfeud. However, if they could not, or would not pay, or if the surviving family refused to accept the recompense, a bloodfeud could ensue. These would sometimes continue for decades, over several generations, with each side of a dispute seeking out and killing members of the other family in a bloody spiral of violent retaliations. Such a bloodfeud famously took place in the eleventh century following the murder of Uhtred of Bamburgh by his rival Thurbrand. That feud lasted sixty years! Some people bear a grudge long and hard, and in the warrior culture of the Anglo-Saxons, such a thing was expected and even admired. However, the bloodfeud is not something that has disappeared in the mists of time. Much later in history and an ocean away, an infamous feud between two families, the Hatfields and the McCoys, almost started a war between the states of Kentucky and West Virginia in the nineteenth century. And in parts of the world today, so-called 'honour killings' and revenge murders, are all too commonplace.

The gory disposal of a witch's body is adapted from many diverse histories and countries. Many accounts come from later in the medieval period when there was an obsession with witches and the occult, but most rituals performed once a suspected witch was dead seem to focus on the fear that they might rise from their tomb and return to wreak their revenge on those yet living. Hence they were often dismembered and decapitated, and running water was frequently used to wash away the evil from them and perhaps confound them with its constant motion.

In *Killer of Kings* Beobrand has found answers to questions that haunted him, and has finally taken the blood-price from some of those who had stood against him. He has suffered much in his short life, experiencing great loss and sorrow. Many readers have contacted me saying they hope he will find some peace. Alas, I don't think peace is something that our hero can know, except perhaps fleetingly. His wyrd is to stand in more shieldwalls. To fight and kill in the service of powerful men who would do anything to become Bretwalda, ruler of the whole of Britain. Beobrand is bound by his oaths and his honour, and he will continue to play his part in the upheavals that shape the kingdoms of Britain.

There are more stories to tell of Beobrand. Great tales of love, passion, ire and the steel-storm of battles.

But that is for another day. And other books.

Acknowledgements

As always, I must first thank you, dear reader, for buying this book and, hopefully, for reading all the way to this point. If you have enjoyed it, please tell your friends and family. The best way to help spread the word is to leave a short review on your online store of choice. A few words are enough, but it really helps new readers to find my books and to make the decision to give them a chance. A huge thank you to everyone who has left reviews for the previous books in the Bernicia Chronicles. The reviews have definitely helped to make the series a success.

As with each book, I sent an early draft to a select group of test readers. They provide invaluable feedback and help me to produce the best book I can. So thank you, as always, to Alex Forbes, Gareth Jones, Simon Blunsdon, Richard Ward, Shane Smart, Clive Harffy, Mark Leonard and Graham Glendinning.

The team at Aria and Head of Zeus has been amazing. Thank you to Caroline Ridding, Yasemin Turran, Nia Beynon, Paul King and everyone else who works hard behind the scenes. I am privileged to be part of such a great team.

Thanks to my agent, Robin Wade, who is ever supportive and knowledgeable.

So many other authors have been helpful and given their time and experience to me over the last few years that there are too many to name, but I'd like to mention a few here who have really stood out. So special thanks to Steven A. McKay, Carol McGrath, Prue Batten, Justin Hill, Angus Donald, Martin Lake, Stephanie Churchill, Samantha Wilcoxson, Giles

Kristian and E. M. Powell. All are great writers, as well as lovely human beings.

And last, but definitely not least, extra-special thanks go to my family, to my lovely daughters, Elora and Iona, and fabulous wife, Maite. I love you all and know I could not do any of this without your constant support. Thank you!

About Matthew Harffy

MATTHEW HARFFY has worked in the IT industry, where he spent all day writing and editing, just not the words that most interested him. Prior to that he worked in Spain as an English teacher and translator. Matthew lives in Wiltshire, England, with his wife and their two daughters.

Find me on Twitter
https://twitter.com/MatthewHarffy

Find me on Facebook
http://www.facebook.com/MatthewHarffyAuthor

Visit my website
http://www.matthewharffy.com

About The Bernicia Chronicles

The Bernicia Chronicles is a series of action-packed historical fiction books set against the backdrop of the clash between peoples and religions in Dark Ages Britain.

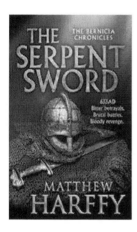 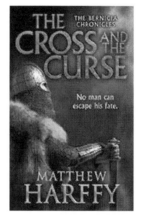 

Find out more
http://headofzeus.com/books/isbn/9781784978822

Find out more
http://headofzeus.com/books/isbn/9781784978839

Find out more
http://headofzeus.com/books/isbn/9781784978846

Find out more
http://headofzeus.com/books/isbn/9781784978846

Kin of Cain, a Bernicia Chronicles novella, is now available

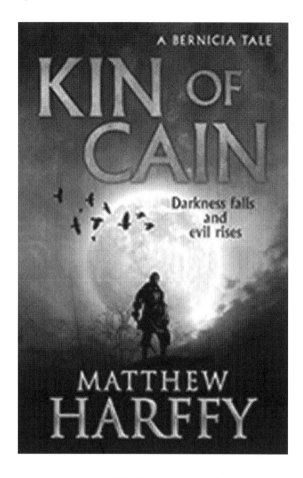

Find out more
http://headofzeus.com/books/isbn/9781784978860

Visit Aria now
http://www.ariafiction.com

Become an Aria Addict

Aria is the new digital-first fiction imprint from Head of Zeus.

It's Aria's ambition to discover and publish tomorrow's superstars, targeting fiction addicts and readers keen to discover new and exciting authors.

Aria will publish a variety of genres under the commercial fiction umbrella such as women's fiction, crime, thrillers, historical fiction, saga and erotica.

So, whether you're a budding writer looking for a publisher or an avid reader looking for something to escape with – Aria will have something for you.

Get in touch: aria@headofzeus.com

Become an Aria Addict
http://www.ariafiction.com

Find us on Twitter
https://twitter.com/Aria_Fiction

Find us on Facebook
http://www.facebook.com/ariafiction

Find us on BookGrail
http://www.bookgrail.com/store/aria/

Addictive Fiction

First published in the UK in 2017 by Aria, an imprint of Head
of Zeus Ltd

9 7 5 3 1 2 4 6 8

A CIP catalogue record for this book is available from the
British Library.

ISBN (E) 9781784978853

Author photo © Stephen Weatherly
Jacket design: headdesign.co.uk

Aria
c/o Head of Zeus
First Floor East
5–8 Hardwick Street
London EC1R 4RG

www.ariafiction.com

15157160R00206

Printed in Great Britain
by Amazon

KILLER OF KINGS

Matthew Harffy

About *Killer of Kings*

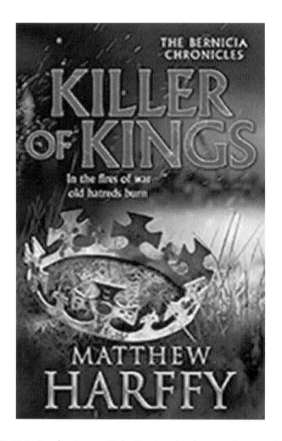

AD 636. Anglo-Saxon Britain. A gripping, action-packed historical thriller and the fourth instalment in The Bernicia Chronicles. Perfect for fans of Bernard Cornwell.

Beobrand has land, men and riches. He should be content. And yet he cannot find peace until his enemies are food for the ravens. But before Beobrand can embark on his bloodfeud,

King Oswald orders him southward, to escort holy men bearing sacred relics.

When Penda of Mercia marches a warhost into the southern kingdoms, Beobrand and his men are thrown into the midst of the conflict. Beobrand soon finds himself fighting for his life and his honour.

In the chaos that grips the south, dark secrets are exposed, bringing into question much that Beobrand had believed true. Can he unearth the answers and exact the vengeance he craves? Or will the blood-price prove too high, even for a warrior of his battle-fame and skill?

For Rich Ward. For all the support and all the laughs.